A Wanton
for All Seasons

Praise for Christi Caldwell

"Christi Caldwell writes a gorgeous book!"
—Sarah MacLean, *New York Times* and *USA Today* bestselling author

"In addition to a strong plot, this story boasts actualized characters whose personal demons are clear and credible. The chemistry between the protagonists is seductive and palpable, with their family history of hatred played against their personal similarities and growing attraction to create an atmospheric and captivating romance."
—*Publishers Weekly* on *The Hellion*

"Christi Caldwell is a master of words, and *The Hellion* is so descriptive and vibrant that she redefines high definition. Readers will be left panting, craving, and rooting for their favorite characters as unexpected lovers find their happy ending."
—RT Book Reviews on *The Hellion*

"Christi Caldwell's *The Vixen* shows readers a darker, grittier version of Regency London than most romance novels . . . Caldwell's more realistic version of London is a particularly gripping backdrop for this enemies-to-lovers romance, and it's heartening to read a story where love triumphs even in the darkest places."
—NPR on *The Vixen*

"Exceptional . . . an intoxicating romp sure to delight fans of historical romance."
—*Publishers Weekly* (starred review) on *In Bed with the Earl*

"Sizzling, witty, passionate . . . perfect!"
—Eloisa James, *New York Times* bestselling author on
In Bed with the Earl

Heart of a Duke

For Love of the Duke
More Than a Duke
The Love of a Rogue
Loved by a Duke
To Love a Lord
The Heart of a Scoundrel
To Wed His Christmas Lady
To Trust a Rogue
The Lure of a Rake
To Woo a Widow
To Redeem a Rake
One Winter with a Baron
To Enchant a Wicked Duke
Beguiled by a Baron
To Tempt a Scoundrel
To Hold a Lady's Secret

The Heart of a Scandal

In Need of a Knight (A Prequel Novella)
Schooling the Duke
A Lady's Guide to a Gentleman's Heart
A Matchmaker for a Marquess
His Duchess for a Day
Five Days With a Duke

Lords of Honor

Seduced by a Lady's Heart
Captivated by a Lady's Charm
Rescued by a Lady's Love
Tempted by a Lady's Smile
Courting Poppy Tidemore

Scandalous Seasons

Forever Betrothed, Never the Bride
Never Courted, Suddenly Wed
Always Proper, Suddenly Scandalous
Always a Rogue, Forever Her Love
A Marquess for Christmas
Once a Wallflower, At Last His Love

The Theodosia Sword

Only For His Lady
Only For Her Honor
Only For Their Love

Danby

Winning a Lady's Heart
A Season of Hope

The Brethren

The Spy Who Seduced Her
The Lady Who Loved Him
The Rogue Who Rescued Her
The Minx Who Met Her Match
The Spinster Who Saved a Scoundrel

Brethren of the Lords

My Lady of Deception
Her Duke of Secrets

Nonfiction Works

Uninterrupted Joy: A Memoir

A Wanton
for All Seasons

CHRISTI
CALDWELL

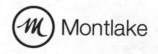

Text copyright © 2021 by Christi Caldwell Incorporated
All rights reserved.

Published by Montlake, Seattle

www.apub.com

Amazon, the Amazon logo, and Montlake are trademarks of Amazon.com, Inc., or its affiliates.

ISBN-13: 9781542032148
ISBN-10: 1542032148

Front cover design by Juliana Kolesova

Back cover design by Ray Lundgren

Printed in the United States of America

To my special girls:
You forever make Mommy smile. You are spirited and
strong and have the most clever wit. You are never
afraid to speak your mind and challenge whatever you
believe is unfair, and you defend those who need and
deserve to be defended.
Annalee's story is for you.

Prologue

"Sylvia is *deaaaadd*."

It was hard to say just which lady of the Mismatch Society that wail belonged to. After all, there were some number of young women making that same ominous declaration about Sylvia, the Viscountess St. John, their fearless leader and founder.

Lady Annalee, her friends Lila and Clara, and Valerie, her roommate on Waverton Street, exchanged looks.

Unlike the majority of their members, the four of them—five, if one included the unconscious Sylvia—were no innocents. Either married or in possession of scandalous pasts, they were all too aware of the ways of the world. The innocent young women who largely made up their society had been oblivious to the details which hadn't escaped Annalee and the mature set: The slight increasing of Sylvia's neckline. The lady's sudden aversion to chocolate when she quite adored that treat. Her fatigue.

Several of the ladies had remarked upon that bone-weary exhaustion as a sign of Sylvia's being overworked with the society.

Nay, to those as innocent as the ladies around them, the reason for Sylvia's current state proved so very foreign as to be mistaken for death.

Valerie leaned in close to Annalee and, cupping a hand around her mouth, whispered, "Do you suppose we should . . . ?"

"No."

"But they think she is dead," the other woman said in hushed tones.

"It is hardly our place to reveal Sylvia's private affairs." Annalee brought her flask up in salute. "Furthermore, they'll learn soon enough that she's very much alive."

Rolling her eyes, Valerie grabbed the flask and set it down.

"Will you just . . . hush." Miss Isla Gately raised her hands, thankfully bringing a brief surcease to the frantic whisperings amongst the women. "Perhaps someone should . . . check for a heartbeat."

"No, I do not think she is dead," Miss Anwen Kearsley murmured. From her vantage point at the back of the settee, she leaned forward. Then, behind her spectacles, the young lady's eyes formed huge circles. "Her chest! I believe it is moving."

The lady's younger sister Cora dabbed at the corners of her eyes. "It is because she is drawing her last br-breath."

Another flurry of cries went up . . . that managed to penetrate Sylvia's unconscious state.

The viscountess moaned.

All the ladies in their swath of white skirts moved like a wave, rolling toward Sylvia.

This was really enough.

Annalee clapped her hands once. "If you could give Sylvia a bit of room to breathe? I daresay she'll live, but with you all crowding her so, she certainly risks suffocation."

There was a brief collective pause, and Annalee gave another sharp clap, effectively dispersing the gathering.

The door exploded open, and a breathless Mrs. Flyaway, the head housekeeper, burst into the room. "Got the dear some mint, I did." Waving her arms, she came racing forward, and the loyal servant handed that remedy over to Clara.

Sylvia's lashes fluttered. There was a moment of dazed confusion, and then she blinked several times, her gaze taking in the fear-filled faces around her. She promptly tossed an arm over her eyes. "I fainted."

"It was . . . more like a wilt," Lila, the lady's sister, said supportively. "You just"—she mimicked a sideways fall—"like that. Right against the arm of the seat. A most splendid way to . . . wilt."

"Do not forget the way her eyes rolled back," Cora Kearsley put in. "More like . . . this?" And with a disturbing—if accurate—imitation, she collapsed herself into a nearby sofa. *"Oww."* Cora glared up at one of her younger sisters. "Whatever was that for? I was just pointing out—"

"That she almost died," Brenna, another Kearsley lady, rejoined in a less-than-discreet whisper. "You do not need to re-create the moment."

"Sy-Sylvia is d-dying," Cressida Alby, the society's newest member, sobbed. And just like that the room dissolved into chaos once more.

Taking advantage of the mayhem around them, Annalee slid onto the edge of the settee beside Sylvia. "Here," she murmured, helping up the other woman. "Are you . . . ?"

"Fine," Sylvia murmured. "Just mortified."

"Oh, hush. This is nothing to be mortified by. Now, getting caught building a champagne tower with a vicar, as I did a week ago?" She waggled her brows. "That is grounds for humiliation."

A little laugh escaped Sylvia, and she leaned her forehead against Annalee's.

"Sylvia is crying!" Anwen said loudly, unfortunately for Sylvia bringing the room's attention back their way.

"Is it because she's dy—"

"I . . . am not dying," Sylvia called loudly, her voice rising above the din. "I am expecting."

Silence met that pronouncement.

Once upon a lifetime ago, Annalee had imagined babes for herself, little boys and girls, a whole gaggle of them, born to her and Wayland, and—

"Expecting what?" Isla Gately blurted.

Annalee didn't blink for a moment, thinking she'd misheard the girl. Except . . . judging by the same blank stares from the other ladies, Isla wasn't alone in her confusion.

Having lost her virginity at the age of seventeen to her first love, and then having eventually found her way on a path of the wicked, it had been so long since Annalee had been innocent that she'd forgotten virtuous women were, in fact, very real. She'd moved out of her family's residence and in with two mature women: one a widow, and the other the lover of that widow's late husband.

Sylvia smiled gently at the younger Gately sister. "I'm with child."

There was another beat of silence, and then the room erupted with excited squeals as the ladies rushed to congratulate Sylvia. Annalee sat there beside her friend, taking in all the bright-eyed joy that filled the other women's eyes. Annalee was absolutely not at all envious about the news. At all. *Liar.* She'd have made a miserable mother, but she'd always . . . liked those tiny humans.

As the chatter died down, Cressida shot up a tentative hand. "How, exactly, is it that a woman comes to be with child?"

All eyes went to Sylvia.

"I . . . I . . ." She cast a desperate glance Annalee's way.

Valerie hopped to her feet and clapped her hands. "That concludes all the excitement for today's meeting."

"But . . ." Cressida was cut short by an elbow shoved into her side by Brenna.

"Her Ladyship might be dying," Brenna said sharply.

"I'm not dying," Sylvia called again as the loyal ladies hurried for the door, not breaking stride. "I'm really quite fine, you know." When most were gone and only Annalee and Valerie remained, Sylvia looked to them. "I really am . . . fine."

"Of course you are, dearest," Annalee said, patting her friend on the shoulder.

"What I am, however, is . . . concerned about . . . all of that. They do not know the ways at all between men and women."

No. Annalee flashed a grin. "Yes, I'd say a good number of our members would stand to benefit from lessons on *les relations sexuelles.*"

Two serious sets of eyes met hers.

Realizing their intent, Annalee was already shaking her head.

"They would, Annalee," Sylvia said.

"And the society has been floundering. We've gotten so very far away from what we started out as," Valerie said earnestly. "When we began, we were a group of women meeting, and our discussions evolved naturally. And I cannot think of a more perfect example than today's talk about babies."

Annalee laughed. "If you thought we had a membership problem before? What do you think your delivering such talks would do?"

"I wasn't suggesting *I* would see to such a task," Sylvia said.

"You always have the wickedest sense of h—"

"I was suggesting *you* could take the society in a whole new direction," Sylvia continued over her.

Annalee's laughter abated as it became increasingly clear that this was no jest on her friend's part.

She looked desperately over at Valerie, and yet . . . there was none of the startlement Annalee felt reflected back. She narrowed her eyes. "You two have talked about this." They'd discussed taking the society in a different direction, and also the role they expected Annalee to play.

"I will be leaving, Annalee," Sylvia said in hushed tones. "The society needs focus, and I cannot think of a more important lesson for the ladies to receive instruction on. These women are going to be making matches soon, and most of them have absolutely no idea what will take place between them and their husbands." The thread of finality in Sylvia's words brought an increasing panic. "Annalee, you tell me how fair it is that grown women should ask questions about how babies are born?"

"It's not." But then there wasn't much that was fair where being a woman was concerned.

"And so it is settled." Sylvia pressed a kiss to Annalee's cheek. "You are a dear." She stood. "Now if you ladies will excuse me?"

"But I wasn't—"

Valerie and Annalee came to their feet.

"I am tired," Sylvia said.

And Annalee immediately held back the remainder of the protestations she'd intended to give.

The moment Sylvia had gone, Valerie turned to her. "It appears as though the society has a new leader taking the helm."

Grabbing a pillow, Annalee swatted her friend in the chest. "Oh, hush."

Valerie laughed once more, and then her amusement faded. She held Annalee's gaze. "Sylvia is correct, you know. We have an opportunity to provide some of the most valuable lessons to ladies who would otherwise have that information withheld from them, and I cannot imagine a person better equipped to lead such bold discussions than you."

"I can't tell if that's a compliment," Annalee muttered.

Valerie smiled. "A compliment. It is very much a compliment. It will be fine, Annalee," she promised, and then took her leave.

Annalee, however, hadn't been jesting . . . about any of this. What did she know about leading . . . anything? She, who at the most random of moments found herself unable to keep control of her faculties?

Except . . . her friends were, in fact, correct. Who was more equipped than her to deliver discussions such as these? Or answer questions bluntly about what took place between men and women, and men and men, and women and women, and on occasion a mix of the three?

Now there was the matter of racking her brain and trying to figure out just how in hell she was going to privately instruct some two dozen ladies on the matters pertaining to lovemaking and marital relations.

Annalee grabbed her flask and downed the contents. If ever a situation called for spirits, this was decidedly it.

Chapter 1

Lord Wayland Smith, the Baron Darlington, had not always been the most dutiful, proper, and reliable sort.

In fact, he'd been slightly wicked and given to pursuing excitement that no proper gentleman should. But then, in those earlier days, he'd also not been a gentleman, either. He'd been the son of a blacksmith, and as the child of a man who'd toiled, Wayland had aspired to a better life. He'd committed himself to the cause of others like him: men and women who'd deserved more and who'd fought for change.

He'd also been many years younger and more foolish, and following a day of folly that had irrevocably changed . . . everything, he'd fashioned himself into one of those reliable sorts.

He'd become that friend and son and brother his family might rely upon. A man who could be counted on to be stable and to provide security, and whom one could turn to when there were struggles that needed sorting. Or scandals.

Never more, however, had he regretted the commitment to being that aboveboard fellow who'd not turn down a plea for help than he did in this particular moment, answering a summons from his best friend, Jeremy, the Viscount Montgomery—and in the middle of the other man's betrothal ball, no less.

"What was that?" Wayland asked in pained tones, hoping that the hum of a sea of guests on the other side of the Countess of Kempthorne's elaborately painted oak panel had merely made a bungle of his hearing and the words—and request—he'd heard were something he'd imagined.

As it was, with no immediate response from his only friend in the world, hope found a place in his chest.

"I need you to help with Annalee."

Alas, there it was, for a *second* time.

I need you to help with Annalee . . .

As in Jeremy's sister . . . but also the first—and only—woman Wayland had ever loved. Of course, Jeremy had never had so much as an inkling. He'd seen the trio of friends they'd been as children. If he'd known the extent of his friend's relationship with Annalee, Wayland would have been the last person Jeremy would have come to about the young lady.

Nay, he'd have called you out and put a bullet through your heart years ago.

Wayland adjusted his cravat—or rather, ruined the folds.

"Are you listening to me, man?" Jeremy demanded on a quiet whisper.

"No."

His friend's eyebrows dipped.

"Yes?" Wayland said quickly.

"I can't help her. I don't know who she is since"—*don't say it*—"Peterloo." Not only did Jeremy mention that nightmare, but he did so with a casualness that, as someone who'd lived the hell of that day, Wayland couldn't understand. "She's a stranger to me."

"What kind of help could I possibly provide Annalee?" An eccentric, after Peterloo she'd ended their affair by refusing to respond to his letters.

"The most important kind." Jeremy held his gaze. "I've tried to reach out to her, and . . . You were there that day, and look at you, chap. You're happy, and hell, you are more proper than ever."

Proper, because Wayland had learned a very important lesson that day on the fields of Manchester: rebellious attitudes and actions brought only suffering and sorrow.

Jeremy's jaw hardened. "Unlike Annalee, who's gone running in red dresses through Almack's, searching for members for that ridiculous club she's started, and who thinks *nothing* of visiting scandalous wagering parties with those men and women she calls friends."

"Has . . . she asked for my help?"

"Of course not." Jeremy's reply was instantaneous, and Wayland wasn't sure how to account for the odd pang of disappointment.

Still, he latched on to that. "There you have it. The lady doesn't want my help." And why should she? Why, when the sole reason she'd joined her friend Lila that day at Peterloo had been so she could go meet Wayland?

"No, Wayland. But she *needs* it." Pacing a quick path back and forth along the luxuriant floral carpet, Jeremy didn't so much as break stride. "If you can remind her of how she used to be, and of the benefits of living a righteous life . . ."

Wayland checked his timepiece. "Jeremy, it's your betrothal ball." His voice emerged strained. But perhaps if he could . . . put him off, the other man would either forget this request or realize the lunacy in what he proposed. "I hardly think this is the time or place to be . . . talking about"—*Annalee*—"this."

"This is the perfect time," Jeremy said. "'Do not invite her,' they said . . . 'It is better if she weren't here,' they said . . . And I insisted they were wrong because, of course, she belongs . . ." Jeremy shot a glance Wayland's way. "She's gone missing during the ball . . . and that does not bode well."

Guilt slithered around inside Wayland.

No, it didn't.

Jeremy abruptly stopped and gave Wayland a meaningful look. "My parents are growing tired of her behavior. It was bad enough when she moved in with two other women. But now the papers are all saying that Annalee is doling out lessons on . . . on . . ." Color flared in the other man's face, and he dropped his voice to a horrified whisper. "Carnal matters. And given"—Jeremy gestured vaguely at the air—"all this, everyone is expecting she's going to cause some new scandal, and she needs to be watched this night, Wayland."

And just like that, this sudden and unexpected request for help with Annalee, in the middle of Jeremy's ball, made sense. Why it was suddenly so important that Annalee start behaving. And coward that he was, Wayland didn't want to know just what the earl and countess had planned for Annalee, should she continue to rain down scandals wherever she went.

"Will you at least think on what I've asked?"

"Of course," Wayland said instantly. The answer would remain a decided *no*. Nothing good could come from renewing a friendship with the woman he'd been so hopelessly in love with.

"When you find her, mayhap you can at least try talking to her . . . as a friend."

"Y—" Wayland stopped. "Wait." When he found her? *What?*

Jeremy's features twisted. "If she's not located, she will get herself into some manner of trouble." *Because she always does.* It hung there, unfinished, but not necessary to be spoken. For they both knew. The world knew. Pain filled the other man's eyes. "And I cannot have that for Sophrona." Ah, Jeremy's fiancée. "Not this time." Once again, his friend stopped, and his gaze fixed on the doorway leading out to the revelries in the ballroom. "Lord knows, she has been understanding and tolerant of . . . of . . . who"—Jeremy grimaced—"*what* Annalee has become."

What she's become . . .

Wayland's stomach muscles spasmed.

Annalee hadn't always been the nonconformist who never failed to shock society. Having been welcomed into the folds of the Spencer family, Wayland knew his friendship with Jeremy, a viscount and the son of an earl, had been an unlikely one. He'd found himself a de facto member of the family, and as such, he'd known Annalee quite well from when she was just a girl of eight and he a boy of ten— only one year younger than her brother. She'd always been sweet and sunny and given to daring, but she'd never been . . . reckless. Or scandalous and shameful. And—

"I have to return," Jeremy said. "As it is, my absence has surely been noted. Will you just . . . see that Annalee doesn't land herself in any scrapes this evening, and bring her back to the ball?"

A pained laugh escaped Wayland. "You are asking me to serve as a chaperone to the lady? My God, man, do you know who your sister is?" Wayland's tone was strained to his own ears. The all-powerful Earl and Countess of Kempthorne couldn't get their headstrong daughter to do as they wished, and yet Jeremy expected Wayland should? "You clearly don't."

"Obviously I do," Jeremy said flatly. "Which is why I'm asking you. You are reliable and can be trusted, and you know Annalee."

You know Annalee . . .

His muscles seized once more.

"You were her friend," Jeremy went on, twisting the blade all the more.

I was her lover . . .

Following that fated day at Peterloo, she'd gone her way and he'd gone his, and they'd become two separate people, with the man now standing before Wayland the only thing in common between them.

The man whose features were a study of misery and worry and—

Wayland briefly closed his eyes. He was undeserving of the other man's faith. *Bloody hell.* He could no sooner reject Jeremy's plea for help than turn himself over to the reckless, rabble-rousing person he'd been in the past.

"Very well," Wayland said, committing himself to the task. "I will do it."

Just then, the door opened, and a figure sailed through.

Pale, her wrinkling features drawn, the countess was a study of worry. "You are missing, and your sister is nowhere to be—"

"I know," Jeremy cut off his mother. "Wayland has been so good as to volunteer."

Volunteer? Was that what they were calling it?

The countess lifted her head in a regal, queenly inclination. "We are indebted to you, Darlington." With that, she looked to her son. "I am so very sorry that you need to bear the hardship of having this on your day, Jeremy."

The gentleman inclined his head. "It is fine, Mother," he assured in placating tones.

"But it isn't. It is . . ." And while mother and son proceeded to speak about that most intimate of matters, Wayland clasped his hands behind him and attempted to make himself as small as possible.

Initially distant, back when her husband had been the one who'd opened their home to a blacksmith's son, the countess had warmed considerably to Wayland after he'd been awarded a title for acts of heroism in his timely rescue of a powerful peer's young daughter. So much so that she, like the rest of the world, hadn't cared—as she should have—about why he'd been there in the first place. For had she known the role he'd played in her daughter's attendance at Peterloo that day—that the sole reason she'd been there was because Annalee and Wayland had been lovers—it was a certainty there'd be no further warmth shown his way by any member of this family. Nay, only the door.

Just as Jeremy would likely end their friendship, were the truth to come to light. And as such, it was the great lie Wayland lived.

Sins that could never be atoned.

Debts that could never be paid.

Crimes that had gone unpunished.

Truths he'd expected, following that fated day of hell, Annalee would share with her family. But she hadn't.

As such, helping the family locate the lady and ensuring she didn't find herself in trouble was the least of the services he could provide in light of . . . all he'd done and failed to do where Annalee was concerned.

"I should go," he blurted.

The conversing pair abruptly stopped mid-discourse and looked to him.

The countess swept over and clasped his hands in hers. "I can never thank you enough for being the friend that you are to this family."

"The best." Jeremy lifted a flute of half-empty champagne in salute.

Friend that he was . . .

Never gladder to quit a room than this one, Wayland beat a quick retreat and set out in search of Lady Annalee. Turning all his focus on the task at hand—a far safer and wiser way to think of his assignment—Wayland went through everything he knew about Annalee.

That was, everything he knew about this new version of Annalee.

She liked hidden corners and fountains and conservatories, and more often than not, when discovered in those places, she was also in the company of some gentleman or another.

Once, the stories coming out of the papers had hit him like a punch to the gut . . . and not for reasons that had anything to do with guilt for his role in her transformation. Rather, his shock stemmed from the thought of her with those bounders. Shameful rogues.

"You're looking for my sister, aren't you?"

That unexpected question called down the hall brought Wayland up short. With a silent curse, he whipped back about.

Some five paces away stood the most fearsome of creatures.

Blunt and direct, and given to mischief, the girl had all the traits of her elder sister.

And with feet planted as they were, with her hands on her hips and her legs slightly parted, giving her the look of a military general squaring off against a less-worthy opponent, she was going to give Annalee a run for her money.

Wayland dropped a bow. "My lady—"

"Oh, stop trying to turn me up sweet, Darling," she said with a roll of her eyes. "Spare me your gentlemanly pomp and circumstance. I'm no lady."

He repressed a smile. "May I caution you from going on about that in the presence of your mother? She would not take well to having you reject the title of a lady."

The girl shrugged. "So?"

So.

Yes, with the spirit this one possessed, if there was an un-grey hair on the earl's and countess's heads after Annalee, they would go fully white by the time Lady Harlow Spencer reached her majority. As it was, the countess had struggled mightily with Annalee's transformation into one of society's most scandalous socialites—the family's turmoil having only grown over the years since that transformation had begun. Guilt, a familiar sentiment where this family was concerned, swirled. "I was only advising you to be careful." To help her.

Lady Harlow narrowed her eyes. "Are you challenging me, Darling?" she snapped, a warning there. Her small hand hovered about the hilt of her rapier.

"I wouldn't dare think of challenging so fierce a warrior. Lovely scabbard," he added, knowing the child well enough to shift tactics and get back in her good graces.

Instantly, the girl's scowl faded, and a smile brightened her plump cheeks. "Annalee's latest gift."

His lips twitched. "Of course," he said, before he could call back the words.

"You dare to insult my sister!" That truce he'd struck with Harlow proved short lived. In one fluid movement, she unsheathed her rapier and thrust the blade at his chest, touching the point to his person.

"I would never," he said indignantly. Not solely because Annalee was his best friend's sister, but because of the relationship they'd once had together. Either way, he'd tarried long enough. There was the matter of seeing to the task his friend had put to him. "If you will excuse me? I do have matters to see to."

Apparently, neither his assurance of fealty to her beloved elder sister nor the pressing obligation he referenced did anything to sway the furious Harlow.

She shot her arm out sideways so that the tip of her rapier kissed the countess's canary-yellow-painted wallpaper and effectively blocked him from walking past. "Halt, sir! What are you doing here? State your intentions."

"Or you will run me through?" he asked with a proper amount of solemnity for his friend's youngest sister.

The blade quivered as she pressed the tip slightly. "Argh, do I detect a note of sarcasm there, knave?"

"Am I to take that as a definite yes in the matter of running me through?" he countered.

"A *very* definite yes, Darling."

And to emphasize that point, she applied another hint of pressure, enough to give the blade a greater bend.

"Duly noted," he muttered under his breath. Apparently it had not been the correct degree of somberness, after all.

"You are looking for her, aren't you?" she demanded, entirely too astute for a girl of her tender years. How much of this child's transformation had been a product of the struggles their family had faced since Peterloo? His chest went tight. "*Theyyyy* sent you. Didn't they? My terrible parents and faithless brother?" She spat that last word as though it were an epithet that had burnt her tongue.

And mature as she was, and appreciating honesty as she did, he gave her the truth. "I'm looking for your sister."

Wary eyes met his. "Because of them?" she pressed, refusing to let him skate by without owning all the reasons for his presence here.

"Do you know Annalee and I were once close friends?"

I will love you until the day I die, Wayland Smith . . .

That whispering of long ago drifted into his consciousness.

Harlow moved her gaze over his face, as though she searched out the truth, indecision marching across her features.

In the end, she proved very much the cynic her sister had become.

The girl hardened her mouth. "Someone needs to defend Annalee from the likes of my parents." She shifted her weapon and wagged the tip of the rapier around his nose as if she were contemplating slicing that slab of flesh clear off. He swallowed hard. Given her penchant for pirates and her threat of moments ago, perhaps she was a good deal closer to separating him from that appendage, after all. "Are you prepared to help Annalee?" And not Jeremy . . . or the earl or countess.

He hesitated.

Armed with an impeccable acuity for one so young, Harlow growled.

"It is your brother's special night," he said gently. "And he wants your sister there."

"Annalee can do what she wants, when she wants."

Was that, even now, where Annalee was? Off meeting someone? An unexpected jealousy sluiced through him.

"And anyway," Harlow said, pulling him back from the black thoughts that had slipped in, "my brother only wants to make sure she doesn't cause him and his bride any trouble." Harlow's heavily freckled face pulled, saying clearer than words just what she thought of her brother's betrothed. In fairness, serene and quiet and calm where the Spencer sisters were a tempest, Lady Sophrona would have never met with the young girl's approval. "Don't make it something more honorable than it is, Darling." She flashed another disapproving look his way before, thankfully, lowering her weapon and sheathing it at her waist. "I, however, never expected this betrayal from you."

That was because she, like the rest of the world, had no idea the depth of betrayal he was capable of. The woman he'd failed. This family he'd subsequently failed.

He was a good deal more skilled at handling his own sister than he was Jeremy and Annalee's thirteen-year-old spitfire of a sibling. Wayland brought his palms up slowly. "No betrayal." Not this time anyway. "Your sister is missing, and your brother asked that I escort her back to the ball. It is nothing more than that. Can you tell me where she is?"

Harlow stared at him for a good long moment.

"And betray her and the good time she's having to the likes of you, Darling?" She snorted. "I think not." She hovered a hand around the holster of her rapier, and he eyed those little fingers warily, more than half expecting and fearing she intended to brandish that blade and off him, after all. "You want her? You find her yourself."

The likes of you . . .

For the truth of it was, Harlow saw what the world did not.

His birthright had made him invisible to all except the Spencer family, and society had come to see him only when he'd been titled. Very few in society shunned him because of his roots. Most accepted him because of his newly minted rank and his connection to the Spencers. But all regarded him as proper and honorable, all the while failing to know of his earliest sins and scandals.

The ones that had irrevocably changed Annalee's life.

As such, she was the last person he wished to be near . . . for so many reasons. But the fact remained: Jeremy had put the favor to him, and he could no sooner reject that plea for help than he could free himself of the guilt of the past.

Wayland held Harlow's gaze with his own.

She gave him a wary look.

"Your brother sent me in search because he is worried," he said gently, in those same tones he'd adopted with his own sister years earlier. Wayland also played upon the one thing or person to match her devotion to her elder sister . . . the girl's love for and loyalty to her brother.

Indecision filled Harlow's blue eyes. They were her sister's eyes, putting him in mind of Annalee when he and she had been younger. She'd been a mischievous girl who'd slip under tables and tie the laces of his ancient boots together.

His chest constricted, and he shoved back those long-ago memories of yore.

"He's not worried for Annalee," she said sharply. "He's worried about his betrothed."

Ah, so devotion to her sister had come to take place above any loyalty to her brother. Alas, having a sister of his own, he'd learned such was the way of sisters.

Wayland stood. "He loves them both. Why can he not worry equally about Annalee and Sophrona?" he cajoled.

And then, with reluctance in her every movement, the girl stepped aside. "Because he doesn't," she said with sadness tingeing her voice. "No one really cares about Annalee anymore. Except me and her friends." Fire lit Harlow's eyes. "To loyal friends!" She unsheathed her rapier and pointed it in a salute toward the small crystal chandelier dangling overhead. With that, she stepped aside so he could pass.

Dropping another bow, he started forward.

He tensed his jaw. Were it anyone else, and not a child, speaking so passionately before him, he would have told her just what he thought of the company Annalee kept.

Those . . . loyal friends.

As in the Mismatch Society, a scandalous league of women who'd come together to challenge society's structure and norms. The club, which met weekly, had become notorious and was also regularly written of and whispered about.

It was so very Annalee.

That was, this new version of Annalee. Annalee of old had spoken of marriage and love and been innocent in ways that she was now only jaded.

Harlow called out after him, stopping him in his tracks. "I don't know why everyone is so unfair to Annalee."

There was a wealth of sadness in the child's tones, and confusion, and a host of so much emotion that he desperately wished to keep walking. To just get on with the task Jeremy had charged him with. A task that he wanted no part of but was helpless to refuse.

Alas, he was also helpless when it came to the misery and confusion there in Harlow's voice.

With a sigh, he turned and headed back the length of the hall. "It is . . . complicated, Harlow."

Harlow snorted. "That was what you came all the way back to say?" She dropped her voice to a deep, slightly nasally intonation. "It is complicated."

He bristled. "I don't—"

"Sound like that? You do. Like you're trying too hard to sound like"—she nudged her chin in the direction of the doors leading to the ballroom—"them."

Because he had spent years practicing so that he might fit into a world to which he'd not been born but always aspired.

He rubbed a hand over his forehead and got back to the initial statement that had brought him over. "The truth of it is, it *is* complicated." This was really a conversation for the little girl's parents or brother. "Life is sometimes—"

"Messy?"

"Yes. And—"

"There aren't always answers that are sufficient to explain?" she correctly supplied.

"Yes. And—"

"And I think I have the gist of it," Harlow said dryly.

The right corner of his mouth pulled up in a wry smile. "Yes, well, I think you have it even better than me," he said, ruffling the top of her tangled curls.

Giggling, she swatted at his hand. "I *know* I have it better than you."

Stumbling back in false affront, he slapped a hand to his chest, all the while walking backward in his retreat.

Harlow's mirth faded as quickly as it had come. She cupped her hands around her mouth and shouted after him, "She is a grown woman and should be free to live her life precisely as she wishes to."

Drinking. Smoking. Wagering. And . . . carrying on with wicked reprobates?

Was that what Annalee was doing even now, during Jeremy's betrothal ball?

Fury sizzled through his veins. Perhaps the embers of those fiery sentiments weren't wholly extinguished, after all.

That outrage was surely a product of her relationship to Jeremy and this family. It had nothing to do with anything Wayland and Annalee had shared in the past. They'd been children. So very different from one another. The chasm between them . . . Those differences had only become an ever-widening gulf as they each coped with Peterloo in very different ways.

"Darling?" Harlow called warningly.

He touched four fingers to his brow in salute. "Your concerns are duly noted."

But not agreed with. He, however, had no intention of debating the child on all the reasons Annalee's actions and behaviors were dangerous and unsuitable . . . not just for a woman, but for anyone.

Perhaps Harlow might help him find Annalee, and he could be done with this chore for the both of them. All of them. He called after her, "I don't suppose you have any idea where I might find . . . ?"

Harlow, who'd already started her retreat, didn't even turn around to face him. "I'm not doing your dirty work for you, Darling."

So it appeared he was on his own in this, after all.

Bloody hell.

Chapter 2

Lady Annalee could puff out a perfect white circle of cheroot smoke with the best of the gentlemen.

She could drink most grown men under the table.

And she'd never lost a wager.

That was, as long as she'd been sober, she'd not lost one.

When she was drunk, she lost any number of them.

At this precise moment, however, she was certainly not foxed. Though she wished to be. Polite affairs tended to have that effect upon her. Add ones hosted by her prim-and-proper, always disapproving mother into the proverbial pot? And then, well, there wasn't enough drink to get a woman through.

It was why, in the midst of her brother's betrothal ball, with all the most powerful and respected members of Polite Society in attendance, Annalee happened to be . . . on the fringe of the festivities. She was well aware of the wagers that had been cast, and the coins that had been flowing, predicting she'd land herself in the middle of a scandal this night.

This time, however, it wasn't an attempt to win a bet herself . . . but rather to keep from fulfilling the expectation the world had of her.

Not that she cared herself what they said about her. After Peterloo, she'd developed a whole new way of viewing *everything*. She'd not given two flying rats what the world said about her or how she conducted herself. She'd *survived*.

Since then, by both the respectable and the reprehensible, Lady Annalee was whispered about, and talked about, to a like degree.

Some whispered stories of wicked escapades, of which she was always the center.

Most spoke freely and frequently about the scandals she found herself in.

None of it, however, was gossip.

Gossip involved unconstrained conversations and included details that were not confirmed as being true.

None of the stories associated with her name were untrue. One witness or another could vouch for the veracity of every scandal she found herself part of.

Nor was she apologetic about a single one.

Following her near death at Peterloo, Annalee had opened her eyes to a new way of looking at the world—at the precarious middling between life and death. One went from blissfully innocent and contented one moment, to nearly trampled by a swarm of panicked people, all bent on survival.

Nay, at the end of the proverbial day, any person—man or woman—who cheated death as she had would stop and reevaluate . . . everything.

As they should. Otherwise, what was the purpose of one's surviving?

Having witnessed and lived through what she had had led Annalee to carefully assess the world around her and, more specifically, a woman's place in it.

Click.

From where she sat on her parents' conservatory floor, tucked behind a table, a forgotten game of whist scattered across the tiles and a cheroot clenched between her teeth, she glanced up.

Annalee trained her ears on the still-invisible-to-her guest.

Silently cursing, she tamped her cheroot on the floor and wafted away the lingering smoke.

A small, familiar figure stepped out from behind the table.

"I thought you weren't coming back," Annalee greeted her younger sibling. Largely barred from seeing Harlow outside of the formal events their parents hosted and expected the whole family to attend, Annalee took every opportunity she did have to see the girl.

"I told you I would," Harlow pointed out, removing the rapier from her scabbard and plopping herself down across from Annalee and the cards laid out between them.

The moon's glow played off the bright shine of that beloved weapon her sister was never without.

As Harlow set the rapier down beside her, exchanging it for the cards she'd abandoned when she went off to see if anyone was looking for Annalee, and commenced with prattling on, Annalee's gaze—of its own volition—was drawn to that flash of metal, her eyes locking briefly upon it. It should so work out that her youngest sibling's fascination and one true love should happen to be . . . that thin-bladed weapon.

Laughter filtered around the conservatory, echoing in Annalee's mind, the exuberant sound mingling and mixing with squeals and screams of the past.

"Isn't that hilarious, Annalee?" Harlow was saying, and Annalee came jolting back to the moment. "Annalee?" Harlow repeated . . . this time questioningly.

Giving her head a slight shake to clear the cobwebs left by the past, Annalee laughed. "A search party, you say?" she said, picking up the few words she'd heard her sister speak. As a rule, Annalee didn't pay too much attention to the rapier. She did, however, support her sister's unconventional love of the thing. Because even loathing weapons as she did, Annalee appreciated far more that her sister was unique enough to have blazed her own way and found a love of something the world would not expect a lady to love.

Harlow's eyes glimmered with a mischievous twinkle that may as well have been a mirror reflection of her own.

And just like that, Annalee's demons fled. It was so *easy*, being with her sister, loyal and loving. There was also something peaceful in the way Harlow accepted Annalee for who she was. She never compared Annalee to the person whom she used to be. And mayhap that was why it felt so very comfortable being with the one person who didn't remember Annalee from back then.

"*Annnnd* there's more," Harlow whispered conspiratorially, leaning in.

She mimicked the little girl's enthusiasm. "*More?* Surely not!"

Harlow nodded excitedly. "Oh, yes!" Stretching out her legs, her sister crossed her ankles, warming to her story. "You'll never guess who's at the center of the search."

"Mother." Annalee paused. "Father." Her stomach sank. "Jeremy." *Please, don't let it be Jeremy.* Jeremy, who should only be at the center of his betrothal ball with his Sophrona, and shouldn't have to be worrying about—"*Oomph.*"

Harlow kicked the bottom of Annalee's bare foot hard with the heel of her boot.

Annalee grunted. "What the hell was that . . . ?"

"Because you're usually better at this. Mother and Father aren't impressive guesses. They're the obvious ones."

"Yes, you're right there," she muttered, directing her focus back on the thirteen cards in her hands. She tossed down a jack of clubs, the highest suited trump card in her hand.

Harlow held up a finger. "I'll allow Jeremy going about like a fogey in the middle of his betrothal ball would be reason to make him a more interesting guess." She added her eight of clubs.

Winning the trick, Annalee collected the cards and added them to her pile. Considering the seven of diamonds revealed, she assessed her hand and paused. "Never say . . . Sophrona."

Sophrona, Jeremy's fiancée, who generally went out of her way to avoid Annalee. Well, as all good ladies did. She tossed down a queen of hearts.

"That is a better guess," her sister allowed. She waggled her eyebrows. "But not the correct one."

Her interest piqued, Annalee raised her gaze to Harlow, who was now intently studying her hand. She nudged her young sister in the foot in much the same way she had knocked Annalee's, and the girl grunted. "You must tell . . . ?"

Haphazardly, Harlow threw down a jack of hearts. "Darling."

The cards slipped from Annalee's fingers, raining down about the makeshift gaming table they'd made of the floor, scattered faceup and facedown.

Her sister scrambled forward. "I know," she said on a furious whisper. "The gall of him." She paused. "I mean, it is interesting that proper Darling is missing the festivities, but all the more so that he'd betray you in this way." Harlow's eyes lit, and she hovered her little fingers over the hilt resting near her left hand. "Unforgivable."

Annalee had accustomed herself to that weapon's unfailing presence with her sister. But that, now coupled with mention of . . . Darling, as society had come to call him . . .

It was a newer name, not the one he'd gone by as a young man or boy, but rather one he had been gifted years later. It suited him. The darling of society, rescuer of innocents. A hero. Who'd happened upon a carriage overturned at Peterloo and rescued the occupants inside . . . while others had been battling for their own salvation on fields run red with blood and echoing with screams and—

Grabbing her champagne flute, Annalee downed the liquid in a long, slow swallow.

"Well?" her sister prodded.

"Wayland is merely looking out for Jeremy." *Wayland,* because she was never going to call him by that silliest of titles or monikers . . .

except when he was near. Then she'd do so just for the sole pleasure it gave her to tease him for it. "It is what friends do, Harlow."

They stuck beside one another, through good times and bad. Through peril and peace.

And despite herself, a cynical smile curled her lips at the corners.

Harlow's eyes bulged. "You'd . . . defend him?"

She shrugged, reaching for the half-empty bottle beside her. She added more of the bubbling brew to her flute. "Don't have much of an opinion of the gentleman one way or another."

That hadn't always been the case. They'd been as close as two people could have ever been. That had been, of course, back when she'd been young and innocent and believed men and women could share a deep, unbreakable bond. With time, she'd come to appreciate that sex was just sex. And there weren't really any bonds that were sacred. And the only love a person was best knowing . . . was a love of oneself.

Her sister's face fell. "But . . . but . . ."

"Leave it, Har," she advised.

"But he was your friend, Annalee. You said that once."

Yes, she had. After a family dinner party when he was in attendance—as he always had been for her family's polite gatherings. She'd been drinking too much and had a discussion with Harlow where she'd *said* too much. And her sister had never let go of that information; she'd seized upon it as a seeming thing of great fascination.

Harlow tugged Annalee's hem, calling back her attention. "There's nothing more important than a pirate's loyalty. It's part of the code. You know," she said on a rush, "where members were asked to make their mark and swear an oath of allegiance or honor . . ."

"Argh!" Annalee drawled in low, guttural tones as she put her spare hand to her brow in a pirate's salute. She let her arm fall to her lap. "But the Darlings of the world, Har?" she began gently. "They're no pirates."

Once there'd been bitterness at what Wayland had become. A living, breathing example of the opposite of the man she'd once loved . . . back when she believed in love.

Harlow dropped her chin into her hand and stuck her lower lip forward in a perfect pout. "He sounded more fun and better then, the way you described him."

"Oh, he was," she said softly, before she could call it back. A wistful smile stole across her face. "You would have liked him very much."

With time, in the days and months and then years following Peterloo, she'd appreciated that the experience had changed them all . . . in different ways. And none of the men, women, or children who'd been caught up in the hell unleashed upon humanity that day should be judged for how they'd come out of that experience.

"But he's not so very bad now, right?" It was a lie. Wayland was a complete stranger to Annalee now, and as such, she couldn't say much about him one way or the other. She knew he was loyal to her brother and their family. He was also kind to her sister . . . which should not be underestimated, given how Polite Society, on the whole, treated women and made invisible young girls like Harlow.

"Yes, I suppose," Harlow said unconvincingly.

And because they'd already spoken too much about the last person Annalee wished to speak about, the one man she'd taken pains to avoid all thought of, she proceeded to gather the cards.

Her sister's head shot up. "Hey! What are you doing?"

"Go. You want to watch the festivities."

A blush pinkened her sister's cheeks. "I'd prefer to stay with you."

"Liar." She softened that with a wink and a tug of Harlow's ringlets.

"Well, most times," Harlow allowed. The little girl flashed a wide, gap-toothed smile. Their mother had long lamented that wide space between Harlow's front teeth. Annalee, however, had forever insisted to her sister, troubled by the gap, that it lent character and intrigue to her.

"But this promises to be more interesting than Mother's usually dull affairs." Her sister hesitated a moment. "You . . . could always come . . ."

"I will," Annalee promised. It was just the longer she stayed away, the less likely she was to shame her family in some way . . . or risk the crowd chasing out her demons. "I'll return shortly."

"No . . ." Harlow fiddled with the hilt of her sword. "I mean . . . *home.*"

Oh, God. There it was.

Harlow rushed to fill the thick silence. "If you did, we could be together. We could sneak off here and not have to worry about Mother's nagging."

And here she'd believed there was no greater misery than the hell of Peterloo. With her sister's softly spoken child's words ripping a hole through her heart, she discovered how wrong she'd been.

"Oh, poppet," she began. "If I were here, there'd only be fighting between Mother and me . . . and that wouldn't be good for you."

"I wouldn't care!"

"And there is . . . the Mismatch Society."

"But Sylvia and Valerie and the others—"

"I've been tasked with leading the society in a whole new direction." One that no other woman in the entire organization was capable of. Not in the way Annalee was. She'd been leading those discussions for almost a week, and yet she still could not fully fathom that she'd been elevated to a leader of the group she so loved.

With a selflessness better suited to a woman ten years her senior, Harlow's entire visage brightened, and she brought her hands close to her chest. "You *should* be a leader. You are one of the bravest, strongest, most wonderful women I know!"

So much love for her sister filled Annalee. Since the society's inception, she'd taken a peripheral role, content to let the others shape the path the group had taken. Not even really believing herself capable to lead. Hell, she wasn't sure she was.

"What are you doing?" Harlow asked.

"I'm helping educate women about relationships between men and women." She settled for honesty—choosing her words carefully, however. "Too many young ladies are unaware of what happens when they get married." Her sexual experience, which had earned her society's condemnation, would now be used to help women who were deliberately kept ignorant learn about marital relations. Her role had been elevated, her purpose there expanding to one where she actually contributed.

Harlow released a wistful sigh. "I cannot wait to be part of the Mismatch Society."

"Someday," Annalee said. "Now, run along before you miss all the fun."

"I'll come back, though," Harlow promised. "Because . . . because . . ." Just like that, her smile faded.

Because it was one of the only times Annalee could steal with the girl. When she chose to live apart from her family, she'd found a freedom that saved her sanity but sacrificed the purest, most loving relationship she could ever hope to know. And yet it was the spirits and wild nights and mindless distractions which had also kept her sane. A wave of melancholy swept through her. Annalee scooted nearer her sister and looped an arm around her shoulders. "Come here." She drew Harlow in close for a sideways hug.

The faintest little sniffling from Harlow hinted at her sister's tears. "I'm staying," she whispered.

"You will not." Annalee squeezed her lightly. "There will be plenty more times for us to see one another, now that Jeremy and Sophrona are to be married. The formal dinner parties between our families. The wedding breakfast. The ceremony. The ball." And as much as she'd rather pluck out her fingernails, and then toenails, with her teeth than suffer through family affairs, she'd happily do so if it allowed her time with Harlow. "Now go," she urged. For all the joy Annalee found being with her sister, neither was she so selfish as to see the girl denied that which brought her happiness, just for her own pleasure.

"Oh, very well," Harlow said with a feigned reluctance Annalee allowed her. "If you insist." With an excited little wave, her sister stood and darted to the front of the room.

Harlow paused briefly at the Jacobean-style oak door that led from the conservatory to the hallway, before letting herself out.

Annalee's sister closed that panel behind her with a firm and damning *thwack*.

The moment she'd gone, Annalee let her eyes slide shut. All her muscles clenched and twisted at the loss of Harlow. When it came to how she'd lived these past years, Annalee regretted little. What would hurt her until she took her last breath, however, was that her decisions also happened to be the reason she was kept apart from her youngest sibling.

Her fingers shaking, Annalee grabbed a cheroot from the pocket sewn along the inside bodice of her gown, and withdrew the scrap. She touched the tip to a candle; the corners curled black and then red as, with a little sizzle, it was lit.

Resting on her elbows, she turned her head and brought a hand up, taking a pull from the cheroot. The first time she'd taken a draw, she'd choked and gasped and fought to see through tears.

With time, the little scrap had come to have a soothing effect. In this moment, however, it didn't help.

Click.

Ah, it had been inevitable.

She'd been found.

The footfalls that drifted closer were as determined as a military man's, marking her guest as one who moved with purpose.

Only one man moved like that.

Then he was there. Stopping above her, his broad blacksmith's frame blotting out the moon's glow that had previously poured through the crystal roof.

Tilting back her head, Annalee raised her cheroot for another puff and then exhaled a perfect cloud of white toward him.

"Tell me, have you taken to subterfuge, stooping to following little girls, Lord Darling?" she drawled from where she lay.

⚜

She'd ask Wayland if he stooped to following little girls? "Of course not," Wayland sputtered indignantly. "I—" He caught the little glimmer in Annalee's crystalline eyes. She was teasing.

Ever so slowly, she pushed herself up from that almost perfect recline she'd been in, and held out her cheroot for him.

He eyed the loathsome scrap a moment and then gave his head a terse shake. "I've not come to smoke with you, Annalee."

"The loss is yours." With a little shrug, Annalee took one more puff before tamping that noxious piece out on her mother's stone floor. She did not, however, make any attempt to rise. "It does beg the question, *Darrrling*," she purred. "Why have you sought me out?"

Unbidden, his gaze slid lower. With her burnt-orange skirts rucked up high as they were, her graceful limbs were put on perfect display. Those long, delicately contoured legs, encased in crimson lace stockings.

He swallowed hard.

Get in quick. Get out faster.

That had been the mantra rolling around Wayland's head from the moment he'd been tasked with finding Annalee Spencer.

The part he'd not added on had been, *With the lady in tow.*

Because that would be the decidedly tricky part.

"Unless"—Annalee let her thighs part slightly, the satin shifting in a hedonistic rustle—"there are other more enjoyable reasons you've come, Darling." She enticed like the Eve she'd always been to him.

Lust bolted through him. Of its own volition, his gaze lingered there . . . on well-muscled thighs, ones that had gripped him hard about the waist as she'd urged him on to completion.

A coy smile on her lips, Annalee caressed a hand over the tops of her lacy garters. He swiftly averted his gaze. But it was too late; the image of her had seared his brain and would remain.

You are as much a bastard as you always were where this lady is concerned.

He slogged his way back to a place of propriety, which had been a near impossible task when they'd been younger and she . . . innocent. Now, with her this siren of sin and seduction, it was a labor not even Hercules would have undertaken. "Of course not," he said gruffly.

Annalee pouted, her lush, crimson-rouged lips forming a perfect moue that put all manner of different, but no less wicked, thoughts in his head. "Oh, come; you weren't always a prude."

"I'm no prude."

"Splendid. You're still bedding young ladies of the *ton*," she purred, and from any other woman there would have been resentment and stinging inflection. Not Annalee.

Even so . . . shame tightened his gut. "I don't bed young ladies of the *ton*," he said tersely. She'd been the only one. And those exchanges hadn't been born of just passion, but love.

"That is a shame," she said in those sultry tones. There came a slight rustle, and unbidden, his gaze slipped lower, and she let her legs part wider, an invitation to sin and decadence and—

She chuckled, a full, throaty sound that sent blood rushing to his cock.

Shifting, Wayland discreetly hid the bulge there.

Annalee hopped to her feet with the agility of his favorite childhood cat, Stew. *Yes, think of Stew. Thoughts of Stew are safer.* "You have lost your ability to detect a jest," she said, her voice laden with humor, which also proved how unaffected she was. "I was jesting, Wayland."

Wayland.

Since he'd been granted a title, she was the only one who referred to him by that moniker of his birth.

That was, when she called him anything. Invariably, they were moving in different directions.

"Forgive me for not finding such matters amusing."

She pouted again. "My, you *are* a prude."

Once impetuous and careless and given to thrills and excitement, he'd ultimately seen the price paid for such flaws in his character. He prided himself on the man he'd become. As such, the lady's genuine disappointment shouldn't matter. And it didn't. Yet, oddly, it grated.

It also brought him back to the matter at hand. Wayland glanced down at the bottle of champagne, the pair of glasses—one empty, the other half-full—and then looked to the rumpled lady before him. He tightened his mouth. Once, it had also bothered him that Annalee Spencer had been linked to any number of disreputable gentlemen. So much so that he'd believed the rumors to be rumors. Until at a family gathering—the most awkward of family gatherings, at that—she'd confirmed the veracity of those stories.

Reclining against the oak worktable with her elbows propped upon it, she eyed him knowingly. "You're passing judgment, *Darllling.*" The extra syllable she tacked on to that husky drawl transformed his name into an endearment.

"I've said nothing," he said tightly. "I don't have an opinion of you and your actions, one way or the other."

She trilled a laugh, and then pushing away from the table, she strolled sleekly over, very much the cat he'd likened her to moments ago.

He automatically backed up a step, but his legs collided with a work stool behind him, and he tumbled onto it. At eight inches past five feet, the lady was taller than most men; being seated as he was, however, managed to put them nearly at eye level.

It was a dangerous place to be, where Lady Annalee Spencer was concerned.

By the coy smile on her rouged lips, she knew it, too.

He swallowed hard. "We have to . . ." His words trailed off as she brought her palms up, pressing them against his chest.

And this time, swallowing, that most reflexive of actions, became an impossibility, and his heart thumped a powerful beat where her hands touched. She tugged free his silken cravat, and his mouth formed the words of a protest . . . that, God help him, he couldn't force out.

She'd always been a siren to him. Forbidden to him by her birthright, and because of his relationship with her brother. And now . . . forbidden to him for altogether different reasons. That reminder was enough to break through his hungering.

She laughed, that husky contralto wrapping around him. "Do you truly believe I'm trying to seduce you, Wayland? Even I would not do that."

His ears went hot. His face. His entire body. The burn of mortification that he'd even thought—

Annalee leaned in, placing her lips close to his ear. "At least not in the midst of my brother's betrothal ball," she whispered, and then she darted out her tongue, flicking that flesh along the sensitive shell of his ear.

He croaked, *"Annalee."*

"Oh, hush, you fusty thing." And then, with an intimacy befitting the wife he'd once yearned for her to be, she gave several firm tugs to the cravat she'd mussed a short while ago. "I'm merely fixing you." She adjusted the folds of that silken article. "Mustn't send you out rumpled, Lord Darling." She clucked her tongue. "Whatever would people say?" And with a greater efficiency and rapidity than even his own valet, she was done. "There," she murmured, and this time, she sounded so very much like . . . Annalee of old. The bold but still respectable lady he'd intended to make his wife . . . until the world had caught fire and their relationship had been devoured by that conflagration.

Annalee rested a hand on his thigh; his muscles went tight under that bold touch. She stilled, a knowing glimmer lighting her blue eyes, and ever so slowly, she stroked her fingers higher. She continued that path, and when she showed no hint of stopping as she reached the place near the vee between his legs, he immediately caught her fingers. Even as he stopped her, that traitorous flesh between his legs sprang harder than ever. "I preferred you rumpled." She winked, the graceful glide of her long, flaxen lashes a different form of temptation, but one no less dangerous.

Firming his mouth and his resolve, he removed her hand from his person. "I'm not here to play games, Annalee."

"That's unfortunate, because I do have cards for vingt-et-un. Or . . . whist? I do believe you were a whist man?"

She knew. She knew because he'd been the one to teach her everything she knew about cards and wagering. Both pastimes she now engaged in freely with all the most disreputable members of Polite Society.

"Your brother has asked . . ." *Bloody hell.* He'd once been smoother with his words. "He said . . ."

Annalee's lips curled up slowly at the corners. She would enjoy his discomfort in this. Determined to just have it done, he got to the heart of the reason for his being here. "He asked that you return to the ball," he said flatly. What would she say if she learned of the other request Jeremy had put to him?

"On your arm?" Annalee slapped her fingers to a daringly low neckline, bringing his focus to the lush flesh straining the lace-trimmed bodice. "Do imagine the scandal, Darling."

He wrenched his focus away. "Not with me. Ahead of me. Just so that—" He caught the sparkle in her eyes. "You're teasing," he muttered under his breath.

She leaned forward and, bringing the tip of her thumb and forefinger together, whispered, "Just a bit. I don't need a nanny or a governess or any other manner of keeper, Wayland." It was the first hint of frosty cool, a deviation from her usual flirting and baiting and teasing. Annalee gave him a once-over, the look cursory. "Not from you, and not from any man." And with that, she filled her arms with the nighttime picnic materials she'd assembled and headed toward the doorway which led outside.

Wayland stared after her retreating frame. "I don't wish to control you, you know," he called after her.

Without looking back, she raised an arm, and giving a wave, she headed for her mother's outdoor gardens.

He should have known this wouldn't be easy. Not with Annalee as the impossible charge he'd been instructed to guide back to the festivities. As she disappeared outside, he hesitated, going back and forth between the favor Jeremy had put to him and the woman who had no interest in being escorted.

With a curse, he started after her.

Chapter 3

I don't wish to control you, you know, he'd said . . .

That had been one of the reasons she'd lost her girlish heart to him. Having a mother who bowed to society's constraints, and a father whose strategy for life was "please thy wife and live in peace," she'd always chafed at her mother's demands that she be a certain way. And for eighteen years, Annalee had been that way publicly. Only when she'd been alone with Wayland had she let herself live freely. And she hated that she remembered any of it. The past life she'd lived.

Setting down her provisions beside the enormous stone watering fountain at the back of the gardens, she grabbed the blanket she and Harlow had occupied and snapped it open. She'd just finished depositing her things upon the edges of the fabric to keep it from blowing and twisting with the occasional night wind when the churn of gravel gave him away.

He stopped beside the fountain. "Annalee, your brother asked for your return."

Goodness, he'd always been obstinate. That tenacity he'd once put toward more important goals . . . like exacting change for the oppressed and improving the lives and lots of people born outside the aristocracy.

"And tell me . . . What if I don't do what I'm supposed to, Wayland-dear?" She leaned forward, putting her bosom on display. "What if I refuse to head abovestairs? Will you"—his gaze fixed on her breasts spilling over her bodice, as she'd intended—"force me?"

He instantly recoiled, jolting. "Of course not," he sputtered.

And Annalee didn't know whether to laugh or be offended. Any other—nay, every other—man whom she'd pressed herself against in that way had gotten tongue-tied, and had been hopeless to do anything but stare at her bosom.

But then, Wayland hadn't looked her way in years. More specifically, since Peterloo. That had been the day that had changed him, and her, and how they'd looked at one another.

Nay, his tastes now ran to the proper, where she'd been running *away* from propriety these past years. And she'd no regrets, and certainly no interest in the man he'd become.

"I thought you said you'd no wish to control me, my lord," she said tightly, surrendering all teasing.

"I don't."

"Splendid." She clapped her hands twice. "Then might I suggest you return and leave me to my"—she nudged at the blanket laid out—"pleasures . . . ?"

He followed her focus to the glasses, one the flute Harlow had drained of lemonade, the other Annalee's half-drunk champagne. The cards. And she knew. By the way his jaw set and the disapproval creasing the hard lines of his mouth, she knew precisely the assumption he'd arrived at: she'd been meeting a lover earlier and now wished to continue her assignation.

Not that he was jealous, nor did she care one way or the other whether he was.

"Under different circumstances," he said brusquely, "it is hardly my affair whom you were meeting"—he flicked a cool, condescending stare over the blanket—"or where . . . but in this particular instance, it is my business."

"Shove off, Wayland," she said, giving him a shoulder.

He slapped a hand against his thigh. "Your being out here in the middle of your brother's betrothal ball isn't proper."

"And you are nothing if not proper," she drawled. Perfect. And prim. A paragon. And every other *p*-word for one of his flawlessness.

All those terms she'd delighted in applying to him in recent years proved a delicious incongruity with the muscular, six-foot form he possessed. *A blacksmith's body* was what she'd always said. With biceps that bulged through his shirts, and sinew in his thighs wide enough to rival a tree trunk.

"I'm here as a friend," he said quietly.

"To whom? Me?" She swiveled back around, facing him. "Or Jeremy?"

"Why can't it be both?"

"Because we haven't spoken in years." In part because she'd never answered his notes after Peterloo. In part because of the contents of those notes. And in larger part because she'd gone out of her way to avoid him.

"That . . . is a fair point." He abruptly quit that distracted thumping of the side of his leg. "Annalee, as I said, I would never presume to tell you who to meet or where to meet them," he began.

So that was what this was to be, then?

A lecture.

To her annoyance, this would prove one of the few times where she hadn't been engaging in the very activities he assumed she had. "I wasn't meeting anyone."

He knitted his brows. "You . . . weren't."

Except, that wasn't quite true. "I wasn't meeting a lover." She didn't know what compelled her to tell him that detail.

Did she imagine the slight sag of his shoulders?

Of course she did.

It was merely being alone with this man, her first love and lover, all these years later, which created an illusion that he might have cared whether she'd been meeting a man.

And furthermore, why should it matter either way what he thought about her or her reasons for being out here? The fight drained out of her, and she slid onto the side of the fountain. "You should just go," she said tiredly.

He hesitated, then took a seat next to her.

"I was playing whist with Harlow, and just talking with her. I . . . don't get to see her anymore." She had to swallow several times around the pain of that.

Annalee couldn't explain how or why she'd shared that piece with him.

"I . . . have heard as much," Wayland murmured.

Annalee glanced over. "From Jeremy?"

He nodded.

Raising her voice a smidgen, she spoke through her nostrils. "I'm a shameful, wicked influence who will only corrupt."

Wayland looked her way. "Your mother?"

And this time, Annalee nodded.

They shared a smile, and it . . . felt oddly wonderful; it was a shared bond with a friend from long ago. *That* was what it was. That was *all* it was. Even so, that connection proved unnerving. Restless, Annalee leaned down and scooped up a handful of pebbles and gravel. Sifting through them, she proceeded to toss the larger stones, one at a time, off into the opposite side of the fountain. Each one landed, pinging droplets. "Whenever I come here"—which was rare—"I find whatever time I can to steal with Harlow."

"She has your spirit."

"Don't let my parents or brother hear you say that." The way he said it, however, made her heart leap in the funniest little way.

"Jeremy is the one who said it," he said. "Numerous times."

"Oh." It had been Jeremy. More of that oddly placed disappointment filled her. "It also seemed better to stay out of the way, as trouble invariably finds me." She glanced his way. "You should have a care. You're going to get your jacket and trousers wet; people will talk."

"No one is going to pay close enough attention to me to notice."

"Because you're the stuffy, proper gentleman?" she asked without inflection.

"Precisely." He winked. "See, there is some good in it. I'm spared notice and free to enjoy myself."

It was a dream she couldn't even imagine. Granted, she'd never conducted herself in a way that would see her permitted the same luxury he enjoyed.

She released her last rock, then dusted the gravel from her palms. "Do you know how to enjoy yourself anymore, Wayland?" Curiosity made her ask the question that, at the most unexpected times, would come to her when she allowed herself to think of him.

"I do."

Did he recognize both the pause between her query and his answer and the hesitancy that made his answer a lie? She spun on the makeshift bench she'd made of the ledge, and facing him, she drew up her knees. "All right. Out with it. What brings the great Wayland Smith, now the Baron Darlington, joy?"

"Annalee," he said, his voice pained.

She swatted him. "Don't be stuffy. I promise to return to the festivities if you answer it."

"Very well."

Annalee snorted. "That's all it took? I should have offered a lesser prize." She motioned with her palms. "Tell. Tell."

"I . . ." His high, broad brow creased. "I . . ."

She pointed at him. "You *don't* know, because you don't really find pleasure in anything."

"I do," he said indignantly. "I . . . I . . . like my coffee," he said on a rush, as though he'd just landed on it.

A laugh exploded from her lips, a great big snorting noise born not of the past years' cynicism but of genuine mirth that she'd forgotten the feel of. And how very good it felt, too. She laughed so hard her shoulders shook, and she leaned against him.

Wayland bristled. "What?"

"Th-that isn't a life's pleasure," she said when she managed to rein in her hilarity. Annalee brushed the moisture from her cheeks.

"It is." He paused. "Though, I'll allow, a simple one." He made to stand. "Now you promised to re—"

Annalee snatched his sleeve and dragged him back to the seat beside her. "There has to be . . . more."

"I enjoy my meetings at Parliament."

She smiled wistfully. "That I can believe." And she could. A man who'd once yearned for a voice had been granted one through the title he'd earned for his heroic act of bravery that day at Peterloo. "Is it . . . everything you had hoped? Having a voice?"

Wayland brushed some of the remnants of gravel that remained from before off the edge of the fountain and back onto the ground below. They rained down with faint little *plinks*. "I find myself, ironically, with a title that allows me to be part of the government and yet unable to exact any real change. I may be amongst their ranks, but I'm not really part of the nobility. The members of Parliament know it, and that matters very much in brokering legislation." He straightened, dusting his hands together. "But . . . I am not as powerless as I once was, and so I take hope in that."

He'd always been driven for greater goals, for the greater good. Even with all the time that had passed and everything that had changed, he had not. Not really.

"You've not yet let them see how daringly bold you might be, Wayland."

43

His mouth tightened, harsh creases forming at the sides. "That *daringly bold* person got himself . . . and others . . . into more trouble than was ever wise or safe."

Peterloo whispered there in the air, in veiled words from his lips that really weren't all that veiled. It was an event they had never spoken of . . . for the simple reason that, after that day, their relationship had been severed.

A breeze stole through, and she rubbed at her arms. To ward off the slight chill as much as the whisper of memories stirred with the most innocuous of words.

"Yes, well, I prefer 'daringly bold' still, Wayland."

She braced for his pompous condemnation. What she wasn't prepared for was the slight softening of his features, or the wistful smile that brought his hard lips up at their corners. "You always were the braver of our pair."

And she knew the moment between them had come to an end. She felt it in the air, and perhaps it was that speaking about the past with her former friend and lover, whom she'd not truly spoken to in years, that accounted for the emptiness that swept through her as he stood. "I should return," Wayland said.

First.

"Oh, yes. It wouldn't do for us to be spotted returning together." Annalee reached for her slippers, and when he still hovered there, she gave him a wave. "Go. I'll be along. I'm not one to break my word."

"I didn't say you would."

"You didn't need to."

Wayland lingered still. "It was . . ."

"It was," she said quietly. He didn't need to complete his sentence. This had been nice, and . . . missed.

Dropping a bow, Wayland left.

With him gone, she set to work tugging on her slippers.

You always were the braver of our pair . . .

"A pair," she murmured, tasting those words on her tongue. That had been precisely what they'd been. No two had been closer than they, as friends and lovers. Everything, however, had changed.

Everything.

Hissss.

Annalee's entire body recoiled, and she whipped around, her skirts snapping noisily about her. She searched frantically for the source of that whistling.

A bright glow lit up the sky, transforming night into day.

Her pulse hammered loudly in her ears. *What was . . . ?*

Booom!

She gasped as the errant echo of that forceful explosion ricocheted, rocking the ground under her feet, and she was jolted to another moment. Another time.

"Chaaaarge . . ."

The thunderous command shouted above the cries of the crowd slipped in.

Biting her lower lip hard, Annalee shoved her fingertips into her temples and frantically rubbed, trying to tamp out memories fighting their way forward—dark thoughts threatening to suck her back to that long-ago day.

Don't let it in . . . You are here . . . You are in London . . . alone. Not in Manchester. You are not about to be overcome by a sea of stampeding men and women fighting their way to freedom.

Breathing heavily, Annalee fixed her gaze out on the expanse of her mother's gardens.

They are empty. No one is here. Just you.

No crowd.

No charging soldiers.

No bayonet blades.

No gun—

There came another loud sizzle, rapidly followed by a sharp pop, and once again the skies lit up brightly.

A panicky laugh gurgled in her throat, and she choked on that empty amusement.

Ah, yes, of course. There would be fireworks marking the occasion of her brother's betrothal. A resplendent, garish display.

How ironic that she'd thought it safer to be away from the crowd, only to find herself thrown into the fire.

Pop-pop . . .

Boooom.

That enormous explosion shook the ground, the force of it so deep that she felt it all the way to her belly, and she was jolted once more from the now and back into the hell of that time long ago.

Frantic, her heart knocking erratically against her rib cage, she searched about for Wayland as the past converged with the present.

He was here.

She'd seen him.

Where was he?

No, that wasn't right.

She didn't want to see him. Not anymore.

Annalee fought through the fog of the past, and falling to her haunches, she clutched at her head again, yanking her hair free of its elegant coiffure.

Panting, she jerked a panicky gaze up, and unblinking, she looked around.

Wait, no, that didn't make sense. None of this made sense. Her hair hadn't been elegant that day. It had been casually plaited, a plait that had so worked against her.

Boom-boom-boom.

Grabbed by passing strangers rushing by her, threatening to pull her under.

She flung her head wildly, left and right, fighting free of the hold they had on her. The memories? Or wait . . . Were there actual strangers with their hands scrabbling in her hair, using her to leverage themselves forward to safety?

Annalee whimpered. *Why can't I get free? Why can't I sort it out?*

And then there they came, the distant thunder of approaching feet. Excited cries.

Or was that laughter? She knocked her head against a stone ledge. A fountain? Why would there be a fountain in the fields of Manchester. Or laughter?

The cries grew louder, closer, and gasping for breath, she lurched to her feet and stumbled around. Her knees caught the crude stone wall on the edge of the pasture.

But stone walls weren't crude . . .

Then the ground was rushing up to meet her.

Nay, not the ground.

Water.

It closed over her head, swallowing her cry and flooding her mouth and nostrils that burnt, bringing her back to the moment.

Not Peterloo.

Through the glassy sheen of the ice-cold water, the fireworks marking the celebratory announcement of her brother's betrothal filled the star-studded night sky.

Annalee propelled herself upright, breaking through the water, gasping for breath, her body shaking from the cold—

To find a wide-eyed audience staring back. Of course, they'd assembled to watch the display of fireworks, only to be treated to an altogether different spectacle—*her.*

Splendid. Just splendid.

She forced a cheeky grin and waggled her fingers at a long line of her brother's betrothal guests, all straining for a glimpse of her, sprawled in her family's fountain.

And then her smile faltered as it landed on a group of five breaking through that line: her parents, horror lighting their faces. Jeremy. His ashen betrothed.

And . . . Wayland.

What must he think?

And why, out of all those people present, did she focus on him first? Here, when she'd gone and made a spectacle of her brother's big night. Her breathing hitched, shame and regret and so much pain making her heart squeeze. This was why it was best if she didn't come 'round the respectable sorts. Her family included. Especially her family.

The quiet proved deafening, made all the more powerful by the intermittent booming of the fireworks. Those same blasted fireworks that had startled her into an inadvertent swim.

Annalee shivered. "Forgive me," she called out into the shock of silence. "I'd invite you to join me. Alas, the water is a bit cold." With that, she stood, her drenched skirts heavy, pulling her back. She faltered.

"Foxed again, she is," a voice in the crowd murmured.

And then someone was immediately there with a hand to steady her.

Through the curtain of wet, sorry curls hanging over her eyes, she stared unblinkingly at the large, white-gloved fingers twined with hers.

Annalee lifted her eyes.

Wayland's gaze met hers. And there was no condemnation or horror, just a gentle concern, and she, who didn't cry as a rule, found herself blinking back the sting of tears as he helped her climb over the edge.

The guests found their collective voices in the form of a gasp as they all locked in on the sight of Annalee with her satin skirts clinging indecently to her body, putting everything on display and adding a layer of transparency to her burnt-orange ball gown, her nipples puckered and revealed by the damp dress. She shivered, folding her arms at her chest. It proved the wrong thing to do; her breasts bobbed up, the flesh climbing even higher over the already daringly low bodice.

A lady fainted with just a handful rushing to her rescue. All the rest stared goggle-eyed at Annalee.

There came a swift rustle of fabric, and a moment later, Wayland brought his jacket down around her shoulders, and she was enfolded in the thickest, most wonderful warmth.

"Not a single word, Annalee Elise," her mother hissed. "In your father's offices. Now."

Oh, dear. She'd called forth the full, ridiculously paired names. This was certain to be bad. Not that Annalee would have expected anything else.

And with as much grace as she could muster, Annalee marched forward, the crowd parting to allow her to pass.

Chapter 4

The night had been ruined for Wayland's best friend in the world. Lord Jeremy's betrothal ball was certain to be consigned to gossip sheets for the whole of the Season, and maybe for Seasons to come.

Before it had been ruined, and scandal-borne, it had been . . . an unexpectedly good night for Wayland.

There'd been the first exchange with Annalee in too many years. Oh, they'd had cordial exchanges and greetings, with her inserting her usual banter and teasing. But they'd not spoken at any length. Until tonight.

Beside that fountain, for a brief moment it had almost been as it had always been between them.

Only to have the evening end so spectacularly awfully, with Annalee an object—once more—of Polite Society's gossip. And he despised it with every fiber of his being. Because the sight of her there, with all the lords and ladies in attendance gawking at her like she was some kind of circus oddity while Annalee herself put on a brave show, knotted his muscles and filled him with a mix of hurt for her and rage for those who delighted in her scandals.

But he knew her, the way she'd trapped her lower lip between her teeth and the brittleness of her smile; she'd been mortified, and he hated that she'd been so discovered.

Now, with most of the guests having filed out, Wayland, collecting his cloak alongside his mother and sister, planned to join their ranks.

"Heartbreaking," his mother was saying as she adjusted the clasp of her cloak. "Just heartbreaking."

"For Annalee," Kitty rejoined.

"Do hush." Their mother stole a look around the foyer, empty of all except the servants. "As it is, I cannot believe you dared to offer your coat to her."

"Oh, yes," Kitty said, her face and voice a flawless deadpan. "Imagine Wayland doing something so ungentlemanly as to rush to the aid of a lady in need."

"*Psst*, Darling."

Wayland was so close. With his cloak on, and with the Earl and Countess of Kempthorne's doorway already hanging open, all he need do was pretend he'd not heard and continue marching right on through.

Between the loaded carriages rumbling on, there was certainly enough noise for him to pretend he'd heard nothing beyond the rattling of those wheels as the guests left for the evening.

The butler, Tanning, gave him a questioning look.

And yet . . .

He and his family followed that frantic whispering to the girl seated above, at the balustrade overlooking the foyer, her legs dangling over the edge. Stretching her fingers through the posts, Harlow waved him up. "You're needed," she said, this time in a near yell that there could absolutely be no mistaking.

"Do go see what Jeremy requires." His mother took him by the arm and steered him toward Annalee and Jeremy's sister. "He will need a friend in this moment."

He'd wager his very soul to Satan himself that it was less the friendship his mother worried after than the prestige that came from the connections provided through Lord and Lady Kempthorne's oldest and most respected of titles.

It spoke volumes of how little his mother knew of this particular family's dynamics that it wouldn't be Jeremy Harlow had fetched him for.

"Did you hear me?" Harlow pointed her rapier downward. "Don't make me come fetch you."

"Get moving, brother," Kitty said, shoving him slightly. A devilish glimmer lit her brown eyes. "Though it would be quite entertaining to see what she did when she came for you."

"What a devoted sister," he muttered.

Alas, it appeared there was to be no escaping.

Damn this night.

He didn't want to do any more damned favors this evening for this family . . . even as he owed them for debts that could not be paid.

Nay, Wayland wished to seek out his own household and sleep in his own damned bed, and forget this night had ever happened.

Alas, the person putting this latest request to him was the last person he could deny.

Unclasping his cloak, he handed the article over to the Spencer family's most loyal of servants. "Please instruct my driver to escort my sister and mother home."

"Very good, and . . . thank you, my lord," the butler quietly murmured as he accepted the garment. And Wayland heard within those four words that it was not the cloak he expressed any gratitude over.

Harlow scrambled to her feet.

Leaning over, she waved her hand, motioning him up. "This way, Darling. Quickly!"

Hastening his steps, Wayland made the climb.

When he reached the top, he met Harlow with a smart salute. "My captain."

Except the young girl stared back with a gravity better suited to a person two decades her senior. Her earlier affront and child's innocence had all faded from their last meeting. An hour ago? A lifetime ago? Time with this family really defied all sense of realness and meaning.

"This isn't the time for games, Darling," she whispered. "There's trouble."

Yes, there'd been any manner of it, this night.

"It's . . . Annalee." A tug on his sleeve brought his attention downward. "Did you hear what happened?"

He hesitated.

"You saw?" Harlow correctly surmised.

"I may have," he allowed. Nearly every illustrious guest had.

Annalee's little sister gave a wrinkle of her nose. "Do you know, that doesn't really make sense." At his questioning look, she clarified. "The whole 'I may have,' when what you really mean to say is that you *did* see. That is what you meant, isn't it?"

"Indeed."

Harlow sank down, and as if she were the queen herself, urging a subject into a proper seat, she patted the floor.

Wayland promptly sank down, claiming the place beside her.

"She didn't do it," she said the moment his arse hit the floor.

"It?"

Harlow rolled her eyes. "Anything. She wasn't misbehaving." There was a slight pause. "Not this time."

No. She hadn't been. She'd been headed back in. She'd given her word, and he didn't doubt she'd intended to follow it. Eventually. The question was . . . What had happened between the moment he'd left her and the moment she'd been caught in the fountain? A disquiet filled him, and he recalled once more Jeremy's favor. "Do you know if . . . something happened to Annalee tonight?" he asked gently.

"She didn't do anything," the little girl said quickly, speaking over him, her words all rolling together. "She was doing everything she could to stay out of mischief tonight. It was why she was in the conservatory. We were playing cards and eating treats and sipping lemonade . . ."

Harlow paused. "Well, I was sipping lemonade. She was sipping champagne, but you get the point, Darling."

He recalled what Annalee had shared. Her reasons for being in the countess's indoor gardens. Not because she'd been meeting a lover, as he'd initially suspected, but because she'd wanted to be with the sister she was prevented from knowing.

In the conservatory she may have been alone with her sister . . . but *what* had transpired in the fountain . . . ?

"Oomph." All the air left Wayland as Harlow sent an impressive fist into his side. "What . . . ?"

"She was alone. I saw her. She fell in. She was leaning over, and just . . . pitched forward."

He wiped a tired hand over his face. "I believe you."

"She needs you." Harlow caught his hand. "She *wants* you to be there for her."

"Did she ask for me?" There was . . . hope within his own question—he didn't know where it even came from.

Harlow rolled her eyes. "Of course not. Annalee doesn't ask for help from anyone. Including me."

She'd always been self-possessed, one who'd never put favors or requests to anyone. When she'd wished to learn something her governesses and parents had deemed unfit knowledge for ladies, she'd taken it upon herself to do the research, finding those answers for herself. What had it been like for her that day at Peterloo? Back when they'd been on different ends of the field, divided by a stretch of land run with chaos and blood? Had she accepted the little help that was to be found that day? Or had she seen to herself as she always had?

His chest hitched, and it hurt physically to try to breathe through it.

"Go to her, Darling," Harlow said softly. "She needs you."

She needed him . . .

For a second time that night, those words had been put to him by a Spencer. Just not the one from whom he wished to hear them. Nay, he suspected he was the last person in the world Annalee needed, or wanted . . .

The youngest, far-too-astute Spencer sibling must have sensed his wavering. "She is in Father's office . . ." Her little features grew pinched. "The Lecture." At his look, she clarified. "That is what Annalee and I call it when Mother and Father bring her in for a scolding."

The girl referred to it as a scolding, and yet, given the earl and countess's searing outrage and fury, that would be a mild way of thinking of whatever was unfolding in the office. Whatever it was, it was entirely too intimate a family moment for him to intrude on.

"I can hardly interfere," he said regretfully. Nay, he couldn't very well go storming into the earl's office and rush to the lady's defense. But that was what she'd desperately needed over the years—a champion. He was seeing that now.

Harlow's eyes hardened. "She should have someone to defend her. It won't be Jeremy, and me, they won't take seriously. At the very *lee-assst*"—in her entreaty she managed to squeeze several syllables into that word—"wait until they are done yelling at her and then go to her. When my parents and Jeremy are done with her, she is going to need a friend. *Please*," Harlow whispered.

Please.

And he was lost.

Wayland came to his feet, and her eyes filled with an adulation he was wholly undeserving of. He'd brought nothing but sorrow and suffering to this family.

"I may allow you into my pirates' club once more, Darling," Harlow said with her usual cheer restored.

Wayland swept a flourishing bow befitting such a benefaction. "I cannot think of a greater honor, my lady."

"Thank Annalee. She was the one who said I shouldn't hold you in ill will and reminded me you were just being a friend to Jeremy when you were looking for her."

He hesitated. "She said that?" She'd defended him? And here he'd imagined there wouldn't be, and couldn't be, a good thing the lady had to say about him. He'd expected her resentment and hatred of him were so strong that there wouldn't be a nice thing for her *to* say. Just as he wouldn't have expected before this night that she'd want him to sit and speak with her outside. Nor had he blamed her for those sentiments. She was not only entitled but also deserving of them.

"Stop woolgathering." Harlow unsheathed her rapier and pointed to the winding spiral staircase. "Now get on with you, and promise that you will not tell her I sent you."

"You have my word."

And for the third time that night, Wayland found himself in the unlikeliest of ways where Annalee was concerned—searching her out.

That hadn't always been the case. A lifetime ago, that was all he'd ever done. That was all they'd ever done—looked for one another. When they'd not been together with Jeremy, Annalee and Wayland had gone about trying to steal private moments to talk and read . . . and simply be with one another. And what had started out as a close friendship had grown to more.

Wayland made his way through the palatial townhouse, headed past the liveried servants standing on alert in their full gold regalia and black epaulets, the epitome of wealth and power.

The moment he reached the hall leading to the earl's office, the first thing to reach him was silence. Perhaps they'd finished with the *discussion*, after all. Perhaps Annalee had already made her way abovestairs.

The young footman near him caught his eye, and there was a regretful glint there as he shook his head, confirming the family still met.

The servants' loyalty toward Annalee was greater than to the lord and lady who employed them, and it was . . . telling.

But then, Annalee had always been warm and friendly to the servants. And like her brother, who'd thought nothing of befriending the blacksmith's son, neither had Annalee turned up her nose at Wayland's station. She'd befriended him and then, years later, when they'd grown up, entertained thoughts of marriage to him.

And so Wayland slipped off, and turning down the next corridor, he seated himself on the floor, resting his back against the wall, and waited for the business to conclude.

Chapter 5

Tension hung over her father's office.

In fairness, tension was the mood of choice whenever Annalee attended a familial gathering. Such meetings had become less frequent since she'd moved out of her parents' home and in with her two equally scandalous friends. They'd collectively been called the Wantons of Waverton.

Her father sat behind his desk like some great, overblown king of yore, her mother, his perfect counterpoint queen, pacing before him. And with the rant she'd been on since they'd assembled, speaking enough for all of them.

From where he stood beside the hearth, Jeremy's features were drawn.

His gaze condemning.

Over the years, Annalee had come to find that, when dealing with the fallout of a scandal she was at the heart of, there was a pattern to her parents' behavior, usually with her mother in charge of the Lecture.

First, there came the cataloging:

"No, it wasn't enough that she was discovered alone with Lady Bedford's vicar son just a fortnight ago, constructing a champagne tower in the middle of *that* family's betrothal ball." Her mother trilled a patently false laugh as she paced. "Or that she was seen accompanying that terrible earl into that outrageous gaming hell just last evening." *That terrible earl* was none other than Annalee's dear friend Lord Willoughby. Willoughby, who'd also proven more loyal than her parents and brother combined.

Then, of course, came the parental woes and lamentation:

"Why must she be so difficult? Why must she live to make our life mayhem?"

"I do not know, dearest," Annalee's father said from his place behind his desk. He slid his gaze Annalee's way, and the sadness within those blue eyes hit her like a kick to the stomach. It always did. For she remembered when he'd swung her around and let her dance upon the tops of his shoes. He moved his stare back to the countess, and Annalee was forgotten . . . once more. "She was not always this way."

No, she hadn't been. As they resumed their parental rant, she stared blankly off to where her brother stood. None of them knew the reasons for her transformation. Of course they didn't. It had been far easier for them to never have to acknowledge what she'd faced that day in Manchester. It had been easier for all of them to make believe it had never happened. And Annalee? She had been the greatest at that game of pretend. Throwing herself fully into a life of distractions.

Her mother's pacing grew frenzied, indicating this latest exchange was coming to a head. "Whatever are we to do with her?" the Countess of Kempthorne seethed. *"Whatever are we to do?"* She repeated that question, slowing each word down to agonizingly precise syllables.

Annalee stilled.

For, on occasion, there was also the most terrifying response to her scandal: her mother's furious musings.

Whatever are we to do with her?

They were the most chilling words spoken by Annalee's mother. For Annalee *knew* she pushed the boundaries of their patience. It had been a delicate dance, conducting herself in a way that allowed her the freedom and escape she sought in life, while not pushing her parents beyond the point of what they tolerated. Keeping company with the fringe members of society as she had, she was well aware of the fate awaiting the daughters and sisters and wives who displeased.

Isolation.

Banishment.

Institutions.

And mayhap that is the perfect place for you . . . You are, after all, stark raving mad.

That silent voice taunted Annalee, as it so often did, with what she'd become. A woman not in control of her own faculties or senses, who couldn't keep the nightmares at bay. A woman who at times forgot where she was and couldn't sort out past from present.

"Annalee." She blinked slowly. *"Annalee."* That furious whisper pulled her from her thoughts, and she looked to Jeremy.

"Are you even listening?" he whispered.

And for another moment, she could believe he was still on her side—her hero, her champion of a big brother.

But then he shook his head in disgust.

That shoulder of coldness was the greatest cut of all.

A pang struck her chest. Her gut clenched.

Her parents' disdain she'd come to expect and accept, but facing that same coldness in her brother? Even if, for all intents and purposes, she was deserving of his outrage and contempt?

After all, she'd gone and turned his betrothal ball to the illustrious, respectable Miss Oatley into a scandal. Annalee's latest scandal, that was.

She couldn't care less about what a single person in attendance this night thought . . . beyond the one six feet apart from her at the other end of the mantel. And yet, if Jeremy despised the changes he saw in her? What would he say . . . ? How would he treat her if he discovered all the times she wasn't in control of her own faculties? Nay, it was something he could never learn. Something no one could ever discover.

"And what is it with her and fountains?" Annalee's father was asking. He sounded on the verge of tears.

"It is *always* the fountains," her mother hissed.

The countess may as well have been reviling Satan himself for the loathing in those five words. "I *love* fountains," Annalee said indignantly, feeling a deep need to defend them.

Her parents gave her a look, and she resisted the urge to squirm as she had when she'd been a child called in for getting grass stains upon her white skirts.

The moment the earl and countess returned to their discussion, Jeremy, where he stood at the hearth, glanced her way. "Really?" he mouthed.

Annalee brought a shoulder up. "What?" she returned silently. "I *do*." At least fountains had given her comfort after Peterloo. They were made of stone but always dependable in helping her chase away the demons and monsters.

Closing his eyes, Jeremy gave his head a shake, and turning dismissively, he returned his focus to their parents' discussion.

Annalee slouched in her seat. She really *did* love all fountains. The small watering ones. The stone and marble sorts.

But she particularly loved the enormous, life-size ones.

She loved dancing in them. Dipping her toes in them. On occasion, she'd even been found sleeping in them. That was, after a night of excess. She loved how the waters within were a cool balm that never failed to wash away the nightmares.

This time, she'd not been caught sleeping in the fountain. But for all the scandal she'd caused this night—of all nights—she may as well have been.

Though in fairness, if they'd learned the truth—that she'd been out of her head in a moment of insanity—it would perhaps have brought even more of their deserved horror.

Or worse . . .

A panicky little giggle bubbled up her throat, and Jeremy fixed a warning glare on her.

Repressing the urge to shiver from her hopelessly wet gown, Annalee edged closer to the blazing fire at her back.

Seventeen minutes already, and an endless tirade of her parents talking about her and not to her.

Yes, this had all the makings of one of the never-ending exchanges . . .

"Do you have somewhere to be, Annalee?" her mother snapped. "Are we keeping you?" she demanded before Annalee could get a response in.

That had done it, then. A possibility loathsome to the countess: that her daughter would dare dictate any aspect of this exchange.

"Of course not," she said with a flourishing hand to her breast. "I would never dare leave my big brother's betrothal ball."

It was the wrong thing to say.

Her brother winced.

"You are a scandal, Annalee Elise," her mother hissed, that hideous pairing of almost identical-sounding names falling from her lips for a second time. "A shameful, wicked scandal."

And that proved the moment Annalee was forgotten. Her mother directed all the rage she felt for her daughter back to her husband. "We have tolerated so very much where she is concerned, but this?" The countess's nostrils flared, giving her the look of a bull Beckett had rented for a raucous summer party when he'd had a bull-baiter waving a red flag. "This is a line too far, even for her."

"Is there any line that is too far for her, really?" her father asked tiredly.

Tired. He always had the air of the exhausted when it came to talking about Annalee, or discussing anything with her.

Not that they'd truly spoken. Not for years and years now.

Her father scrubbed a hand beginning to wrinkle across his forehead.

His disappointment had also become familiar enough that the evidence of it had hurt, until it hadn't. Now it was just accepted.

And were it just her disdainful parents, she would have been all too happy to meet them with the flippancy she reserved for them and their lectures and disappointment.

But this wasn't about them. Or her.

It took a physical effort to turn her head once more and face her big brother. "I am sorry, Jeremy, for the scandal," she murmured. "It wasn't my fault."

"Not this time" would certainly apply.

After all, many, many, many times before this one, it had invariably been her fault. Nor was she the guilty sort, taking ownership of actions that weren't her own. She was quite aware of her sins and scandals.

At his silence, she stretched out a hand, which only managed to set the crystal beads dripping from her sleeve shaking and drips of water flying. Water caught her brother in the cheek, and he flinched.

Pulling a kerchief from his immaculate sapphire wool jacket, he patted the moisture from his person.

"It wasn't her fault, she says," her mother seethed, pacing back and forth, the only hitch in her stride the moment she faced her elder daughter and had her in her sights.

Annalee looked once more to her brother, Jeremy, hopefully. Hopeful that he could see not only her sincerity but also her regret.

Standing at the hearth, his hands clasped behind him, he caught her glance.

He gave his head a slow, slight shake, a disgusted one. It was a barely perceptible flick of the head Annalee had also become well accustomed to over the years. Not, however, from her brother.

And not for the first time since she'd been caught sprawled in the fountain with her family's most prominent guests as witnesses, guilt burrowed deep in her chest.

Alas, there'd be no rescue this time, in this place.

Not that she could blame her elder brother; it wasn't every night a young gentleman had his betrothal ball before all of Polite Society . . . and had that grand affair spoiled by his drunken sister.

Though, in fairness, this time she wasn't three sheets to the wind, she'd been well on her way to it, and quite happily. Her family's tedious, always proper, invariably boring affairs had that effect upon a lady.

Wicked ladies anyway. Of which she was decidedly one.

With a sigh, Annalee withdrew a cheroot from her pocket, and heading over to the nearest sconce, she raised the scrap to light it.

"What is she doing?" her mother squawked.

"Smoking," she said needlessly. "You might find it helps with your nerves."

"I don't have nerves," the countess snapped.

And with a great deliberate show meant to rile, Annalee took a long draw of the smoke, letting it fill her lungs, and then exhaled a perfect ring of white.

Her mother's eyes bulged. "The only frayed nerves I do have are because of you. You are the source of all the woe of this family."

Annalee dropped a hip against the wall. "*Ohhhh*, would we *realllly* say there's familial woe? Jeremy is in love. You and Father are obscenely wealthy and well received. Why, some might say that our family is blissfully blessed." Annalee took another pull from her cheroot.

"What are we to do with her?" her mother demanded as Annalee became invisible to the exchange once more.

"The only thing we can do. The ball is concluded. We return with Jeremy and speak to Sophrona and her family, and she"—her father cast a long, sad look Annalee's way—"she will not attend. She will return to her residence—"

"'She' is still here," Annalee pointed out gleefully, waggling her spare hand.

Both parents continued to ignore her.

"Yes, yes. You are right. We must try to smooth this over," her mother murmured to herself, as if she'd just heard words so profound that they now fueled her courage and confidence to face the great challenge of meeting Polite Society after this scandal. "They will be devastated." The countess pinched her pale cheeks, bringing an immediate splash of crimson to them. "Come along, dear." Her husband immediately sprang to his feet like a dutiful terrier, and together, the pair made to march from the room.

They lingered at the threshold, casting a questioning glance at Jeremy.

"I'll be along shortly," he vowed.

With that they left, and Annalee was, at last, alone with Jeremy. Her elder sibling, and her only brother. Her champion. Or, rather, the former still applied. Much had changed over the years. Everything had changed over the years.

"Well, they took that better than expected," she said dryly when the door had closed behind them.

"It isn't amusing," he said, his tone rich with the same disappointment their parents expressed toward Annalee. "And need you really do that?"

She followed his glance to the scrap between her fingertips. She immediately stubbed out her cheroot. Annalee may not give two damns about her mother's opinion on the habit, but she quite adored her elder brother. "It was an accident, Jeremy," she said earnestly, using really the first words he'd spoken to her as an invitation to join him.

"There's always an accident and some such . . . The time your hair snagged on Lord Wembley's buttons."

"It looked worse than it was," she lied. She'd been doing with Lord Wembley precisely what the whole world had taken it for when they'd come upon her and the earl in Lady Stanhope's gardens.

"Your being discovered alone at Vauxhall Gardens' pleasure paths?" he went on.

And if she could still manage a blush, being called out by her brother for when she'd been caught enjoying a different sort of fireworks on those famed grounds would certainly be the time for one.

But she wasn't a young girl. Or naive. Or innocent. Not in any way.

"I was alone this time," she pointed out brightly. Surely there was something to be said for th—

Jeremy pressed at his temples. "Is *everything* a game with you, Annalee?" And had his tone been as outraged or disgusted as it had been throughout this whole discourse, and not this, this resignation, it would have been a good deal easier.

Apparently there wasn't something to be said for it, after all.

But then, after having his betrothal ball turned into a source of gossip, Jeremy wasn't one to receive such an empty reminder as the one she'd given him.

It didn't matter that she'd been donning her slippers when those fireworks had erupted; it didn't matter that a memory of a different time, a long-ago, darker one, had intruded. When memories so rarely did. Or that they'd had the same potent, crippling effect and left her facedown in that fountain she'd once so very much loved.

"No. It's not," she said quietly. Almost everything was. Her more-loyal-than-she'd-deserved-over-the-years brother? Anything surrounding him and his life was not. Annalee swept over to his side. He'd been the only one there for her following . . . Peterloo. Following that foolish, fateful decision to go to the fields, where chaos had reigned supreme. She caught Jeremy's hands and gave them a squeeze. "I love you. You are my brother."

"It isn't about love, Annalee," he said in that same tired voice, draw-ing back his hands. "It is about you making decisions that are dangerous . . . ones that hurt yourself . . . and now . . ."

And now, him. "How can I fix it?" And yet, even as the question escaped her, she knew the answer. There was no fixing a scandal. Once born, forever there, and gone only when replaced with some other juicy morsel. One that she more often than not provided.

"Don't you see, Annalee? I don't give a jot about how it reflects upon me. I care about Sophrona."

She'd once imagined to have a love like the one he knew now. Once upon a lifetime ago, when she'd not been aware of the ugliness in the world, she'd dreamed of marriage . . .

And she'd almost had it.

Annalee gave her head a slight shake, pushing aside thoughts now as unwelcome as the memories of Peterloo. Nay, somehow worse. Because those belonged to a naive girl, so very green, and entirely removed from the reality that was life. At least the thoughts of Peterloo, as unpleas-ant as the memories were, harkened to a time when she'd ceased being a girl and had become a woman with eyes wide open about what the world truly was.

"I am sorry," she said, weakly, hearing within the words their inher-ent uselessness. "For so much." So very much.

He looked at her for a long while, his blue-green gaze so faintly pitying and sad and resentful that she had to look away.

From within the crystal panes abutting her father's desk, she caught Jeremy moving with swift, purposeful steps, quitting the room.

Well, that could have been worse.

Liar.

Lighting herself another cheroot, Annalee headed out of her father's offices, leaving a soggy trail upon the hardwood floor which had previ-ously been cleaned of the water she'd left on her way in. She headed for the foyer, eager to be free of her childhood household. The moment she turned the corner, Annalee stopped.

Halfway down the hall, seated on the floor with his back propped against the wall, was Wayland. Casual in his shirtsleeves, because she'd, of course, stolen his jacket. Nay, he'd given it to her.

He immediately stood, springing to his feet with an ease uncommon for a man as tall and broad as he was.

She briefly considered the path behind her. Of course the great witness to her latest misery should be Wayland. Putting on a brave face, she continued toward him, the dark wool jacket he'd given her slipping open at the front.

He watched her approach warily.

But then that was the way most eyed her—with unease from the proper ladies and sorts. Interest and appreciation from the less proper *gentlemen.*

❧

There'd been a time when Wayland had felt he knew the woman approaching him even better than he knew himself.

Then Peterloo . . . and time . . . had divided them. They'd gone from two lovers as close as any souls could be to people who, on occasion, ended up at the same social affair and exchanged nothing more than a polite greeting before going their separate ways.

Only for him to discover as she came toward him, exaggerating the sway of her hips, infusing a siren's stride into her stroll, that he knew something else about this grown-up, mature version of Annalee.

Her sexuality was a shield. Did she even realize it was a barrier she kept up?

And just like that, the favor Jeremy had put to Wayland came whispering forward . . .

You were there that day, and look at you, chap. You're happy, and hell, you are more proper than ever.

His friend had been right about a part of that statement.

Wayland had been there. He'd survived the hell of that day and battled the same demons Annalee no doubt did. Perhaps Jeremy's request hadn't been . . . so far off, after all. Perhaps Wayland might rekindle a friendship with her and, in so doing, make up for past wrongs.

Annalee reached him. Clamping her cheroot between her teeth, she freed her hands and shrugged out of the now wet garment that hung huge upon her frame. "I trust you're here for this, Wayland-dear." *Wayland-dear.* That special name she'd once had for him. How very much he'd adored hearing it fall from her lips, and yet this was what she thought of him?

That the only reason he'd come was to collect his jacket? What did that say about how she'd been treated by others through the years?

"No, I'm . . . not here for my jacket. You are . . . free to it."

She lingered there. "I . . . thank you for your assistance earlier, Wayland," she said softly. She took another draw from her cheroot. "You did so much for me this night. Between you and Harlow, you were the only friends I had here."

Those sad and surprisingly frank words were a kick to the gut . . . and also a reminder of Jeremy's favor. "You needn't thank me." Perhaps he hadn't tried enough all those years ago to reach her. What if he had? Would they be together even now? Would that sad smile have been the exuberant, joyous one he'd loved to tickle her lips into giving?

Annalee looked at him with a sudden suspicion in her eyes. "Why *are* you here?"

When other ladies tiptoed around plain speaking, she veered to bluntness. She'd always been direct. It had been just one of the many things he'd loved about her. "I'm here because I wanted to be, Annalee," he said, opting to leave out mention of Jeremy and the request the other man had put before him. She took another draw from her cheroot. "I wanted to be certain . . . you were all right." And it wasn't untrue.

Annalee puffed a little cloud of smoke out from the corner of her closed lips.

When she didn't speak, he was encouraged to continue. "What happened?"

"I don't know—"

"Come, Annalee." He infused a gentleness into that interruption. "I was with you just moments before."

Her eyes instantly grew shadowed. "I don't know what you're talking about," she said tersely, and turning, she headed down the corridor.

Wayland stared after her slender form as she slipped inside her father's offices.

He'd tried.

She'd left.

His obligation to Jeremy was surely complete.

Only, as he stared after the place she'd been, he knew he could no sooner walk away from her than he could cut off his own limbs.

Wayland entered the earl's offices, closing the door quietly behind him . . . and immediately found her.

But then he'd always had an uncanny way of knowing when she was near. Apparently, for everything that had changed between them, that had remained a constant.

Annalee, however, gave no indication she heard him. She rummaged through the drawers, bypassing papers and ledgers and pens. She was methodical in her search.

Finally, she paused. "Don't you have . . . other more pressing responsibilities, Wayland?" she asked tiredly, wiping a hand over her brow.

"I've nowhere to be at the moment, Annalee." Somewhere along the way, his being here, however, had less to do with Jeremy's favor and more with a genuine need to know that Annalee was well.

"Well, then . . . how fortunate for me." With that, she dismissed him once more and continued looking . . . and then finding. She withdrew a bottle of brandy from the earl's hidden stash and then straightened. "Nothing to say, Darling?"

"What should I say?" he asked quietly.

"Nothing," she said. "Nothing at all."

As she removed the stopper, her hands shook. Even with the length of the office between them, he caught that tremble. Her eyes locked with his, and she glared at Wayland, daring him to speak. Daring him to say anything about that quiver.

She tossed the crystal cork onto the immaculate surface of the mahogany desk, and perching her hip on the edge and not bothering with a glass, she drank from the bottle.

She drank deep.

How easily her throat moved as she swallowed.

She was a woman accustomed to spirits.

Wayland ventured deeper into the room, joining her at the front. "You hated liquor," he noted softly, the way he'd spoken with his father's fractious stallion. They'd tasted their first brandy together—he, Annalee, and Jeremy. They'd all spit out their drinks and laughed uproariously about the gentlemen who indulged.

Annalee brought her bottle up in salute. "I judged it unfairly."

Another change wrought by Peterloo.

As if she attempted to horrify or offend him, she took another swig, then wiped the back of her hand over her mouth, smudging upon her fingers what remained of her crimson rouge.

Wordlessly, she held out the bottle.

Her eyes shot up as Wayland came forward and seated himself in a like pose beside her.

He took the decanter and set it beyond her reach. "What happened tonight?"

"You saw it all," she said, not pretending to misunderstand. "I was discovered in the fountain."

He'd wager his very soul he hadn't seen it all. "I mean when I left you, Annalee."

Her lips grew pinched at the corners, and she stared over at the bottle she'd been drinking from. "I was startled by the fireworks." She stared at that carafe as if it contained the answer to mankind's existence. "I should have anticipated my parents would have had such a garish display commemorating the night."

He shifted closer. "The noise," he murmured. "It bothered y—"

"La, do not be such a killjoy." She pouted. "I don't want to talk about my latest scandal."

Except, it wasn't her scandal he spoke of. It was whatever had landed her in that fountain after he'd left her.

Jeremy's urgings from earlier rang clear in his head. Annalee's need for a friend. And help.

"Loud noises still startle me, Annalee. They always will," he said, attempting to rekindle a bond that would always be between them. One she refused to acknowledge. "I've found there are far better ways to find joy than in a bottle," he said without inflection.

Annalee scooted closer, pulling herself near until their legs touched. He tensed.

"Tell me more about those better ways to find joy, Wayland," she whispered, resting her fingers on his thigh. "I want to know all about them."

"Annalee," he said hoarsely.

Step away. She was only attempting to distract him.

But the Devil take his soul, he'd always been hopeless where this woman was concerned. He did not resist, as he should. Annalee continued to glide her fingers up and down, stroking him.

His mouth went dry. She caressed her palm up, higher, along that expanse of his thigh, moving it higher still, closer to that bulge pressing at the front fall of his trousers, as she'd done earlier in the conservatory.

This time, however . . . This time, he did not pull away.

His breath hitched noisily, and like a siren, empowered and emboldened by his surrender, Annalee slid off the desk and stepped between his legs.

"Annalee." He repeated her name, a guttural prayer. For more? So that she would stop? It was all jumbled in his thoughts.

"I love the sound of my name on your lips, Wayland," she whispered. Raising her head, Annalee took his mouth, and there was . . . a sense of coming home in these, the first lips he'd ever kissed.

Annalee caught her hands in the fabric of his shirt and dragged him closer, and God help him, he went.

"I want to taste you," she breathed against his lips, nipping at that flesh, suckling his lower lip, urging him in every way to allow her entry.

With a groan, he let his mouth open and granted her that which she sought.

He gripped her firmly by the hips, his fingertips sinking into her flesh with an intensity and possessiveness to his touch, firmer than it had been all those years ago, and she reveled in that primitive grasp he had upon her. Then he was drawing her closer to his cock, and she pressed herself against him, rubbed along him.

There grew a franticness to their kiss, and he stroked his tongue against hers, that flesh gliding along Annalee's, and she rocked her hips in time to the erotic dance they now engaged in with their mouths.

And then, knowing what she'd once loved, he drew up her skirts, and she let her legs fall open and settled herself atop his thigh. With a breathy sigh signaling a sybaritic relief, she rubbed herself against the perch he offered.

And just as he'd done long ago, he caught her by the waist and helped guide her on to the pleasure she found from this simplest and yet most erotic of acts.

"So close." She panted. "I'm so close." And he swallowed the remainder of her words with his kiss.

Wayland's mouth slid from hers, and he trailed a path of kisses down the curve of her cheek, lower to her neck.

He suckled that flesh, and on a long, low groan, Annalee let her head fall back, opening herself to his worship.

How he'd missed these moments in her arms.

Annalee's breathing grew labored, and her movements more frantic as she rode him, grinding herself against him in a bid to reach her peak.

It was so good. It had always been good between them . . .

Biting her lower lip, she buried her head in the crook of his shoulder. "Wayland."

And then suddenly he stopped; the sound of his name wrenched from her lips brought him crashing back to earth . . . and the moment.

He blanched. Good God, what manner of cad was he?

Wayland remained with his hands upon her waist, and a growing horror filled him, knotting his insides. His fingers clenched and unclenched reflexively upon her before he caught himself.

As if she'd caught fire and he'd been burnt, he yanked back his hands. "Annalee," he said hoarsely, shame coursing hot where desire had once raged. "I shouldn't . . . That is to say . . ." He held up his hands.

"Shame," she murmured, her lips forming a sardonic twist. "What a cute emotion." Annalee straightened and pushed down her dress. The satin skirts, still damp from her tumble into the fountains, fell around her in a noisy rustle, their descent slowed as the article caught on his knees. He immediately pushed that fabric from his person.

As she casually went about straightening her garments, Wayland did so as well, with a rapidity born of his horror.

When they'd both finished righting themselves, they stood across from one another.

"Annalee," he began gruffly. "Forgive me," he stammered. Jeremy had asked him to go to her as a friend, and this was how he behaved? Nearly tupping her . . . and in the earl's offices, no less. "I . . . Please—"

Annalee caught him by his shirt, effectively silencing him in an instant. "It was nothing," she whispered against his mouth. She managed to give him an up-and-down look, then freed him. "Truly."

And with that incisively delivered insult, she swept off.

Standing there alone in the earl's offices long after she'd gone, Wayland was reminded all over again of the danger that came in being close to Annalee Spencer, and why Jeremy's favor was an impossible one.

Chapter 6

Leave it to members of the Mismatch Society to each find themselves presented with a copy of *Thérèse the Philosopher*, the salacious but eminently informative book, and to not have a single question on it.

"If I might direct you to the title page," Annalee said, turning the book around and revealing the scandalous sketch of the voluptuous woman bent over while a priest caned her.

Alas . . . not a single woman was compelled to open her volume.

Loud chattering filled the room.

"I for one believe if Annalee wished to go swimming in a fountain, then that was her choice to do so. She was fully clad."

"But what if she wasn't clad? Should she be open to society's condemnation, based on that?"

Annalee *used* to believe nothing was more fascinating for young, virtuous ladies than the mysteries of men and matters pertaining *to* sex.

Except her scandal. It appeared that was the one thing.

In the past fortnight since she'd begun leading the discussions and sharing literature, she'd fielded questions about everything from what took place in the marital bed to just how, exactly, what she'd explained could be in any way pleasurable.

"If I might bring you back . . . If I could . . ." But her calls were to no avail.

Mayhap this had been a disastrous idea, after all. The idea that she could lead. Because she was decidedly not a leader.

Since its inception, there'd been any number of scandals faced by the Mismatch Society, an organization dedicated to promoting a world where women lived freely and challenged society's norms and expectations for them.

Conceived by Miss Emma Gately, who'd severed a lifelong betrothal, and spearheaded by the former Lady Sylvia Norfolk, now Viscountess St. John, this society was the living, breathing persona of *ton*-ish scandal.

Why, even the idea of three young women living together was perceived as wicked.

Granted, one of those women was a former fighter who'd also been the lover of Sylvia's late husband—but that was neither here nor there—and the other was Annalee, who was, well, *Annalee*.

At every turn, their venture was met with outrage from angry parents whose daughters had found their way into the society's folds. Or horror and fear from brothers and guardians who were more concerned with marrying off their charges and being free of their responsibility to those women than with each respective lady's happiness.

The papers printed exaggerated stories of their wicked intentions.

All the while, gentlemen were allowed their meetings and their opinions and their clubs.

But then, such was the way of the world. Men could have, run, form, and visit any manner of club or establishment, but the minute women formed such a venture, society was up in arms, and there came the calls of shutting it down.

Sylvia took command. "We've certainly faced scandal before."

Murmurs of assent went up from the other members.

Those other members, however, issued their assurances from behind the newspapers that so consumed their attention.

Yes, they had faced scandal before. But not when they'd been on the cusp of creating something of the nature that they were. Not when *Annalee* had been on the cusp of finally stepping forward into a leadership role, capable at last of truly contributing something to the ladies of society.

Sylvia caught her eye, and Annalee couldn't even feign her usual droll humor. Nothing. Just an aching regret and panic at what she might cost their members. "It looked a good deal worse than it was."

Anwen Kearsley tossed down her paper, where it hit the table with a loud *thwack*. "But neither should it have mattered if it was," the bespectacled lady asserted with as great a firmness and boldness as Annalee had ever recalled of the quietest, usually meekest of the many Kearsley sisters. "Why should she not have been dipping her toes in a fountain or dancing in those waters with a dashing gent?"

Annalee cleared her throat. "If I may?" She lifted what remained of her cheroot. "I'd also reiterate that I was not dancing in a fountain. This time." It bore pointing out and repeating because she was a scandal, but she'd not have her friends believe even she would go about conducting herself as she'd done countless times before in the middle of her brother's betrothal ball.

"Then what were you doing in the fountain?" Miss Isla Gately asked, the intonation of her query and the roundness of her eyes a model of intrigue.

As one, all the younger girls shifted on their seats and angled their attention on Annalee.

"Yes," Cora Kearsley pressed. "I trust it was something outrageously fun and delicious that sent you into the waters."

Fun and delicious . . .

Screams pealed around her mind, the distant echo of gunfire melding with the distorted cries of a confused crowd.

A panicky little laugh built in her chest and tumbled free of her lips.

Brenna Kearsley clapped her hands happily. "I knew it was something wonderful!" With a sigh she dropped her chin atop her hands, and all the other girls sighed in return.

But the stares remained from a sea of young women who believed they'd worked themselves to the answer, with no input needed from Annalee herself to either confirm or deny.

And suddenly, Annalee's palms slicked with sweat—nay, that perspiration coated all her body—and she wished she'd kept her damned mouth shut. That she'd been content to let even her closest friends and supporters to their ill opinions about her and what she'd been up to. Because any of that was better than admitting her past had any hold over her still.

Her hands shook slightly, and to steady herself, Annalee took comfort where she so often did, in the remaining bit of her cheroot. Raising it to her lips, she sucked deep, filling her lungs, welcoming the way it warmed her.

Feeling Valerie's and Sylvia's gazes, ones filled with concern and not the rabid curiosity the others possessed, was somehow . . . worse.

"What else would it be, dear girls?" Annalee said to the room at large, her rhetorical question still met with a bevy of answering nods and murmurs of assent. "After all, you each know my love of fun . . . and good times." Grabbing the flask resting beside her, she raised it, toasting herself.

Then Annalee heard it. Even through the noisy chatter of their approving members. "I wish I could be her." Brenna Kearsley's soft sighs and quiet murmurings reached Annalee. Along with the agreement that came from her sisters seated beside her.

For so long, all the years since that fateful day in Manchester, Annalee had thrown herself fully into living an existence free of the constraints that had once bound her, the ones that shackled ladies to rules so very one-sided where the genders were concerned. Only recently had there been a feeling of . . . emptiness to it all.

Sylvia cleared her throat. "There is, however, still the matter of our membership to consider," she said cautiously. As their members slid looks her way that were equal parts disapproving and stunned, she rushed to clarify. "I am not saying that we should change our ways—"

"Then what are you saying?" Isla Gately demanded of their apparently not-so-fearless leader.

"I am saying that there is a difference between asserting our views of the world and being mired in scandal. These constant scandals? They threaten everything we've established. Everything we hold dear."

And yet . . . Annalee's stomach sank. The truth remained—they did have to pay some mind to what the world said . . . not for themselves, but rather . . . for one another. For the young ladies who were here to learn new perspectives and challenge the norms and think for themselves, out from under the thumbs of their domineering mamas and papas, could do so only if they didn't offend the world too greatly. It was a delicate waltz they danced. Challenge the existing order, but do it too wildly or too outrageously and the very existence of the society would be threatened. And the young ladies who attended could find themselves instantly recalled by a disapproving parent.

"I for one do not want Annalee to change," Anwen Kearsley announced to the room at large. "I'd have her just the way she is."

And perhaps Annalee was tired from the endless night that had been her brother's betrothal ball. Or mayhap it was simply that she was going soft, but at that gentle show of support from the young woman, a wave of emotion filled her throat. The polite sort didn't defend her. Why, even the members, until now, had viewed and treated her as more of a fascinating oddity. Or that was what she'd believed anyway. Clamping the cheroot at the side of her lips, Annalee looked to her friends. "There are no worries; I've no intention of changing. Now, if we can return to *Thérèse?*"

And this time, the ladies took out their copies, and Annalee found herself spared from any further questioning or concern about her latest descent into madness.

There was only one certainty . . . The women here were dependent upon her, and she'd an obligation to get her bloody mess of a life together and start behaving in a way that didn't jeopardize everything they'd created.

Chapter 7

"Nothing exciting happens here."

Standing on the side of Lady Sinclair's ballroom's crowded dance floor, with guests throughout the room sipping tepid lemonade and conversing amongst one another, Wayland couldn't agree more with that unusual-for-her whining pronouncement from his sister.

For Wayland, however, "nothing exciting," following Peterloo, was what he'd come to strive for, and had also committed himself to.

"Nothing at all," Kitty continued muttering to herself. "With the exception of last evening at Lord Jeremy's, that is."

Alas, his spirited sister proved of a wholly different mindset.

He tweaked a dark, perfectly formed curl. "And here I believed you couldn't imagine anything more exciting than attending a London ball."

His sister's mouth puckered with her annoyance. "That was before," she muttered. "Must we remain?"

He had opened his mouth to tease once more when he caught the strain at the corners of her eyes and the tension on her lips. And he followed her stony gaze out . . . across the ballroom to where a quartet of young ladies stared boldly back, tittering behind their hands. The white-clad misses made no attempt to conceal their mockery.

His gut clenched.

"Stop it, Wayland," his sister whispered.

"I'm not doing anything."

"You're looking at me all pityingly, and you're only going to make it worse."

Make it worse, as in the bullying that had been directed her way—rather, their way—from the moment he'd been granted a title. The bullying toward him? It had faded . . . mostly. He had a title. It eased Wayland's way, but still did not make it better. His sister would always carry the stigma of being, to Polite Society, just a blacksmith's daughter . . . unless he made a respectable match. One that his mother and the world desperately wished to be with Lady Diana for the romantic roots attached to their connection. Of course, only Wayland seemed to realize there was nothing heroic about him or what he'd done that day . . .

He steeled his jaw.

But he would not fail Kitty. His sister, whom he could spare pain and hurt . . .

"It will get better, Kitty," he said quietly.

She rolled her eyes. "No, it won't. We will never belong. You will. But certainly not me. And they will never be kind, and that is fine." She patted his shoulder. "Now, if you will please let it rest."

Let it rest.

Let her suffer unkind cut after unkind cut? He'd sooner lop off his own limbs. Nay, it was why the match his and Lady Diana's mothers expected him to make was vital. That union the *ton* cheered for would be that which made it so for Kitty. He knew that. He'd resolved himself to ultimately making that match. For his family. He didn't love Lady Diana. He'd already given his heart. But he admired her. He respected her. And he didn't doubt, in time, there could—or would—be more. "I'm going to make it better for you, Kitty."

She snorted.

"I promise." He gave another curl a playful tug.

"And furthermore, don't go about pulling my curls." She frowned. "Though, if I had my way, I'd yank all these ridiculously tight ringlets out."

Their mother should choose that precise moment to join them. "You'll do nothing of the sort. Your ringlets are lovely. The most perfect of all the ringlets. Tell her, Wayland."

"They are—"

His sister gave him a look that singed and threatened all-out burning if he so much as agreed with their mother.

Their mother was new to the nobility and, in her quest for their family to fit into this new world, determined to turn Kitty into a model of ladylike decorum and propriety in every way, down to her presentation.

"And do hush," Mother said on an outrageously loud whisper as she turned this way and that, layers upon layers of noisy crinoline crackling loud enough to be heard over the racket of the ballroom. "I'll not have either of you offend our host and hostess." She wrung her gloved hands together.

She, herself, was as garishly and ridiculously attired as Wayland's unfortunate sister.

"Well, I should say it hardly makes a difference one way or another if we are invited to attend this or any other ball when I don't even have invitations to dance." As if to emphasize that very point, Kitty lifted the card dangling on her wrist. The neat bow twisted and twirled forlornly, a kaleidoscope of blank spaces where there should be names of a suitor or partner.

Their mother slapped at Kitty's wrist. "Do put that down, dearest," she whispered. "We cannot go about drawing attention to . . . to . . . that."

That, as in the empty card which highlighted the dearth of suitors.

"I'd argue you're making a good deal more of a show by hitting my arm and hiding that which everyone already knows, Mama," Kitty muttered.

Their mother balked. "Mother. You know—"

"That is right. 'Mama' is too plebeian," Kitty murmured in the flawless, crisp tones of a lady. "However could I have forgotten?"

Over the top of their mother's head, brother and sister caught one another's eyes and shared a look.

"Where are they?" Their mother wrung her hands again. "Where are they?" she repeated under her breath over and over. "I have it on authority that they've arrived in London. And yet they've not appeared at a single ball." She was referring to none other than the Duke and Duchess of Kipling, two of the most powerful peers, and also parents to Lady Diana . . . the girl Wayland had rescued years earlier, now grown up. "Given everything we've done for them, the very least they might do is throw their support behind us for your sister."

"Given everything we've done?" Kitty drawled. "I daresay *you and I* were not present on the fields of Manch— *Ouch*." Their mother delivered an effectively silencing if discreet pinch to her younger child.

"Hush. Do not diminish what your brother did that day."

What he'd done that day was coordinate to meet up with Annalee, only to have the world turn itself upside down. Running frantically in search of her, he'd come across a flipped carriage being overrun by a fleeing crowd. He'd plucked the small girl, her maid, and her mother out, managing to save three that day.

All the while, Annalee had saved herself.

Nay, there'd been nothing truly romantic in his actions that day, even if the world had been determined to see them in that most favorable of lights.

And then it was as though he'd summoned her.

A buzz filled the ballroom, that din drowning out the orchestra's playing and ending the previous chattering of gossipy guests.

But then she always had that effect upon any room she entered.

Nor was that response born of her scandalous reputation. Not solely. Nay, the sight of her was enough to bring any room to a halt.

"I wish I might go about dressed like her," Kitty breathed.

Their mother gasped. "Never say something so scandalous. You would never, and will never, wear something so . . . outrageous. Ever. Have I made myself clear?"

And while his mother proceeded to launch into a lecture for Kitty, Wayland found himself drinking in the sight of Annalee. Attired in a lacy, black gauze gown over a silver satin, with a silver bow tied about her that accentuated her cinched waist, she was curved in all the most splendid places for one to be curved—deeply rounded bosom, generously flared hips, and equally generous buttocks. She was a lush fertility goddess.

And with a tiara done in collet-set, table-cut rose diamonds affixed to a crown of lush golden curls hanging loose about her shoulders and waist, she was very much a queen in every way. A potent wave of lust went through him.

And God help him, Wayland proved the bastard of a friend he'd always been where Jeremy was concerned, because in that instant, he saw Annalee as she'd once been with those curls draped about her shoulders as she'd ridden atop him.

Nor was he the only one aware of her . . . of the sight she presented.

And he, who'd believed himself long past jealousy where this woman was concerned, found the lie he'd fed to himself all these years. As she glided down the stairs, the crowd parted for her, making room as if she were Athena herself, mingling with mere mortals.

And mayhap they were. Perhaps this was Annalee's world, and the rest of them merely lived in it at her whim.

She found a place on the edge of the dance floor, alongside a pillar, and rescuing a glass of champagne from a passing servant, she sipped at that drink, all the while taking in the ballroom.

She was . . . a study in boredom. Perfect boredom.

Or mayhap it was simply that he'd once known her so well, and so the crease between her eyebrows and the pinched set to her mouth were ones he recognized from when she'd been bored at her family's events.

"It is absolutely shameful that she is here. Shameful, I say," his mother said. And there could be no more effective killer of lust than one's mother's disapproving utterings.

"I daresay she has as much right to be here as anyone else," Kitty defended. And he'd always loved his sister, but he found he loved her all the more for that defense of Annalee. "Certainly more than we do."

Mother gasped. "That is utterly preposterous. She may have been born an earl's daughter, but she does not conduct herself in a way befitting a lady. Just the opposite."

"Mother," Wayland bit out, infusing a warning into those two syllables. He'd be damned if he tolerated his own mother's disparagement of Annalee.

She released a beleaguered sigh. "I know. I know. Lord Jeremy is a dearest friend, which is why we tolerate her."

Tolerate her. "We don't . . . tolerate her," he said gruffly. "Tolerate" would suggest they merely put up with Annalee for self-serving reasons. "She is a family friend." And deserving of their loyalty and support, regardless of what behaviors she engaged in or events she attended or how she conducted herself.

And leaving his mother there sputtering, he set out across the room to the last person he should be joining . . . and for so many reasons.

Wayland cut his way along the sidelines of the room, bobbing and weaving between the countess's guests in a bid to reach Annalee. No one paid his hasty strides any heed; nay, they were too focused on the same figure whom he now headed for.

Lady Annalee.

Annalee, who rarely attended proper balls or soirees, and who, when she did, did so only because of any connection she had to the host or hostess.

Except this time.

A figure stepped into his path, forcing him to a stop.

"Lord Darlington!" Mr. Chester greeted. "A pleasure to see you here."

"Yes. Yes, always," Wayland lied, his focus shifting beyond the greying merchant's shoulder to Annalee. Annalee, who herself had been waylaid by another. "If you'll . . . ?"

Alas, Chester launched into a long-winded accounting of his latest business ventures, and Wayland silently cursed, never regretting more having committed himself to being the always respectable gentleman.

As the old fellow spoke, Wayland had to remind himself to murmur at the correct moments. And yet . . . with Chester rambling on, he frowned. Tall and wiry, with an impressive set of whiskers—if one was the facial-hair-wearing sort—Annalee's companion, Lord Cartwright, had an arm up above the pillar so he'd framed half the room off from Annalee.

What was she doing, speaking with Cartwright? Not that it was Wayland's business. Not anymore.

His frown deepened. But surely she wasn't friendly with . . . with . . . that one? That *cad* with a reputation for being pompous as the London day was long. A pairing between Annalee and a cur like Cartwright hardly made any kind of sense.

"We do have to stick together at these affairs, don't we?" The rotund gentleman leaned in and up, whispering, "Us self-made sorts and all."

Self-made sorts.

Wayland bit the inside of his cheek to keep from pointing out that there'd been nothing self-made in what he'd acquired. Luck. It had been pure luck where he was concerned.

His gut twisted. Not that there'd been anything lucky about that day in Manchester. More, it had been a trick of the fates that had seen Wayland titled, and yet he would have happily given it all up to return to life as it had been before that tragic day.

With Chester's droning on and the hum of the ballroom, Wayland's eyes were brought briefly closed as the past ushered in a remembrance.

"I will love you until the day I die, Wayland Smith," Annalee whispered against his mouth.

"Let us hope that day isn't for a long, long time, love . . ."

When he made himself open them, the sight to meet him wasn't the glowing, adoring gaze of a woman who'd always loved him more than he'd deserved . . . but that same woman, now standing too close to a man who deserved her even less.

Just then, Cartwright's gaze dipped low, and the bastard made no attempt to conceal his interest in her daring neckline. Whatever the lady said raised a booming laugh from the bounder.

A low growl worked its way up his chest.

"Might I introduce you to my wife and daughter?" Mr. Chester was saying.

"If you'll excuse me?" Wayland said curtly and with a brusqueness that brought the other man up short for a moment.

"Of course. Of—"

Wayland was already stepping around the merchant. This time, he marched with purpose, refusing to be waylaid by those guests whom he'd otherwise never have cut, powerful lords whose approval he'd sought so that his family might achieve the respect not automatically afforded them because of their birthright.

"Perhaps we might find a . . . fountain through which to waltz together, sweet." The gentleman danced a bold finger along the sleeve of her dress.

A blanket of rage fell over Wayland's vision, a crimson-black veil the color of death and blood that he'd like to pound the other man into. And it was a fury that came from Wayland's friendship with Jeremy, and his devotion to Annalee's family.

"I couldn't think of anything I'd rather do less," Annalee drawled, a study in boredom that she elevated with a practiced yawn, and some of Wayland's anger dissipated under that bold and beautiful rejection of the uncouth lout.

Cartwright's cheeks went florid. "Given your predilection for dancing in fountains during proper affairs, I'd daresay a jaunt out with me would be more to your—"

"The lady said no," Wayland said coolly, and the pair whipped about to face him. "And lest you make any more of an ass of yourself than you already are or have, might I suggest you take that dip in a fountain by yourself?"

The dull flush on the other man's too-sharp cheeks grew heavier. "Shove off, Darlington. The lady doesn't have any interest in, or need of, you," Lord Cartwright said, curling back his lip in a sneer.

"Ah, but she hasn't said as much to me, and she has given every indication that she wants nothing to do with you," Wayland drawled.

Cartwright looked down his long, noble nose at Wayland. "Apparently you're not as nice a fellow as the papers paint you to be, eh?"

Wayland took a step closer so the shorter man had no choice but to look up. "And this from a man who doesn't know how to honor the word 'no' from a lady."

The other man's cheeks grew splotchy, and he tripped over himself in a bid to put space between him and Wayland. Then, turning on his heel, Cartwright raced off.

The moment he'd gone, with her champagne flute dangling awkwardly between her fingers, Annalee gave a little clap. "Impressive stuff, Wayland. Well done." She leaned close. "Defending my honor, and publicly," she purred, running a finger along his lapel. "I am touched."

A muscle twitched at the corner of his eye. Had she thought he'd not defend her against the scurrilous pursuit of a man in whom she'd revealed no interest? Or was it simply that she made light of him? "Were the roles reversed and my sister found herself so accosted, Jeremy would have responded exactly as I've done." It was not untrue, but it was also not the sole reason he'd involved himself.

Annalee's lush mouth formed a perfect pout, lips that made a man imagine any manner of wicked thoughts for them, that flesh parted and wrapped about his length. An imagining made all the more real by the memories he carried still of her taking him in that hot, moist cavern.

"My big brother's best friend coming to my rescue." Annalee gave him an up-and-down look filled with so much mockery and judgment he knew precisely how Cartwright had felt to be shredded by her. "How . . . honorable, my lord."

And Wayland's ears went hot in that moment as she rightly called him out. Wayland, the man who'd bedded his best friend's sister. More times than he could remember . . . and then coordinated to meet with her in Manchester.

The lady made to leave.

"It's not because of your brother," he said gruffly, and that managed to stop her retreat. Though everything in this moment was confused. Perhaps he should have just let her to the opinion she'd formed, and they could have gone their own ways, as they'd done since Manchester, instead of him admitting that she was, in fact, the reason for his intervention.

Annalee turned back slowly. *"Ohh?"*

"Come, Annalee. You know we are . . . friends." Except, was that what they really were? Certainly, it was what they'd once been.

"Friends?" That syllable rolled off her tongue like a sinful invitation.

Sadness cleaved his chest. For all that had come to pass between them, and all the tragedy and heartbreak that had divided them, what right did he have to claim that place of friendship? To her . . . or her family?

"I'm teasing, Way," she said, punching him lightly in the arm in a lighthearted gesture that drove away some of the tension, bringing them back to a place of familiarity and recalling the friendship they'd been speaking of. "I know you're a friend."

She spoke with the ease of a woman who believed those words.

And yet, had he truly been a friend to her in a long while? Even when he'd sought her out at Jeremy's betrothal ball, he'd been motivated by his loyalty to the lady's brother.

Annalee gave a roll of her eyes. "Oh, stop."

He bristled. "I've said nothing," he said indignantly.

"You didn't need to. You've gone all melancholy. Your lips are drawn, and your muscles all bunched." She discreetly dusted her fingers along his coat sleeve.

Those muscles jumped reflexively at a touch his body had never been able to not respond to. Annalee gave him a knowing smile.

From her tempting, barely there caress on down to her words, it was unnerving to have become more strangers than anything these past years, and yet to have her still know him so very well. Whereas Wayland? He couldn't make out heads or tails or up or down or left or right where Lady Annalee was concerned.

Annalee went about sipping her champagne and eyeing the crowd once more. "Oh, dear," she murmured, licking a remnant of those bubbling spirits from the left corner of her lower lip.

He followed that gesture. "What is it?" he managed, completely captivated by that delicate pink flesh. Hell, the ballroom could have been on fire and he would have stood there, consumed, before he could pull himself away. But then Annalee had always been a master when it came to seducing him with subtleties. With . . . anything, really. Where the other was concerned, they'd both been skilled in that regard.

"Your mother."

The last thing he cared to think about in this moment was . . . his mother.

"She quite disapproves," Annalee murmured from the corner of her mouth.

"Not at all. She's . . . she's . . ." Yes, there could be no disputing or doubting; his mother was less than pleased.

Annalee winged up an eyebrow. "Usually glowering?"

"It could be the countess's lemonade," he pointed out, discreetly motioning to the untouched glass held in his mother's hand.

An adorable little snort filtered past her lips.

"It could be," he said as they engaged in a private little jest about his glowering mama across the room. "Why, she *does* look like she's sucked a lemon."

Joining in the false somber contemplation, Annalee captured her chin between her thumb and forefinger and made a show of studying Wayland's mother. "Yes. Yes. I daresay, you might be right. There's something—"

"Tart?"

"—about her. *Hmm.* Yes . . . exactly that! Why, even—"

"Sour-faced?"

Even clear across the room, he made out the way his mother's eyes bulged.

He and Annalee shared a smile . . . a real one. A private one that came from a teasing and mirth they'd shared long, long ago.

Capturing his sleeve, Annalee pressed herself against him. "Should we give her something to really be scandalized by?" she whispered in a throaty contralto and his shaft stirred.

It was all a game of pretend and jest, and yet his body knew nothing of games.

Her words were a tempting proposition that ushered in more wicked thoughts, recent ones with her straddling his thigh, panting and moaning, as she'd sought a climax. A climax he'd desperately wished to provide her.

She cast him a look, and through that haze of lust, he recalled an answer was needed. "No."

"Methinks your protest is half-hearted and belated," she rightly noted on a full, husky laugh that ended on a regretful sigh. "Alas, it appears our fun has come to an end . . ."

Fortunately, Kitty came to the rescue, pulling at their mother's arm, forcing her to look away from Wayland and Annalee. His sister, God love her, caught his gaze and winked before tugging the older woman off.

He firmed his jaw, annoyance coursing through him at a mother so concerned with their reputation and standing that she'd be publicly cold to Annalee. She'd not always been that way where Annalee was concerned. Once upon a lifetime ago, she'd even urged him on to a match with his best friend's sister, seeing it as an entry to a better life.

"You do know you're tempting scandal by conversing alone with me," she remarked.

He scoffed. "I'd hardly call it a scandal."

"For me, no," she allowed. "For you?" She waggled her perfectly shaped golden eyebrows. "Absolutely."

He stole a glance about, realizing the number of stares now upon them. Most of the earl and countess's guests stared baldly on at him . . . and Annalee. Slightly curious, but not the rabid gawking that usually was directed her way. Some of that a product of the *ton*'s knowledge of his connection to her family.

Annalee held out her half-empty champagne flute.

He waved off that offering.

With a little shrug, she finished the contents of her glass. In one fluid movement, she deposited it upon a passing servant's tray, all the while, with an impressive simultaneousness to her agile movements, retrieving herself another.

Folding her arms at her chest, she inadvertently plumped that already voluptuous bosom, and his mouth went dry as he stared at the olive-hued flesh of a woman who'd always loved the sun on her—

"I take it you're doing reconnaissance for Jeremy. Keeping an eye on his most wicked sister."

He laughed . . . before she sluiced a sideways look his way, and it hit him. "You're serious." He was unable to keep the indignation from creeping into his response.

"Generally, as a rule? No. In this—"

"Of course I'm not here because of your brother," he snapped, now having a taste for what ole Cartwright had felt.

"La"—she pressed a satin-gloved hand against her bosom, and this time, he fought the pull to gaze upon that glistening skin like the enrapt schoolboy he'd once been—"how utterly silly for me to think so, given the fact that you searched me out three times last evening."

"My hide-and-seek skills have improved exponentially from when we were younger," he said.

Annalee stared at him for a long moment, and then tossing back her head, she laughed. It was the unrestrained, freeing sound of a woman content in her right to surrender to her own happiness and amusement. It was also one of the things he'd first fallen in love with about her. And with her cheeks flushed from laughter he'd brought her to, he was reminded all over again just how much he'd loved her laugh and, more, making her laugh.

When her mirth faded, she gave her head a wry shake. Annalee finished off her drink, and then summoning a servant, she deposited her empty flute. Instead of taking another, however, she issued a word of thanks and waved off a third glass.

"Though I am surprised to see you here," he admitted when they were once again alone.

"Where should I be?"

"I . . ." He felt his neck go hot. "No, that is not what I mean." What had happened to the ease with which he'd once been able to speak to her? Or, for that matter, anyone? Since his entry into the peerage, he'd lost the ability to be comfortable in his own words. "I'm, of course, glad to see you here and—"

"Not at a more wicked affair?" she supplied.

"No. Yes. I—" He reached for his cravat, but Annalee deftly caught his fingers.

"Relax, Wayland." She leaned close. "I'm teasing," she whispered, her body arching toward his, and as it did, he detected a hint of rose blossom upon her. It was a different scent than that which she'd used to dab behind her earlobes—apple blossom.

There was a sultriness to the fragrance that filled his nostrils; it tempted.

"Of course," he said, his voice hoarse and rough to his own ears.

He recalled belatedly that he still held her hand in his. For at some point when she'd grabbed his fingers, he'd curled them around her palm. He made to draw his hand quickly back, lest he bring them any more attention than he already had . . .

But Annalee gripped him more tightly. Retaining a hold upon him, she brought her other palm to rest on his sleeve.

"I would be honored to dance this set with you," she murmured, perfectly skilled at steering them away from scandal . . . and onto the now filling dance floor.

And as they took their place amongst the sets of other dancers, he wasn't certain which posed the greater danger: the risk of scandal they'd raised this night or the taking of Annalee into his arms.

Chapter 8

Dancing with Wayland seemed like the safest way of touching him while still avoiding scandal.

Not that she would have much cared.

He, on the other hand, would have.

For all their earlier repartee and teasing about his mother, Wayland cared very much about fitting in amongst Polite Society.

This world she'd been born to—that she'd be more than happy to be without—he'd been attempting to bind himself to since he'd been titled.

Mayhap it had really been long before that.

When she thought about the future they'd imagined, and the talks they'd once had, there were signs that he'd cared: His fear of revealing the nature of their relationship to Jeremy. His insistence that he'd be something more . . . that he'd create an existence greater so that she could have the life she deserved.

Even as she'd assured him that he was all she wanted.

In retrospect, as a woman fully grown, matured by time and struggle and suffering, she could now see Wayland had been fighting for a grander life for himself as much as for her. Mayhap even more than.

But it was her business, however, to care now, too. For the reasons Sylvia had raised.

Still, it did not keep her from wishing that she and Wayland could go back to the more comfortable sparring they'd been enjoying moments ago.

Nay, he was all stiff and proper, once more.

Her body, however, didn't seem to care . . . or even mind, for that matter.

Quite the opposite. It reveled in the challenge he posed with his decorous self.

There was a tautness to his powerful physique, to their nearness. To the eyes now trained upon them. It hadn't ever been this way when they'd danced. "I daresay your dancing instructor did not do an adequate job in teaching you that relaxing one's body and feeling the music is the most important part of the waltz, my lord," she murmured.

A lifetime ago, a smile would have grazed his lips; nay, they would have turned up in a wide grin. "I had the finest instructor."

Those lessons had come without the benefit of music, just what she'd hummed and sung while guiding him through the motions and movements. The strains of the orchestra muted the noise of the room, and Annalee closed her eyes, surrendering herself to the music and the joy that had always come in dancing.

Liar . . . in this man's arms. There'd always been something splendorous about the way their bodies had moved so beautifully in time.

And yet . . . it was also not the same, and she silently and secretly mourned this change that time had wrought.

Annalee opened her eyes.

Wayland's gaze remained directed at the top of her head, and his lips moved faintly, the way they had when he'd counted steps. "Relax, Wayland," she murmured, careful to not let her mouth move lest the world now watching saw his name falling from her lips. "It is just a dance."

Nor was her concern wholly about him, if she were being honest with herself. Since Sylvia's talk earlier, Annalee had committed herself to proper behavior.

"I know," he said stiffly. "I'm not concerned."

She snorted. Surely he didn't believe it. "You're *always* worried about your reputation." Annalee lightly stroked her fingers at his shoulder; the muscles rippled and rolled under her touch.

"Some of us don't have the luxury of not caring, Annalee," he said quietly.

Annalee followed his pointed stare across the room to where his mother stood alongside a white-skirt-wearing young lady, who smiled, where the older woman was scowling. Eyes as warm as they'd always been when Annalee had come 'round to visit. "She is all grown up," Annalee said, more to herself. Kitty was near an age to Annalee when she'd gone off to meet Wayland on the fringes of that Manchester field.

"She is. And she is not received. And while I don't give a damn about myself, I do care about Kitty."

"What a devoted brother you are," she murmured.

His mouth tightened. "You'd make light."

Because he, like the rest of the world, believed Annalee incapable of solemnity or somberness.

In fairness, over the years she'd given little reason for the world *to* believe. She'd lived a carefree existence, one where she put her own pleasures and needs and happiness first, and yet neither did that mean she was an empty-headed person who didn't take anything seriously. She held his eyes. "On the contrary, Wayland," she said softly. "I do believe you are devoted to your sister and family, and I can only find that honorable . . . But do you know what else I think?"

He adjusted his hold at her waist, his fingers dipping a shade lower as he glided her through a perfect turn, a dizzying one that left her faintly breathless. Or perhaps it was the feel of his palm on her person.

He searched his gaze over Annalee's face. "What is that?" His fingers moved almost reflexively at her waist as he drew her faintly closer. Or was it that she leaned into Wayland, drawn as she'd always been, a moth to that fiery flame?

"I believe there is a part of you, perhaps one you're not aware of or capable of acknowledging to yourself, that cares very much"—perhaps just as much as he did about his sister and mother—"what the world says about you and thinks about you."

His fingers curled almost reflexively as he clasped her. "That's not true." He paused. "But if I did, would that be so very wrong?" he asked brusquely.

"That you deny yourself happiness? There is a lot bad with that."

"I don't deny myself happiness. I live with caution and care."

As he hadn't before.

The message and meaning were clear as day, even as those words went unspoken.

"And there is something to be said of that, Annalee," he added.

"Ah, unlike me, who plays with fire?" she purred.

She stroked her fingers along his sleeve, that caress born not of a deliberate need to taunt or tempt, but rather to fulfill this insatiable need to just . . . touch him. With every back-and-forth glide, those muscles tensed and eased. The heat burning through her had nothing to do with the crush of the crowd or the thousands of candles drenching the countess's ballroom in light.

Her husky urging of years past whispered forward. *"Waltz with me, Wayland . . ."*

"We're naked, Annalee." And yet he came to his feet anyway and gathered her in his arms, their bodies pressed close as they danced a different, forbidden dance together that morning.

An ache pulsed between her legs, a throbbing need born of those erotic thoughts of the past.

Their eyes locked; his eyes glinted and glimmered, reflecting his desire and her own within those greenish-blue pools. Wayland's gaze slipped to her mouth, and seeing his focus where it was, where she wanted it, Annalee slowly, deliberately flicked her tongue along the middle portion of her lower lip, inviting him to look.

His chest moved fast, and reveling in that display of his desire, Annalee continued to glide that tip of flesh he was so focused on to the corner, and then up and around.

Wayland dipped his head lower. She knew propriety was the night's effort, the sole reason for being here, and yet she was hopeless against the magnetic pull that brought her neck back as she lifted her mouth.

His gaze continued to linger there.

He wanted to kiss her.

Annalee's heart pounded.

He was going to kiss her.

Wayland, her first lover and London's most proper gentleman . . . Here, in the middle of the earl and countess's ballroom floor.

And she wanted it. Desperately. She shifted her hips to alleviate some of the ache between her legs. Her efforts proved futile.

But then Wayland's gaze slid away from her mouth and back to that point of her tiara. And as a woman with a knowledge of men and desire and gaming, she now knew that to be his tell. When he didn't trust himself, he stared at the top of her head. It was a new action from a man she'd once known so intimately as to have had the exact count of freckles and birthmarks upon his naked chest and bare back.

As he guided her through another deep, sweeping turn, one that left her light-headed with passion, she whispered huskily, "You remember dancing in the fields of Manchester?"

A flush dulled his cheeks, and his jaw rippled, his mouth tensed. But straitlaced as he was, he still did not confirm that which she already knew to be truth anyway.

"And you loved it." She pressed herself closer; near as their bodies were, she detected . . . every subtle nuance of his movements—his audible swallow, the way his throat worked. "You loved every single moment of it, Wayland Smith. I think you miss those days when you were free."

"No," he said so sharply she almost believed his denial. "No, I do not. There is nothing good that comes from being careless or impulsive, Annalee. I matured, and I learned what I wanted, and . . . this is it."

She followed his glance out to the swarm of dancing partners, and to the even greater swarm of people watching on the sidelines.

This was what he craved. This, as in Polite Society. As in acceptance amongst the *ton*. A people he still had yet to learn never truly accepted anyone because they'd rather cut a person off at the knees and subsist on the scandals and gossip that came when they ultimately fell.

In short, he wished to belong to a world that she never, ever would truly belong to. Not again.

And something in that left a bitter taste on her tongue.

"You might profess to having matured with . . . life." Odd that Peterloo had been such a part of their lives, the final moment they'd shared as young lovers, and yet they had never, and likely would never, speak of it. "But you were never content with being a blacksmith's son. You were always determined to be viewed and treated differently, Wayland. And have more." After all, hadn't that been why he'd been at Manchester in the first place? Fighting for a seat at the proverbial table? Calling out—and justly so—for a voice in a world that reserved speaking for those born to the most privileged class? "You were always craving . . . this." As a naive, lovestruck girl, she'd believed she was what he wanted most. *Foolish, foolish child.*

His nostrils flared. Wayland of old would have called her out, gone toe to toe to challenge Annalee of her opinion, unconcerned about being viewed as polite, instead treating her as an equal in debate or discourse . . . It had been one of the things she'd loved about him. And also, apparently, one more thing that had changed about him that day.

The music came to a stop, and Annalee and Wayland glided to a halt amidst the other partners.

"I found my way, and I'll not make apologies for who I've become, Annalee," he murmured as the lords and ladies around them lifted their hands to politely clap at the efforts of the orchestra.

"And without blood on your hands or talks of revolution or sedition, my lord." She inclined her head. "Imagine that."

He jerked like she'd struck him. The color leached from his cheeks. And if she were a better woman, perhaps she'd feel some compunction about so wounding him. But damn him, she didn't feel bad. She was angry with him for passing judgment on her when he had become . . . become . . . *this*.

And alas, because he was ever the gentleman he prided himself on being, Wayland dipped a stiff but still polite bow. "My lady," he said tersely, and then stalked off, leaving Annalee alone.

The hum of whispers immediately went up . . . as they invariably and inevitably did.

With a smile, Annalee lifted her shoulders, and with her head back, she cut a path across the ballroom floor, waving and smiling as she went. Because to hell with them. She'd not be made to feel less. Not when she'd come to find herself and realized she was deserving of more.

God, how she was done with all this already.

Suffering through politeness was a torment she'd take on only for her sisters of the Mismatch Society.

Once she reached the foyer and her carriage was called, she shrugged into the cloak handed over by her hosts' dutiful servant. Annalee fastened it at her throat; however, a short time later, after she'd boarded her carriage and the conveyance rumbled onward, she wrestled off those fastenings, suffocating.

How she despised those stilted affairs. Not because she was every person's favorite object to gawk at and whisper about. To her mother's horror, Annalee had never really cared about that. She'd cared even less after Peterloo.

Rather, it was the tiredness of the affairs, a place where women's souls went to die. At the respectable events, ladies were expected to behave a certain way, and anyone who didn't found herself cast out of the *ton*'s good graces.

As though there were even such a thing as "good graces" where the *ton* was concerned.

And yet oddly, this night, Annalee hadn't found herself minding Lord and Lady Sinclair's ball so very much. She hadn't minded it at all.

Reasons that had to do with the thrill that had coursed through her from being in Wayland's arms.

Back in his arms, rather.

It was the first time they'd ever publicly waltzed. When they'd been all but children, playing at pretend, imagining what they thought life would be, she'd taught him the steps they'd danced tonight. Motions and movements they'd practiced only in private, he with his hand gripping her tighter, closer than the world would have ever deemed wicked. And she'd reveled in it. Those dance sessions that had ultimately dissolved and seen her on the grass with him above her, moving within her as they'd partaken in the most primitive of dances.

Her body grew heated.

That was the only reason she'd needed out of that ballroom and away from Wayland . . . and the memories. Because he'd aroused within her a hungering that was strictly based on the sexual.

Even so, restlessness fueled her strides as she climbed the steps of Lady Wilmot's palatial residence. Dutiful servants threw open the doors, allowing Annalee entry into that which was most familiar to her: a world of sin and decadence.

Handing over her satin cloak, she headed inside.

Long-standing gold candelabras lined the corridors, the light lent by those tapers casting a bright-orange glow upon the crimson carpeting. And as always, whenever Annalee walked these halls, she marveled at the hostess's boldness in lighting such a path, when the ones who would be wandering it were the most intoxicated, most unsteady members of Impolite Society.

As she passed parlor after parlor, each room converted into a makeshift gaming hall, she didn't bother looking. Instead, she headed for the room most familiar to her.

The moment she arrived, she glanced about.

A pair of lovers tangled in one another's arms availed themselves of their host's pretty pink settee near the front of the parlor. Sparing barely a glance for the couple engaged in far different pursuits than card play, Annalee found her way to the table set up directly by the hearth.

The two gentlemen looked up from their game of whist.

"Deal a lady in," she drawled.

A cheroot clamped between his teeth, Lord Willoughby grinned up at her. "A joy to see you, love."

A strapping footman drew out a chair, and Annalee slid herself into the comfortable leather folds.

Muttering a slew of black curses, Beckett tossed a hefty purse across the table, which the other man happily scooped up. "Beckett was of the foolish and incorrect opinion that you wouldn't be coming this night," Willoughby explained at Annalee's questioning look.

In fairness, she hadn't planned to visit this night—the whole proper-behavior business and all that. Even so, devoted friends with Lord Willoughby for eight years now, she still found herself unable to utter that particular truth. One that would be met only with questions she'd no wish to answer. Eventually she'd have to. But not now. "Where else would I be?" She tapped the table, indicating again that she was ready for the game play.

Flawlessly and quickly shuffling the stack, Willoughby proceeded to deal the cards, letting them fly, until an ace landed and Beckett found himself the dealer for their game of vingt-et-un.

As Annalee gathered her hand, Lord Willoughby leaned forward, his own forgotten. The first friend she'd found in her descent into free living and wickedness had been Willoughby. "Well, that is a question, isn't it? Where have you been?"

She resisted the urge to squirm under the attention paid her by the gentlemen studying her entirely too intently, and she made a show of arranging and studying the cards she'd been dealt.

A fabulous hand.

"Lord and Lady Sinclair's."

There was a beat of silence, and then both men promptly dissolved into laughter.

"Granted, I'd expect Sinclair's would be a place you would have attended," Willoughby said through his amusement, "ten years ago when the fellow was a proper rogue and not the proper, devoted papa and happily married gent." He surrendered to his mirth once more.

She lifted her finger in a crude display that only added to both fellows' amusement.

"What in God's name were you doing there, love?" Willoughby demanded when he'd gotten himself under control.

"I'll have you know," she murmured, straightening the card Beckett had dealt her, "that I was being respectable."

She registered more silence and looked up. Both men exchanged a look, then proceeded to howl once more.

"Oh, hush. The both of you." She dealt them each a kick under the table.

"Wh-what . . . ?"

"It is for my Mismatch Society." She proceeded to outline the latest trouble faced by her group. A servant came over with a glass, and her mouth dry from the hell that was this night, Annalee accepted the crystal snifter with a word of thanks.

Leaning forward, Willoughby filled her glass.

She and her tablemates lifted their snifters in toast, clinking rims and then drinking deeply.

Imbibing was certainly not in the "proper" column, and yet neither was attending Lady Wilmot's household card parties. The night, however, called for it. She tossed back a long swallow, welcoming and relishing the comfortable burn as the silky liquor glided down her throat.

"Seems like a lot of trouble and not a lot of fun," Beckett remarked, motioning for the card play to resume.

"I enjoy it," she said, swirling what remained of the contents of her glass several times. "It brings me pleasure."

"And you are ever one for your own pleasure," Willoughby purred in silken tones.

She wrinkled her nose. "I'm not in the mood." She paused. "Tonight."

Surely later she would be. But for some reason, after her dance with Wayland and being held in his arms, she couldn't think of being embraced by Willoughby . . . or any man, for that matter.

They each looked at their cards and staked their bets.

Annalee added three counters.

"So tell us, how was your first foray into respectability?" From around the cheroot clamped between his teeth, Beckett asked that question conversationally.

"It was . . ." A memory slipped in . . . of Wayland with his palm upon her waist, his fingers curled into the satin fabric of her dress. She grew wet and shifted on her seat. "As tedious as one might expect," she lied. "Now if we might return to our hand, gentlemen?"

And fortunately, the game resumed, and the questions about Lord and Lady Sinclair's ball were at an end, along with the whole discussion about respectability. And yet, as Annalee sat there long into the early-morn hours, wagering with two of society's most notorious rakes, she could not push back the thought of Wayland.

Chapter 9

In the world of Polite Society, the slightest thing brought scandal raining down.

In this case, it appeared, nothing more than a waltz with Annalee had resulted in the *ton*'s latest sick fascination.

> Given her appreciation for the wicked, Polite Society could not help but notice the unlikely attendance of a certain Lady A at the unlikeliest of events—the Earl and Countess of S's latest ball.

> Polite Society also noted the sole—and unlikely—figure whom the lady danced with: Baron D. Given the illustrious Lord D's reputation, theirs was an unlikely partnering. Yet given the gentleman's close connection to the lady's brother, perhaps it was nothing more than friendly devotion to the family. Or perhaps . . . there is more? If there is . . . it would throw into doubt all hope of the match society has waited with bated breath for between Lord D and Lady D . . .

Wayland sat there, staring at the two short but very damning paragraphs. Over and over.

This was bad.

It shouldn't be.

And it wouldn't be . . .

If there weren't the expectation that he would wed Lady Diana. A union that was increasingly urgent for the misery Wayland's sister was suffering through.

"Ahem."

Lowering his copy of *The Times* slightly, he looked at Kitty, seated beside him.

"I would like to point out that it's all really just rubbish. Why, it features a whole *host* of redundancies," his sister said helpfully and devotedly. Leaning in, she jabbed at the tiny printed words. "One-two-*three* 'givens.' And as if that wasn't bad enough? One-two-three-*four* 'unlikelies'? In just two paragraphs and six sentences." Kitty lifted a finger. "And if I may also point out, one of those sentences is incredibly clunky and long and awkward, and could have very easily been broken into several sentences. Terrible writing, that."

Yes, it was terrible writing, as his sister pointed out. Terrible, however, for a whole host of reasons.

"Should I keep going?"

"Please," he said, swiping a hand over his face.

"Not everyone is waiting on that match between you and Lady Diana. I couldn't care less whether you wed the duke's daughter."

And ironically, Kitty was the main reason he ultimately needed that formal union.

With a curse, Wayland tossed down the gossip pages.

"Now, that there would really scandalize them, brother," she said, waving a heavily buttered biscuit his way. "You swearing at the breakfast table in the presence of a lady—" She laughed as he grabbed up the newspaper and playfully swatted her on the arm with those sheets. "Oh, come, brother dearest. It's really not so bad as all of that. Why, I think this is perhaps the most interesting thing about you in . . . in"—she wrinkled her nose—"why, years!"

"Thank you for that devotion," he said wryly, picking up his coffee. He blew on the still steaming contents.

She patted his hand, leaving a greasy bit of butter atop. "You're quite welcome."

She'd always been hopelessly inept when it came to identifying sarcasm, and any other time her innocent response would have raised a smile. This time . . .

It was the likeliest outcome—gossip. Gossip followed Annalee, trailing her like the king's finest bloodhound on a hunt.

Wayland glanced down once again at the same newspaper he'd been reading that morning. The same blasted one now being read all over London, at every table in every polite household. Including . . . Jeremy's. The duke and duchess, as well as Lady Diana, were reading that gossip.

His gut tightened.

Bloody, bloody hell. This was bad. No matter which way one looked at it.

"I for one do not think there was anything wrong with it, brother," Kitty said softly, cutting into his panicky musings. "It was just a dance, and it was just Annalee. Why, you were friends when you were children." She wrinkled her nose. "They don't mention anything about that now, though, do they?"

His response emerged tired to his own ears. "No, they didn't."

But that was because, to the *ton*, Wayland's life before Peterloo may as well have not existed. They knew he was a blacksmith's son, but beyond that, no one delved into the life of a common man. No, they were content to focus on the title he'd been granted, and forget the past he'd come from.

"And you looked happy, Wayland."

Happy . . .

There'd been the same thrill that had always been there when taking Annalee in his arms for a waltz or quadrille or country reel. She'd always been filled with an effervescent joy, radiant like the sun, but that orb had blazed brighter, all but consuming her since Peterloo.

The furious echo of footfalls reached the breakfast room, and he and his sister looked up.

"This is a disaster," their mother cried, brandishing a thoroughly rumpled version of the same scandal sheet he and Kitty had been speaking over.

Kitty held up the remnants of her chocolate pastry. "I agree most strenuously. There were but three chocolate-covered biscuits . . . three . . . and they are *gone*." And in a grand flourish, she slapped the back of her spare hand across her brow.

God love his sister. His lips twitched in the first real humor he'd felt since waking up to find that damned gossip sheet.

"Biscuits." Their mother's lower lip trembled. She grabbed the chair on the other side of Wayland before one of the two footmen could, a suspension of decorum from a woman who'd committed herself entirely to it that spoke volumes of her upset. "I am not talking about *biiiiiscuits*."

Any other time he would have been impressed with the extra three syllables she'd managed to squeeze into that particular word.

Kitty cupped a hand about the side of her lips, visible to their mother, and mouthed, "Sorry . . . I tried."

He winked.

"Are you paying attention to me, Wayland?" Mother cried, jerking his focus back her way.

"Yes, yes. Of course."

Kitty ripped off another piece of her biscuit. "As though he could be focused on anything else with your yelling," she said around that mouthful.

"All anyone is talking about is the fact that you danced with that woman."

"'That woman' is Lady Annalee," he said tightly. "Also Jeremy's sister, and—"

His mother shoved the newspaper with the words he'd already committed to memory in his face, interrupting the rest of his defense. "I know who she is, but she is not respectable."

No. He tightened his grip upon his cup. Her reputation was not what it had once been. Even so . . . "She is an earl's daughter."

"Who drinks, Wayland." His mother proved unrelenting. "Who drinks and smokes cheroots and wagers."

"*IIII* think she is quite fun," Kitty said casually. Having moved on from biscuits to toast, she was now buttering a thick slice of bread.

Their mother gasped, her eyes bulging enough that he worried they might actually pop from their sockets. "Not another word, Kitty Smith."

His entirely unrepentant-looking sister made a show of marking an X across her closed lips, before returning to her toast.

Dragging her chair closer to Wayland, his mother continued on in her tirade. "This will never do, Wayland," she said quietly. "We are outcasts as it is. You . . . well, you are largely fine. Accepted enough. But me and Kitty . . ." She gave her head a sad shake. "We shall never be welcomed unless everything about us is above reproach, and that includes you not engaging that woman so . . . so intimately," she said on a hushed whisper.

Now she opted for discretion. As though she'd not just come screeching into the room, airing their family's business before their servants.

"It was one dance," he said, as much a reminder for himself as for his fretting mama. It shouldn't result in this level of scrutiny . . . even if it was Annalee. "One dance," he repeated.

"And he danced two with Lady Diana." Kitty's reminder came muffled from the bite she still chewed.

Their mother leaned around Wayland so she might better turn a frown upon her daughter. "Do not talk with your mouth full. It is very plebeian. And I'll remind you both, there are certain rules and expectations which must be followed by respectable members of Polite Society . . ."

With that, their mother proceeded to dole out essential lessons that they need remember. As though he weren't entirely aware. As though he hadn't dedicated himself these past years to being respectable and honorable and proper. He gritted his teeth. And now because of one dance with Annalee, he'd find himself not only the subject of gossip throughout every breakfast room and parlor but also the recipient of a lecture from his mother.

His sister leaned in and whispered, "What is more plebeian than a blacksmith's kin, though, eh, big brother?"

"Indeed."

Even as they shared another commiserative-sibling smile, his gut clenched.

Blacksmith's children was what they were, and what they would always be. And while he'd come to accept how the world viewed him, he'd never be at peace as long as Kitty was treated as she was by Polite Society. Shunned. Mocked. Nay, there could never be humor in those words she'd uttered. Not when she was an outcast amongst the ladies, a wallflower without even a dancing partner or suitor.

His mother spoke, bringing him back from his troubled musings. "Two dances with Lady Diana is still only one more than a set with . . . with . . . Lady Annalee." She wrung the edges of that paper in her gloved fingers, staining the white satin with ink as she did.

"But three"—Kitty waggled three of her fingers—"is tantamount to an offer of marriage."

"Which is the *goalllll*," their grasping mama whispered furiously. "The whole world knows that."

More than anyone amongst Polite Society, his and Kitty's mother had bought into the romance of a future match between Wayland, the heroic rescuer, and the duke's beloved daughter. When Diana had been a child, it had been easy enough to not give any real thought to the expectations society and his mother had for them. But now that the lady had made her Come Out, he was being forced into a place of having to actually commit—or not—to that union.

Kitty furrowed her brow in an overexaggerated confusion, and even with the misery of the day, Wayland found himself smiling. "The goal is . . . marriage?"

Mother threw up her arms. "Of *course*."

His sister sat forward, dropping an elbow on the table. "So marriage between Wayland and Annalee is the goal?"

He promptly choked on his swallow, and the force of his paroxysm sent the black brew spilling over the sides of his cup.

"Oh, dear. I've gone and given you a fit, brother. I was simply teasing."

Teasing about him and Annalee . . . when no one knew anything of his former relationship with the lady, no idea that marriage had been something they'd dreamed of and spoken of before . . . life had interfered.

Kitty thumped him hard between the shoulder blades, only sending more droplets splashing.

"Do not kill your brother, or else where will we be? Precisely as we were. It's all very precarious, you know."

"Yes, my dying young is certainly secondary to all that," he said when he managed to get a proper breath.

His mother gave a curt nod. "Precisely."

She was nothing if not honest in her aspirations and views about her children's usefulness.

"Your brother must marry Lady Diana, Kitty," their mother went on to explain. "It was ordained."

Ordained.

Had anything other than blood and heartbreak and ruin been born on the fields of Peterloo?

"Ah, how could I forget?" Kitty made a show of sitting back in her chair, a study in revelation. "Isn't it enough that Wayland's a lord and you're the mother of a baron and I'm a baron's sister, and that Wayland has estates in England, and Scotland, and wealth to our name?"

"*Nooo.*" Their mother eyed her youngest offspring as though she were half-mad.

"Of course not. Foolish me," Kitty said under her breath. She waved them on. "As you were."

"It was noted that you were there, dancing attendance upon the lady, Wayland."

"I am aware," he said tersely. "We have discussed it ad nauseam."

Their mother swept to her feet. "We cannot afford this, Wayland. Not when our reputation is"—she glanced at the servants lined over at the sideboard and dropped her voice—"what it is."

He gritted his teeth. As if he needed any further reminders. Sometimes, however, he wondered how much of her ambition came from a desire to climb that damned social ladder, and how much of it was really about Kitty. "Your concerns are duly noted," he said. Anything to be rid of her.

Her shoulders rose and fell in a tangible display of her relief. "You are a good boy." With that, she gathered her newspapers and left.

The moment she'd gone, there were several beats of silence . . . that Kitty broke.

"Do you know she used to speak the same exact words to our old hound, Mr. Jumbles," Kitty remarked, pulling a laugh from Wayland.

She winked. "That is better, brother. You mustn't let her get you down, and you shouldn't let her decide whether or not you dance with Annalee. In fact, given how magnificent Annalee is, why should you not?"

Because when he held her, he recalled . . . all manner of sins they'd committed together, ones that these past two days had reminded him he wasn't so very honorable as to be above committing again. Because it made him want to forget the easiest path forward to his sister's happiness—a union with Lady Diana—and instead, focus on the greatest path toward his own.

"Are you all right, brother?" Kitty asked, giving him a look. "You've gone all . . . queer. I didn't make you sick from your coffee, after all . . . did I?"

"Visits from Mother ofttimes have this . . . effect upon me." The reason for his upset had to do with the pressing need to help make the world right for Kitty, and guilt for having failed Annalee all those years ago.

Footfalls sounded at the entry, and they looked up.

His butler, Belding, attired in gold and the most ridiculously high powdered wig, as insisted upon by Wayland's mother, stepped forward. "My lord, you have a visitor."

Thank God. Anyone. Absolutely anyone, as long as it was not his mother returning, would be preferable to sitting here, enduring more of what he'd suffered through that morning.

Belding stepped aside.

"I took the liberty of showing Lord Montgomery here."

Wayland's stomach sank. *Oh, bloody hell.*

And then his gaze went to the very damning copy of *The Times* tucked under Jeremy's elbow.

He'd been wrong. There had been one person whose company he'd rather not face at this particular moment. *Bloody, bloody hell.*

Kicking him under the table, Kitty hopped up, springing Wayland into belated action.

He rose, the legs of his chair scraping along the hardwood floor, while Kitty dipped a curtsy. "You must forgive my brother. He just had the most unpleasant visit from— *Oww*." Her words cut off as she glared at him. "Did you just step on my foot?"

He briefly closed his eyes. "I was shifting my boot."

"Onto my foot?" she demanded indignantly.

God love her loyalty, she was still hopeless when it came to subtleties.

Jeremy stared at them bemusedly.

"Yes, well, then . . . I trust that my brother stomping my foot most viciously now had something to do with something I wasn't supposed to say, which also undoubtedly means there are other matters that you gentlemen have to discuss that make my presence a bother."

"Your presence could never be a bother," Jeremy murmured, sweeping another bow.

"Oh, splendid," Kitty said, her expression deadpan as she perched herself on the edge of the table. "Then I'll stay."

Over the top of her head, Wayland leveled a scowl on the other man.

Jeremy, with his spare hand, wrestled with his cravat. "Uh . . ."

A smile widened Kitty's lips. "I'm teasing." She hopped up. "I'll let you both to your"—she dropped her voice, deepening it several shades—"very serious business." With a wink, she headed out . . . and closed the door behind her.

Jeremy stared at the panel a moment. "She's a bit of a whirlwind, isn't she? When did that happen?"

"I think . . . forever?"

Alas, it was too much to hope that his closest—also his only—friend in the world had come to discuss his sister.

"I can only . . . imagine the reason for your mother's upset." The other man tossed his newspaper down on the table. It landed with a decisive *thwack* alongside Kitty's empty plate.

Wayland winced. Could he, though? Could Jeremy know precisely what his faithless mother had said? "You know my mother," he said carefully. Though that was likely the lesser offense to worry about. Nay, his having danced with Annalee had raised questions amongst Polite Society. And it was to be expected that Jeremy might have those same—

"Because you know my sister," Jeremy said, and the unexpectedness of those words sent heat up Wayland's neck, and he prayed for a second rescue. This time, he'd even take it from his damned status-climbing mother. Anything. Anyone.

"Uh . . ." Nothing. Wayland had absolutely no response to that. For he did know Annalee. Intimately, in ways that would have likely ended not only his friendship with Jeremy but also Wayland's life.

Jeremy looked him in the eye. "Annalee brings scandal on all she comes into contact with." The other man began pacing. "And now she's brought scandal to you."

So caught up in his own guilt and musings about Annalee, Wayland took a moment to register what the other man had said. He blinked slowly. "Come again?"

Jeremy abruptly stopped that annoying back-and-forth stride, and grabbing the chair vacated by Kitty, he seated himself. "You were gracious enough to dance with my sister, and I'm grateful to you for extending that courtesy. But I also came to apologize for . . . for . . ."

Wayland fell into his own seat. "You are thanking me for dancing with your sister . . . ," he echoed dumbly.

"And apologizing, of course."

Apologizing.

Wayland attempted to sort out which was worse from a faithless brother . . . the apology or the gratitude. And between first his damned mother and now Annalee's disloyal brother, all the earlier unease at having his name in the papers faded. "I don't need an apology or your words of thanks," he said curtly. Nor did he point out that Annalee had pulled him onto the dance floor because, well, hell, it really didn't matter.

Jeremy rested a hand on his shoulder. "I don't deserve your friendship, old chum. This"—he grabbed his well-worn copy of *The Times* and held it up—"I know is everything you seek to avoid. Scandal. Shame."

Yes, after Peterloo, Wayland had pledged himself to everything his friend now spoke of. And yet, to hear him speak so . . . of his sister? Of Annalee . . . Even if there was truth to what he said, it grated. "Nothing shameful transpired last evening," he bit out. *But plenty shameful transpired years before it,* a voice jeered and taunted, calling him out for that faithlessness that he'd never paid a proper price for. He stormed to his feet. "Nothing at all. It was a damned dance."

The other man blinked up at him. "No. I . . . I wasn't suggesting that it did. I didn't mean to. Rather, I was just saying that simply being with my sister—"

"I know what you're saying," he snapped.

Jeremy continued to stare wide-eyed.

Oh, bloody hell.

In the end, Wayland found himself rescued.

The door burst open, and they both looked over.

Kitty had returned, like an avenging warrior. "I require saving."

The hell she did. His sister could have saved Wellington's men better than the old general himself. "Mother is attempting to squire me to the modiste, and you know when she does, she attires me in"—she lifted up her arms—"this."

Both men looked to the entirely unremarkable blue satin day dress.

"Uh . . . I fail to see anything wrong with your dress," Jeremy said, cocking his head.

Sweeping over, she patted him on the hand. "You're just being a dear because you are Wayland's best friend and a gentleman." She clapped her hands. "Now, if you'll excuse Wayland and me?"

"Uh . . . of course." Jeremy shoved to his feet. "We . . . can speak about this later?"

"Indeed."

But for now, Wayland had been granted a reprieve.

Chapter 10

Annalee had grown accustomed to people leaving rooms when she entered them.

That was, when she entered places where the respectable sort mingled.

Mamas dragged their daughters away when she came near.

Wives held their husbands' arms all the tighter.

Though if those respectable wives would have cared to know the truth, Annalee didn't bother with married men. Faithless bounders who couldn't respect their vows were hardly the manner of men she kept company with. Nay, at least unentangled rogues and rakes were honest in their dealings and what they wanted.

At that very moment, the latest room she was responsible for clearing was . . . a shop.

A modiste's, to be exact.

Silence continued to fill Madame Bouchard's as the mothers and their daughters present stared on at Annalee and Valerie.

And then, almost as one, clutching their daughters the way they snatched their pearls when she was near, the ladies filed past.

"And here I was worried about having to mingle with the *ton*," Valerie said with her usual drollness. "Now it appears the only worry is as to whether we'll be served."

Together, they looked to the modiste and the shopgirls, hovering at the back of the shop and eyeing them with the same wariness they might have reserved for a visit by some specter. "Oh, they'll attend us." Annalee made that prediction with complete confidence. "Furthermore, you'll never have to worry about mingling with the proper members of the peerage when I'm about." Removing her flask, she uncorked the piece, saluted her friend, and raised the spirits to her lips. "Particularly after my latest scandal."

"They left because of me," Valerie said as they moved down the aisles, assessing bolts of fabric.

Annalee snorted. "Do not flatter yourself, dear. I and I alone possess the power of clearing places of polite people. And particularly after last evening." She sighed. Alas, her first real attempt at a return to politeness and properness . . . which had, of course, descended into her leaving a ball early and attending Lady Wilmot's and drinking and—

Valerie lifted a swatch of orange, examining it. "I do not see what was so scandalous about your dancing with a respectable lord. That seems the manner of activity that would put rumors to rest."

For another lady, perhaps. But that waltz . . . Annalee's heart kicked up its cadence as she—and her body—recalled the feel of Wayland's hands upon her, the slightly possessive grip he'd had at her waist, a fierce hold that had always left her breathless. And that place between her legs ached . . . even though she'd brought herself to pleasure last evening, thinking of that same dance that now consumed her. Because no one danced like Wayland. Her body never moved more perfectly than when he held her for something so simple as a waltz, and yet more erotic than lovemaking itself.

"It is splendorous . . ."

"Yes," she breathed . . . There was nothing more splendorous—

Across a bolt of pale green, her friend smiled.

Wait . . . what?

Valerie wagged the nauseating fabric in her hands.

Annalee followed that slight rustle and blanched. "Do put that down." She plucked the fabric from her friend's fingers. "I'd look like a plate of peas made into puree in that one. And I hate peas. They hardly belong on a plate, let alone a person."

Valerie looked wounded. "I thought you said it was splendorous," she protested, picking up the swatch.

"I was being sarcastic." The lie came entirely too easily, born of a need to keep from mentioning how special that moment had been to her. "This fabric offends me." It had been blasphemous to have—even in error— applied the same word she had for dancing with Wayland to a material such as the one her friend encouraged her to have made into a proper dress.

"There's hardly anything scandalous about peas," her friend pointed out. "Well?" Valerie gave it another shake, waggling her eyebrows like she was one of those vendors hawking their wares on the streets.

Together, they stared with a renewed interest in the satin.

Annalee looked at the fabric dubiously. Perhaps Valerie was correct and she should consider an entirely different aesthetic for her wardrobe. Particularly one that couldn't or wouldn't attract the looks that crimsons and blacks and golds invariably did. Simultaneously, she and Valerie cocked their heads in opposite directions, eyeing the fabric still. Why, attired in a shade such as this, it was a certainty that absolutely no one would lust after her or look at her.

That was, look at someone in such a shade of green for any reasons beyond horror.

She sighed. Mayhap that was the very reason she should consider it, then.

"*Hmm?*" Valerie caught her eye and gave the bolt a little shake.

With reluctant movements, Annalee stretched her fingers toward it, then promptly drew them back. "I can't do it. I just . . . cannot wear *that.*"

"You're trying to be proper," Valerie persisted.

Yes, but the line had to be drawn somewhere. "I'm trying to be proper, not"—Annalee swept her fingers in a little circle, gesturing in the direction of the item in question—"put myself through any self-flagellation." Good God, this was going to be even harder than she'd anticipated. All of this. Removing her flask from her reticule, she uncorked the desperately needed spirits.

Valerie stared pointedly at the silver flask, and Annalee returned the object in question to her bag.

"This is different."

"Drinking spirits in one of the most posh, well-respected modiste's?" Valerie promptly dropped that hideous fabric. "This I have to hear."

"Well," Annalee began in the elevated tones she'd used years earlier, when she'd been a girl instructing her brother and Wayland on some point that they'd needed to know, "it is simply that . . . we are"—she stretched her arms wide—"alone. Uh . . . with the exception of the modiste."

Again, they looked to the still dawdling shopkeeper.

The modiste tensed her mouth.

Valerie tipped her head in the young woman's direction. "And the only reason we're alone is because we drove everyone away."

"And because of that, I'm certainly free to indulge in a bit of whiskey."

"And it's also the reason you should be of a mind to pick a fabric like—"

"You are nothing if not tenacious." With a laugh, Annalee claimed the material once more from her determined friend's clutch. "No."

Valerie glanced about for the still tarrying shopkeeper. "You know we're only moments from being thrown out, don't you?"

Pouting, Annalee helped herself to one of the decorative feathers from the table. "Ah, but I do not know that," she said, wagging that pink scrap in her friend's direction. "Because Madame Bouchard is in a pickle. She doesn't want to have me sully her steps, but also, she recognizes that I'm the daughter of one of her greatest, most free-spending patrons. And as such, she won't throw me out." She tapped her friend on the nose. "Yet."

Eventually the woman would get around to it. Eventually, all the respectable sorts tired of her. But Annalee rather suspected Madame Bouchard would come over, grant her the quickest of quick appointments, and rush her off.

"She is upset that we've driven off all her patrons."

And that she'd women of Valerie's and Annalee's reputations in her shop.

The bell tinkled at the front, followed by the click of an opening door. Annalee lifted a finger. "Not everyone."

Valerie rolled her eyes. As they resumed their stroll down the aisles, her friend collected a swath of brown muslin. "This?"

"Egad, *noooo*. Brown? *Valerie*." Annalee lamented her dearest friend's very terrible taste. She did a search of the table and then widened her eyes. Quitting the other woman's side, inexorably pulled to the very end of the table at the farthest end of the aisle, Annalee stopped. With reverent hands, she reached for the shimmering scarlet silk and lifted it closer for inspection. That slight movement sent the material rippling, and the light streaming through the shop windows played off the fabric, giving it a glossy sheen that added radiance to—

"No."

Annalee jumped and clutched the scarlet silk protectively to her chest. "But—"

"No," the other woman repeated more emphatically. "It's red."

Her friend guided her hands back down.

Annalee turned a pout on Valerie. "You are no fun."

"Which is why I'm the perfect person to help you with this particular decision."

With a last sorrowful look, she laid the article down. "I'll have you know it's more a shade of scarlet. Not exactly the same as red," Annalee mumbled as they continued their quest.

Valerie fingered the lace fringe of a pale-yellow muslin. *"Hmph,"* she said, her gaze not on that fabric but on the front of the shop. "It is tiresome," she remarked.

Annalee chuckled. "There is much tiresome about modistes and Polite Society. You have to be more specific, dear."

"It's just that she's still debating whether to serve *you*, and yet she's rushed off to provide assistance to a man and his mistress, so mayhap she's not as respectable as all that."

A man and his . . . ?

Endlessly intrigued, Annalee looked to the front of the shop and froze, her heart thumping funnily in her chest. For the pair on the floor now, speaking with the modiste, were no wicked woman and her protector. It was . . .

"Wayland?" she whispered.

She felt Valerie's questioning stare.

After all, she'd have to be looking at the other woman to have seen it. As it was, all her focus was entirely reserved for the broad-muscled figure conversing with Madame Bouchard.

What brother bothered to accompany his sister to a place as tedious and miserable as this one?

Between being oblivious to her relationship with Wayland and returning from the Continent all those years earlier and finding his sister the talk and scandal of London, Annalee's own brother couldn't have been bothered to defend her honor. Nor, for that matter, would she have ever wished him to do something as foolish as duel because of her. He'd been more of a friend, even when they'd been children, treating her as one of "the lads," as he'd called the three of them. He'd enjoyed her company when she'd been fishing and shooting and racing him and his best friend. But neither had Jeremy been the manner of devoted brother who'd go about escorting her to fittings.

"Is he one of your lovers?" Valerie asked curiously.

"Hmm?"

And then it registered what her friend was asking—whether Wayland was one of the men she'd taken to her bed.

Oddly, the answer was both . . . yes and no. It had been a lifetime since she'd made love to Wayland. He'd also been her first, the man she'd happily surrendered her virtue to. "No," she finally brought herself to murmur.

Those moments belonged to another time, between a different woman and a different man from a lifetime past. "He is . . . a friend of my brother's."

"Ahh."

Valerie's murmuring belonged to someone who thought she'd pieced together a connection, and yet . . . she couldn't know, truly. Because no one knew about the years Annalee had been head over heels in love with the gentleman. Back when she'd believed in love.

Just then, Madame Bouchard squired off Wayland's sister, a bundle of blushing cheeks and guileless eyes and so much innocence and—and the oddest pang struck, and for the oddest reason. She didn't miss the woman she'd been. And yet . . . Annalee's gaze locked on the crimson fabric she'd haggled with Valerie over.

The young woman's eyes landed on Annalee, lighting not with the disdain so familiarly turned Annalee's way.

"Annalee!" she exclaimed, and with an absolute lack of ladylike decorum that Annalee fell a little bit in love with her for, the girl rushed over. "It is ever so good to see you here in London! I have missed seeing you."

"I . . ." A swell of emotion filled Annalee's throat at that unexpected pronouncement from the younger girl. "May I introduce my friend, Miss Valerie Bragger."

All of London knew Valerie Bragger—at least they knew of her name from the scandal sheets. And given Wayland's full immersion in Polite Society, there could be no doubt his sister was well aware of the other woman's reputation.

"How do you do?" Valerie murmured with a deep curtsy.

"Oh, no. None of that at all!" Kitty Smith brushed off that politesse with a wave of a gloved hand. "I forbid it. I despise that formality!"

Surprise lit Valerie's eyes.

Kitty turned back. "Wayland!" The young lady waved her arms exuberantly. "Look who I have found!"

Annalee's eyes slipped over to the devoted brother, who paused in his conversation with the head shopkeeper. His gaze slid away from Madame

Bouchard, and he froze, and in that moment, it was as though time ceased moving altogether, and everyone else within the room melted away but for her and Wayland.

Annalee's mouth went dry as recognition flared within those striking green-blue depths, and her body recalled all over again that slight tightening of his fingers as he'd sunk them into her hip. And Lord smite her for the wicked creature she was, her imaginings took an even more forbidden turn as she imagined straddling him and him gripping her that same way. She bit her lower lip hard, and even with the space of the shop between them, she caught the narrowing of his lashes as his focus locked on her mouth.

The moment was shattered, and time resumed its movement, with a dizzying rapidity. "Wayland!" his sister called out as she once again motioned for him. "Do come over."

Wayland murmured something to Madame Bouchard, and a pretty blush stained the young shopkeeper's cheeks.

A tart taste filled Annalee's mouth, and she followed his approach. He'd always been a charmer. From the girls in the village where they lived to, by the reports she'd read within the papers, all the most respectable ladies in London. He'd always possessed a way of making a woman feel as though she were the only person present. She'd not, however, witnessed . . . that charm in action. On other women, that was.

Wayland reached their trio and immediately doffed his hat, tucking the elegant article under his arm. "Look, Wayland," Kitty said happily. "I've found Annalee."

"I see that," he murmured, his eyes sliding to Annalee's once more, and doing all those dangerous things to her belly, flutterings and flips that she'd forgotten with time's passing and then buried with the jaded course she'd set. Apparently, those butterflies had been resurrected by the power of Wayland's piercing eyes.

He sketched a bow. "My lady."

Alas, that singular focus proved entirely one-sided as he slid his attention away all too easily.

Madame Bouchard swept over. *"Viens, viens, mon cher. Il y a beaucoup à faire."*

Kitty beamed, offering another enthusiastic wave. "Perhaps you would be so good as to keep my brother company for a short bit?"

"That won't be necessary," he said quickly, *too* quickly, as his sister rushed off.

"Forgive me," Annalee said after the girl had gone. "Lord Darlington, allow me to introduce my dear friend, Miss Valerie Bragger."

She reflexively positioned herself closer to Valerie. Wayland of old would not have ever been anything less than welcoming and warm to a woman of Valerie's reputation. The new Wayland, married to respectability and his good name—and reputation—was a man she didn't know. And as such, she knew even less how he'd receive—

"Miss Bragger," he murmured, offering a deep, respectable bow. "It is a pleasure."

"My lord," Valerie said with the usual cool she reserved for men.

"I have read much of yours and Annalee's work with the Mismatch Society."

Annalee tensed.

"I think it is admirable that you and she have taken on such an important venture."

He did?

"Do you?" the other woman said gruffly, though without the same amount of her earlier vitriol.

Wayland lifted his head. "Indeed."

"Thank you. It is . . . a pleasure meeting you, as well, my lord," Valerie murmured.

He dropped a bow. "Any friend of Lady Annalee's is a friend of mine."

And if she were capable of falling in love again, it would have been in this moment, with this man who didn't cut her friend, and who might disapprove of her society but had also spoken respectfully of it to Valerie.

Dropping a hasty curtsy, Valerie slipped off.

And with that, she left Annalee and Wayland . . . alone.

⚬⚬⚬

Leaving was the wisest course.

He'd exchanged the suitable degree of politeness, with greetings and proper formality. As such, dropping another bow and heading in the opposite direction while he waited for his sister was the safest thing to do.

Particularly after the scandal that had come from just a dance.

Whatever would the world say to a coincidental meeting the next afternoon following the set that had the *ton* talking?

A meeting that was, in fact, chance, but the world wouldn't see it that way.

And yet knowing all that and committed to avoiding scandal for the sake of his family, still, something kept Wayland frozen to the floor.

Go.

He made to bow . . . but the earlier hesitancy had cost him.

"I daresay the world would be agog if we were seen here, conversing," Annalee murmured. "As such it would be best for you, Lord Darlington, if we parted ways as quickly as possible."

A challenge dwelled in the slight up-tilt of her intonation.

She'd always dared him.

Nay, they'd always dared one another in various pursuits or games.

"You expect that I will leave."

"I expect you will," she said. "But then, I expected you should not have anything nice to say about my Mismatch Society, and you proved me wrong just moments ago." And that quiet murmuring didn't contain the usual brash confidence and jest.

"I surrendered my rebellious roots, but that does not mean I cannot admire what you have created and what you attempt to do for women."

Her jaw slipped and her lips parted, and standing as close as he was, he caught the breathy little sigh. "I liked your rebellious roots, Wayland," she said softly.

"No good came from them." Certainly this woman, more than any other, should have realized that.

"Yes, well, not all of us have the luxury of abandoning our rebellious ways. Women aren't afforded the same luxuries as men."

"No. I am aware of that."

"Speaking of rebellious ways," she whispered, leaning close. "What will the world say to your speaking here with me now?"

Absolutely nothing good. It would fuel the gossip, and throw further fire upon the *ton*'s fascination with him and Lady Diana, and the frustration that the romantic match the world craved was being so thwarted.

Given the state of his sister's ostracism by Polite Society, all that should matter most.

And yet . . .

"I don't care," he said quietly.

And found . . . there to be truth in that admission.

Annalee started.

Be her friend . . . she needs you . . .

All Harlow's and Jeremy's separate urgings slipped forward.

She dampened her lips. "Well, that . . . is quite surprising."

Sadness swept through him. "Then that is because I've been the most miserable of friends." He'd failed her . . . not just at Peterloo. But after, too. He'd made so many mistakes.

"Not the most miserable," she protested. "The most absent, perhaps." She gave him a slight playful nudge with her elbow. "Well, then, as you are interested in stepping forward as a friend, I must really insist you help me." And then she slipped her arm through his, and with that one exchange, he may as well have transported them back a lifetime ago to when they'd been both friends and secret lovers. "I am going for respectable, and the modiste is otherwise busy," she said as they began a stroll through the shop.

Together, they looked over to where the shopkeeper tended Kitty. Kitty, who'd arrived after Annalee.

She'd been given the cut direct by the damned modiste. He'd been so consumed with how Kitty had been shunned, only to have failed to see that Annalee had found herself . . . suffering that same cruelty? How had it taken Jeremy pointing out just how much Annalee was and had always been deserving of his support?

He glared at the modiste.

"Oh, do stop. It's really quite fine," Annalee said on a rush, so very accurately reading him and his outrage.

"It isn't," he gritted out. *In any way.* "She's no reason to deny you service."

"She's not denied me. She's just . . . made me . . . wait." She smiled up at him, the radiant expression that dimpled her cheeks and lit her eyes, and always made a muddle of his mind. It never failed to.

Except . . . this time. This time, rage consumed him. "I'll not tolerate it."

"Well, you have no choice," she said firmly, "because I do, and I've found that it is best to know which battles are worth taking up. And this? This is decidedly *not* it."

He remained there, his entire body tense, staring at the modiste. Warring with the need to stomp over and demand she respect a woman deserving it, when Annalee lightly squeezed his arm.

"She's done me a favor, Wayland."

A muscle ticked at the corner of his eye, and he forced his gaze away from that viper and over to the woman at his side. "I daresay you'll have to enlighten me as to how."

Annalee briefly leaned her head against his shoulder. "Why, there isn't a better person to help me achieve proper than you."

"Thank you," he said dryly as they started their walk around the edge of the shop.

"I meant that as the greatest of compliments. I do have a need for respectability, you know." She brought them to another stop, this time alongside a table littered with fabric. Collecting a crimson bolt in her long fingers, she held the material aloft. "Eh?" she said, molding it to her frame.

Images slithered forward, of her draped in that shimmery red silk and him tugging it free and kissing each swath of skin exposed. He resisted the urge to tug at his cravat. "Uh . . ."

"I'm teasing." She tossed it down and gave a roll of her eyes. "I'm not quite so hopeless." With that she held up another, bringing it close to her person. A blue so pale it was as though the weaver who'd created the fabric hadn't known whether to wish for a white or sky blue, and had managed to meld those shades and hues along with several others within. She cleared her throat. "What do you think?"

He stared, riveted—frozen. Completely captivated by this . . . vulnerable, hesitant woman before him. Wayland's gaze locked with hers. "Perfect," he said quietly. "Utterly and completely . . . perfect."

And along the way he'd ceased to speak about the fabric and was capable of seeing and talking about only her.

Her arm wavered, the bolt slipping, and she drifted close, and just several days ago . . . he would have cared. He would have cared so very much.

Somewhere at the front of the shop, he registered a slight tinkling of a bell.

Perhaps those were warning ones in his brain?

The slightest whisper of rose water wafted over him, filling his senses. It was the delicate scent of her, gardens and glory.

"Annalee," he began hoarsely.

"Wayland!"

And just like that, the moment came to a jarring and miserable halt.

They looked as one to the owner of that voice.

A bright-eyed, white-skirt-wearing young lady rushed through the shop to meet him, waving as she went.

Oh, hell.

His stomach sank.

"I thought I spied your carriage outside, Wayland, and I hoped to see Kitty, but you are here, too!" Diana's smile wavered as she looked to Annalee. Annalee, who'd gone silent and made an impressive show of studying the fabric. "Oh . . . hello. You have . . . a friend."

And ironically, there it was. That term applied yet again to his former lover, and from this woman, whom Polite Society all expected him to wed. He cleared his throat. "Forgive me. Yes. Lady Diana, may I present Lady Annalee. Lady Annalee, Lady Diana."

Annalee dropped a curtsy. "How do you do, my lady?" she murmured.

"Ever so well." And much the way Annalee had done moments ago, Diana joined her arm with his. "Now that I've seen Wayland. Our friendship runs deep"—she lifted a simpering gaze to his—"does it not?"

Oh, God. I am going to throw up.

"You know one another through Lord Jeremy . . . do you not?" The duke's daughter chatted happily, as though she were not talking to his first and only love. Because she couldn't possibly know. No one ever had.

"We do," Annalee said, the stronger one of the pair of them, who was actually able to formulate coherent words. "Jeremy and Wayland were the dearest of friends, and they were"—she looked his way briefly—"good enough to allow me to tag along."

Diana sighed. "He is ever so thoughtful, isn't he?"

"Ever so," Annalee murmured, and Wayland couldn't sort out heads or tails of what she was genuinely thinking in that moment.

"Diana!" That sharp call from the duchess cut across the shop.

Diana pouted. "Oh, dear. Mother calls. It was so lovely meeting you."

Annalee curtsied. "The pleasure was all mine."

Another smile lit the girl's face as she turned her adoring gaze up to his. "I promise to return after I make my selection, Wayland."

"I . . . look forward to it."

Giving him another little wave, she hastened off.

The moment she reached her mother's side, the duchess started speaking quietly and sternly. Then Diana stole a stricken glance over her shoulder toward him and Annalee, and his stomach fell all the further.

He'd never allowed himself to really imagine a match between them. She'd been a child at their first meeting, and in his mind that was how she'd remained. And yet that didn't erase the possibilities that came for Kitty from a marriage between him and Diana.

"I . . . I should go. I"—Annalee picked up the bolt of blue—"did not anticipate just how quick this trip would be, but it was, thanks to your help."

"Annalee." Except what in hell was he to say? "I . . . it was"—*perfect until Diana arrived*—"good to see you," he finished weakly.

As she left and he remained with Kitty and Lady Diana and her mother, a pit settled in his gut at the realization that if he pursued that match his mother and the whole world sought for him, then it would mark a complete and final end to his time with Annalee.

Chapter 11

Well, hell.

This was bad.

The latest edition of *The Times* stared up damningly, while Annalee, Sylvia, and Valerie stood around Sylvia's desk, contemplating the latest scandal Annalee had found herself embroiled in . . . and all because of a visit to Madame Bouchard's most prestigious of modiste shops.

From the corner of her eye, Annalee peeked at the two women flanking her and the newspaper.

As usual, Valerie's expression was a carefully crafted mask that gave no indication as to what the other woman thought or felt.

Sylvia, however, wore her strain in her eyes and the corners of her mouth, and whether that fatigue was a product of Annalee or the fact she was expecting a babe was hard to say.

A healthy amount of fear snapped through Annalee. Eventually all tired of her. People tolerated only so much where she was concerned. From nursemaids to governesses to lovers . . . to even parents, ultimately everyone tired of her and her "antics," as Mother referred to them.

Perhaps this would prove the last straw for Sylvia. Though that would be the height of irony, indeed. What would bring her down wasn't the orgies she'd attended or running in her chemise through fountains or her friendship with the two greatest rakes amongst Polite—and

Impolite—Society, but her association with the estimably proper and honorable Lord Darlington.

She would have laughed. If she could have. If she weren't filled with a hellish terror that she'd be forced to return home, where her dowry had been withheld, dependent upon a family who despised her, who would constantly remind her that her own actions that day in Manchester had been a stain upon the family, just like all her wild behaviors.

Annalee wrenched her stare away and back over to the front page of *The Times*.

And with every click of that Griotte-marble-and-bronze clock punctuating the pregnant silence, an inevitable sense of doom swelled and rose, threatening to engulf her. She couldn't go back. She didn't belong there. They didn't want her. Panic ricocheted around her breast, pinging back and forth like the staccato echo of the bullets that had flown that day in Manchester.

Except that remembrance only brought out a sweat upon her palms and skin, and bile burnt her throat, climbing higher, and she swallowed quickly several times to keep from casting up the contents of her morning meal right there on that damning sheet that was her source of woe.

Annalee's gaze slid to the silver flask she'd foolishly set on the center table as she'd entered the room. Her throat ached, and her mouth went dry, parched for the smooth heat of the liquor that invariably managed to dull the edges of the most unpleasant aspects of life. She eyed her flask covetously. Given the severity of these latest circumstances—with her fate and future in this household and as part of the society that met within this residence, however, all in question—this was hardly the time to draw attention to her love of spirits.

At last, the silence broke . . . in the form of Sylvia's sigh. "Well, this is . . . certainly . . . not wonderful." The recently married viscountess pressed her fingertips against her temples and rubbed them in small circles.

Or that was another, more polite way of saying it. And if Annalee were capable of a smile or a laugh, that startling contrast between her uncouth thoughts about the situation and Sylvia's more polite, optimistic one would have been reason for it. But she wasn't capable of either, beyond the weight pressing down on her like so many bricks, stealing her ability to breathe.

"I'll fix it," Annalee said quickly. She didn't know how. As it was, each effort she'd made to not be scandalous had been met with only greater scandal.

"Fix what?" Valerie snapped. "You did nothing wrong." She turned to Sylvia. "She didn't do anything. She merely spoke with the baron. Why . . . why . . . He was just as polite and pleasant to me."

And yet, neither had Wayland strolled through the shop on Valerie's arm or helped select fabric, all of which had been reported in the gossip columns.

Sylvia scoffed. "You don't have to fix this, Annalee," she said, her eyes glinting with the passion of her defense. "You visited a respectable modiste, and with a friend at that, at the same time one of London's most respectable gentlemen should have also attended with his sister." With a sound of disgust, Sylvia shoved the paper. "As though the perfect place for an assignation is a modiste's."

"Yes, imagine that," Annalee added weakly. Because, of course, her reputation preceded her, and she'd not always been innocent where modiste shops and gentlemen were concerned.

"This is what is wrong with society and how women are treated . . . *mature* women." Valerie amended her word choice and overemphasized those two syllables. "They see Lady Diana and imagine her, the perfect innocent, to be his *perfect* match in every way, and then there is the big, bad, terrible wanton, ruining all the good plans between them."

"I'll allow 'big' and 'bad,' but a 'terrible wanton,' too, Valerie?" Even with her attempt at jest, a vicious jealousy snaked around her gut at Valerie's words.

For she, like everyone, nay, more than everyone, had heard the tales of Wayland's heroic rescue that day in Manchester. She'd read those newspapers with his name, admiring him and loving him for who he'd been to that mother, her daughter, and her maid that day . . .

"Well, either way, it is preposterous," Sylvia was saying, pulling Annalee out of her own head.

"Their linking you romantically to one such as Lord Darlington? *Darlington?*" A snorting laugh spilled past Sylvia's lips, and she shook her head. "It's ridiculous."

Annalee forced herself to add a chuckle, joining in Sylvia's mirth, the sound of her own slightly strained. Yes, it was rather hard to conceive. The world would have never dared pair Annalee with one such as Wayland, but the world also didn't know a thing about the man he'd once been or the passion and fire he was capable of. Where he'd doused that light, however, Annalee had let herself be consumed by it, and those changes from their once equally passionate selves accounted for Sylvia's incredulity.

"However much truth there is to it," Valerie said brusquely, "there still remains the fact that the *ton* has once more turned their focus on . . . on . . ."

"My influence," Annalee quietly supplied. "It is me." She, who was supposed to be leading the Mismatch Society, had thrown the group into tumult once more. And this time she'd actually engaged in nothing scandalous. Well, not to her usual level of scandal.

"Yes, well, either way," Valerie continued, "that doesn't change the fact that the gossips are talking, and the mothers and fathers and overprotective brothers of our members will certainly have something to say to their daughters and sisters . . ."

"I said I will fix it."

"And just exactly how will you fix it?" Valerie shot back.

How would she . . . And then Annalee went still. Why, yes, of course. Society saw her as the "other woman." But . . . what if she were, in fact, not the other woman, but rather, "the woman"?

Only . . . what if Wayland does, in fact, have feelings for the girl? As soon as the thought slid in, her stomach muscles again clenched. Surely . . . he didn't. He couldn't. Why, he was well over a decade older than the duke's daughter.

But then, that was what a proper, respectable gentleman would seek in a wife: one who was perfectly virginal and young and not as jaded by life as Annalee was.

"What are you thinking?" Sylvia asked gently.

She was thinking she had a sudden urge to cry. "I'll . . . strike a proper courtship, and by establishing a respectable image, I'll be free to lead the meetings and continue educating the other members."

Another round of laughter, this time from both Sylvia and Valerie, met that pronouncement.

"What?" she asked indignantly.

And then both women's amusement faded, and a like understanding dawned in their eyes.

"You are . . . serious," Sylvia said on a quiet exhale.

Annalee resisted the urge to squirm. "And why not? It should work."

Sylvia found herself. "Because you shouldn't have to—"

"You did it." Annalee interrupted her friend with that reminder. "You enlisted the aid of a respectable gentleman to save the Mismatch Society; why should I not do the same?"

"Because it's not the same." Sylvia frowned. "In fact, it's entirely different. Clayton and I had a friendship that went back, and he was willing to take part because of our past relationship."

And yet . . . not unlike Sylvia, Annalee also had a former friendship with a gentleman who was—if possible—even more proper than Sylvia's husband, the Viscount St. John.

"Then I shall strike a courtship with the most proper of lords."

"Who are you thinking of?" Sylvia asked.

Her friend still didn't realize.

Annalee spelled it out precisely. "Lord Darlington."

"Darlington?" Sylvia echoed, her gaze going to the newspaper and then to Annalee, and back once more to the copy of *The Times*. "As in"— she tapped a fingernail in the middle of the page—"this Darlington?"

"Why, he makes perfect sense as a choice," Annalee said, her words rolling together as she warmed to her quickly evolving plot. "He is my brother's closest friend. We knew one another as children. And in striking up a courtship, I shall turn what the world sees as scandalous into that which is not only acceptable but also respectable . . ." Annalee spread her arms wide. "A proper courtship."

Another round of silence fell. Then, chewing at her fingertip, Sylvia began striding before the table, her pace unhurried, the lines of her brow creased in contemplation. Suddenly she stopped and lifted the copy of *The Times*. "Why . . . it may just work," she said quietly.

"And what happens when your proper courtship comes to an end?" Valerie asked with her usual bluntness. "What then?"

"Oh, do not be the slayer of optimism and ingenuity." Annalee softened that scolding by looping her arms about the other woman and hugging her.

Valerie shrugged her off. "I'm not," she said flatly. "I'm being realistic."

"Perhaps we realize our bond has never moved beyond the deep friendship we had as children. Perhaps he or I discover a desire to travel that the other one helped"—she framed her face with her hands—"open our eyes to."

Valerie drew back. "You'd do that?" She looked stricken. "You'd go travel and leave the Mismatch Society?"

"To save the Mismatch Society? Yes, yes, I would," Annalee said without hesitation, that declaration coming from a place of love and devotion to this group which had saved her. It would break her heart to miss out on so much as a single moment with the ladies, but for as selfish as she was in so many ways, to save the group, she'd leave. "Even if it means I have to separate from the society altogether."

Valerie gasped, visibly recoiling.

Sylvia lifted a hand. "No one is going anywhere." She scrunched up her nose. "Other than me to the countryside, but only temporarily. We are a family, and we weather storms and scandals as friends do, damn it," she finished, punching a fist toward the floor.

So much love for this woman filled her. Tears pricked Annalee's eyes, and she tossed her arms around Sylvia.

"Come now, Annalee," Sylvia said softly as she folded her in her embrace, stroking her back. "We are friends."

Ones of whom, with the way Annalee had decided to live her life, she was undeserving.

"And there will be no parting with one another," the viscountess went on. "Ever."

Sniffling, Annalee stepped out of her friend's arms and swiped at her cheeks. "You are entirely too good to me." A resolve strengthened her spine and brought her shoulders back. "I will make this right," she vowed. If anyone might restore her reputation and paint her in a new, favorable-to-Polite-Society light, that man was Wayland. "You may rest assured the Mismatch Society will not only be fine in your absence but will also thrive, and you will return to find us flourishing even more than ever."

Sylvia smiled. "I do not doubt it. First, however, there is the matter of Darlington and petitioning him for his help. Do you think he will be amenable to assisting us?"

Petitioning him for his help . . .

This was a mistake . . . Forgive me. Us, being together . . . It cannot—

"Annalee?" Sylvia asked hesitantly.

"Yes! I . . . I expect he will," she lied. Now came the impossible task of convincing the estimable Lord Darlington to dance with the Devil in a deal that would only darken his reputation.

Bloody hell.

Chapter 12

Following his mother's invasion of the breakfast room the morning before, when Wayland found his name splashed all over the front pages of *The Times* for a second time, he knew better than to leave himself like a target at that table.

He eyed the closed door covetously. His clubs.

Jeremy's.

Any place was safer and better than this one.

Eventually he'd be found.

"You have time," his sister said, walking a path about the table, contemplating the red velvet surface, "before she discovers us."

Yes. Because the last place she'd think to find him was in the billiards room. His offices, yes. His library. His rooms. The breakfast room. Certainly not the billiards room. At least not in broad daylight without gentlemen to entertain.

He made one more appeal. "You know, if you really were the devoted sister you pride yourself on being, you'd leave me to my escape."

Kitty snorted. "And leave me with the mess of your making?" she murmured distractedly as she leaned over the billiards table, eyeing her shot. "I think not." His sister drew back her stick and pressed it forth several times. "I'm a devoted sister, not a martyr, Wayland." She let her cue fly.

Crack.

The balls perfectly split, and two of her whites sailed into opposite end pockets.

He winced.

His sister glanced up. "Oh, don't be a fogy. I don't *really* think you did anything," his sister said with a roll of her eyes. "But what I think doesn't matter."

Nor for that matter was it about what their status-climbing mama believed, either. It was about Wayland's reputation. A reputation that had to be above reproach. For even as it hardly mattered for himself, it mattered for Kitty and her future. Having lived in a one-room household with meager payments earned for the backbreaking work his father had done, Wayland would see her secure so there was not even the slightest possibility that she found herself back where they'd been.

Kitty took another shot; her target ball knocked into the one she'd been eyeing, which sailed and then stopped just shy of the pocket. She recoiled. "Oh, bollocks, I've missed."

This was the last thing he needed, his mother discovering him playing billiards with his sister, and her cursing like a sailor as they did. "You shouldn't say that," he said, stealing another glance at the still thankfully closed door.

Kitty drew her back straight, and flipped over her cue so it thumped angrily upon the parquet floor. "And whyever not? They're just words."

"Words that ladies don't say."

As it was, the papers had been unkind enough about the uncouth daughter of a blacksmith mingling amongst their elite numbers.

In one fluid move, Kitty flipped her cue back over and brought it down hard over his hand.

With a curse, he drew his wounded knuckles close. "Christ, Kitty. What the hell was that for?"

Kitty batted her eyelashes. "Oh, dear, how uncouth of you, brother dearest. *Tsk, tsk.* Swearing in the presence of a lady."

He shook his hand out, flexing his palm in a bid to drive back the pain.

She widened her eyes. "Never say I've hurt you?"

"Would it matter if you did?" he countered, shaking his hand again.

"Only as so you might recall this moment and why you shouldn't go about being so stuffy as to think it matters if a lady curses."

Wayland set his cue down on the side of the table. "It isn't about what I think—"

"No, it's about what others think," she interrupted. "Which I find all the worse, Wayland."

The door exploded open.

Winded and perspiring, his mother drew to a sudden stop. "You are playing billiards with your sister?"

"Well, in fairness, I've been playing. Wayland has been doing a whole lot of watching and talking."

Ignoring her daughter, their mother swept over. "This outrageous behavior fits very much with your scandalous escapades these past two days."

Kitty leaned in and spoke in an exaggerated whisper. "Two days that we know of, Mother. Why, who is to say how many more days or weeks or even months Wayland has been behaving so?"

"Kitty," he mouthed silently.

She winked.

He was so glad one of them was enjoying this.

"Kitty, a moment."

And by the way their parent didn't so much as remove her fury-filled gaze from Wayland, he was in for it with a lecture.

Kitty gave him a last pitying look before taking herself off.

The moment she'd gone, his mother pounced. "Not one word. Not one single word, Wayland Winston Wallingford Wilks Smith." His mother clipped out each syllable of that ridiculously long name she'd fashioned for him after he'd received his title. Adding three in between the more common Christian name and surname he'd been born with because, of course, lords deserved more, and alliterative ones at that. "How could you?"

He folded his arms at his chest. "I'm afraid you must be a trifle clearer."

She sputtered. "As though you do not know? Do not play games with me, Wayland. This is nothing to make light of. We have a reputation to consider."

"And I'm forbidden from being in any of the places that Lady Annalee is?" he drawled.

"Yes. Do you truly believe I think this was a coincidence?" she demanded. "You took your sister with you and met that woman, and you'd flaunt her in front of Lady Diana?"

A curtain of rage briefly hazed his vision. "'That woman' is Annalee Spencer," he said in quiet tones, icy enough that it seemed to penetrate the boldness his mother had stormed in here with.

She faltered. "You would defend her because of your relationship with her."

"Tell me this, Mother . . . Why was it, when I was nothing but a blacksmith's son, you were always encouraging me to pursue a relationship with her, but now that I'm a titled gentleman, you don't have need of her?"

"Because she is not the same woman she was, and you know that," she said quietly.

He jerked. Restless, he wanted to flee. He wanted to run from this talk about Annalee and his mother's reminder about the changes that had overtaken her . . . after that day in Manchester. "I will not cut her. I won't do it."

"She didn't want anything to do with you following Peterloo, Wayland."

It was a testament of how dire his mother found his suspected relationship with Annalee for her to mention that day. The only references she allowed their family about Peterloo had pertained to how his hero-ism had "saved them," and the beautiful friendships they'd forged because of it.

He remained there, frozen to the floor, his arms locked at his chest, unable to call forth a single word in response. But really, what was there to say?

"You wrote her," she reminded him viciously of memories he didn't need. Ones that had haunted him for years. "You sent her notes." His mother's scent for blood was even greater than the Duke of Kipling's hounds', and she was as merciless, maternal bond be damned. "And did she ever write you? *Hmm?*" She didn't allow him a chance to answer; neither, however, did he suspect she needed or wanted one anyway. "And do you know why?"

No, and it had broken him. Left him shattered and more crippled than the broken ankle he'd suffered that day. A wound set by the duke's finest doctors, healing so that the scars were invisible to all . . . but Wayland.

"She didn't write because the same way you committed yourself to being a different man, living respectably and honorably, she commit-ted herself to shameful, hedonistic pleasures, putting only herself first."

"You don't know that," he said, his voice toneless and dead.

"How else do you account for her shameful living, *hmm*?"

He couldn't.

He couldn't understand why she'd ended their affair by refusing to respond to his letters. He couldn't understand the scoundrels she opted to keep company with.

Pain cleaved through his chest, like a fiery lance that slashed him open, and let free all the agony, all the resentment, and all the jealousy that he'd bottled up within him, emotions he thought he'd ceased to feel. And in that moment, it wasn't Annalee he resented, or even himself for his failings of her.

It was his mother.

"I'm not certain what you want me to say that will appease your worrying. Nor am I certain I altogether care," he said coolly, wringing a gasp from his mother.

"Wayland," she whispered.

"However, I've told you numerous times now that there is nothing between Annalee and myself. So do not come to me with scandal sheets and your baseless worrying, built on nothing more than gossip and your own aspirations."

Tears gleamed in her eyes, and she clutched a hand at her chest. "I just want to know that you and Lady Diana will find the happiness her family and I all know you can achieve together." She rested a hand upon his sleeve. "That was your fate, Wayland. She was your destiny." On that note, she left.

Diana was his destiny.

They were words he'd heard entirely too often where he and the young lady were concerned. At the time, she'd been a child. Now, a woman grown, that expectation had morphed into something more real . . . for her family. For his mother. And . . . even for him.

Because marrying her made sense. They were compatible. They had a shared past. And yes, there was the fact that her connection would only provide a greater security for his own family.

And yet, these past two days, he'd not thought of all that he'd committed himself to: respectable, honorable living. Instead, he'd been walking around in a haze of lust and confusion because of Annalee.

She'd exploded into his life all over again with all the passion and exuberance she'd always moved about with. A veritable firestorm that consumed anything . . . and everyone . . . in her wake.

Only, there could be nothing respectable with her. For the simple reason that she didn't want that . . .

And if she did . . . ?

His mind shied away from that . . .

Because she didn't. She'd been clear in her silence all those years ago, and her avoidance of him, and her movement in other circles, that she and he were entirely different people and the furthest thing from a suitable match.

A knock sounded at the door, and he glanced up.

A bewigged footman entered. Clutched within his white-gloved palms was a silver tray with a sheet of vellum upon it. "A missive arrived, my lord," he announced.

Wayland straightened, his heart knocking a quicker beat when the young servant stopped before him.

He quickly grabbed for the note and then froze as his gaze took in the harsh, bold strokes of an unfamiliar hand.

Not the sweeping and almost airily fun and light strokes belonging to a certain woman. *And also a woman who hasn't written you in years. Pathetic fool.*

The servant blinked. "Beg pardon, my lord?"

And she had him talking to himself. "I . . . was just remarking upon the *academic rule* that's surely responsible for such . . . impressive pen strokes. Always been something of a connoisseur of good handwriting." *Stop. Just stop.* He winced at his own pathetic explanation.

"Uh, yes, right, my lord," the young man said with a suitable—and certainly appropriate—degree of perplexity.

"That'll be all," Wayland said quickly, and considering the speed with which the footman bowed and raced off, it was hard to say who was more relieved by that reprieve.

The moment he'd gone and Wayland was alone, he returned his focus to the note belonging to not the person he'd initially hoped—that was, thought—it had belonged to. "You are a fool, you know," he muttered under his breath as he slid his fingertip under the seal.

What foolish nonsense was this? Thinking that she'd written him? He gave his head a hard shake meant to dislodge that fleeting insanity.

Cracking the seal, he unfolded the page and read.

Darlington,

I'm aware of your opinions on the proposal of Lord Lansdowne's Act in Parliament. I thought we might speak of my thoughts on the proposed legislation, along with several changes that I'd like to put forward. As there is a matter of urgency, I'd request your presence this morn quarter past eleven o'clock.

~St. John

An urgent summons from the Viscount St. John.

One requesting Wayland's consideration of a bill he was attempting to see passed. There couldn't be anything more different or more proper than this particular missive.

And it was a timely reminder that it was best, and safest, to continue the course he'd set himself upon. Not the scandal he'd flirted with at Madame Bouchard's. Or in the Earl of Kempthorne's conservatory or hall with Annalee.

Steeling his resolve and commitment, Wayland quit the billiards room, and a short horse ride later, he found his way to the viscount's residence. The viscount's very bustling residence. Servants streamed about, carrying trunks and valises past him, to the three carriages waiting outside.

Furrowing his brow, Wayland took in that activity, then allowed himself to be shown in by the butler. A footman immediately came forward to take his cloak.

"I don't like this. I don't like this one bit." Even over the noise made by the servants at work, that less-than-quiet announcement echoed around the spacious foyer, and Wayland followed it up . . . to a bevy of girls lined at the balustrade above, who frowned down at him. Well, not all of them. One had her head buried behind her book.

The girl next to her, an identical match marking her a twin, threw a sharp jab. "He's here," the lady whispered, and the book was instantly lowered, and he found yet another glare turned his way.

The youngest one, however. It was the youngest one, with her angry little stare, who inspired the most unease. And then, she took a little finger and made the motion of drawing a line . . . across her throat . . . and then jabbing that same finger Wayland's way in a message that couldn't be clearer. By God, he was amassing quite the collection of young ladies who seemed to have him on their lists.

"Worry not." That emotionless tone came from St. John's sister clad in all-black mourning skirts. The young lady stepped forward and leaned slightly over the railing. "You'll not die at Eris's hand."

He forced a laugh. "Well, that is certainly reassu—"

"It'll be in a garden," she murmured. "When you are old and very wrinkled and very grey."

"More's the pity," one of St. John's ruthless sisters muttered, her lamentation met with a flurry of agreement.

"There'll be a dog, too," the eerie Kearsley sister continued with her enumeration of his demise.

The youngest—Eris?—stamped her foot. "He doesn't *deserve* a dog."

Anwen Kearsley patted her shoulder. "No, he doesn't, dearest. You are right."

Nay, he'd been wrong. Each of St. John's sisters was a bloody terror in her own right.

He gulped and briefly eyed the door out of this madhouse. St. John's sisters certainly took his parliamentary work very seriously and . . . very personally.

The rules where propriety were concerned surrounding an exchange such as this eluded even him. "Uh . . . good morning." He dropped a bow.

Only more glares came his way.

A whistle echoed.

"Girls, come away from there." The Dowager Viscountess St. John swept over to the gaggle of girls still glowering.

"But—"

"I know. I know," the woman interrupted one of the identical twins at the middle of that row.

The butler cleared his throat. "This way, my lord."

Never more grateful for a reprieve, Wayland sprang into motion and followed the servant. And he'd thought the woes were great with the challenge of one spirited sister. God help St. John. It was a wonder the man hadn't bypassed grey and white and gone straight to bald with that merciless crew.

As they walked the corridors, frame after frame of each of those young ladies' likenesses followed, and he found himself quickening his step. The Kearsleys were a decidedly terrifying, and also interesting, lot.

The butler brought them to a stop at the end of the hall. "Here we are, my lord," the servant murmured, letting Wayland in and hastily backing up, closing the door behind him.

Wayland stepped forward. "My—" His words died quickly, and he stopped even faster in his tracks.

It took but one glance in the viscount's offices to ascertain one key detail.

It wasn't the viscount who awaited him. The enchantress wore a silk creation of seafoam, trimmed with a white lace along the bodice of her gown that accentuated generous orbs that didn't require any embellishment. She was lush, a veritable Venus, and a man's gaze needed no further urging when she was near. With the viscount's desk a perch behind her, it immediately put Wayland in mind of Botticelli's rendering of that goddess born of the seafoam, emerging from her shell. "You are not the viscount," he said hoarsely.

Annalee's lips tipped up. "Decidedly not." And then, temptress that she was, Annalee played with the deep vee between her breasts, stroking a finger along that crevice.

He instantly went rock hard.

Her knowing gaze slowly dipped and then lingered upon that telltale tenting, an uncontrollable response he had whenever she was near. It appeared even when he was slated to meet with one of London's most respected, powerful gentlemen.

Annalee's smile widened, and she advanced, her movements a cross between a march and a glide, those steps graceful, her efforts determined.

Oh, hell. This was . . . bad.

With a quiet curse, he glanced frantically behind him.

"Annalee, you cannot be here," he said sharply. All the while he backed up, scrabbling behind him for the door handle. "You're courting ruin." Hers and his. "If the papers have commented on a dance between us and a chance meeting at a shop on New Bond Street, what do you think they'll say about . . . about . . . this?" he asked.

She stopped when she reached him. "Well, interestingly, Wayland," Annalee murmured. She brought her hands up . . . but she was only adjusting a cravat he didn't recall rumpling. "That is what I'd like to speak with you about." Then she began to smooth her palms over the front of his jacket.

"Courting ruin?" he croaked.

She trilled a laugh. And then abruptly removed her hands from his person and stepped away. "Please . . ." She motioned to the viscount's pair of wing chairs. "If you would?"

He followed her gesture. "If I would . . . what?"

"The chairs, Darling. I'm indicating the chairs. I'm urging you to sit." She swept off, making for those seats.

And fortunately, with the fragrant rose scent of her not invading his senses or her tempting touch distracting him, his desire faded, and he'd a firm grip again on his self-control. "Annalee," he said tersely. "Our being alone together is scandalous. I'm meeting the viscount." Fishing out his watch fob, he consulted his timepiece. "In fact, he's overdue and will arrive any—"

"You're not."

He paused.

"You're meeting me."

His patience snapped. "Damn it, Annalee." He stalked over. "Not everything is a jest. I was summoned by the viscount about matters pertaining to Parliament and—"

"You're not understanding me, Wayland," she said calmly, without her usual teasing and seductive whispers, but rather all business. "You were not summoned by the viscount."

That brought him up short again. "I . . ."

"You are here because of me. The viscount and viscountess were so good as to coordinate a private meeting."

He rocked back on his heels. "You're jesting."

"Usually, yes. But in this, no. This time, I am deadly serious." With that, she settled herself onto one of the leather chairs and stared expectantly at him.

Chapter 13

Annalee wasn't a woman who found herself unsettled often. Or really, ever.

She didn't give in to nervousness—certainly not about or around a gentleman.

She was confident in who she was and all her actions, and in all meetings and exchanges.

Until now.

And with . . . Wayland. A man whom she'd known since they were children, the man who'd been her first lover and her one true love—back when she'd believed in a thing called love.

Now, with Wayland unmoving and the time passing, she wasn't at all certain whether he intended to follow her requests, after all.

Except, this was, of course, a new Wayland. A Wayland who was a stranger to her.

Wayland of old would have not only hopped onto one of the viscount's luxuriant seats but also pulled her atop his lap for whatever discussion she'd intended for them to have.

And as such, this stark difference in him and the way they'd been together only heightened the unease that came . . . not just from meeting Wayland but from her chances of success. She'd promised Sylvia he would take part in her ruse, but . . . Annalee really hadn't had any place giving such assurances. He owed her nothing. And they were . . . nothing. She was merely appealing to him as a friend of old.

At last, he sat, and immediately spoke. "Annalee, is this a game—"

"I've already told you," she interrupted. "No game. I've asked you here on a matter of some seriousness."

His brows drew together sharply, the harshly beautiful angles of his face becoming a perfect mask of concern. "Are you in . . . peril?"

And that transformation stirred the flames of hope that perhaps it wouldn't be so very difficult after all to convince him to take part in this ruse. He also offered Annalee the perfect opening with which to put her request to him. "Well, funny thing, that, isn't it? There are many different types of peril." She just happened to be more aware than most respectable ladies of the deadly kinds. And the wicked ones.

Wayland sat forward on his seat; his penetrating gaze did a sweep of her face. That stare. It was the stare that had first made her once girlish heart beat all the faster, eyes that sliced through one's soul, stealing in like measure a woman's breath . . . and her secrets. And even now, though she'd known sexual pursuits of all kinds, his eyes still had the ability to leave her breathless and weak.

"Annalee." He spoke her name, and there was a greater urgency, and a deepening of the worried lines at the corners of his entrancing green eyes. "What is it?"

"My Mismatch Society is . . . facing some difficulties. Temporary ones," she rushed to assure him. The whole world, her family—they'd all expected she'd bungle it. And she already had and would no doubt continue to do so.

"What is it?" he asked again.

"Recently, with the support of the Viscountess St. John, the Countess of Scarsdale, and Valerie, whom you met just yesterday . . ." Except that was the wrong thing to say, as it resurrected that moment at the modiste's when he'd been moments away from kissing her, before the young Lady Diana had entered and Annalee had been left with questions about the lady's relationship with him. "We founded a society of women, by women who—"

"I'm aware of your group's work."

Yes, that was right. Her heart thumped extra fast and hard in her chest at the reminder he'd not only been aware of her work but also had not judged it, as she'd expected.

"Uh . . . yes. Then you're no doubt also aware of the disapproval we are occasionally met with."

"I am."

"You would be," she muttered under her breath before she could stifle the utterance. Women of every station rising up and challenging the existing institutions was something he'd have approved of, and likely joined in support of, years earlier. As he'd done at Peterloo. Not anymore.

A frown ghosted the edges of his lips, and Wayland angled in closer, raising a hand to his ear. "What was that?"

Annalee made a clearing sound with her throat. "That is, you would be impressed by our commitment to the improvement of the lives of women."

He narrowed his eyes.

Of course he'd sense that lie. But he was too polite to say as much.

She flashed her most beatific smile.

His hard features remained a mask.

But he isn't entirely as apathetic as he'd have you or the world believe. Nay, he'd draped his jacket over her at the fountain, and strolled with her through the shop.

"We've recently learned that the young ladies of society are not knowledgeable in the ways they should be."

He stared blankly at her.

She nodded.

He shook his head.

Annalee briefly closed her eyes. "Sex, Wayland. I'm speaking about sex."

He immediately jumped. "Yes, I . . . uh . . . of course." There was a brief pause. "And that is a problem?"

She stared incredulously at him. "*Of course* it is a problem, Wayland." Jumping up, Annalee began to pace. "Young women have no idea of anything that takes place between a man and a woman. They are expected to marry and go into their unions knowing absolutely nothing. Nothing. And that is wrong. I've recently been charged with delivering lectures and lessons to the young women."

"Lessons," he ventured, his voice strained.

She stopped abruptly. "Don't be a prude. If you've made love, and you have"—color bloomed in his cheeks—"and you're educated on what happens, then women should be afforded that same education."

He choked.

Annalee rolled her eyes. "The knowledge, Wayland. I'm speaking about the knowledge."

Wayland scrabbled with his cravat, thoroughly crushing the fabric. "Annalee—"

"Here," she murmured. Gliding closer, she pushed his hands out of the way and adjusted the lines of the fabric.

"Are you asking me to"—he dropped his voice to a furious whisper—"to serve as a guest lecturer?"

She froze, and then a laugh exploded from her chest. God, how she'd missed him. Lowering her brow to his, she shook her head. "You, dear man? No. I assure you, I have that covered all on my own, no assistance necessary."

A vein bulged and ticked at the corner of his temple the way it had when one of the village boys had attempted to steal a kiss from her during the May Day festivities. "What is it, exactly, you are asking of me, then?" he said curtly.

Surely, he wasn't . . . jealous? Nay. He'd ceased loving her long ago. But he had remained a friend, and that was what allowed her to continue.

She retook her seat near him. "The papers have been speculating on the nature of our relationship, and none of it is good. There is a greater forgiveness of behavior generally deemed unsuitable for young women when ideas and actions and events are sanctioned by leading members of Polite Society. And with Lady Sylvia and by her marriage to the viscount and her husband's association to the Mismatch, the *ton* turns up their noses but still allows their daughters to attend."

"Annalee, I . . . fail to see what I have to do with this."

Had he always been . . . this direct? This to the point?

Perhaps with others. Never with her.

"Lady Sylvia will be retiring to the country," she said softly, divulging that intimate secret with the other woman's consent. "And the membership will fall to me. If society continues to believe that I'm . . . the wicked, awful wanton who is seducing you, then I'll never be seen as respectable. But if they . . . believed . . . there was . . . is . . . something"—she held his stare and gave a slight nod his way—"respectable between us . . ."

"You want me to speak out in support of your club?" he asked slowly, the hesitancy of a man desperately trying to work through—and struggling with—exactly what she was saying.

"I want you to court me."

He went absolutely motionless.

"Not in truth," she said, hurrying to put him at ease. "Just . . . in pretend, and only as long as Sylvia is gone. When she returns, you may go your way, and I will go mine."

⁂

This was why he'd been called here.

Not because the Viscount St. John wanted to discuss legislation with him, but because Annalee had wished to see him and put this favor before him.

He should be disappointed. He, who was on a never-ending quest to find partners for his progressive legislation in Parliament that concerned men and women belonging to the station he'd been born to.

And yet, he couldn't think of anything else beyond the great lengths Annalee had gone to, soliciting assistance from the recently married Lord and Lady St. John.

There'd been a time once when he wouldn't have denied her anything. And yet . . . this? Taking part in a ruse when he *knew* that there was nothing there? When he knew Polite Society would all turn their eyes to them, and he would be putting on a facade, one made all the more dangerous for the passion that blazed between them still. And by the secret hungering . . . for more. And it was also that secret hungering that didn't make him immediately reject outright that which she requested.

She stared intently at him, and he searched her always sparkling eyes, and then it occurred to him. This wasn't a test. Or a game.

His stomach churned.

Coward that he was, it would have been a great deal easier were she making light.

"I am capable of . . . seriousness, you know," she added, and by the solemnity of her declaration, he wasn't sure whether she was attempting to convince him or remind herself. Her expression hardened. "People think I can't . . ."

"I don't think that." He moved closer in his seat. "I'm not one of those people." And without realizing what he did, his fingers moving as though of their own free will, he collected her palm in his.

He froze, as did Annalee; both of them looked down at the same moment to the sight of their joined fingers. Taking her hand was an act so natural, one he'd done so many times in his life as to lose count, and yet he had not done it in so long that there was a . . . new awkwardness to locking his digits with hers. One that he mourned and regretted and resented.

Reluctantly, he disentangled their hands, and Annalee formed a steeple with the tips of those gloveless digits. How he missed the warmth and naturalness that had once existed. A naturalness that was no more.

"I do not see how my courting you will help . . . your club."

She chuckled, that sound low and husky. "Of course you do. I'm the villain. The seductress setting out to ruin you. But . . . if they believe that there is something proper between us . . ." Annalee's fingers pinched at the lacy overlay of her seafoam muslin, and she briefly dropped her gaze to her lap. When she glanced up and caught his focus upon that nervous movement, she immediately stopped. Her eyes locked with his. "Then they will cease speaking ill of me . . . at least for now . . . and I will be free to run my lectures. Furthermore, a lady who is courted by a respectable man is different from one who has a vast collection of lovers."

A vast collection of lovers.

How casual she was with that.

She may as well have kicked him in the teeth, then punched him hard between the legs for good measure.

His facial muscles froze. His entire body coiled, and he tried to breathe. And he failed.

Because he well knew the stories about her and various rakes and rogues, but . . . hearing her speak it aloud, lending a real life to what had previously been gossip, shredded him inside.

"I don't, you know," she said, the slightly strained quality of her contralto at odds with the airy show she put on. But he knew her. Even all these years later, how to pick out the telltale tension, the way she dipped her head ever so faintly. Her slightly tucked chin. "Have a collection of them."

But she did have lovers, and that truth would break him and then break him down all over again with each time he let himself think of it.

He pinched the bridge of his nose. "I want to help you, Annalee."

Her eyes lit so bright, those blue depths vibrant with such joy and hope that he wanted to give her what she sought. "Splendid! I knew I could rely upon you, Wayland."

He tried to interject but it proved impossible.

"You're worried." She rightly identified that emotion but misunderstood the reason for it. "Rest assured, the arrangement needn't be for long, and I will be entirely well behaved." She laughed. "As much as I'm able, of course."

God, she was determined to make this impossible for him.

"Annalee," he began quietly.

That managed to penetrate her elation.

"What . . . is it?"

He wanted to give her what she asked of him.

And yet . . .

He briefly closed his eyes.

He couldn't.

When he opened them, he found Annalee staring back without her usual show of confidence, and it was the hesitancy there that made him falter once more.

Quitting his seat, he fell to a knee beside her. "Annalee," he said. "I . . . don't want a ruse."

Her lips slipped a fraction, and then she moistened her full lips. "You want a real courtship, then?"

Color splotched his cheeks, and he instantly fell back on his haunches.

Her pretty blue eyes sparkled with a glimmer that had shades of sadness contained with that sparkle. "I'm teasing, Wayland." She laid her palm over his gloved one. "Obviously you don't."

He stared blankly at her hand resting on his, eyes fixed on the leather of his glove—a stark contrast against her flesh.

Of course he'd once hungered for a relationship with her, one with a permanence to it and not the clandestine secret they'd been forced to keep because of their different social statuses and his relationship with Jeremy. There hadn't been anything he'd wanted in the world more than that future with her. She was all he'd ever wished for. But time had divided them; it had stuck a great big wedge between them that they'd only just begun to peek around to see the other person still standing there.

"And of course, I don't want a real courtship with you, either," Annalee said, wielding those words like a master swordsman laying the blade upon a weaker opponent. Her lips twitched. "Or any gentleman, for that matter." She grew serious once more. "I . . . This rejection . . . Is it because of . . . Lady Diana? Is there something more between you?"

"No." He surged to his feet. "Yes." Only in some small part.

"Oh," Annalee said, her voice soft and sad.

Surely he imagined that sentiment.

He tried to explain. "Diana . . . she is still a child, but there remains an expectation . . . and I have to be careful in all my dealings with her." If he didn't make the match the world expected . . . if he made missteps in that relationship, he would be vilified, and his sister would pay the price.

Annalee's lowered lashes concealed whatever she thought of that.

Wayland swiped a hand through his hair. "Annalee, nothing good can come from us playing games before Polite Society." He tried to make her see reason. "There's nothing I can truly contribute to this . . . or you."

"Actually," she said calmly, sliding forward in her seat. "Something very good can . . . My reputation stands to benefit, and because of that, the Mismatch Society's, which stands to improve the lives of women, and as one who dedicated much of his earlier years to improving the lives of people, then yes, I think very much it is something you could and would get behind."

He ran his eyes over her face. He'd never before seen her this . . . solemn. Not even when she'd been a young girl and young woman had she been so . . . serious. This didn't fit with the new Annalee the world had come to know. And for that reason alone, even if there hadn't been so many other reasons before this, he wanted to give her what she sought. "Annalee," he began, carefully picking through his words, "I am honored you think I might help."

Her eyes hardened. "Please do not take that appeasing tone with me. I'm not a child."

"I don't think you are," he bit out. "I'm trying to be polite."

"Well, you're failing. Try harder. Your tone is coming across as pompous."

"Very well." He spoke flatly and plainly this time. "Your society is scandalous."

She eyed him for a long while. "Scandalous."

"And that is . . . fine," he said on a rush. "I respect your convictions and your spirit, and what you wish to do. But I have only just managed to establish respectability for myself." She recoiled. God, he was making a muck of this. Wayland scraped his hand through his hair. "Even as much as I wish I could help you, I don't have the same luxury of just doing what I want. Having been born outside the peerage," he explained, needing her to understand, "I am not afforded those choices." Even if he had been, however, putting himself in close quarters any more than he already had with Jeremy's sister would prove a disaster because of Wayland's own weakness. For her. He'd always been weak where she was concerned. These past days had proven just how dangerous it was, being with her. Every moment spent with Annalee, he remembered just how much he'd missed her . . . And yet, there could not be a future between them.

Annalee frowned. "And you care so very much about your reputation." There was a trace of scorn within that statement that wasn't even really a question, and yet he answered anyway.

"Yes, I do," he said instantly. "But what I care about more is Kitty's reputation. She is an outcast, and I worry about her being accepted by society. And I care about yours. Even if—" He stopped himself from finishing the remainder of that, but she was entirely too clever to miss his intended meaning.

"Even if I don't?" With a sound of disgust, she came to her feet.

"That isn't what I meant, Annalee," he said.

"Yes, it is. Don't be a liar on top of a coward, Wayland," she tossed back.

Fire suffused his cheeks; that insult from this woman struck a perfect blow to his gut.

"Annalee, there is Kitty to consider."

"Don't hide behind your sister," she spat.

He recoiled. "I'm not. She has even less of a luxury than I do, Annalee." His voice rose as he spoke. "At least be honest and acknowledge that. She is and will always be a blacksmith's daughter, treated with derision and shamed because of circumstances that were always beyond her control."

Annalee drifted closer, angling her face up toward his. "Tell me this, Lord Darlington," she rejoined. "Is it Kitty who is bothered by society's condemnation . . . or is it you?"

"I . . ." He opened his mouth to confirm the former, but something froze that response on his lips.

Annalee smiled. "I thought so." Then that luminescent smile faded, and it was as though the sun's rays had been snatched from the sky, leaving the world dark. "You might say I don't care how the world views me, Wayland," she said softly without the earlier vitriol. "But that isn't altogether true. I've had to listen to what people say about me." She took a step closer, and he immediately backed away. Annalee stopped, a small, knowing smile on her lips as she looked him up and down. Only, no . . . It wasn't entirely knowing. Disgust and disappointment poured from her person, spilling onto him all those sentiments she had for the man he'd become. "I care about the recent gossip surrounding my reputation, but do you know the difference between you and me?

The difference is you have just your sister to worry after, but I? I have to think about almost two dozen ladies who are trying to find their place in this world, Wayland. Women who do not have the benefit or protection of a loving, loyal brother." Like Jeremy, who'd cut her off . . . She'd been looking after herself, and now had taken the responsibility of helping ladies who found themselves in a similar way.

Wayland curled his hands so sharply his nails marked up his palms.

Giving him a derisory up-and-down look, Annalee swept off.

He should let her go. He wasn't going to change his mind . . . no matter how much he wished he might be able to help her. She'd accepted his rejection, and they were better off parting ways sooner. And yet—

"It *is* about Kitty, you know," he called after her, an exclamation that would have halted any other person, but Annalee continued her march across the viscount's offices.

And something about that . . . Her not even breaking stride. Annalee not so much as glancing back his way.

That she didn't even care what he intended to say, or what defense he'd give for his declination, proved the greatest insult he'd been dealt, an insult without words. Or worse, that she didn't believe him. All of which was saying a good deal, given his treatment by Polite Society through the years.

And yet, as she left, with her accusations lingering in the room where they'd met and still ringing in his mind, a part of him deep inside that he didn't want to acknowledge or confront whispered that mayhap it wasn't just Kitty he was so very concerned about, after all. And he hated himself for that buried truth that Annalee had so effortlessly wrenched out of him.

Chapter 14

That had turned out to be a disaster. Annalee's meeting with Wayland had decidedly not gone as planned.

At all.

Even as she'd told herself it would be difficult securing his coopera-tion because he was a new, proper, always decorous gentleman. In her mind's eye, she'd seen that exchange playing out altogether differently. He was to have said yes, and they were to have followed through on the ruse she'd promised Sylvia he would.

He was always going to have said yes.

But he hadn't.

And Sylvia was gone to the country, with Annalee left to oversee the society . . . with really only one course and recourse available to her.

All her muscles seized under this greatest of losses, a loss made all the more agonizing, having voiced it aloud.

Seated around the parlor with the other Mismatch Society mem-bers, Annalee finished explaining all the latest troubles to the group. Because they had a right to know. Because they should have been told from the start. Neither she nor Sylvia nor Valerie had any place with-holding from them matters that pertained to the health of the overall group.

Anwen Kearsley was the one to speak first.

"He rejected your offer," she whispered, and Annalee appreciated the shock and disbelief from the eldest Kearsley sister. She really did. After all, it bespoke a confidence in Annalee's abilities. Granted, one she was undeserving of, but a generous and kindly sign of her friendship.

That also was the part the young lady would focus on—the betrayal, or if not betrayal, the rejection by Annalee's friend. Or former friend. They weren't friends any longer. Oddly, that was meant to ease the frustration and hurt, but it only added a stone to those already weighing on her chest.

Annalee cleared her throat. "Yes, he did." And he'd been quite decisive in his rejection. That, however, was neither here nor there. She'd not mention that Wayland saw them as too scandalous to link himself to. "As a result, I have called this emergency meeting to share with you my . . . decision . . ." Oh, God. She couldn't do this. It was impossible. This was the one place where she felt a sense of true belonging with other women. A sisterhood. "The only conclusion I've been able to draw," she continued, stumbling, attempting to get the words out. "The only safe and wise course for the society is that I step back and step down, and . . . remove myself from the household."

Silence came quick, but the thunderous tide of shocked exclamations and declinations came on the heels, even louder and more forceful.

All the words blended together, with the occasional shout piercing the noise of the upset membership.

"Absolutely not . . ."

"You cannot . . ."

Cressida promptly dissolved into copious weeping, crying into the shoulder of Brenna Kearsley beside her. Brenna patted the other young woman on the back, while also swiping the moisture from her own cheeks.

Annalee's heart lurched.

And tears. There were tears, too. For her?

And blast if a sheen didn't film across Annalee's own eyes. She fought desperately to drive them back, digging her nails hard into her lap, distracting herself with a different pain.

"What about *Thérèse*?" Anwen whispered.

"If you read the book . . . it will answer most of what I would have shared anyway," Annalee assured.

The Dowager Viscountess St. John shot up a hand. As one, they looked to her. The oldest member of their group, the mother of the Kearsley sisters, with daughters who ranged from five to twenty-five, the respected if eccentric matron did not make all meetings, but she'd proven devout and devoted. She was positioned on a pale-blue settee, seated between two of her daughters, Cora and Anwen. "If I might make a suggestion," she began. "As dear Emma is off traveling for her honeymoon and Clara is otherwise busy with her music hall and—"

"Get to it, already, Mother," Cora urged.

"I volunteer to lead the discussion pertaining to sexual relations," the dowager viscountess finished.

The woman's daughters visibly recoiled.

"Absolutely not," Cora hissed. "I forbid it."

The Kearsley mother bristled. "I beg your pardon. I have seven children and am quite adept at answering questions about the pleasure I found with your fath—"

Cora stuffed her fingers in her ears. *"Laa-la-laa."*

"I'll quit again," Anwen vowed, her voice inordinately loud for the fact she had her palms clamped firmly over her ears.

"Well, I shall gouge my eyes out," Brenna swore.

"I daresay that won't help with what you'll hear," Isla Gately pointed out.

Valerie brought the gavel down hard, pounding it until the room had fallen quiet. "Sylvia would not approve of this," she said quietly.

"I agree. She'd be as horrified as all of us at the idea of my mother instructing us on such matters," Cora muttered.

Lady St. John frowned. "All women should be so lucky as to have a mother so free to speak of 'such matters,' as you call them." A murmur of agreement rolled around the room, and the dowager viscountess preened. "Eh—see?" she asked, pointing out the other members to her daughter.

"I was speaking about the possibility of Annalee leaving," Valerie said impatiently. She glared sharply at Annalee. "And neither do I approve."

Another round of agreement rolled around the parlor.

It had been inevitable—with the spirited crew amongst them, the initial upset had been destined to give way to rebellion.

"This isn't for Sylvia to know about," Annalee spoke firmly, intending to quash those efforts. Sylvia, one of her dearest friends, was with child. Despite the world's low opinion of Annalee—most of those ill thoughts true—she wasn't so selfish as to be a burden for Sylvia at this delicate time. That was, any more selfish than she'd already been. "And . . . and . . . it doesn't have to be forever." It would just *feel* like forever. "I will go, and then . . . when she returns, I'll come back." She smiled. "It is that simple." That was, if her soul managed to survive her departure.

Nay, there was nothing, absolutely nothing, simple about it.

Valerie took to her feet, drawing everyone's attention her way. "First, I will say I do not believe you should go," she said to the room at large. "It is not who we are."

And yet, they were also *nothing* if the ladies present were barred from attending because of Annalee.

"It is my decision," Annalee murmured, speaking the one statement she knew these women could understand and respect. Ultimately, they, who were denied choices over everything in life, honored one another's control of self and their decisions.

Flattening her mouth, Valerie wrenched her gaze over to the window and shook her head, her disapproval more palpable than had she spoken it aloud.

"Where will you go?"

Oh, God. Isla's quiet murmuring forced Annalee to think about the one thing her mind had been shying away from. Because . . . there was one place she'd have to go . . . because there were no other options. Not ones that didn't compromise the women here, or their society. Annalee drew in a shaky breath, getting the air into her lungs to expel the loathsome words. "To my parents'," she said, infusing all the tranquility she could manage into them.

If one had dropped an embroidering pin, one might have heard it strike the walnut planks, as quiet as the room fell.

"They will . . . have you?" Isla Gately asked the better, if blunt, question.

Olivia shoved an elbow into the younger woman's side.

"*Whaaat?* I'm just asking," Isla groused.

"No one is going anywhere." That pronouncement echoed around the room. The dowager viscountess came to her feet. "My dear, we do not need a gentleman to salvage your reputation."

"What are you suggesting, Mother?" Anwen asked, hope tingeing her query.

With all the members' attention resting on her, the dowager viscountess glided across the room, headed on a path toward Annalee. "I'm suggesting Annalee go about as she has these past several days, attending respectable . . . if dull"—the dowager viscountess added under her breath—"affairs and reputable establishments." Lady St. John reached Annalee's chair.

Annalee craned her neck back. "I've attempted that. All I've managed to create is gossip." That was, even more gossip.

The dowager viscountess's eyes twinkled, and she slipped onto the arm of Annalee's white upholstered French fauteuil and placed her hand on Annalee's shoulder. "Ah, but that is because you, my dear, are a unicorn. Rare sightings do not make it a horse. Being a horse makes it a horse."

"Unicorns are fictional creatures," Brenna Kearsley, the bluestocking member of their group, and also one of the most literal-speaking ones, called to her mother. "Mythical."

Mythical. Fictional. Both perfect words to describe the charade Annalee had attempted to take part in. Only . . .

What if she transformed herself? Yes, a partnership with the highly esteemed and prim Lord Darlington would have been the easier course, but if she continued to show herself in a new light . . .

"Rome was not built in a day, my dear," Lady St. John murmured, squeezing Annalee's shoulder gently.

"That is another cliché," Brenna pointed out. "One that is—*Owwww!*" she exclaimed, glaring at her older sister Cora. "Whatever is that for?"

"Because Mama is making good points. Important ones. And you are taking away from her very vital messaging for Annalee," Cora shot back. Cupping her hands about her mouth, she yelled across the room, "As you were, Mama!"

The dowager viscountess lifted her head. "Thank you, dearest."

The older woman would not only support her daughters and join them in the revolutionary group but also fight to keep Annalee within the membership ranks? What would it be like to have a mother such as her?

"Now, my dear, he has rejected your offer, and to that I say . . . pooh on him." The dowager threw her arms wide, like a veritable Cleopatra thwarting her male counterparts and calling her people to join her insurrection. "When they bring you a battle, the only course is to declare an all-out war!"

Wild hurrahs went up, feet stomped. Clapping commenced, along with whistles and cheering.

With the Mismatch Society come undone over this rebellion, Lady St. John leaned close and whispered in Annalee's ear, "Instead of that defeatist attitude, dear, I'd think about how you can one-up the gentleman and make him regret ever daring to reject you."

Annalee shook her head. "I don't know . . ."

Lady St. John smiled. "First"—she shot up a finger—"you hold your head high at a respectable *ton* event." She lifted another digit. "And two, you bring within our folds the lady of the gentleman's household."

An image popped in her head: Wayland's straitlaced shrew of a mother. She strangled on a laugh. "His mother?"

Lady St. John shook her head slowly. "No, my dear. Think again." The dowager viscountess looked about the room to the other ladies present. "Who holds the real power over a gentleman?"

Different answers all rolled together from the members.

"A wife."

"A daughter."

"A mother?"

"Yes, well, it does differ from family to family," the dowager viscountess allowed. She brightened. "Perhaps I might offer a group lecture on that topic someday?"

"Mother," Anwen called over impatiently.

"Oh, yes. Right. Right. As I was saying, as to which woman holds most sway over a household . . . it varies."

Annalee froze.

What I care about more is Kitty's reputation. She is an outcast, and I worry about her being accepted by society . . .

"Sisters," she whispered.

Why . . . of course. Why had she not thought of it? She could bring Kitty within the fold and, in so doing, connect Wayland's sister with women who would be true friends . . . And also Wayland would have to lend his support to Annalee and the society. A smile curled her mouth upward.

Lady St. John patted her affectionately on the shoulder. "That is better, dear. Much better."

❧

That same night
Mayfair, England

Wayland and his sister had often jested in private that if the whole world were on fire and they'd also been invited to a powerful peer's formal gathering, their mother would have dressed them all in garments soaked in water and gotten them through the conflagration to the respective ball, and on time, no less.

It would appear, that night, that not even an invitation from the Duke and Duchess of Fitzhugh had an effect.

And it was also a testament to the lengths to which he'd go to avoid a discussion with his mother that he'd rather attend a ball where he felt about as comfortable as a pig in church.

As his mother whipped back and forth, pacing, Wayland latched his gaze to the clock across the room.

"Might I point out that we are going to be late, Mother?"

Not even that reminder had an effect.

Nay, instead she just quickened her pace, back and forth, over and over again. "You may not. This is dire, Wayland. Dire!"

It certainly was not good.

Of course he should have expected, knowing Annalee, tenacious and spirited and stubborn as the English day was rainy, that the lady would have never taken his rejection lightly. But this . . . sending around an invitation for Kitty to join her league? Well, this was a battle he'd little hope of winning. "You must do something."

"We must do something. We have the ball—"

"Enough with the ball, Wayland," his mother cried. "I command you to forbid her from attending."

"The hell he will." Kitty's voice came muffled but clear through the locked door of his offices.

He pressed his fingertips against his head. *Bloody hell.* He should have expected there'd be hell to pay for refusing to help Annalee. She'd invited his sister into the folds of her society.

She had landed the upper hand, after all. But then, had there been any other way with her?

"Why are you smiling, Wayland?" his mother squawked.

"I . . ." He hadn't realized he'd been. It appeared Annalee still had that effect upon him.

Quickening her pacing, his mother wrung her hands as she flew back and forth. "How could Annalee invite our Kitty to take part in that . . . that club?"

"It is a society." His and his sister's still muffled responses came as one.

Furthermore, he knew exactly what had been behind Kitty's invite. He also knew he'd sooner cut out his tongue than mention he'd inadvertently been the one who'd prompted her receiving one.

"Open this bloody door this damned instant."

As one, Wayland and his mother looked to that closed panel his sister had set herself at, periodically jiggling the handle.

Horror rounded their mother's eyes, and this time when she spoke, she did so in the most hushed of voices. "Do you see? She's already become wicked."

"Kitty has always cursed," he felt inclined to point out.

"That is right, Mother. I have," came Kitty's latest reply.

"Furthermore," he continued, stalking across the room and past his mother to unlock and open the door. "This is no new phenomenon," he said, letting Kitty in.

His sister immediately scrambled inside.

"And," he went on, closing the panel once more behind them, "she's not even yet met with the club." He paused. Or . . . "You . . . haven't yet joined their ranks?"

Kitty shook her tightly coiffed head.

"See?"

"Not yet," Kitty added with a wink.

Wayland briefly closed his eyes and dropped a curse in his mind.

Their mother's eyes rounded until her irises bulged, and she released an ear-piercing shriek. Stalking past her daughter, she stopped before Wayland. "You must speak to that woman. Tell her that you absolutely forbid her from allowing Kitty entry. Do you hear me?" And with that, she stormed off. "Now, come," she ordered, not looking back. "We have the Duchess of Fitzhugh's ball."

The moment she'd made her exit, he looked to Kitty.

Damn his mother for making this . . . worse. If that was possible.

Actually, it was. He knew that very well. She may as well have gone and thrown down a gauntlet, and dared Kitty to do her best.

"Kitty," he began tiredly, sinking a hip onto the desk.

"No."

He furrowed his brow. "I didn't say anything."

"You didn't need to. You were going to pretend your weak defense was a legitimate one."

He bristled. "It wasn't a *weak* defense."

"Neither was it a strong or admirable one," she countered. "When all the while, you have no intention of gainsaying Mama." Her mouth pulled. "Or as she likes to think of herself"—Kitty raised the timbre of her voice and put the pitch in her nose—*"Mottther . . ."*

Reflexively, his lips formed a smile.

Kitty punched him hard in the chest, instantly killing that amusement. *"Oomph."* He rubbed where she'd landed her blow. "What was—"

"Because you don't get to smile or speak." She stuck a finger under his nose. "Not so much as a word, Wayland Smith. Not a single word." And then she must have seen something in his eyes. She gasped, recoiling from him. "Surely . . . you aren't going to speak with Annalee about barring me."

Kitty's reputation was that of a blacksmith's daughter who'd found her fortune but would never have a superior bloodline. Living their lives above reproach was the one way to find a semblance of fitting into this new world they'd landed in. Joining the ranks of society's most scandalous women . . . would never serve her or her future well.

"Wayland," she whispered.

"Kitty, this . . . change for us, from blacksmith's children to peerage, it isn't a temporary one. It isn't the party thrown by the duke and duchess after . . . after . . ." His gut kicked.

"After you saved their daughter," she supplied, filling in the easier words. But then, child that she'd been, and entirely removed as she was from Peterloo, she'd not ever think of it in the same light or terms as people like he . . . or Annalee . . . would.

"We"—she waved a palm back and forth between them—"are not on the same team. You are on Mother's side."

"I am on the side of seeing you safe and cared for," he said in solemn tones, willing her with that gravity to both see and hear his sincerity. "And your future secured, and if that makes me a bad brother, Kitty, then so be it."

Silence followed his quiet pronouncement. She searched her eyes over his face for a long while.

Perhaps . . . she could be reasoned with, after all. Kitty was emotional, but she also possessed a keen logic and mind. Perhaps—

Kitty released a shriek, fit to challenge the perseverance and quality of every piece of crystal in the room. She punched him harder in the chest this time, in one-two-three rapid succession, and stormed off.

"Kitty!" he called after her.

"Go to hell." She swept out into the hall and slammed the door hard behind her, rattling the frame and sending the crystal adornments upon the sconces tinkling.

Wayland dug his fingertips against his temple.

It was his lot in life to fail where all females were concerned.

Looking forward to the upcoming carriage ride with his mother and sister with the same eagerness as a man might feel facing a firing squad, he made his way to the foyer, where he found the tense, unspeaking mother-daughter pair. Grateful when they arrived a short while later at the duke and duchess's residence, they made their entry, waiting in stiff silence to be announced.

Wayland glanced around the packed ballroom.

When he'd first entered events hosted by members of Polite Society, the crowds had gawked with fascination at him, an interloper amongst their ranks. A king might grant a title, but that title did not automatically transfer societal approval. Far from it. Originally, almost always and only met with the cut direct, he had felt that coldness recede eventually, and the people thawed—somewhat.

In time, with the support shown him by Jeremy and his family, and some of the more benevolent lords and ladies, a greater courtesy had been extended to him. But that approval was contractual . . . dependent upon how well he adhered to the expected steps. A requirement made all the more important by the fact that his sister had never really found herself the recipient of the acceptance Wayland had been shown.

"Not one word from you this night," his mother said as the party before them prepared to be announced, and she, Wayland, and Kitty slid into place behind them.

"I've not said anything. Not that I would say anything to you anyway," Kitty said from the corner of her mouth, her lips unmoving. "There is nothing I wish to say to either you or my traitor of a brother."

Traitor of a brother? "Oh, for the love of—" Wayland's clipped challenge was cut short.

"The Right Honorable Lord Darlington, Miss Smith, and Mrs. Smith."

"Smile, dears," their mother urged, plastering the most painful-looking one on her lips as she swept forward.

And as he trailed behind, with a furious, unsmiling Kitty on his arm, he cursed this night . . . that undoubtedly could not get any worse.

He reached the bottom of the steps and froze, his gaze landing on the tall, statuesque lady with one of the duke's Doric columns as her only company.

"Annalee is here!" Kitty exclaimed animatedly, the happiest he'd seen her that night. She gave an exuberant wave, and across the room, Annalee lifted her fingers, giving them a little wag. All the while, her taunting stare remained locked on Wayland.

His heart thumped hard.

After she'd quit the Viscount St. John's offices, he'd thought their paths wouldn't again cross. But it appeared, between this and the invitation she'd extended to Kitty, the lady wasn't quite done with him.

He was in trouble. There was nothing else for it.

Chapter 15

Annalee had, as a rule, come to appreciate that one could never truly rely upon other people completely.

Oh, it wasn't cynicism that lent her the belief. It was life. And simply put, the reality of it.

Her parents hadn't a use for her, following Peterloo. Her brother, well, he'd even less use of her upon his return from the Continent, when he'd discovered her transformed from the innocent sister he'd called friend to a wicked wanton whose honor was long past defending by that point.

Why, even the Mismatch Society hemorrhaged its members to the marital state—first Sylvia was gone and married, and now gone altogether. And then it was Emma.

Even that group of some dozen ladies staunchly defended her and supported her, but neither were they and their families rushing to send any invites Annalee's way to their respectable affairs.

It was also that cold, hard reality that accounted for Annalee dusting off Wayland's rejection, as the Dowager Viscountess St. John had encouraged, and continuing without his help.

Proper and respectable. She could do that. At least until Sylvia's return.

Hell, since Peterloo, Annalee had mastered both.

And she'd been doing swimmingly this evening at the Duchess of Fitzhugh's ball . . . until Wayland had been announced.

Of course, it made sense that he would be here. At one of the most respected events, hosted by the estimable duke and duchess. It was the perfect affair for him to attend.

When she'd coordinated an invitation for herself that night with the assistance of the Dowager Viscountess of St. John, Annalee had only had one purpose in mind—rehabilitating her image.

She'd not allowed herself to think about seeing Wayland here.

Now, she was as hopeless as she'd always been where the gentleman was concerned to do anything other than drink in the sight of him.

For all the ways in which he'd set to fit in with Polite Society, he'd forgone the puffs at the sleeve heads as favored by nearly all lords. In his figured silk waistcoat, snuff brown in shade, he stood apart from the many gentlemen who donned black, thinking themselves dashing in darkness. Deep-brown breeches. A wool jacket in emerald, and wide cravat and loose bow, on the arm of his sister as he was, he epitomized the role of devoted, loving brother.

He always had.

It had been one of the reasons she'd so admired him. Contrary to how some older brothers went out of their way to avoid an under-the-foot sibling, Wayland had been the kindest, sweetest big brother when Kitty was nearby.

Not unlike Annalee's brother.

A wave of unexpected melancholy filled her.

Kitty offered another exuberant wave for Annalee, which she returned. These events amongst the members of Polite Society were deuced uncomfortable, and . . . lonely. It was a rarity that she was welcomed, and it was kindness that meant so very much to her.

The girl slipped her arm from Wayland's, and leaving his side, she joined their mother.

Annalee forced her focus away from that trio.

Wayland's mother had once been so welcoming but had since made a habit of giving Annalee the cut direct whenever their paths crossed.

Nay, she'd hardly approve of Annalee. Not now. Not anymore.

Just as her son didn't.

He wouldn't have approved of anything where she was concerned since Peterloo. Those unexpected moments of madness that seized her, crippling her mind and paralyzing her to all except the horrors of that day.

God, she desperately needed a drink. Her throat ached for it.

She followed the trays being carried about the room, those flutes bubbling and sparkling with the pale, frothy spirits within.

Annalee bit the inside of her cheek and repeated the mantra she'd set out with this night:

No champagne.

No brandy.

No whiskey.

No cheroots.

Annalee had rattled off that litany while Valerie had helped her make her dress selection for the Duke and Duchess of Fitzhugh's overflowing ballroom.

Get in. Be respectable. Get out.

A handsome footman with a tray aloft came closer, and everything within her arched toward his offerings.

Her tongue heavy, Annalee stretched out her fingers.

Mayhap just one champagne flute.

An elegant figure stepped into Annalee's path, stealing that opportunity for the relief brought through libation, and killing temptation's pull. "You're doing splendidly, my dear," the dowager viscountess said, flanked by her three eldest daughters.

This was doing splendidly? Hanging out on the fringe of the ballroom, a pariah to the respectable? And barred from the pleasure of drink? "There isn't anything that feels good about any of this," she said, unable to call back those mutterings.

"Well, I for one would have you stay unchanged— *Oww*." The dowager viscountess killed Brenna's defense with a decisive pinch that was even less discreet than the young lady's shriek.

"We are not attempting to change her. We are attempting to"— Lady St. John lifted a palm, moving it higher as she spoke—"elevate her."

Annalee smiled for the quartet, more loyal than her own family, and certainly a good deal more loving. "Thank you," she said softly.

"Nonsense," the dowager viscountess scoffed—slashing that same hand prone to wild gesturing up and down. "No thanks necessary. Now, if you'll excuse me for a moment, I must coordinate partners for these three."

"Mother!" Anwen implored.

"Yes, yes. I'll be discreet about it," the eccentric matron promised, also ruining that vow with her less-than-careful tones.

"Would you like to join us?" Cora asked hopefully. "I'm certain Mother would dearly love to find you a match."

"Just for dancing. Just for dancing," Lady St. John said exasperatedly. Like they were two peas in the pod of the same exact opinions, she held Annalee's eyes and rolled her own. "Unless there is love, men only serve two purposes: one"—she stuck up a finger—"a good dance partner, and two . . ." The older woman waggled her brows, earning blushes and groans from her daughters and a laugh from Annalee. The first real one she'd managed that night.

Clapping her hands, the dowager viscountess marked the discussion at an end, and her three daughters fell into a neat line behind her like devoted little ducks, trotting off.

And for a second time that night, Annalee was riddled with envy at that evidence of another loyal, loving family. Not unlike Wayland and his sister, the Kearsleys exuded a deep, abiding love for one another.

They were a family whose devotion wasn't contractual, dependent upon one's child's or sister's obedience to the rules of decorum and propriety Polite Society held so dear.

Alone once more, Annalee turned her attention out to the crowd.

Get in. Be respectable. Get out.

No champagne.

No brandy.

No whiskey.

No cheroots.

She could do this. Nay, she was doing this. And she would do it without—

Him.

Her eyes collided with Wayland and his family. Nay, not just his family.

Also the Duke and Duchess of Kipling and their daughter, Lady Diana.

Had there ever been a more perfect pairing than those two?

The woman Wayland had saved, and received a title for rescuing. In those earliest days following Peterloo, Annalee had lain in her bed, staring sightlessly at the window. Maids would slide in and out, bringing trays and offering to assist her with her daily ablutions. She'd bathe, change, and then climb into bed, not eating, and then repeat that same routine over and over. All the while, she'd remained trapped inside her head, a prisoner of the hell of that day, the gunshots pinging around her mind, blaring as loud as they had on those fields that had run with blood.

She'd tortured herself with thoughts of the hell Wayland had faced. Wondering what those moments had been like for him. Because though they'd experienced that same macabre scene of suffering and strife, there'd been enough infinitesimal differences to mark each experience, each person's own personal hell.

When she'd fought through the stampeding crowd, abandoning her friend Lila, her only thoughts had been to get to Wayland. Even as her instincts had screamed to flee, recognizing the futility of her search, she'd been compelled deeper and deeper into the melee.

The crush of bodies, threatening to pull her down and suffocate her.

The numerous times she'd slipped, thinking she was about to meet her end, only to somehow find her way back to her feet.

After that, she'd never believed she could face a crowd again.

Which was, ironically, why she'd first sought out the biggest, noisiest, wickedest affairs. Because the only way to control her demons was to confront them.

And she'd been successful with it.

Sweat coated her skin, slicked her palms.

Perhaps it was the sight of Wayland here with his Lady Diana. Perhaps it was that she'd made herself relive those darkest minutes of her life. But the weight was back in place, a thousand bricks upon her chest, crushing off her breath, and with every struggle to get air into her lungs, little pricks of light flickered before her vision.

The laughter swelled, distorted in her ears like a macabre twist of poisoned mirth. The smiles on the faces of the guests around her at odds with the terror winding like venom in her veins.

A servant came close, and panting slightly, she grabbed for one of those crystal flutes. Her movements clumsy, Annalee splashed several droplets over the side, staining her gloves. And she downed the glass, welcoming its trail. Welcoming the bubbling warmth.

Oh, God. It didn't help.

No champagne.

No brandy.

No whiskey.

No cheroots.

Stand down . . . stand down . . .

Ping—ping—ping.

The ricocheting gunfire popped and peppered her mind. Or the air? Were those shots coming from here? Except that didn't make sense. She was in London. In a ballroom.

You've done this before. You've talked yourself through it . . .

Except she'd only found that distraction through the very things she'd vowed to avoid this night.

Stop. You have greater self-control.

Have you seen my baby . . . ?

My baby? That didn't make sense in the duke's ballroom. But then perhaps that meant she wasn't in the duke's ballroom. Perhaps she'd been transported back to that field of evil and ugliness.

A sweat broke out on Annalee's skin.

"My lady . . . or tell me . . ." A hand tugged her sleeve, and wild-eyed, Annalee stared blankly at that appendage gripping her.

Nay, it wasn't gripping her. It was stroking her. That was different. And it was a man's hand, not the callused, bloodied one of a woman in search of her child.

"Tell me what I should do . . . pleeeease." The mother's pleas as she'd screamed over the rioting crowd, begging Annalee for guidance in finding the lost child, filled her mind.

And then suddenly, she came crashing back from the past, breaking its hold over her, her entire body jolting from the shock of her return.

She registered several things, all at once.

Lord Welles's less-than-discreet hand, stroking the curve of her hip. The leer on his face. And the looks from several nearby guests.

"Hmm?" Lord Welles purred. "Tell me what you'd like to do, love . . . where you'd like me to meet you . . ."

Annalee stared dumbly back, registering all the details that had found clarity through that moment of madness and that she'd just succumbed to Baron Welles making bold of his touch.

"Somewhere away from the noisy crowd, yes?" The baron leaned down and whispered in her ear, the brandy scent on his breath only making Annalee hunger for those spirits all the more. And he mistook the hunger that brought her lips apart for something more than it was. "Oh, yes . . . let's find a place, love."

Her skin pricked and burnt, the feel of a thousand stares upon her in that moment. Nay, it was just one. One person, one man whose gaze had the power of a touch upon her. She glanced past the yammering baron's shoulder and found him almost instantly.

Wayland.

Stricken.

Like he'd been physically hurt, but by what?

It was preposterous.

Why, when she'd even teasingly suggested a real courtship, he'd been a study in the word "horror." He wouldn't care whom she kept company with.

Furthermore, in the unlikely chance that he had felt . . . something . . . about seeing her with Welles . . . if either of them were given to such sentiments in that moment, it was her witnessing him and his Lady Diana. Diana, who'd been with him at Peterloo, and who'd shared all these years in between with him, too. The "post life," as Annalee had come to think of it. Everything before that summer's day in Manchester. And then everything to come after it.

Except, it was the wrong thought to let creep back in.

Nausea roiled in her gut.

She wasn't going to make it this night.

Oh, God. It was too much.

Tripping over herself in her haste, Annalee took flight along the perimeter of the guests.

Her fingers shook as she pressed her flute into the baron's hand. "Splendid," he purred. "Where shall we . . . Lady Annalee . . . ," he called after her. "Lady Annalee?" That query grew more distant and blurred in her mind as she rushed along the side of the dance floor, taking the first doorway out and not breaking the pace she'd set for herself. She ran and kept on running until she'd found a way out.

Her breath grew raspy in her own ears, the pounding of her heartbeat deafening.

She reached the end of the hall that spilled outside, and fumbling with the handles, she managed to get herself free.

The air, thick and hotter than usual for a London spring, however, proved no balm. It only further blended the lines between past and present, where it was the oppressive heat of an August day weighting the air and sucking the breath out of her.

Panting hard from her flight, she staggered to a stop, and hunching over, she let her palms rest atop her knees and fought to breathe. She fought for control.

Then she heard it.

The faintest gurgling.

The tinkling pitter-patter of drops of water striking water. Distracting and soothing as they'd come to be, and they called.

As she walked, Annalee hopped on one foot and freed herself of first one slipper, then the other.

The moment she reached the side of the palladio garden fountain, she hiked up her skirts and stepped over, dipping her feet in. The icy-cold water closed over her ankles, and gooseflesh rose on her legs and arms, a balm that instantly cleared those cobwebs from her mind.

Mayhap this was what those mermaids pulled from sea felt when they returned to the waters—a homecoming. A baptism that cleaned the soul, if even just briefly.

She felt him before she heard him, knowing his footfalls and sensing his presence in the same way that she'd felt his gaze in the ballroom. "Lord Darlington," she called, not glancing back.

There was a moment's hesitation, and then the slight crunch of gravel, indicating he'd moved.

The moment he reached her side, she rested her palms on the limestone edge of the fountain and glanced up, smiling at him.

"Am I . . . intruding?"

Was she meeting Lord Welles?

That was the question he was really asking.

"No," she murmured. Would he even believe that denial? And why did she care if he did?

What was he doing here? Why had he come? Why had he left his Lady Diana's side?

So many questions rolled through her mind, ones that she could not ask and desperately wished to know the answers to.

Wayland clasped his hands behind him, staring at the mighty Aphrodite that stood at the top of the fountain, letting water fall from her fingers.

Annalee hated this silence between them. "Never say you've sought me out." She kicked her toes, splashing him slightly. Several drops landed on the front of his jacket, and he frantically wiped them off as though he were scrubbing lip rouge from his person.

She couldn't help the sad smile. How she missed the rebel he'd once been.

"Wayland of old would have sat beside me, shucked his boots, rucked up his trousers, and joined me in soaking his feet."

"Wayland of old also wouldn't have joined you at a formal ball hosted by a duke and duchess," he said quietly. "But here we are."

Annalee drew up her knees and folded her arms around them. "Yes, here we are."

Then, he did the most unexpected of things: he . . . joined her, seating himself beside her on the edge of the fountain.

And . . . strangely, for all the tumult this night had brought, there came a sense of peace in being here, alone with this man, now.

"Tell me, Wayland," she said conversationally. "Why do you think I'm always off meeting a lover?"

"Are you?"

She tried to make out anything in those syllables. "No." Annalee turned her head, studying the upside-down version of this tensely aloof Wayland. She looked him over. "You don't believe me. Do you know the truth?"

He hesitated, and then gave his head a slight shake.

Annalee leaned in, whispering against his ear, "I've never met a lover at a fountain." She raised her mouth to claim a kiss.

"But you've had lovers," he said, just as their lips would have met.

"And haven't you?"

She wasn't so naive as to have failed to hear the places he'd once visited with her brother. His cheeks went red with splotches of color. A blush. Of guilt? Embarrassment? Shame? What accounted for it?

Chapter 16

Wayland knew the very moment he'd fallen in love with Lady Annalee Spencer.

He'd been swimming in her family's lake, and she'd scaled an enormous oak, climbing to the highest possible branch. The moment she'd reached the top, she'd shucked all her garments until she was nude. And then, with a stunning grace and elegance, she'd brought her arms above her head and launched herself into a flawless dive, disappearing beneath the serene water's depths before breaking through, splashing him and declaring that neither he nor any boy could or would ever dive as perfectly as she did.

That confidence, that gumption—her sense of pride and the knowledge she'd possessed of her own accomplishment—had fascinated him.

But that had been when they'd been children. And his life from that moment on had never, ever been the same.

As he'd grown up and become a man, and she a woman, he'd learned the real reasons he'd been so hopelessly and helplessly in love with her: her strength. Her belief that people, regardless of station or gender, should have a seat at the table that was the world.

He'd never known there could be a woman like her.

Hell, he didn't know a single person like her.

It only made sense that they should meet now, beside water, when it had always beckoned to her.

And yet, that love of water had also become something that wasn't just intimately known by him. These fountains that had come to represent trysting spots.

And fire seared his veins at the thought of her meeting Welles . . . or anyone else . . . out here.

"Do you want to know why I'm always in fountains, Wayland?" she whispered, leaning close.

He shook his head tightly.

"It is because I like them. I search them out because they relax me. They soothe me."

They relax me . . . They soothe me . . .

Those weren't the same reasons she used to give.

"Because of Peterloo," he said somberly.

She stiffened, and his body tensed alongside hers.

It was the first time they'd ever spoken of it. In those earliest days, when her family had rushed her off to London and he'd been left behind in Manchester, he'd written note after note. Pleading forgiveness. Swearing to atone for having placed her in the path of danger that day.

At last, she spoke. "Because of Peterloo," she said softly. "It was hot that day."

"So hot," he added needlessly, his voice rough, and yet echoing that reminder forged the memory in his mind.

They were speaking of it. And it felt . . . right. And freeing. Speaking to her, the one woman whom he'd loved more than anyone else.

"Oppressive. Like the crowds."

The crowds. Yes, when he'd left her, she'd been far in the distance on the side of the road, but the crowds had swelled and soared and been dispersed in every direction that day. She fell silent. They *both* fell silent. And he knew she wanted to let the discourse die.

Only he'd always been selfish where Annalee Spencer was concerned. And now that they'd begun speaking of that summer's day in Manchester, he didn't want to let the moment of closeness go. A fledgling bond had been kindled, forged from that day of hell. He wanted to keep talking with her about it. Because then, mayhap if they did, it would bring them back to a place they'd once been—if not lovers . . . then friends.

"I never saw that many people in my life," he murmured, staring vacantly at his image beside hers reflected in the duke's watering fountain. "I couldn't imagine there was anything more exciting than all those men and women, come together to advocate for change." The pings raining down from Aphrodite's fingertips, little teardrops upon his and Annalee's frames, were so very fitting, a metaphor for both that day and what had happened to their friendship. "A damned fool, I was." Bitterness lent a hard edge to that utterance.

There was a slight rustle of satin, indicating Annalee had shifted closer. "Because you sought to bring about reform to the existing way of life? A way that is unfair?" She rested a hand on his sleeve, her fingers finding a purchase upon his person as though it were the most natural thing in the world to touch him so. "What you saw, what you spoke of, Wayland," she said, her voice impassioned enough to let him know she actually believed the words she spoke, "were all the men who were and are unfairly denied the vote. You spoke up and out against a law passed to pay for a war on the backs of the most oppressed, the ones with the least financing the luxuries of the few." She looked up at him. He saw it in those same waters, a reflective mirror that allowed him to look upon the two of them together, but also to avoid her eyes as the coward he was. "Those were your words, Wayland. You spoke them."

He swallowed painfully past a wad of bitterness. "I was a naive schoolboy who resented that I didn't have more."

"And there was nothing wrong with expecting you should be afforded the same rights," she said calmly.

A woeful smile brought his lips up. "When did our roles become so reversed?"

She let her arm fall from his sleeve. "I *always* believed those things you were fighting for, Wayland. You were the one who stopped."

When he'd been granted his title.

She didn't speak with recrimination. She didn't speak with anything beyond a relaxed matter-of-factness. So why was he unable to meet her eyes, even in that watering fountain? Why did shame turn in his belly?

"I don't suppose that is why you've come?" she gently prodded him, dropping her chin atop her knees and rubbing that dainty point back and forth along the yellow fabric. "To speak about Peterloo?"

"No," he said gruffly. And he found he'd been wrong earlier. With her gentle challenges and questions, ones that made him think about those aspects of Peterloo and his own life which he didn't wish to contemplate, he was grateful for the shift away from talks of that August day.

"What is it, Wayland?" she asked softly, trailing the tip of her right toe along the surface of the water, writing a little line with the ripples she made, then erasing it with the heel of her foot. "You are serious." She paused, smiling up at him. "That is, more serious than usual."

He'd not always been the stuffy, grave figure she now took him for. She'd known him back when he'd been lighter, and life easier. But her remarks also served to remind him of why he was here. "I wanted to speak to you about Kitty," he began, hating himself even as he got those words out, because he knew they'd sever the brief but beautiful connection he and Annalee had found here.

She smiled. "I adore her. She's grown into—"

"She cannot be part of your club," he said flatly before she mistook this meeting for anything other than what it was.

And just like that, all the warmth they'd shared, the kindred connection they'd forged of their past, and the high opinion she'd once carried for him, died a quick death. All the light in those eyes went dark. And in that instant, he wished he could call back the real reason for his being here. Restore them back to that connected plane they'd existed in. A place he'd never again thought to be with her.

"*That* is why you've sought me out?" Annalee narrowed her eyes upon his face, and the glint icing her eyes, a shade of blue that would forever captivate him, marked the death knell for any further closeness between them. "Bah." She stormed to her bare feet. "Of course that was why you came looking for me. The stuffy, always proper Lord Darlington would *nevvver*"—she wagged her palms—"seek me out unless I served as some possible threat to you and your precious reputation."

His cheeks fired hot. "That is not the case." He paused. "Not entirely."

He'd always been a terrible liar. "The hell it isn't," she shot back, giving him a derisive once-over. "You've come to tell me . . . what? That I should rescind my invitation and turn your sister away?"

When she put it in those terms . . . he certainly heard the damning sound to them. And yet . . .

"Oh, my God." Annalee recoiled. "That *is* why you've sought me out this evening."

She went absolutely silent, her features frozen, and his heart ached because of her hurt.

And then . . . Annalee burst out laughing. Her laughter doubled her over, and she clutched at her sides as tears of mirth streamed down her cheeks.

He brought his shoulders back and looked straight ahead. That amusement at his expense grated. It was mocking and condescending, and looking at this exchange from her perspective, she was within her rights to that condescension. It did not, however, make it any less . . . acute.

Regaining control of her hilarity, Annalee dashed the moisture from her cheeks and met his gaze.

She promptly dissolved into another gleeful fit.

Wayland beat a hand against the side of his leg. Oh, this was really enough. "I'm glad you find this amusing."

Her amusement receded, and the ire came back in her eyes so quickly that he perversely found himself preferring the lady's earlier sarcasm. She took a step toward him. "I find it amusing that you know me so little as to believe that I would ever dare bar your sister because of something any man has said to me."

He jerked. At Manchester, he'd witnessed men being run through, and the sharp way in which her words knifed him, he'd a taste of that unexpected pain. Hell, with the way she'd referred to him—"any man," despite all they'd shared—he'd have preferred it to the way she severed any connection between them. "You think so little of me," he said quietly.

"I don't even know you," she replied with a lightning quickness, an unflappability at odds with the tumult running amok inside him. "Not anymore."

They didn't know one another. That appeared to be something they did find common ground on.

"But you? Seeking to interfere in your sister's life? Choosing the activities that you deem proper and attempting to cut off those you don't? In this? Yes, my opinion of you is not a good one, my lord."

My lord.

From the moment he'd learned he'd be granted a barony because of his act of bravery at Peterloo, he'd hated everything about that title. For Wayland, it had become synonymous with that day and everything he'd lost.

But this? Hearing those two little syllables fall from this woman's lips was like another blow to the belly. It shouldn't matter what she thought, and yet it did. It mattered so much. He tried to make her understand.

"My father toiled. He worked until his hands bled, and we still had but a one-room household, one that was cold in the winter and blazing hot in the summer. And when patrons found another who could do work cheaper, there was even less security. I don't want that life. And I'll see my sister settled so she is secure, and yes, if that means behaving a certain way and being"—someone he wasn't—"the stuffy lord you take me for"—his jaw flexed—"then by God, I'll do that for her."

Annalee took a step closer, and continued coming until the tips of his boots brushed her bare feet. "Are you speaking about your sister's security, Wayland?" She looked him squarely in the eyes. "Or your own?"

"I . . ." Her question confounded him.

Heat blazed through him, as it always did when she was near.

She wasn't finished with him, however. "Who are you, even?" she asked sadly. "You, the great voice of those without ones in their government. The men and women struggling for food, and striving for a leg up in the world . . . That you should so quit, because why? *Hmm?*" Annalee slashed a hand back toward the duke and duchess's palatial residence that could have fit a thousand of the hovels he'd lived within. "Because your life improved? Because you are now included amongst the ranks of the people who once shut you out?"

And he was grateful for the cover darkness provided to keep from revealing the stain of shame on his cheeks. Except . . .

"You don't know what it is to be without that security, Annalee," he said, willing her to understand. "You have always belonged to this world, one that is secure and safe." In fact, the only time it had proven not to be the case for her had been when she'd ventured into those fields and mingled with the riotous masses of Manchester. The guilt of that would follow him until he drew his last breath.

She stared at him for a long moment, and he tensed, bracing for the sting of her next biting attack.

That didn't come . . .

"Don't I?" she asked curiously. "If I wed, I'm at the mercy of a man, nothing more than his property. And even as a grown woman, I've had my dowry withheld, and any monies that were to be mine remain locked away. I'm at the mercy of Lady Sylvia's generosity, and any funds I do have are because of any wagers I've won."

"My God," he whispered. "They cut you off."

"They cut me off," she confirmed, "because I bring much *shaaame* to the family name." Those words flowed so freely from her tongue, there could be no doubting she'd had them tossed her way. "So much shame that they've pleaded with me and threatened to send me away, back to their country house in Ma-Manchester." Her voice broke, and his heart cracked along with it.

He took a step closer to her, but she shot up a palm, forcing him to stop, telling him with that brusque flip of her hand just how much she wanted or welcomed comfort from him in this moment.

"They would send me back to the place of my nightmares," she whispered, "just to be free of me."

And it was the first time in the course of his life that he hated her family. Her parents, for cutting her off. Jeremy, for allowing it to happen. And . . . himself, for not having known. Wayland fisted his hands tight.

Her eyes sparked with a determined glint, but her gaze was one that moved through him as though he weren't there. As though at some point she'd ceased speaking to him and spoke only to herself.

"You see a woman with more freedom than I truly have, Wayland," she said, her eyes fixed beyond him to that fountain she'd been perched beside. "You see a lady who, because of her birth to a noble family, has security. But I don't. Not really." Annalee slid her gaze back to his, holding his eyes with her own. "No woman does."

"I . . . never quite thought of that perspective," he said softly, his shame compounded by the truth of that admission. "I . . . simply saw members of the peerage, all of them . . . as secure. Free from strife." Because as a boy born outside her world, he'd been an outsider looking in.

Annalee moved her eyes over his face. "I don't have any real control of my life, Wayland," she said matter-of-factly. "And neither does your sister. When she marries, she'll have even less. As such, you should support her in whatever pursuits or endeavors she wishes to avail herself of." While she was able. Before Kitty was constrained by the husband who was supposed to represent security.

He ran a hand over the side of his face. Everything was confused in his mind. Why was it confused?

Annalee. It was because of her.

Annalee had always had the ability to challenge him and make him see angles of discussions he'd missed. That hadn't changed.

"I always respected you," Annalee said sadly. "I admired you, because you wished to change the world. Where is that man?"

And something within him snapped.

He took her lightly by the shoulders, gripping her, his fingers curling into her arms. "And what did that get either of us?" he hissed. "Was the world made better? For you? For me? For anyone that day?"

"The world is what we make it."

"You'd condemn me, but what did you make it? An Eden for you to sin all day long in."

Her lips parted slightly and moved, but no words were forthcoming.

Oh, God. He recoiled from his own words. And he shook his head. "Annalee . . ." *I'm sorry. I didn't mean to hurt you. I didn't mean to have ruined your life that day . . .* That was the apology she deserved, but that stuck in his throat.

⌘

You'd condemn me, but what did you make it? An Eden for you to sin all day long in.

Her chest . . . ached and throbbed. And for the oddest reason, at that. Wayland spoke words of truth before her, about her. He wasn't wrong.

After Peterloo, she had committed herself to her pleasures and pursuits, to bury the memories of that day. To feel again. To feel something that was different from the terror and agony that had consumed her.

To forget him.

Instinctively, she folded her arms around her middle and hugged herself hard, trying to ward off this pain.

Perhaps this was merely a reminder that the wild life she'd dedicated herself to had been for naught.

Annalee drew in a soft breath through her teeth, and letting her arms fall, she stepped away. This wasn't about her . . . and him. They'd just made it so. "You might think the Mismatch Society is wicked, for no other reason than because of my involvement with it."

He tried to protest, but she touched a finger to his mouth, stifling that lie. For that was precisely what it was. Even if he couldn't admit as much to himself. "You know nothing about us, Wayland," she said through the pain knifing away at her still. "You read about how we are scandalous and challenging norms, and yet I would say to you, that is a good thing. You don't know how we have helped women avoid marriages to men who would have beaten them." Some emotion she couldn't identify filled his eyes. Once she would have been able to make sense of it. Not anymore. "Or how we've helped other ladies once afraid to share their opinions to share them, and to do so proudly." She pressed a finger against his chest. "There is good in what we do. And I'll not have you besmirch my society."

They stood there, chests heaving, their gazes moving swiftly over one another's faces. And then, Wayland's eyes slipped, falling to her mouth. He lowered his head slightly, then drew back, but then—like that magnet she'd once observed the bluestocking member of the Mismatch Society, Brenna Kearsley, playing with—he was compelled forward, lowering his lips once more. His lashes swept low, and she proved her desire for this man would be forever greater than her pride.

With a moan, she lifted herself up on tiptoe and kissed him.

His hands were immediately on her buttocks, dragging her close to the hard ridge of his shaft tenting his trousers.

Afire, she stroked her palms up and down the sleeves of his jacket, gripping those blacksmith's muscles he'd not lost, that were as hard and large as ever.

"Why am I mad about you still?" she rasped against his lips.

He slipped his tongue into her mouth, and mated it against hers. Twisting and tangling with Annalee's.

He lusted after her, but he'd never want anything more. Why, he didn't even want his sister near her. The sharp edge of that truth gave her the power to wrench herself free of his arms.

"Is this some sort of test, Lord Darlington?" she taunted, adjusting the bodice of her dress.

The color of his cheeks, flushed from their embrace, deepened. "Of course not."

"But it does feed your ill opinion, doesn't it?" she purred. "Wicked, whorish Annalee."

"Do not call yourself that," he said harshly.

As though he were offended . . . for her. "Isn't that what I am? To the world. To you?"

He appeared stricken. "Never," he whispered. The slight knob of his Adam's apple moved. "I've *never* . . . seen you that way." And by the force of the emphasis he placed upon that word, she . . . could almost believe him.

But his opinions and his demands for her and his sister, Kitty, however, were proof enough.

"But that is the way I am," Annalee said gravely. "Men can bed who they wish freely, but the moment a woman does it, they cast all manner of hideous labels upon her." With a sound of disgust, she stepped away from him. "I may be a sinner, but I'm not so bankrupt inside as to try to interfere in the lives of those I love because of a fear of what people who don't truly care about anyone but themselves have to say about those I love." She gripped him by the lapels, dragging his face close. It was a mistake; she faltered, his breath wafting upon her lips, and remembered the feel of his mouth. She wrestled through the pull he'd always have over her, and released him suddenly. Annalee gave him a long look. "And we are not a club. We are a society, Lord Darlington." She grabbed up her slippers.

"Annalee," he said quickly.

Not breaking stride, she lifted her finger in a vulgar salute and dashed off.

She flattened her mouth.

To hell with stuffy, overbearing, and oppressive brothers . . . and fathers. Nay, to hell with all men.

More specifically, to hell with Wayland Smith, the illustrious Lord Darlington.

With every step that carried her away from those gardens and down the halls of the duke's carpeted corridors, her frustration and ire grew.

Wayland, with his pompous, judgmental views on her Mismatch Society. A group he would have once fully supported and applauded, he should now condemn.

Because of you.

And she hated with every fiber of her being that his low opinion should cleave through her heart. That she was still weak for him.

She stole a glance over her shoulder to be sure he'd not followed her.

As though he would.

Why, he was likely out of his mind, elated at being free of her company.

And to hell with this fancy affair she had no part of and wished she'd never come to . . . not even to rehabilitate her reputation.

To hell with it all.

All of it.

She wanted a drink, and she needed it.

Her whole body hungered for the numbing satiation spirits brought.

Annalee raced around the next corridor and crashed headfirst into a solid wall; the velocity of that collision expelled all the air from her lungs.

Her slippers flew from her fingers, and she sucked in a silent gasp as she was flung backward.

But firm hands were on her waist, catching her before she hit the floor, keeping her upright on her feet.

Dazed, Annalee gave her head a slight shake, registering that she'd run into not any wall, but a leering lord.

Lord Welles's fleshy lips peeled back in a grin that was more smirk than smile.

Bloody fabulous.

"There you are, sweet," he purred. All the while his hands remained firm at her waist.

Oh, bloody hell. The absolute last wish she had or thing she wanted was a run-in with a *gentleman.*

I don't have time for this, Welles, she wanted to screech. Except screeching would summon spectators, and spectators would spread salacious gossip. And that would mean more scandal, and . . . She gritted her teeth. No, she really did not have time for this. Annalee firmly disentangled his fingers from her person. "My lord, if you'll excuse me?"

Shock brought his fiery eyebrows shooting up.

God, give her the confidence of a pale, doughy-faced man of the peerage.

"Excuse you? When we've only just met up?"

"Yes, yes. That is it. You have the right of it. Now if you—"

A sudden understanding dawned in his eyes. "Ah, I see."

What exactly it was he thought he saw, she neither knew nor cared to know. All Annalee knew was the need to escape. Damning this night all over again, she stepped around him.

He shot out a hand, catching her firmly by the arm, wringing yet a second gasp from her this night: outrage. It burnt like fire in her veins, and she glared at him. "Release me this instant, Lord Welles." She'd almost been a victim before. Since that night of Willoughby's arrival, she'd not found herself so accosted. Some of that was no doubt a product of the protection afforded her by her close relationship with Willoughby and Beckett.

The baron sniggered. "You like the chase, do you? I heard as much. From Lord Gravens."

Lord Gravens, who'd spread stories of her wickedness during that, her first foray into the decadent. Her rejection, followed by her departure from that event with Lord Willoughby, had stoked the rumors of her sordidness.

Until the myth became the legend, and she was a whore forevermore to Polite Society.

She fixed another glare on him. "Step aside, Welles. As it is, I bed men, not pathetic, begging boys," she taunted, and wrenching her arm free of his grip, she hurried around him.

He proved quicker than she'd expected. But then, when they had assault on their minds, there was little to slow them down.

He cut her off once more.

And this time, his tenacity recalled the past terror. It came raging back. That feeling of helplessness, once experienced, was one a woman always recalled. It never left one, and always reared its head. Briefly crippling, a paralysis of the mind and body that slowed one's flight and cast one further into peril. Annalee shoved off that fear, a useless sentiment that saw no person saved.

This was not one of the wicked affairs she preferred to frequent, where everyone in attendance had the same expectations of debauchery and there wasn't a risk of ruin. "The duke and duchess would hardly appreciate your engaging in such scandal in the middle of the only ball they throw," she said coolly.

His smile widened, revealing two rows of crooked teeth. "I trust one such as you is better at clandestine trysts."

"Better than whom? You? Certainly. But my first rule is always a willing partner. Of which I am decidedly not."

Like a child denied a treat, he stomped his foot. "Ah, it is simply that you've met someone else," he whined, his already nasal tones pitching a decibel higher. "I was too late to scratch your itch, was I? I've also heard that," he jeered, scraping a stare over her, one that sought to strip her of her dignity. "That you'll take anyone between your legs when you're foxed—"

A roar of primal beasts thundered around the hall, bringing Welles spinning around. Wayland launched himself at Welles.

Several stones heavier, and several inches taller, he easily took the wiry man down.

Annalee gasped. "Wayland."

But it was as though he didn't hear. And mayhap he didn't. He was a man possessed, pounding the other man again and again. Blood sprayed from Welles's nose, staining Wayland's brown cravat with crimson drops that turned the fabric black.

Grabbing Welles by his lapels, Wayland dragged the shorter man up until his feet dangled several inches from the floor. "Say it again," Wayland snarled in the other man's face. "I dare you to say a single god-damned word about her."

"But everyone kn-knows what sh-she is," Lord Welles blubbered, tears and snot and blood painting his already purpling face into a hideous mask. The baron glanced to Annalee. "T-tell *himmm*."

"Tell him that I'm a whore? I'd rather not. Even if I was, I was never meeting you," she spat.

"She's lying! You lying wh— *Ahhhh*," Welles cried out as Wayland knocked the man's forehead with his own, a veritable battering ram.

His lips drawn back in a snarl, Wayland had the look of a medieval warrior come to life, eager to end the life of the man before her. In all the years they'd known one another, she'd seen him many ways, but never . . . like this.

"You will not go near her." Propelling the smaller man hard so that his back collided with the wall behind him, Wayland stuck his face in Welles's. "You will not speak an unkind word about her. In fact, you will not speak her name. Am I clear?"

Sobbing, Welles nodded, the tears falling down his cheeks converging with the blood dripping from his bulbous nose and turning into a sanguine river that emptied onto his powder-blue cravat and waistcoat, staining those silk articles. And then Wayland punched the other man hard in the stomach. All the air exhaled from the baron's swollen lips, and he slid slowly to his knees.

Annalee stood motionless, shocked into immobility. He would do this . . . for her? This volatile show went against the gentleman he'd become, who didn't display emotion. She didn't want this for him. And certainly not because of her. "Wayland," she said quietly. "Wayland," she repeated, this time more insistently. He brought his arm back once more, and she caught it between both of her hands, gripping him tightly in a bid to break through whatever insanity now gripped him. *"Stop."*

He glanced back, his gaze locking on her fingers upon his elbow.

His eyes glinted with a half-mad sparkle, and then he blinked slowly, and she knew the moment she'd penetrated whatever murderous rage had so consumed him. "He insulted you," he said on a furious whisper.

"A lot of people have."

His eyes frosted over all the more. "I'll kill them all."

And she caught the inside of her lower lip hard at that defense—an undeserved one. "Oh, Wayland. You need to stop. You'll kill him, Wayland."

"And happily." Because of her. When no one, not even her own brother, had believed her honor was worth defending.

At their feet, Welles curled his arms over his head and rolled into a fetal position.

"I don't want that," she whispered. "It is not worth it. He is not worth it." *I am not worth it.* All held true.

She'd ruined so much in her life. She'd brought unhappiness to so many. Her parents. Her brother. His betrothed. Her friends. She could not see Wayland and his family added to that list of those to whom she brought hurt.

In the end, it appeared it was her lot to bring scandal and shame.

Footfalls came quick, and murmurs and cries of horror grew louder, as a sea of the duke and duchess's guests converged upon Wayland, Welles, and Annalee.

"My *gawwwwd*," someone in that crowd cried out.

Annalee briefly closed her eyes. When she opened them, she found some ten or twelve guests around them, most familiar. Several not. And from the ranks of that audience, Wayland's mother shouldered her way through and staggered to a stop.

"What is . . . going on here?"

There was no doubting what opinions were already being formed. Which ones had already been formed.

Bloody hell.

Chapter 17

The following morning, Annalee lay in her bed, sprawled on her back. She stared overhead at the lacy film canopy that draped across the four posters.

Through that translucent, gauzy fabric, she remained fixed on the naked gods and goddesses painted there, locked in their own play.

She'd always loved this particular rendering; it was one of the reasons upon her arrival at Waverton Street that she'd asked Sylvia and Valerie if she might have this room. Because it was like a . . . homecoming of sorts. Not because she felt powerful like the gods. Far from it. Rather, she'd felt a kindred connection to this moment of hedonism they partook in. This wicked play they surrendered to made sense to her.

He disapproved of her.

He disdained her.

It was what she'd always known.

Nay, not always.

Before all the sin and ugliness that had exploded like hell had been unleashed upon mankind—and womankind—in Manchester, he'd respected her.

But then, what reason would a man like Wayland—a gentleman—have to respect you? a voice taunted. Over the years, she . . . had taken lovers. More specifically, in those first months following Peterloo, she'd attended orgies and other scandalous affairs.

After a year of sinning, however, she'd tired of men who didn't fill the void that existed within her. Instead, there'd been a greater thought to whom she bedded and why.

And then there was the smoking.

Granted, Wayland had been the one to teach her how to smoke a cheroot. He'd sneaked them from his father so that she and he and Jeremy might attempt it. They'd been children then.

Wayland of now didn't smoke. Or drink.

And the one venture she was most proud of, the one thing she'd done with herself that actually felt purposeful and meaningful, he didn't even approve of that. In fact, he was so horrified by it, and her efforts and what her society sought to accomplish, that he'd become one of those oppressive elder brothers who attempted to stifle their sisters' wills and wishes.

Because those honorable good girls, those respectable ones, had no place entering the household of Annalee Spencer.

And last night? She'd gone and ruined him. Granted, he'd ruined himself by storming the corridor and fighting for her honor.

Why? Why would he do that if he didn't respect her or care about her anymore?

A strained laugh gurgled up from her throat. But then, whatever of those sentiments had lived last evening had likely died after the scandal that had rocked London after she, Wayland, and Welles had been discovered.

Her gaze locked on the mural of the goddess Methe. In one hand she hoisted a glass of wine in salute to the revelry unfolding, while her other fingers were twined with Dionysus's. Together, they celebrated with Amphictyonis, that deity of wine and friendship.

What is honorable about what you do, Annalee?

And because of who she was, who she'd become, Wayland would bar his sister entry to the Mismatch. And that, oddly, hurt the most of all. That had she been just Sylvia or some other respected lady, he'd not only consent but also would likely gladly have Kitty mingle with the Mismatch members. And now Kitty should pay the price, being denied the opportunity to grow and challenge and be challenged by women who'd said "enough" to society's institutions . . . because of Annalee.

Wrenching her stare away, Annalee curled onto her side and directed her attention to the window, a safer place that didn't conjure her life that Wayland saw as a failing.

Why should she care anyway? She, who didn't give a goddamn what anyone thought of her? She, who'd deliberately built herself up so that she couldn't or wouldn't care?

Only to find that . . . she'd not done such an impressive job with those defenses as she'd thought. Not such an impressive job, after all. Not when Wayland had so easily penetrated them, raising insecurities she'd not known she'd possessed. Weaknesses she'd not known she had.

Mayhap it was because of the one who'd called her out, challenging her.

Mayhap it was because a lifetime ago, he'd been her best friend and her lover, and the one man whom she'd entertained marrying. Nay, the man whom she'd been determined to marry. Even if her parents would have fought that match—as she knew they would have. Even if Jeremy would have likely resisted it, too. She and Wayland had been fated for one another.

Or that was what she'd told herself for so long, what she'd believed for so long. What a naive fool she'd been.

RapRapRap.

There wasn't a pause long enough for her to utter an "enter" before the door opened and then closed.

There came a light tread that she knew too well, even before the young woman identified herself.

Valerie's black skirts came into direct line with Annalee's vision. "Are you jug bitten?" Her friend's question came without recrimination. It was so very matter-of-fact, and somehow . . . all the worse for it.

"No."

Annalee flipped onto her back, but that proved the wrong direction to look, as Dionysus and Methe partnered with Amphictyonis. With a sigh, Annalee rolled the other way.

"You do know you are late. You're never late. Even when foxed."

Which she so often was.

The mattress dipped as Valerie set herself on the edge, and Annalee rolled back. "It is a terrible idea."

Her friend's golden brows dipped a fraction. "Being in your cups? I must admit I've never understood your love of sp—"

"No. Not that." Annalee's love of spirits, as her friend referred to it, wasn't what she spoke of. Though if she were discussing that, she'd explain it was more a need than a wish. She sat up quickly. "My being part of the Mismatch. I'm a terrible fit," she went on, and as she spoke, her words all tripped and rolled together. "The key piece is allowing women a forum to come together and fight for a better place for themselves in the world, and yet, as long as I'm here, I'm an impediment to that. Ladies will continue to be barred, and after last night . . ."

"Ah, the fight."

Her friend knew about it. Had no doubt read about it. But then, if just being in the same modiste's as he and his sister had been a source of scandal, all of London was surely whispering about that exchange in the duke's corridor. "I am a magnet for scandal," she said, flipping once more, lying on her back.

"That's never bothered you before," Valerie pointed out, not attempting to deny Annalee's description of herself, and it was that honesty she so loved her friend for. "Should I . . . ask what the fight was over?"

Annalee made herself sit up; drawing her knees close, she folded her arms around them. "A gentleman accosted me. Wayland interfered . . . beating the baron quite viciously."

"Good," Valerie said without hesitation.

And shamefully, in that moment . . . it . . . had felt good to have some-one who believed her worthy of defending. Even if she wasn't. Wayland had. And she'd ruined him.

"You do know staying in here will not undo what's happened?"

"I know that." That was, however, not the reason she was here. Not really.

There was only one certainty. She couldn't remain on Waverton Street. She had to leave. At least until Sylvia returned. And coward that she was, she didn't want to climb out of this bed and go down to the meeting and share this with the friends she'd come to love. Women she now needed to protect. Why, if Wayland, who'd once loved her, refused to let his sister join their ranks, what chance did they have for the others?

And so Annalee made herself get out of bed and, with Valerie's help, rushed swiftly through her ablutions and made her way downstairs.

The moment she stepped inside . . . Annalee froze.

Her eyes went to the figure in the middle of the room, engaged in a discussion with the Kearsley sisters.

"Kitty is here," Annalee whispered.

"Should she not be?" Confusion wreathed Valerie's query.

As though she'd sensed she was being discussed, the other young woman looked over. The girl's entire face lit as she waved at Annalee and then quit the side of the Kearsley sisters to join Annalee and Valerie.

"It is . . . so very good to see you," Annalee said. For now. For as long as she was able to remain without her family's interference. "I didn't expect you would be here." Another wave of guilt twisted at her belly.

Kitty's brow wrinkled. "And whyever not?"

"Because . . . because . . ." Annalee floundered, caught between not wanting to say too much as to what she'd suspected about Wayland, and also not wanting to be responsible for creating a potential rift between brother and sister.

Understanding filled Kitty's brown eyes. "*Ahh*, you mean you thought I wouldn't come today because of Wayland."

That was precisely what she'd thought. It really wasn't her place to question and yet . . . "You defied him, then."

"My brother?" Kitty snorted. "Hardly. Not that I wouldn't if the situation required it," the spirited young girl tacked on. "But it was not necessary." Her smile widened, a mischievous twinkle in her eyes. "This time. This morning, Wayland sent me on my way with his blessing and an urging to have fun."

Annalee's heart slowed, then resumed a rapid rate. "He . . . did?" Annalee couldn't contain the breathless quality of that question that slipped from her. She felt Valerie's eyes form pinpricks as she narrowed her gaze upon her, but couldn't bring herself to care. He'd . . . not tried to interfere as so many oppressive papas and brothers had?

"Oh, yes," Kitty said, and proceeded to fish around inside her reticule, only half attending to Annalee. And turned upside down by the information the young lady now shared, Annalee was grateful for her distracted movements. "And not only that, he also even offered to distract Mama, falling on the sword so I might make my escape. And if that isn't a sacrifice, I don't know what is," Kitty said, adding that last part under her breath. "Ah, here it is!" She produced her notebook, and waved it about.

Let it go.

It doesn't matter that Wayland hadn't proven as overbearing and insufferable as most of the other male figures associated with the women in the Mismatch Society.

All that mattered was that Kitty was here now and they were free to begin the day's meeting.

Only, Annalee could not free herself of the curiosity. "But . . . I believed Way—the baron did not approve." *Or perhaps it is only you whom he takes exception with . . .*

"Oh, Wayland does not want me to take part in"—the girl rolled her eyes—"scandalous activities. He's concerned because, well, *you* know how he now worries after his reputation and *our* reputation. But no . . . for all his commitment to propriety, he remains more committed to not attempting to live my life for me." The younger girl leaned in close, whispering, "In fact, I believe Wayland likes to think himself different from how he used to be. But he's not. He's the same man who always appreciated a good challenge to the rule of order and inequity in the world."

With every word uttered, Annalee's heart pounded all the harder, her pulse beating loud in her ears. And he'd also known his sister was suffering for friends.

Cora Kearsley joined them.

"Cora, you remember Miss Kitty Smith," Annalee said.

The young ladies exchanged greetings, and in a moment it was as though they were fast friends. "You must borrow my copy," Cora was saying. She waved the little leather volume and gave a sly look. "Why, I've already read it." She grinned. "Twice!"

And as they laughed, Annalee's heart continued swelling at Wayland's having supported her society, and for his having supported Kitty and their friendship.

"I am ever so . . ." Kitty's words slowed. "Whatever is she doing here?" she blurted.

Perplexed by that abrupt turn, Annalee followed the other woman's focus to the front of the room. Or rather, to the tableau at the front of the room. Wearing white silk skirts with an enormous train, and a tiara stuffed with a feather that gave her height an ostrich would envy, a young lady with a bevy of servants entered the parlor, ushering in a brief, noticeable silence followed by whispers. Annalee's stomach muscles clenched tight.

Valerie rushed off to greet the elegant guest.

"Whoever is that?" Cora asked.

Kitty lowered her voice. "*That* is none other than *the* Lady Diana Regan . . ." Wayland's sister pointed her eyes toward the ceiling.

The Lady Diana Regan.

Kitty slid closer, angling her body in such a way that she turned her back to the woman in question and conversed in private with Annalee and Cora. "Surely you know of her . . ." As Kitty spoke to Cora, her voice wove in and out of focus for Annalee with only certain words periodically registering.

From her lungs on down to her toes, every muscle clenched and squeezed in a shock of unexpected pain. Having seen her before, having conversed with the young lady in the modiste's, proved so very different from this. Now.

That day, Annalee and Wayland had gotten on as they'd always done before Peterloo, teasing and so very . . . comfortable with one another. She'd not let herself imagine anything more between him and the young woman.

Mayhap it was because it had been easier not to. Mayhap she'd let herself be blinded to that which her eyes had no wish to see.

But now, with Lady Diana laying command of Annalee's parlor and Mismatch Society, there could be no hiding or escaping. Particularly not in light of Wayland's rejection.

"King's goddaughter, and she takes care to be sure that everyone knows it," Kitty was saying. "Do you know what I think?" she whispered loudly.

Cora leaned in. "Yes?"

Annalee made herself shake her head, riveted by that regal command of the room. She found herself equal parts admiring that girl for such authority and unnerved by that strength. And more than a bit wanting to cry. Was there any wondering now the reason Wayland had denied Annalee's request?

Lady Diana lifted her head in acknowledgment of those women she passed. Periodically she'd pause and speak, exchanging brief pleasantries, before sweeping off.

"Years ago she got it into her head that there's a romantic connection . . ."

Annalee had the sudden urge to vomit. Or drink.

Nay, drinking was the better course. It was always the more steadying one.

She searched about for her flask, finding it—

213

"Do not look now," Kitty muttered in hushed tones just as Annalee grabbed the silver jug of whiskey.

"Kitty, dearest," Lady Diana greeted in elevated, crisp English to rival the queen's, lifting her head. "It is always a pleasure to see you." Diamonds dripped from her dress and ears and headdress. She exuded a wealth and extravagance most young ladies reserved for their Come Outs, never again rising to the level at which this woman wore and flaunted her prestige.

"The same," Kitty said with a flatness that filled her tonality with an absolute insincerity. Wayland's sister lifted her notebook and made a show of flipping through those pages.

The Duke of Kipling's daughter slid her focus back to Annalee. "If I may, Kitty . . . and Kitty's friend?" None would have ever mistaken the young woman's words for anything other than the order they were. "Lady Annalee, we meet again."

It did not escape Annalee's notice that the other young woman hadn't mentioned it as being any sort of pleasure to be in her company.

Kitty hesitated, vacillating between standing shoulder to shoulder with Annalee and escaping.

Annalee knew it was certainly the latter, because she had that same desire to flee.

In the end, Kitty and Cora dropped a quick curtsy and bustled off.

Not that Annalee would ever blame them.

Lucky girls.

The moment they'd gone, Diana adjusted her full-length satin gloves. Gloves that were entirely too formal for the time of day, and for the meeting. But then, so was the silly—if extravagant—train now being hoisted up by two servants. Suddenly, Lady Diana gave a smart clap. Her lady's maid brought forward her train and draped it over the young lady's forearm before curtsying and retreating several paces.

"I have . . . recently heard much about you, Lady Annalee," the girl said the moment they were alone.

"Most people have," she said dryly, and winked.

Lady Diana's nostrils flared the tiniest fraction in hint of her disdain. "Yes, well, that is one of the reasons I am here . . . I have heard much about your . . . club." She flicked her gaze about the room to the conversing women before recalling her focus over to Annalee.

"We are a society," Annalee said.

"Is there a difference?"

It was the first true hint of curiosity, and because of it Annalee found herself releasing some of the tension that had dogged her since the girl had arrived. "Yes," she explained. "To the women here there is. A club is a smaller group dedicated to entertainment and the amusement of its members. A society—our society—is an organization dedicated to the purpose of larger goals than simple pleasures as found in those clubs of White's or Brooke's."

"*Hmm.* Yes, anyway, I'm quite friendly with the Smith family."

"Your relationship with Miss Smith positively exuded warmth," Annalee said, keeping her features deadpan. The duke's daughter had all but ordered Kitty gone, treating her like the inferior she clearly saw her as.

"Indeed." Lady Diana adjusted her already perfectly straight diamond tiara. "I have a way of making all young ladies feel welcome."

Annalee strangled on a laugh, converting it to a cough that she caught in her fist. "Forgive me. I . . . had something in my throat." It wasn't untrue. Disbelief and humor had both set out to choke her.

The young woman gave her a strange look.

Annalee cleared her throat. "Forgive me. You were saying . . ."

From across the room, Valerie caught her eye and jabbed a finger to the clock at the mantel. "Late. We. Are. Late," her friend mouthed perfectly.

And even as there was nothing she'd like more than to end this exchange with this woman, part of her remained compelled by whatever it was she'd come here to say.

"Do you know how Wayland and I met?" Lady Diana asked suddenly and so unexpectedly that Annalee froze.

Wayland. The girl called him by his given name. Given the ceremony the lady stood on from appearance to presentation, Lady Diana's use of that given name proved all the more . . . telling of their connection. Somehow the intimacy of that proved far . . . closer, and far more agonizing for it.

Agonizing? You silly twit. Wayland, Lord Darling, is free to carry on with whom he would whenever he would. Including this five-feet-nothing, white-skirt-wearing proper miss, whom he'd saved and earned a title for.

A coveted title he'd always yearned for . . . that hadn't mattered a jot to Annalee. But it had to him, and this lily-white, innocent miss with her flawless ringlets and flawless skin . . . It would matter to her, too.

"My lady?"

Annalee started from that rumble of thoughts, all mixed together. "Annalee," she supplied. "You should call me Annalee."

Lady Diana smiled, a measured one that highlighted her dimples but did not crease her eyes or mouth with laugh lines. Everything about her was practiced. "I declare we shall be friends, then." Friends. Annalee had made it a point of counting as friends only those who'd met here with kindness and had spared her from the judgment she was so used to having heaped upon her for behaving . . . well, exactly as she chose to behave. "Might we . . . take a turn about the room?"

Annalee hesitated a moment, before accepting that proffered arm.

"It is my understanding you are . . . close with Wayland. Or that you have been." The young woman cast a glance her way. "Yes?"

Yes, indeed.

What in hell was Annalee to say to this?

Gone was any hint of warmth that had been there when they'd first met at the modiste's.

And it was as they made a pass halfway about the room that she realized one key detail where Lady Diana was concerned: Annalee had underestimated her. The kitten had claws, and she was prepared to use them. And had it been any other woman, and any other man whom they were discussing, well, then Annalee would have admired her that show of spirit and character.

That it was this woman, however, and Wayland whom she'd sought her out to discuss, only brought Annalee's back—and guard—up. "Forgive me, I didn't realize a response was expected of me here."

The lady smiled that same beatific smile of delicate amusement that grated on Annalee's last nerve. "I do suppose you are correct. All the papers can and do talk about is your relationship with Wayland. Therefore, it isn't really a confirmation I'm seeking."

Had she really considered her . . . a kitten? That was the last time Annalee would make that underestimation. A tiger. A ruthless tiger, not unlike the one Annalee had observed in rapt horror and fascination at the Royal Menagerie who'd made quick work of devouring his lunch.

From across the room, where she stood conversing with Lady Scarsdale, fresh from her honeymoon, and her sister, Isla Gately, Valerie caught Annalee's gaze, a silent offering there. One that said the former boxer had not only sensed Annalee's disquiet but also that she would cross the room and apply those former pugilist skills.

Alas, just as Annalee had looked after herself that day in Manchester, so, too, would she handle her own proverbial battles. "What is it, exactly, that you are seeking, then, Lady Diana?"

Lady Diana stopped so quickly that the change in motion brought Annalee stumbling. "Why, I would like to join you."

"Join me?"

"No, as in a permanent membership with your club."

Her stomach sank. *Bloody hell.* "As I told you, we are a society," she said coolly.

Alas, caught up in her plan and chattering as she was, either the determined young miss failed to hear that correction or she didn't care. And small as Annalee was feeling that day, she would wager on the latter.

"I want to join you," she said, throwing her arms open.

Nay, Lady Diana wished to keep an eye upon Annalee. Having dealings with some of the most ruthless and shocking sorts, Annalee had become an excellent judge of character, and as such, she knew that was what the other woman truly meant.

Lady Diana gestured to the parlor, indicating the other women engrossed in discourse, before settling her focus on Kitty. "Why, Wayland clearly admires those of you attending this . . ."—she curled her lip in an impressive sneer—"venture, and as such, I would be part of it and learn how the other half lives."

"There is no other half," Annalee said coolly. "There are just women who come together, discussing the inequities of the world and looking to improve our place within it."

Lady Diana beamed. "Splendid. I look very much forward to being part . . . of that, and learning whatever it is Wayland likes about . . ."—she gave a wave of her hand—"this."

"I wasn't saying—" Annalee needn't have bothered. The buxom beauty had already clapped her hands, signaling to the dutiful servant poised close by. Together, with her lady's maid trailing at the noxious but respected distance expected by Polite Society's standards, Lady Diana took her leave.

Annalee stared after the lady . . . the woman Wayland was intended to wed.

Valerie joined her. "Who was that?"

"It would seem our latest member," she muttered under her breath.

God help them all.

Chapter 18

The carriage ride would eventually end.

"It is grievous that you were involved with such a scandal . . ."

It had to.

"It could have been a good deal worse . . ."

Alas, until it did, Wayland was forced to endure the never-ending jabbering of his mother and her thoughts on Wayland's attack of Lord Welles the evening prior.

And Annalee.

"You *knowwww* we must be above reproach . . ."

And Wayland and Annalee together.

"And to dare risk our reputations for her, of all people . . ."

Wayland balled his hands into fists.

"Why, the lady's own parents will not tolerate her," his mother said. Snapping open her fan, she fluttered it before her face.

Wayland's patience broke. "Will you have a care and some respect for the lady and the family," he said tightly, "who, if I might point out, have been welcoming of us from before we were titled, and who were gracious enough to extend us an invitation this evening?"

"Gracious enough." She sniffed. "Roles are reversed, and we are hardly the scandalous ones any longer. Why, I would say in going to their musical that we are doing them a favor."

"Oh, yes, honoring them with our presence," he said dryly.

Sarcasm, however, had long proven lost upon his mother.

Kitty shot up a hand. "With the exception of me, if I may point out, who is now part of the Mismatch Societ— *Owww*."

Their mother snapped open her pearl-handled fan once again and waved it slightly. "You may point out no such thing." Angling her head, she attended the passing streets out the carriage window. "The only reason I'm even tolerating your participation is because Lady Diana has joined."

He frowned. Lady Diana had joined Annalee's group? The radical nature of what Annalee and those other members did didn't fit with what he knew of the duke's daughter.

"She's not a real member, though. She is only there because she's heard Wayland has been dancing attendance upon Annalee and fears that he won't come up to scratch where she is concerned," Kitty mumbled.

Their mother gasped. "Kitty! You should not speak so disparagingly of the duke's daughter."

This time Wayland's sister was wise enough to draw her fingers close, sparing her knuckles a second thrashing. "Oh, hush. It's the truth."

"Yes, well, even if that is, then it would be commendable for the lady to be watching after her future husband's activities and guarding herself against the interference of another . . ."

Wayland's body went stiff.

"I for one would rather pluck out my lashes than see Wayland marry Lady Diana," Kitty continued over her mother's horrified gasp.

"Kitty!"

"What? I would. The lady is cold. The last thing Wayland needs is more coldness."

Fire in her eyes, their mother surged forward on her bench, jabbing her fan under Kitty's nose. "A connection through marriage to that *cold* lady, as you refer to her, will be what saves you in Polite Society, Kitty

Smith. They may be hesitant to join you now, but when your brother weds His Grace's daughter, then your path will be smoothed, as will all of ours." With every word she spoke, their mother's voice climbed in a rare lapse in self-control from a woman who went through every day desperately fashioning herself as a proper lady. "So just hold those insolent words inside your head and be grateful that, for whatever reason, they've graced us with their approval, and that your brother will do the right thing and marry Lady Diana!" His mother fell back on her bench, her chest heaving, her words ringing in the confines of the carriage, managing to silence even Kitty.

His entire body tense, Wayland scrabbled with his cravat, the fabric choking him, and then he caught his actions reflected in the window-panes, the thorough rumpling he was giving the folds his valet had meticulously made of the silk. He forced his hands to his sides.

The words his mother uttered really weren't all that different from ones she'd spoken so many times over the years. There had been . . . an unspoken understanding between their families that someday Wayland and the lady would marry. Given her tender years at the time of the attack in Manchester, and until recently, he'd not put much thought into a match. The reality of it, however, had been something he'd not entirely shied away from, either. Why, then, should Wayland, of a sudden, be fueled with this . . . restlessness?

Nay, he knew.

The reason for it was because of the sudden resurrection of a lover from the past. Nay, not just a lover, but a woman whom he'd desperately loved, and who'd loved him in return.

And also a woman who'd refused to respond to his notes after that day in Manchester. From that rejection to the life she'd lived afterward, she had indicated it was entirely over.

There'd not really been a closure, however. And mayhap that was what accounted for his mind and soul suddenly balking at the expectations his mother—and society—had for him where Lady Diana was concerned.

He'd do well to remember all of Annalee's rejection, and the lessons from it. No good could truly come from anything between them. And even less good could come in throwing over the relationship he'd fostered between his and Lady Diana's families on nothing more than memories of how wonderful it had once been with Annalee.

Annalee, who, for that matter, didn't even tend to frequent the same events as Wayland, and therefore running into her these past several days, coincidences offered by fate, was playing games with his mind and his memories.

The carriage rolled to a stop outside the stand-alone residence, more manor than townhouse, its size and positioning on Mayfair's streets marking the wealth and power of the family who lived within.

Their driver drew open the door, and Wayland's mother immediately placed her hand out first, always one to lead the way into formal affairs. It had been a role she'd reveled in since their change of circumstances.

Wayland stepped out and held up a palm for Kitty. They continued at a slower pace behind their mother.

"I think it was gallant," Kitty murmured as they started the ascent up the earl and countess's limestone steps.

Wayland gave her a quizzical look.

"What you did for Annalee."

Ah, beating Welles senseless. "Violence isn't an answer," he said gruffly. Or that had been a guiding principle he'd adhered to after the British government had turned their swords and gunfire on the masses.

"Do you regret knocking him out?" she asked as they made their way inside.

He looked her in the eye. "No."

He'd resolved to be proper, and to conduct himself honorably. But he'd quite happily thrash the bounder again on the altar of Westminster

Abbey on Sunday were Wayland to discover him so much as looking sideways at Annalee.

Kitty smiled.

They were shown to the music room, where guests had already assembled and now milled.

Wayland did a sweep of the room, spying Jeremy alongside his betrothed. He tensed. Jeremy, who no doubt had questions, and coward that he was, Wayland had given thanks when the other man had not shown up that morn to discuss . . . Annalee, or what had transpired. Because too many other questions and explanations were owed along with it.

Then the crowd parted, and his gaze landed upon a lone figure off to the fringe of the gathering, close enough to not be seen as standoffish, but still removed as to not truly be part of it. And yet, how could every eye not be upon her? Clad in gold, with her flaxen tresses worn down, hanging loose about her shoulders, she was very much the goddess of beauty herself.

Annalee chewed at her fingernail, a distracted habit she'd had since she was a girl. He couldn't help the smile.

A hopelessly bored-looking Annalee . . . and nervous. Because he knew her gestures of old as sure as he knew the lines upon his palm. That habit of biting at her nails. The slightest bend to her right shoulder in how she postured herself that lent her an uneven stance.

It was an incongruity. Lady Annalee, as she existed now in his mind, was wholly confident, unbothered by opinions from the mere mortals around her.

She passed a stare over the room.

And then their gazes met.

Letting her arm drop, she inclined her head, lifting it the slightest fraction, and several curls bounced at her shoulders, bringing his gaze to her neckline, modest, and yet, Annalee had forever been splendorous in whatever garment kissed her skin.

"If you'll excuse me?" he said distractedly.

"Wayland?" There was a question in his mother's tone. "Wayland?" she repeated. "Get back here this—"

Kitty slid between them, preventing their mother's attempt to block Wayland, and he made his way across the room, pausing occasionally to greet familiar members of Parliament and other gentlemen whom he'd made acquaintances with through his years. None of them really friends.

Only two in the whole room.

Only one at the moment whom he cared to see now.

Even with his mother's lecture and the silent warnings he'd given to himself about Annalee.

He reached her side.

She straightened. "Wayland Smith, Lord Darlington," she said by way of greeting. "You see tales of my corrupting the innocent hold truth, yet you continue to invite scandal . . . again."

By speaking with her.

Wayland dropped a bow. "Conversing in the middle of a musical hosted by your family? I daresay I'll take my chances."

They shared a smile.

"I am surprised to see you," he remarked. And more than a little . . . happy to see her here. A good deal more than was safe, and a great deal more than he was willing to admit to himself.

"Alas, so are my mother and father." She tipped her head ever so faintly in the direction of the countess, conversing with one of her distinguished guests; all the while the evening's hostess paused to watch Annalee. "I fear I've crashed the affair."

He frowned. Crashed the affair? Which suggested . . . Surely not. "You did not receive an invitation?"

"A lady of my reputation?" She snorted. "Certainly not."

Their own daughter. Jeremy's own sister. But then, after what she'd shared about her family cutting her off from her dowry, and turning her out, he shouldn't be surprised . . . and yet . . . In an instant, Wayland proved a liar in all the beliefs he'd held in terms of brutality. He was filled with the sudden urge to do violence once more to the lady's faithless brother. Because goddamn it, a brother was supposed to protect his sister before anyone else. And yet where the hell had the other man been when Annalee's life had fallen apart, and rakes and cads had begun to be her company of choice?

As though you have grounds to pass judgment when you robbed the lady of her innocence without the benefits of matrimony.

Guilt sluiced through him, commingling with his rage.

"I never had an opportunity to thank you," she said softly, pulling him back from a dark place that involved him hunting down all the men who'd ever taken advantage of her . . . and then finishing himself off . . . because he was included in those ranks. "For what you did last night."

Wayland clenched and unclenched his fists. "I didn't do it for thanks. I did it because he deserved it for how he treated you."

A sad little smile played with the corners of her lightly rouged lips. "I do believe you are the only person to have felt that way where I was concerned."

God, how he hated the outcast she'd become. The way in which she was treated . . . by all. Including her own family.

"Why would you come?" he asked, sliding closer.

"And put myself through the joy of my parents' displeasure? I'm on a path to proper, Wayland." She lifted a hand. "I'll not be deterred."

Because of her Mismatch Society.

It bespoke a devotion to the women who were members that she would endure the hell of this room and the unkindness of strangers. She was braver and greater than all the women present, combined.

And it made him wish he might have given her a different answer. If he had been able to.

"You're rumpled," she murmured, shifting so that she was concealed by the back he'd presented to the room. Reaching up, she tenderly adjusted the folds of the cravat he'd ruined on his way here. When she'd finished righting the article, she patted it gently. "There." And there was such an intimacy to those almost casual actions, ones that a devoted wife might have seen to, that a wave of longing spread through him. "You're being summoned," Annalee murmured.

He blinked slowly, and then he followed her stare.

And the magic of the moment was shattered.

From across the room, where his mother stood conversing with the Duke and Duchess of Kipling, she waved a hand impatiently, urging Wayland over. He furrowed his brow deeply. "Where?" He made a show of glancing about. "I'm afraid I do not see her." Lifting his fingers to his forehead, he continued his over-the-top perusal of the music room.

A startled laugh spilled from Annalee, tinkling and clear and bell-like, not the jaded, husky one he'd come to recognize as her feigned humor.

He winked. "She is . . . nothing if not . . . obvious."

"Yes, one might say that." Annalee nudged him slightly with her elbow. "Go."

Yes, he should go. He'd lingered here alone with her certainly long enough to merit looks, particularly following the recent pairing of their names. He hesitated. "Is that what *you* want?"

"Lila and her husband are due to arrive!" Did he imagine there was a forced cheer to that pronouncement? "You should go. I'll be fine. Truly."

And yet as she rushed off, it didn't escape him that not only had she not answered his question . . . she'd also given every indication that she was not fine.

Chapter 19

The night was destined to be miserable.

Not only was she at a musical hosted by her parents, but her brother and his betrothed wouldn't look at Annalee, let alone speak to her.

Lila, who'd been scheduled to attend, still had not arrived.

The only briefly bearable moment had been when Wayland had come to speak.

He'd sought her out, and he'd been willing to stay despite his mother's tangible outrage. He'd also risked the wrath of the powerful Duke and Duchess of Kipling.

Is that what you *want?*

Despite the scandal that had followed his attack on Lord Welles and their being discovered, he'd still come over, and ultimately left the decision as to whether he should stay or go in Annalee's hands.

Given the changes to his demeanor and the way he carried himself, the last thing she'd expected was that he would boldly cross a room and greet her, and offer to defy a duke and duchess for her.

Of course, she'd also not expected he'd ever lose control and beat a man senseless, and certainly not for her. But he'd done that, too.

If she were as selfish as the world believed, she would have asked him to stay.

Instead, she'd sent him on his way, for him . . . and his family.

And now had the pleasure of watching Wayland charm that very innocent, stunningly beautiful diamond.

Ah, this was the misery she'd expected for the night.

"How could you?" her mother clipped out.

And more misery on top of it. At some point the countess had extri-
cated herself from her guests and found time to greet her daughter.

"I'm afraid you'll have to be more specific, Mother," Annalee drawled.

"I specifically told you no, Annalee Elise."

Yes, her own mother had rejected her request to attend a respectable
affair she was hosting. Annalee draped an arm about her mother's shoulders—narrow, almost bony shoulders that tensed. "Ah, in fairness, Mama,
you didn't *tell* me anything. You sent a note."

The countess squirmed and shrugged to be free of her touch. "Do
not be common."

Annalee touched a finger to her chin, and sticking out a foot, she
fashioned her features into a contemplative mask. "Tell me, do you take
familial affection to be as grievous an offense as indulging in spirits and
smoking cheroots?"

Color splashed her mother's high cheekbones. "I do not find you
amusing. Having you about brings nothing but problems for this family."

"Because I'm amusing?"

"Because you cannot help but find yourself in a scandal," she said
on a furious whisper. "You continually bring shame and humiliation to
this family. It wasn't enough that you ruined your brother's betrothal ball.
There is the scandal you dragged Lord Darlington into as well."

It was on the tip of her tongue to point out that she'd in fact not
dragged him into that one. That he'd come hurtling, leaping, and bounding all the way forward himself. But she swallowed the words, ones that
would put any part of what had transpired last evening in Wayland's lap.
Not when he'd defended her.

"Fighting Lord Welles as he did has only set tongues to wagging for
him and his family now. There are those who automatically assume he did

so because he is involved with you, instead of realizing his deep devotion to Jeremy and this family, and now the Duke and Duchess of Kipling have their eyes upon our family, and unfavorably, because they see you as a threat to their families' partnership."

Their families' . . . partnership.

As in Wayland and the Lady Diana.

Her gaze slipped across the room to where he now stood speaking with the lady in question.

It made sense.

The papers had abounded with tales of the heroism of a young man who'd put himself between the angry masses and an overturned carriage, and plucked each beloved member of the duke's family from it and seen them to safety. Now, the girl had grown up, and in properness and decorum, the lady was Wayland's match in every way.

Annalee knew that. She'd also accepted long, long ago that anything and everything of a romantic nature between her and Wayland had died as sure a death as the souls who'd been cut down on the fields of Manchester.

Just then, the young lady rested her fingertips upon Wayland's sleeve and leaned up and close, whispering something into his ear, and Annalee wrenched her stare away from that handsome pair.

"It is not my intention to bring shame or scandal this night," Annalee said, infusing a solemnity into that promise. "I will be a model of propriety." That was, after all, the goal. She crossed an X over her chest. "You have my promise."

Her mother's brows came together. "Why are you so determined to be here?" And then she froze, doing a hurried search of the room. "If you dare say you're intending to meet one of the gentlemen present . . . ," she muttered.

"*Tsk, tsk.* Come, Mother, you know I'd never dare engage in a tryst with one of the staid fellows you've invited."

Except . . . unbidden, her gaze slipped across the room, over to Wayland. Her former lover . . . and love.

Wayland, who was also now thoroughly engrossed in discourse with the dainty, delicate, and undoubtedly innocent Lady Diana.

"You need to leave."

Annalee recoiled. She'd toss her out. Her own mother. Hurt and heartbreak jolted through her. Even as she shouldn't be surprised. Even as she knew her family despised her and was ashamed of her.

Mustering all the pride she could, Annalee tipped her chin up a notch and made her way through the crowded music room, stares following her as she went.

Since Peterloo, Annalee had made many marches of shame—most of them deserved after some scandal she'd caused or improper situation she'd found herself in. But never before had she been set to walking by her own mother. This really was the unkindest cut of them all.

And then, Wayland and his Lady Diana's gazes landed on Annalee.

She smiled at that happy couple and lifted her hand in a wave.

God, she'd faced horrible walks before—sloppy, drunken ones. Ones with cruel insults hurled in the form of jeers as she'd passed, but none of those had ever felt . . . like this.

Perhaps it was because her own mother was behind her ejection.

Or perhaps it was because Wayland was witness to it.

Either way, she'd never found herself more grateful to be free of a room than she was the moment she reached the foyer. The butler, Tanning, her family's oldest servant, stood there in wait with a sad glimmer in his kindly eyes and her cloak in hand.

Ah, so there'd been no chance of her staying. Her mother had always planned to turn her out. "My lady," he murmured as he helped her into the garment.

She climbed her gaze to the balustrade above.

"Her Ladyship has instructed Lady Harlow's governess that the little lady is to remain in her rooms."

Annalee's entire chest hurt.

So she'd not even be permitted to see Harlow this night.

All this had been for naught.

"I, for one, think every event is more festive for your presence, my lady," he whispered. Some inches shorter than herself, his shoulders, stooped with age, made the old servant even smaller. Leaning down, she kissed his cheek.

He immediately blushed.

"I fear I'll scandalize the household and cost you your post if you are discovered with a kiss from the infamous Lady Annalee," she whispered.

He leaned in. "It will have been worth it," he returned in nearly noiseless tones. He winked.

Resisting the urge to break down crying, she patted the old servant affectionately on his lapels.

"Thank you, Tanning," she said, her throat clogged with tears, and stepped outside.

Just down the street, a carriage rolled closer toward Annalee's family's household . . . and Annalee's stomach sank as her gaze landed on the familiar crest—the Duke and Duchess of Wingate.

Annalee bit her lower lip. *Now* her friend would arrive. But then, what right did Annalee have to expect anything from the other woman? Lila had been the one with her that day at Peterloo—because of Annalee. Oh, Lila had been the one to ultimately suggest that visit, but Annalee had planted the seeds, talking about the grand event, enticing her to go, so that Annalee could, in turn, meet Wayland there. And not so very long ago Lila had retreated from the world . . . and just as Wayland had, she'd left Annalee alone, trying to figure out how to navigate the hell of this new existence.

Hurrying down the steps, Annalee headed quickly for her waiting carriage. Not wanting to face the other woman, a person who not so very long ago had praised Annalee for having gotten on so well after Peterloo.

A panicky whimper gurgled up her throat.

How damned laughable that was . . . How bloody wrong Lila had been.

For it had been *Lila* who'd gotten her life in order. Just as Wayland had.

Annalee was the only one still floundering to find her way back.

"Annaleeeee!"

Keep walking.

Keep walking.

It would be all too easy, after all, to pretend she hadn't heard Lila calling. Because goddamn it, Annalee didn't want to see her other friend who'd lived through the hell she had and managed to pull herself up and be an actual person.

Alas, she ground her feet to a stop on the pavement and made herself face Lila.

Lila reached Annalee's side, the lady's husband hanging back.

"Forgive me," Lila said, out of breath, her chest heaving. "Hugh and I were late." A blush filled the other woman's cheeks.

Hugh and I were late . . .

Once, Lila had been the friend whom Annalee had confided nearly everything in. All that had ceased, and those confidences had become even fewer since Lila had put her life in order and fallen in love. "It is fine," Annalee murmured softly. She'd not begrudge the other woman the happiness . . . or connection . . . she'd found. It didn't mean, however, that she could stop herself from envying that lifeline, either. "I was just leaving." Which seemed exceedingly more vital now, when presented with all the reminders of her great failings.

Lila frowned. "Please, do not. I did not mean to leave you in there, all alone. I'm so glad I caught you before you left."

Before she left . . .

Lila reached for Annalee's hand. To lead her back inside?

A little giggle built in her chest, and she held her fingers out of reach. "I didn't leave."

Confusion wreathed her friend's brow as her arm dropped uselessly to her side. "I don't . . . understand?"

She didn't understand. But then, wasn't that the crux of Annalee's whole miserable, pitiable existence? Her patience snapped. "I was thrown out," she cried, her heart racing. "My mother had me shown the door in the middle of it all."

Lila sank back. "Annalee," she whispered. "I am so sorry."

Sorry.

So was Annalee. About so much.

"She wasn't wrong," Annalee stammered. "I am a mess."

"The women in the society adore you," Lila said, taking her hands. "You bring joy to so many."

"I'm an oddity. They admire me because I do things that they don't and shouldn't do." Her voice grew pitched. "But the truth is, Lila," she cried, "I'm *not* okay. I'm not *dealing* with Peterloo well, like you once said . . . like you think. And so if you and the ladies would just stop admiring me for flouting the rules of society, because I'm a bloody mess." She wrenched her hands from Lila's and took off racing for her carriage.

"Annalee!" her friend cried. "Please . . . come back."

Calling up orders to her driver, Annalee allowed a servant to help her inside.

Following Peterloo, there'd been only one place Annalee had been able to go, one person she'd been able to turn to . . . at any time.

And never more had she been in need of that safe space than she was at this moment.

A short while later, her carriage hadn't even rocked to a full stop before Annalee was tossing open the door and jumping down.

Just in time.

Cloak donned, hat upon his head, Lord Willoughby stood on the steps, the door still hanging half-open behind him. "I am headed—"

Marching up the steps, Annalee gripped her longtime friend by the arm and steered him back inside.

"Out," he said under his breath.

"Pipe down, Willoughby," she muttered, storming his household. The moment she was inside, Annalee shrugged out of her cloak.

A strapping footman was immediately there, relieving her of the article.

"I gather I am not going out, then," Willoughby said with a sigh. He gave his head butler a look and then a slight nod.

The servant instantly pushed the door shut behind them.

She'd never been turned away. He'd never turned her away. Ever. And she didn't expect him to now. That was the manner of friend he'd been through the years, and it was the manner of friend she needed, especially now. Following her visit with the latest Mismatch Society member, the perfectly perfect and prim Lady Diana and—had Annalee already said "perfect"? Because that's what the lady *was*. Grinding her teeth, Annalee cut a path through Willoughby's household, heading straightaway to the room she was most familiar with in this posh residence.

The moment she reached the billiards room, Annalee made for the sideboard. She stopped before it, pausing to eye the sparkling, glittering crystal perfection contained upon that smooth mahogany surface. Glorious perfection.

Peeling off her gloves, Annalee tossed them atop the velvet-lined billiards table and turned all her attention back to her drink selection.

Settling upon a bottle of whiskey, she grabbed a glass and poured herself several fingerfuls; the tinkling of crystal touching crystal, and the smooth stream of liquid pouring, had the same soothing effect as a good cheroot.

Or it always had.

Not this time.

Annalee pushed the door shut. "Take off your cloak; you're not going out."

He smirked, his fingers making quick work of the clasp.

"It's not that kind of visit," she snapped.

"Unfortunate that. I've never seen you in such a state, love," he drawled, leaning against the heavy oak panel.

Which was saying a good deal, given he'd seen her in nearly every state, even retching over a chamber pot from a night of too much drink.

"We have a new member."

He gave her a look.

She tossed up her hands, her quick movement sending liquid spilling over the rim of her glass and spattering the floor. "The Mismatch Society. What else would I be talking about?"

"I really have no idea, love." He paused. "And that is problematic."

"No. Yes. No."

He winged a chestnut eyebrow.

Yes, it absolutely was.

"She is perfectly ladylike."

"Who?"

"Lady Diana." Her mouth tightened in the corners in a reflexive scowl.

Willoughby shuddered. "God forbid. I'm well aware of the lady's reputation. With necklines that nearly reach her chin and a properness not even the sternest matrons could muster, she doesn't fit with your usual scandalous members."

God love him for attempting to follow, and yet . . . Annalee bristled. "We're not *all* scandalous. There are the Kearsley sisters, and the Gatelys and Sylvia." She frowned. Come to think of it, aside from the Countess of Waterson, a former courtesan and music hall owner, just she and Valerie had reputations that preceded them.

"So if the lady is not one you wish to have amongst your members, then don't." Willoughby glanced at his timepiece.

"Do you have somewhere to be, Wills?" she snapped.

He immediately dropped the chain. "I wouldn't dream of it, dearest."

Holding out her filled glass, she pointed it in Willoughby's direction. "Do you know the problem with being a lady?"

"I could only begin to guess," he drawled from the other side of the table.

"The expectations. Everyone expects us to be a certain way and behave a certain way. But what is worse, Willoughby," she whispered, "is the ladies who allow themselves to be so changed." As she'd once allowed herself to be. And now she was doing it again . . . for Sylvia, of course. For their membership. But she was changing, and didn't recognize herself. And today had only highlighted . . . no matter how much she did manage to change, she still would never be . . . Lady Diana. "And what is it for?"

"The ladies allow themselves to be changed," he agreed. "Unlike you, love," he said without recrimination. Following Peterloo, he'd been the first friend she'd found. At a club not fit for any lady, it had been Annalee's first foray into the world of sin and wickedness. When a drunken Lord Gravens had attempted to take that which she'd been unwilling to give, Willoughby had been there . . . From that moment on, he'd taken her under his wing and safely opened up that world to her. Over the years, their relationship had been a friendship, but also one that blurred and straddled the line of lovers.

"I wasn't always this way," she said, more to herself. Nay, there'd been a time when she'd been bright-eyed . . . and innocent. Innocent in every way. She'd been that, too.

"I couldn't imagine you any other way than as you are now, Anna."

Willoughby's words should be a compliment, particularly coming from a man who detested innocence even more than Annalee.

Odd, that it should strike a pang in her chest. Because, well, goddamn it, Annalee didn't want to be like the others. She wanted to be her own woman. Not the simpering debutante and the revered lady lords sought to marry. Lords like Darlington, who cared so very much about his title and his reputation, and such a man would countenance a life and a future with only a flawless, biddable, and unsullied-in-every-way lady. One such as Lady Diana.

Annalee tossed back her drink, grimacing at that enormous swallow which burnt her throat.

"What is it, love?"

She started, having failed to hear Willoughby's approach. "Have you come for a diversion?" He lowered his lips to her neck, and Annalee briefly closed her eyes, tilting her head to allow him that access he sought. He brushed a kiss there. How many times had she come here in search of the very distraction he now offered? And yet, even with his breath, hot and brandy-tinged, a sough upon her skin, this wasn't why she'd come. Not this time.

She drew back slightly, eluding his efforts. "Darlington."

Willoughby paused, his mouth still close to her skin. "*Tsk, tsk.* Calling me by the wrong name, love. Even for you, that's bad form."

She grimaced. "No. No. I was . . ." She caught the teasing glimmer in his eyes. "I was speaking about Darlington."

Willoughby straightened. "I assure you, you're looking in the wrong household if you think I'd have Darlington, or anyone like him, here." He chuckled quietly, and Annalee felt the stirrings of annoyance at that jaded condescension.

Why? Why, when she'd silently jeered and mocked Wayland through the years? All the changes he'd undergone from a blacksmith's bold, deter-mined-to-rise-up-and-change-the-world son to a tied-up, proper-in-every-way baron?

Mayhap, however, it had been easier to pass judgment upon him than accept he was all that was good and honorable while she'd made a full descent into sin and sinning.

"What is it, Annalee?"

"I don't like him." *But that isn't altogether true,* a voice taunted. *You like him just fine. You always have.*

"I know that."

He knew that. "You never asked why."

Willoughby shrugged. "It never seemed like my place."

It never seemed like his place.

And she appreciated that. Or she had. He'd never probed too deeply. Not very deeply at all.

Unlike Wayland, who, in this recent time together, had put any number of questions and challenges to Annalee. Wayland, who'd probed and pressed her about how she'd lived, forcing her to think about decisions she'd made, and making her think about whether this was the life she wished for herself.

Of course it was. Of course there was only one life for her, anymore. She'd picked a path, and this was the road she now traveled. But that . . . he'd asked her. That he made her think and challenged her . . . Wasn't that . . . friendship?

It was all so confused. Everything in her mind.

She dug her fingertips into her temples and began to pace. But then, Wayland had always flipped her thoughts and world upside down. "He was the one," she said.

Willoughby stilled.

"At Peterloo," she clarified, even as she turned and caught the unlikely-for-him gravity stamped in his features, and knew he knew. "I was . . ."

"Meeting him," he murmured. "The dashing love of your life."

"The very same," she muttered, her cheeks heating with a blush. And yet, just like in their every dealing, he didn't pass judgment, instead urging her on with his silence. "And he has a fiancée. Or an *almost*-fiancée."

"And this bothers you?" he asked, his tones belonging to one who sought to sort it all out.

"No. Yes." She stopped abruptly and scraped a hand through the curls hanging about her shoulders. "I don't know," she confided.

He pushed away from the table. "Do you know what I believe, Annalee?"

She shook her head. "No." It was part of the reason she'd come. In the hopes that he'd have the answers she most desperately needed sorted out, when she couldn't speak to Valerie or the ladies of the Mismatch.

He stopped before her and glided his knuckles down her cheek and along her chin, bringing her gaze up to his. "I believe he makes you remember a different time. And you see yourself as you once were . . . and the life you might have had."

I will love you until the day I die, Wayland Smith . . . We shall have the most glorious babies . . .

Her throat muscles moved under the memory of that last day that life between her and Wayland had existed as a normal courting relationship, when the possibilities had been endless and the future bright with the dreams she'd carried for them.

Willoughby continued. "But you aren't that girl, and he isn't that man," he said with a bluntness that brought her crashing hard back to earth and reality. "He is a proper bore who, at best, if he'd entertain a future with you, would seek to change you."

She'd had the very same thoughts and opinions about this new version of Wayland. Why, then, did hearing Willoughby speak those words make her want to plant him a facer?

"And Annalee," he said, recalling her to the moment, "that is at best. As you've indicated yourself, he's already set his sights upon the proper miss who will be his bride. And you?" He brought her hands to his mouth, pressing a kiss upon the tops of them, one at a time. "You will only find yourself hurt, and I'd not see you as you once were."

Her gaze caught on the soft fire blazing in the hearth, following those flames as they danced and bobbed.

Lost.

She'd been lost.

Searching for herself.

"Precisely," he murmured, and she started, having failed to realize she'd spoken aloud. "And now, you are found." Willoughby wrapped an arm about her waist and drew her into the vee between his legs in a way he'd held her so many times before this one. "Now, let me give you the release you desperately need," he whispered against her neck. He pressed another kiss there, and she shivered. Her lashes fluttered.

He'd always been able to bring her satisfaction, offer her, as he called it, a distraction, if even for just a brief moment in time.

Just take it . . . Take what he is offering . . .

For soon, her time with Wayland would be at an end; he'd go his way, marrying his perfect Lady Diana, and Annalee would be left . . .

Her mind balked and shied away from imagining what her life would be when he was again gone. Everything would go back to what it had been since Peterloo. And she wanted that. She did . . . didn't she?

She dimly registered Willoughby trailing a path of kisses along the bodice of her dress, and as if she were watching another, she stared down at his bent head . . . wholly unmoved.

Willoughby brought his mouth to hers, and just as their lips would have met, Annalee turned. His kiss fell upon her cheek. "Not this time, Wills."

He stilled, then dropped a kiss atop her forehead. "This is even worse than I feared, love." He patted her on the hip and set her away. "Have a care, Annalee. You're playing with fire where that one's concerned. He'll happily bed you, but he's never going to wed you. And thinking that it might be more is only going to see you brought back to that point you were . . ." When he'd found her.

Broken. And even worse off than she found herself now.

"I know what I'm doing, Wills," she insisted, though she wasn't sure if she sought to convince him or herself.

And for that matter, she wasn't sure she entirely believed the flimsy lie she fed herself, either.

Chapter 20

The Times

The Notorious Lady A's reputation precedes her. So
wicked she was turned out by her own mother and
father, none were surprised to discover her entering,
and then exiting, a certain Lord W's household. What
one is left to wonder is about a certain and seemingly
forgotten Lord D . . .

She'd gone to Lord Willoughby's.

The following morn, Wayland sat at the breakfast table . . . frozen
inside. Numb.

The man was a rake whom Wayland saw on occasion at White's; they
weren't friends. They weren't even acquaintances. Hell, in the rare instances
they were in attendance at the same events, neither of them so much as
acknowledged the other with a bow or inclination of the head.

And mayhap it was because Wayland had known, and read the sprin-
kle of sentences within newspapers, about Annalee and the marquess.
Known that she had given herself to that man in a way that Wayland had
once known her.

Fire licked slowly at his insides, and like a spark, it sizzled through his veins, a furious heat born of the taste of his own jealousy. As potent as any poison, and powerful enough to devour.

With a snarl, Wayland wadded the sheets of the damned gossip rag and hurled it across the breakfast table. The bottom of the page caught the flicker of the candle; the edges of *The Times* immediately curled and then went up in flames.

Much like Wayland's damned mood that morning.

Bloody hell.

He exploded to his feet.

Alas, several of the more quick-footed footmen were already there, tamping out the fire eating up the silk tablecloth.

That was the manner of damned day he was having, one where he'd set his own damned household ablaze.

A certain Lord W who was certainly not Wayland.

Not Wayland.

A *W* belonging to a different name.

All these years, he'd denied feelings of jealousy about whom Annalee took up with. He'd denied any and every feeling. All these years, he'd come across Annalee's name just as he had now in some scandal sheet or another. But he'd forced himself to read on. He'd told himself he didn't care. They and what they'd shared were in the past.

He'd done such an impressive job of lying to himself all these years that he'd actually come to believe it. Until now.

Now, when presented with an image of Annalee . . . entering some bloody bastard's apartments and—

His mind recoiled, his entire body shuddering from the insidious thoughts that intruded.

But it was too late. The vicious tentacles took root and wrapped and twisted their poison, imaginings of her in the throes of passion with another.

A man who, thanks to the goddamned *Times*, wasn't even a stranger, but a very real man with a name and an identity and a blasted face.

And a good-looking one at that.

Wayland slammed his fist down on the table, and his plate jumped. He did care.

There came the frantic rush of footfalls outside the breakfast room. Splendid.

This was exactly what else the day called for—a visit from his mother. She stopped quickly and sniffed the air. "Was there a fire?"

Grabbing his coffee, he took a swallow of that bitter, black brew. "I knocked over a candle," he said tersely. Which wasn't untrue.

Humming happily to herself, his mother set a new, unwrinkled copy of *The Times* beside his setting.

He stared blankly, unblinkingly, at that page.

"There," she paused long enough in her song to say. She pointed to Annalee's name tangled with Lord Willoughby's.

With a gleeful and gross smile, she plopped herself down on the seat a servant drew out for her. "I trust you've seen that already?" she remarked, buttering a piece of toast with a smug smile that, had she been a man, he would have happily wiped from her face. And it was too much to hope that his mother, abreast of all *ton* gossip and knowledge, should be speaking about some other on-dit, one that didn't have to do with the one woman Wayland didn't want to think of in this particular moment.

"I've seen it. Though I hardly know—"

"Oh, hush. Do not take me for a ninny. You know and I know that I am speaking about the reports of Annalee's whereabouts last evening."

Her whereabouts.

After she'd left her parents, she'd gone and . . . visited another gentleman.

And just like that, his mother's words, coupled with those he'd read inked upon *The Times*, painted a picture all over in his mind . . . of Annalee . . . and that bloody Lord Willoughby. Tall and wiry and born a proper gentleman, a man the papers had paired her name with through the years. The two of them twisted in one another's arms as he moved between her legs. Coaxing those breathless little gasps from her—

Nausea roiled.

Wayland tossed back another swallow of coffee.

It proved a mistake. The brew slid down his throat.

I'm going to be sick.

"I've told you to have a care around that lady. It doesn't do for you to be seen with her as you were last night."

"I wasn't with her," he thundered, slamming a fist down upon that damning scandal sheet. "I was conversing with her because she is a damned friend, and because I'll not treat her as a goddamned social pariah when the lady's own parents would do so."

His mother stared wide-eyed at him.

His chest heaving from the force of his fury, Wayland sat back in his chair. He never lost his temper. Good God, what was happening to him?

Oh, you know, a voice taunted. *You know.* These past few days had stirred reminders of feelings he'd carried, and they were running amok, torturing him with what would never be.

Fortunately, an interruption came, cutting into the tense debate with his mother.

A servant came forward with a silver tray and held it out.

Wayland stared at the familiar scrawl.

Splendid. Absolutely splendid.

He grabbed the sheet and broke the seal. Unfolding the note, he read the two concise sentences scrawled upon the page.

> Urgent. I require your presence.
> -Jeremy

Bloody hell.

Wayland came to his feet.

"Where are you going?" his mother called as he started for the doorway.

"I have business to see to," he said, not glancing back.

"Surely, you see that it is as I said . . . She is not for you, Wayland. She is . . . damaged. She is not the girl you knew and played with. She is not the lady you loved."

Blocking out her grating voice, he quickened his strides, calling out for his mount.

He was no more eager to speak with his mother about Annalee, or his relationship with her, than he was to sit there thinking about that.

Jealousy and fury lent his strides an increased frenzy.

He turned the corner and collided straight with his sister.

Kitty cried out; the newspapers in her hands went flying, raining down around the corridor floor.

Cursing, Wayland caught his sister to keep her from falling. "Forgive me," he said on a rush, and waving off the waiting footman who ran over to help, Wayland fell to a knee and proceeded to stack his sister's newspapers.

He gritted his teeth. Though were they really newspapers? It was gossip. Bloody gossip was all it was.

"I am quite fine, dearest brother," Kitty assured, joining him on the floor. Collecting the newspapers from him, she proceeded to tidy her collection. "I trust you read about Annalee."

God help him. Not his sister, too.

"I don't care to talk about it, Kitty." He stood. "If you'll excuse me? I have a meeting."

"Yes, yes." However, Kitty hopped into his path. "It is just I think you should . . . keep an open mind."

Oh, his mind had been opened that morning, all right. With all manner of dark, unwanted, unwelcome thoughts. He gave his head a hard shake.

"So what?" Kitty shrugged. "The lady was spied visiting a gentleman. They are . . . friends. I'm sure. Women can be friends with men."

"They absolutely cannot be," he replied in an instant.

Invariably the friendship became confused; entangled within were romantic sentiments, and then more. He knew that better than anyone. Of course, he couldn't as well say as much to his sister.

Kitty threw up her hands. "Lady Sylvia was friends with the Viscount St. John."

"And they married."

And this wasn't Lady Sylvia or any other damned lady they were speaking about.

It was Annalee.

Annalee, who, following their exchange last evening, had left her family's household to visit another.

Nay, not another. Stop letting your mind shy away from what it was: a man. A rake of the first order. A cad.

His sister touched his sleeve, jerking him back from the silent, tortured hell of his own mind.

"I'm simply saying that just because she visited him does not mean anything untoward happened. And that . . . you should trust her."

Trust her.

He inclined his head. "I—"

"I know. I know." Kitty shoved him lightly. "You have a most important meeting. Off you go, then."

A short ride through Mayfair later, Wayland found himself climbing the Earl and Countess of Kempthorne's steps. The doors were drawn open by a more-somber-than-usual Tanning with a rapidity that indicated this household had been awaiting Wayland's visit. Nay, not visit. A visit suggested an amicable meeting between friends.

That was not what this was about. Not this time.

The moment he entered, a servant came to relieve him of his cloak.

"This way, my lord," Tanning murmured after Wayland had handed over the article. When they reached the billiards room, Tanning announced him.

The moment Wayland entered, the servant immediately rushed off, closing the door quickly, leaving Wayland alone . . . with Annalee's brother.

Oh, God. He knows. The other man had finally deduced all these years later that Wayland had been the one to take Annalee's innocence. That he'd cared about her. That it was why he'd involved himself with Welles.

And yet, even with Tanning having called out Wayland's presence, the other man remained unmoving.

A hip rested on the side of the table, but that was where any hint of casualness ended. His shoulders stooped and his head lowered into the palm of his right hand, Jeremy had the look of a man with demons.

But then, didn't they all?

Wayland cleared his throat. And when there was still no movement from the other man, he made another clearing sound.

Jeremy jerked his head up, blinking slowly.

He looked haggard, his cheeks rough with a day's worth of growth; his bloodshot eyes locked on Wayland, but his stare was sightless, going through his friend.

Wayland had been wrong. He didn't want this meeting. He wasn't ready for it.

His hands forming reflexive fists at his sides, he made a slow walk over to his oldest, longest friend. And aside from Annalee . . . Wayland's only friend. Were he and Annalee friends anymore? They had been. But it was all confused now. She'd been clear in her disdain of him. For him.

Wayland reached his side. "Jeremy," he said quietly.

The other man instantly straightened. "You came."

"Of course I did," he murmured.

This was what the meeting had been called for—Annalee.

"I'll not waste time with it," Jeremy said tiredly, dragging a hand down his stubbled cheek. He let his arm drop. "I've called you here to speak about what transpired at Fitzhugh's."

And there it was. Having known it was coming, and having mentally braced for it, his mind still ceased to function.

"Yet another scandal." Jeremy's face spasmed. "I asked you to help, and because of it, this time she's involved you. I am so sorry that you found yourself dragged into"—he slashed a hand about—"this."

She'd involved him?

"I thought you might reach her"—a pained laugh burst from Jeremy's lips—"never thinking in asking you to help that she would ruin you. I should have expected there was only one outcome where Annalee was concerned."

Ruin him?

Was the other man out of his goddamned mind?

And that increasingly familiar rage that had besieged Wayland since that night reared its head once more, slipping and twisting around inside him, this time for the man before him. "You're apologizing to me?" he demanded. "My God, man, for Welles's affront on your sister," he hissed, "he deserved to be called out and felled with a bullet at dawn."

Jeremy blanched, the color leaching from haggard cheeks. "I . . ."

On the heels of Wayland's charged words, the accusation he'd inadvertently leveled registered too late.

He briefly closed his eyes. "Forgive me. It was not my intention to call you out—"

"But you're right." All the life seemed to drain from Jeremy as he sank once more onto the edge of the table. "I have been a shite brother to her," he whispered, his voice threadbare. "You defended her two evenings ago when I did not. You tarnished your carefully protected reputation with scandal."

And he'd gladly do so all over again—

"You are the best of friends."

This was too much.

The long blade of guilt twisted and wrenched once more.

Unable to look his friend in the eye, Wayland looked past his shoulder to the mustard-colored, velvet curtains that hung from the ceiling to the floor. "I am . . . *not* the friend you think I am," he finally managed to say, uttering those long-overdue words at last.

He felt Jeremy's stare. "I don't . . ." Out of the corner of his eye, he caught the slight movement as his friend shook his head in confusion.

Inhaling air into his lungs, he spoke on a rush. "I . . . loved your sister, Jeremy."

There it was.

He'd said it.

Jeremy stared at him for a long while, then gave him a peculiar look. "Of course you did. We were three peas in a pod, we were." My God, had the other man been this oblivious? Or had he been willingly blind? "She was like a second sister to you, tagging about. I care for your sister in that same—"

"No," Wayland said curtly, determined to disabuse his friend of that erroneous assumption. "Not like that. Like . . ." His tongue grew thick and heavy in his mouth. "Like . . . in a romantic sense."

Silence reigned supreme over their exchange.

Jeremy's lips slackened; his jaw fell. "I . . . oh."

Wayland's heart pounded hard. At last, he'd set that revelation free. "I . . . before Peterloo. We'd spoken of marriage. We were in love. She'd come that day to meet me."

And then it had all fallen apart. His life. Hers. The future they'd imagined for one another.

"I . . ." Annalee's brother scrubbed a hand down the side of his face once more and released a sad sigh. "She was always reckless," he said sadly. "And either way, she is not the girl she was, and . . ." His friend sucked in a shaky breath and shook his head. "Your defense of her brought you scandal."

Disbelief kept Wayland momentarily motionless. That was what he'd say. "I beat him because he deserved it. Because he disrespected your sister." Just as Jeremy should have pulverized every single bastard who'd ever done so. Just as Wayland should have. Just as Wayland wanted to beat Jeremy to a blasted pulp now for his absolute . . . indifference to what Wayland had revealed.

"Either way, Darlington, my parents have reached their limit where Annalee is concerned. They've run out of their last shred of patience." Sadness filled Jeremy's eyes, his gaze distant. "It was inevitable," he murmured, that last part more to himself.

Yes, the earl and countess, with their commitment to social standing, weren't ones who'd tolerated Annalee. Those words she'd shared two nights earlier whispered around his memory.

Even as a grown woman, I've had my dowry withheld, and any monies that were to be mine remain locked away. I'm at the mercy of Lady Sylvia's generosity, and any funds I do have are because of any wagers I've won . . .

All these years, he'd appreciated the Spencer family because they'd accepted him. When most other noble families would have turned up their noses at Wayland for his humble origins, they'd allowed his friendship with Jeremy and then thrown their support behind him when he'd been titled.

Because of the generosity they'd shown him, a blacksmith's son, he'd let himself remain blind to . . . just how much they'd wronged Annalee.

But there were so *many* who had wronged her.

Wayland, Jeremy, her parents . . . They were all guilty.

"I asked you here because the responsibility of speaking to Harlow has been ceded to me," Jeremy said, slashing through his musings.

Harlow. Annalee's like-spirited sister, who wasn't quite a small child, but certainly was many years from being a woman. An age by which family struggles and pain couldn't be kept from her, the way they would have been were she still a babe. Nay, she'd be aware of the gossip.

"Speaking to her about what, exactly?" he asked, straining to follow.

"Annalee's future."

Her future? Warning bells clanged in his brain.

Jeremy frowned. "You're like another brother to Harlow . . . and me." Pain ravaged the other man's features. "And I need help with this, man," he whispered. "I cannot do this alone."

"Can't do what?" he demanded.

"My parents are sending her away."

The other man's quiet pronouncement knocked Wayland back on his heels. They'd shutter her away in the country, stripping her of her choice of remaining in London.

They cut me off . . . because I bring much shaaame to the family name . . . So much shame that they've pleaded with me and threatened to send me away, back to their country house in Ma-Manchester . . . They would send me back to the place of my nightmares . . . just to be free of me.

"My God, man," he said on a furious whisper. "You cannot allow that." To force her back to that place, of all places? Did they love their daughter so little? Did his friend care not at all for the demons Annalee battled? "She will be haunted." More haunted than she was. All those who'd lived through Peterloo had ghosts and demons they battled daily.

"With the life she is living here in London, how she conducts herself, the drinking and the smoking . . . What else can they do?" The strained lines at the corners of Jeremy's eyes and the brittleness of his mouth spoke of a man who'd wrestled with his parents' decision—but ultimately capitulated. "Perhaps had she wed you, she wouldn't be in this . . . situation," Jeremy said tiredly.

"Would you have supported a match between us?" Wayland asked, the curiosity he'd carried all these years bringing him to ask the question he'd always wondered.

And he knew by the way Jeremy's eyes slid away from his, and by the hesitancy in his response, everything he'd always known as a young man desperately in love with Annalee: his suit would have never been accepted. It had been destined to be met with nothing but resistance from her powerfully connected family. Even his best friend.

"I don't know," Annalee's brother said.

Lying to himself, and to Wayland.

Did the other man even know it?

The door exploded open.

And just like that, Wayland found he'd been wrong earlier. There was a meeting worse than one with Jeremy. One with Annalee's young sister.

Harlow stormed inside, her rapier drawn. She shoved the door shut with the bottom of her bare foot and stormed over.

Donning a strained smile, Jeremy straightened and made to greet his youngest sister. "Har—"

"Not one word." She stuck the tip of her rapier against her brother's throat, ending the remainder of his words. "I'm not pleased with you and will decide when you talk." She turned all her thirteen-year-old ire Wayland's way, and he tensed.

Except . . . she smiled, her eyes soft. "You defended her."

"I . . ."

"Annalee," she said, as though there'd been a bevy of other women for whom he'd intervened and the matter required clarifying. Harlow tapped the side of her blade onto his right shoulder. "I knight thee."

"I thought you were more the pirate sort," he said solemnly, and bowed his head to accept that high praise she'd conferred.

"Yes, well, in matters of heroism and heroics, a certain ceremony is required. I reserve the pirate's wrath for"—her features immediately went dark as she swiveled her focus over to an unfortunate Jeremy—"dastards like *youuu*," she seethed.

"Harlow," Jeremy began again.

The girl brought her blade slashing down close to her brother's face in a decisive *X* she wrote in the air. "I've not given you permission to speak. I'm still recognizing Wayland's valor and honor."

Nothing could be further from the truth. The moment he'd really needed to save Annalee had been at Peterloo. It was a failure that could never be forgiven.

Harlow smiled. "Thank you," she said softly, her lower lip trembling, and in that moment, her tender years were on full display.

"I only did what was right, and what she deserved."

Harlow nodded. "She did deserve it. Because she is a good woman who just happens to be surrounded by disloyal kin." She fixed another glare on Jeremy, pointing her rapier at her brother's heart. "What do you want?"

Bringing up a hand slowly, Jeremy guided the tip down. "I thought we might speak."

She folded her arms, her weapon dangling menacingly at her side. "Well? Out with it, then."

"There are . . . concerns about Annalee."

"What kind of concerns?" Harlow asked for the both of them.

Jeremy dropped to a knee. "You know when you caught that fever five years ago?"

She hesitated, and nodded.

"You were sick," Jeremy said. "Well, there are many different types of sick. When you've got an upset stomach, or when you've a fever or—"

Unease tripped along Wayland's spine.

"Would you spare me the child's explanation," Harlow snapped, as impatient as Wayland was to understand just what the other man was on about. "I know what sickness is. Who is sick?" She peered at him a moment. "Is it you?" Not waiting for him to respond, she switched her attention over to Wayland. "Are you? You do have a queer look about you."

"I'm . . . not." Though he did feel close to casting up the contents of his stomach.

"There are . . . sicknesses of the spirit and soul," Jeremy continued in what rang as a scripted explanation he'd run over time and time again until memorized.

That apprehension grew in Wayland's gut. His mind slipping down a path it didn't want. Praying he was wrong.

"Will you just get out with it?" Harlow shouted. "Who is—"

"Annalee."

All the air left Wayland on a swift, noisy exhale.

"Annalee is sick." And with that, Jeremy began speaking quickly, all the words tumbling from his lips. "And she has been making decisions that are not safe, and so Mother and Father—we," he amended, "have made the decision to send her away to a place where she will be cared for."

And there it was.

The cruelest place to ever consider sending her. The one place she didn't wish to be.

"Where is she going?" Harlow whispered.

"Not . . . one of those places," Jeremy said quickly.

Wayland blinked slowly, knocked off course by that response, which was decidedly not "Manchester."

Not one of those places? Surely his friend wasn't saying what . . . Wayland thought he was? That they were thinking of . . . Nay, planning to send Annalee to a goddamned institution? A place where men and women were locked up and stripped of their dignity and beaten and abused, all in the name of reform and—

Wayland squeezed his eyes shut.

I'm going to be sick . . .

Harlow scrunched up her brow. "What places?" When neither gentleman spoke, she looked back and forth between them, ultimately settling on her brother. "What. Places?"

Jeremy buried his face in his hands.

"Perhaps we . . . adjourn," Wayland said tightly, casting a pointed look in the little girl's direction. Because the things he intended to say to the other man about this decision weren't fit for a child. None of this was.

"Who are you to say?" Harlow shot his way. "I have more grounds of being here than you. After all, I'm family."

"Of course you do," he said soothingly, placatingly. What in hell was the other man thinking in allowing the thirteen-year-old girl to attend this discussion?

"Oh, hush. You clearly don't mean that." Folding her arms at her chest, she glared. "This is why Annalee is the way she is," Harlow muttered under her breath, speaking to herself. "Independent and bold and strong. It's because all you men go about trying to cut us out of important discourse."

Jeremy cleared his throat. "In fairness, I was of the opinion you should be here," he pointed out in a moment of cowardice, making that concession which spared him some of the little girl's wrath.

Over the top of Harlow's head, Wayland gave his faithless friend a long look. "Thank you," he mouthed dryly.

"My apologies," Jeremy responded in equally soundless tones.

Not that Wayland much blamed the other man at all. He himself was deathly terrified of Harlow on good days. When her hackles were up . . . ? Best stay clear.

With a sigh, Jeremy rubbed at his temples. "Perhaps we can cease arguing and put our attention where it belongs?"

On Annalee.

And for the first time in all the years that he'd known her, Harlow remained silent and nodded slowly. It was a signal and sign of the young girl's devotion. Suddenly, Jeremy let his arms fall. "Mother and Father are of the opinion that Annalee would best be served . . . living away for a short while."

Lines of confusion puckered Harlow's high brow. "But she already lives someplace else. With Valerie." She frowned and grabbed her brother's arm. "What. Is. This. Place."

"A quiet, lovely place in Lamel Hill for . . . people who are sick."

A quiet, lovely place? Wayland's gut roiled, and bile burnt the back of his throat. With an utterance such as Jeremy's at that moment, there was only one Spencer sibling proving to be mad, and it was decidedly not Annalee or her sister.

Harlow's mouth moved. "But she's not sick," she blurted.

Except there were different forms of sickness. And there could be no doubting or disputing that Annalee's dependency upon drink was in fact a sickness of its own sort.

One a product of him and Peterloo . . . and . . . He squeezed his eyes briefly shut.

"As I said, there are different types of sickness. Perhaps . . . it is best . . . ," Jeremy murmured. "In this . . . one rare instance, Mother and Father are right, and that it would best serve Annalee . . . if even for just a short while . . . if—"

It hit Wayland all at once.

Why, this wasn't a *discussion*. That was why the other man had insisted on Harlow's attendance in a topic difficult for most adults, let alone a girl of thirteen. Jeremy hadn't requested his presence here as a collaborative participant in a discussion about what the earl and countess planned. Rather, Wayland was here to help break the news and be a voice of support for Harlow . . . on a matter that had already been decided.

Oh, God.

"What are you saying?" Harlow demanded, fixing a glare on her brother.

"Just as I said, Harlow. Perhaps it is best if she goes away for a . . . short while."

Silence descended upon the billiards parlor.

"What?" Harlow whispered.

Or mayhap that was Wayland. Perhaps he'd spoken aloud the only response or thought he was capable of, following his friend's pronouncement.

Harlow recoiled. And in that instant, her cheeks pale and her eyes enormously rounded, she was very much a scared child and not the fearless pirate warrior who battled the world.

"It's not fair. And it's not right. You get to do what you want," Harlow cried.

Jeremy tried to speak. "Harlow."

"Where are you sending her?" Harlow pointed the tip of her rapier at her brother's chest.

"It is a hospital."

There it was. Spoken into existence by Jeremy, converting what had just been a horrified fear in Wayland's mind into reality.

Wayland's entire body recoiled; a buzz, like the thousands of bees he and Annalee had inadvertently released from their hive while jumping from that old oak above the river, filled his ears. And then sound became as muffled as when they'd dived under the water, swimming far until his lungs felt close to bursting to be free of those angered insects.

Harlow's little arm quavered and then fell to her side.

While Jeremy attempted to ease Harlow's worrying, the words the other man spoke moved in and out of focus. "Not like other institutions . . . minimal restraints . . . It is run by Quakers, and it is a place where she will be treated with kindness."

"Treated with kindness," Harlow whispered. The rapier slipped from her fingers and clattered to the floor. "Treated with kindness?" she repeated, raising her voice, and she screamed her brother into silence. "You are a monster. You are all monsters. You hate her because she is spirited. You hate her because she lives her life as she pleases. You hate her because of who she is." Grabbing her brother by the shirt, Harlow shoved him with all her might, knocking him down.

And in that moment, the little girl shouting and fighting was Wayland on the inside.

Jeremy shoved himself up onto his elbows and got to his feet. "Harlow, you don't understand—"

"Oh, I may be thirteen, but I understand perfectly. Annalee isn't like other ladies. And Mother and Father hate it. And you're too busy with your fine Lady Sophrona to worry about the sister you should be protecting. You never protected her. You never looked after her." Every word she shouted sent Jeremy recoiling. "You will all send her away because she doesn't act the way every other woman does. But do you know what?"

Seething, the little girl, a veritable tempest, stormed forward. "I don't want her to be like everyone else. I love her for who she is. And you don't. And someday, you and Mother and Father will send me away, too."

Jeremy's face crumpled. "I would never—"

"Wouldn't you?" She cut him off, sneering with a vitriol no girl of her tender years should know. And yet . . . she was right to her resentment. "Aren't you trying to send Annalee away? And someday, when I'm not the proper lady, you'll let our parents send me away, too."

"I wouldn't."

"Excuse me if I don't believe you," she spat, and with a sound of disgust, she headed for the door.

Wayland stood there stiffly. He'd been so very certain there was nowhere in the world worse than Manchester. Every utterance Annalee had spoken, every challenge she'd issued at the Fitzhughs', about her place in this world and lack of security, was actualized in this hideous moment with a cowardly Jeremy. Her family would send her to York, and after that . . . when . . . nay, if she were freed? She'd never recover. Her soul would wither and die, and he couldn't bear it.

"There is another way." Before he could talk himself out of it, Wayland called out, his voice hoarse. He wouldn't.

That brought Harlow to a jarring halt. She whipped around, facing him with such hope that it reached all the way across the room.

"I will court her," Wayland said to the room at large, breathing his idea aloud.

It made sense. This was the only way.

Harlow ventured over with a tentativeness that bespoke a fear of believing too hard that her sister had been saved.

"What are you saying?" Jeremy asked.

He'd been the reason she was at Peterloo. He'd been the reason her life had fallen apart after that fateful day. And yet . . . this time . . . it was different. What was at stake was Annalee's freedom . . . and her future. To shut her away would be to put her through a different kind of death. And she'd suffered so much already. "I'm saying . . . I was with her last night. My name has been linked to hers, and . . . a courtship can kill that gossip." And he would also be providing Annalee with precisely the favor she'd put to him. Only now, its purpose proved . . . twofold.

"But—"

Wayland glared the other man into silence. "What the hell would you do? Send her to a bloody institution?"

All the color bled from Jeremy's cheeks. Good, let the bastard feel guilty. Wayland had made enough mistakes where Annalee was concerned. He'd be damned if he'd sit idle and allow her family to silence her, punishing her and hurting her in a way that she could likely never recover from.

"If she'll allow me to court her, I will." He glanced between the pair. "And none of this is spoken beyond us three. Is that clear? If it is, then all of this is for naught, and the earl and countess will succeed in . . . in . . ." Wayland couldn't get the rest of that out past the fear and horror of it clogging his throat.

Brother and sister exchanged a look, and then Jeremy nodded.

"You are a hero, Wayland," Harlow whispered, and then going up on tiptoe, she pressed a kiss upon his cheek. "I was right to have knighted you."

A hero.

It was the last thing he'd ever been where Annalee was concerned.

But mayhap, in this, this time, he could make it right.

Chapter 21

That morning, following his meeting with Jeremy and Harlow, one matter took importance above all others: making himself seen.

As someone who'd sought to avoid and steer clear of scrutiny, it was a new way to find himself . . . and singularly miserable.

Wayland's first order of business had been to go to one of the most famous, and even more importantly, the most frequented, hothouses in London, and now with a ridiculously large—and also deliberately eye-catching—bouquet of fuchsia and pale-pink peonies in hand, he descended the steps of his crested carriage and marched a deliberately slow path up the steps of the infamous Waverton residence.

He was no hero, as Harlow had called him that morn.

But he was determined to help Annalee out of this mess she found herself in, in some part because of his violent outburst at the Duke of Fitzhugh's ball.

Cresting the stairs, Wayland looped the velvet-tied flowers behind his back, putting them on display for the passersby, and raising his spare hand, he collected the ring and brought it down hard.

He was going to make this right . . . for Annalee.

He'd never be absolved of his sins that day in Manchester, but he could spare her this pain her family would inflict upon her.

Puzzling his brow, he stared at the pretty painted pale-green door.

That was, if a servant bothered to open the door and he had the opportunity to put his suit to Annalee.

At last, footfalls fell on the other side of the panels, and Wayland straightened.

"I'm coming. I'm coming," an impatience-filled voice called out.

The doors were jerked open, and the most unconventional of servants glared back. Tall as Wayland's six feet, and as broad of shoulder, he fit more with the laborers Wayland had grown up alongside, and Wayland himself, than with the usual scrawny fellows stuffed into grand uniforms and wigs propped atop their heads.

The man gave him an annoyed once-over. "Which one are you?"

Which one? Which meant . . . Annalee was accustomed to fielding suitors, and for a minute his pretense in being here, the real role he played at pretending, was forgotten by the rush of jealousy for—

"Well?" the butler demanded, taking a step forward. "Which daughter or sister are you trying to claim?" And then, with a menacing slowness, the servant locked his fingers together and cracked his knuckles.

"Daughter or sister?" Wayland repeated back slowly. And then it occurred to him . . . The man wasn't speaking of men who'd come here in pursuit of Annalee, but rather of the outraged papas and other protectors who'd come to claim their daughters from attending her society.

"Uh . . . neither?"

"*That's* the correct answer." The butler grunted. "I thought so." He made to close the door in Wayland's face.

Oh, bloody hell. Wayland reflexively shot out the hand with Annalee's flowers, the enormous bouquet preventing that panel from closing, but also subsequently suffering the beheading of three of those blooms and badly rumpling the others.

"Now, see here," he began firmly.

"Are you looking to threaten me?" And by the gleeful relish there in the bulky butler's eyes and voice, he was decidedly hoping the answer was in the affirmative.

"Of course not," Wayland said, calling for calm to defuse a situation that was rapidly getting away from him. "I'm here to call on Lady Annalee."

There was such a long break in silence, with only the rattle of passing carriages and the clip-clop of horses' feet, that Wayland suspected the older man may have not heard him. He tried again. "I am here to see—"

The butler found his voice. "I heard you," he snapped. "The lady ain't receiving. Not of the gentleman sort. Not of *any* of the man sort." And this time, Annalee's loyal servant slammed the door shut so hard it shook the frame.

There came the slight *thwack* of a lock falling, and just like that, Wayland found himself barred entry, standing there with nothing but one empty hand, the other holding an increasingly tired-looking bunch of peonies.

Glancing down at the forlorn heads chopped off by Annalee's front door, he muttered a curse under his breath.

Well, this wasn't going to plan. This wasn't going to plan at all. Wayland was to arrive and be shown to a formal parlor, and she was to come down immediately. At no point in how he'd played this out in his mind had it gone the way of him being barred entry and denied the right to see her.

And now, here he stood . . . with no access to Annalee . . .

Feeling gazes upon him, Wayland glanced over his shoulder . . .

At some point an audience had assembled to watch the show that Wayland had found himself putting on for their benefit.

But there was the attention from members of the *ton* that he'd managed to gather himself that morning. In fairness, that was one thing that had gone to plan about all this.

People had noted his arrival with flowers, and as such, some of the day's goals had been achieved.

The most important piece of this whole charade, however, the one that would ultimately spare Annalee from a fate she didn't deserve, was speaking to the lady herself.

Firming his jaw, he took a step forward and pounded again on the panel. Any other time, he would have appreciated that Annalee had a butler who scared off male visitors. But he'd be damned if he was turned out. Not with what her brother had revealed to Wayland that morning.

Alas, after three solid minutes of knocking—as confirmed by his timepiece—it became clear there'd be no entry.

Not through the front door anyway . . .

Christ in hell. He'd have to become one of the criminal sorts, then. Finding a different entry. Wayland had started down the steps when, suddenly, there came the scrape of the latch lifting, and the door opened a fraction A birdlike woman ducked her head out, her white hair frazzled, her buglike eyes round. "You there," she called, and Wayland immediately came bounding up, taking the stairs two at a time.

"Yes," he said quickly.

She jabbed a finger through the opening and wagged it in warning. "Don't think to break in, or I'll clout ye good."

"I wouldn't dream of it," he hurried to assure her. He lied. If it meant sparing Annalee from what her family sought to do, he'd do it. Scandal be damned. Broken promises to this woman or anyone be damned.

The servant's gaze went to his flowers and then back to Wayland. She glanced over her shoulder. "You looking for Her Ladyship?" she asked on a loud whisper.

"I am," he said calmly.

"Are your intentions honorable or not?" she asked, peppering him with questions.

He bowed his head. "The most honorable."

Her eyes immediately narrowed, suspicion blazing from within the tiny pinpricks they'd formed. "Don't trust the honorable sorts. They're always coming in here with their fancy speech and stately manners, and causing nothing but trouble for the ladies here."

Wayland mentally filed that revealing bit away. "I am a . . . friend of Annalee's?"

The old woman angled her head, eyeing him with a new interest. "Never 'eard of you before," she said, her voice slipping between Cockney and a proper King's English. "And just because you used to be friends before doesn't mean your intentions are good now."

Ironically, what the old servant couldn't know was that he'd been driven to this doorstep, and this moment, by only good intentions.

It had been everything else that had come before this moment where Annalee was concerned which had proven dishonorable.

"I'm a friend still," he said quietly, and . . . he was. He realized that the bond between them hadn't been broken by the divide Peterloo and time apart had wrought. That, to Annalee's question of just this: Were they friends? They had been and always would be.

The servant peered closer. She must have seen something there in the sincerity of what he spoke. "You're not looking to shut the misses' society down?" she finally asked, revealing the first hints of wavering.

Wayland raised the bouquet in his hands, touching it to his chest. "I wouldn't dream of it."

"Wouldn't be able to do it if you wanted to anyway," she snapped. "Other men have tried. They've all failed."

And with Annalee's spirit and strength and courage, those men had been destined for defeat. Admiration filled him. "I don't doubt it," he said, a wistful smile on his lips. She'd gone and taken on the most powerful peers of Polite Society, and Wayland, who'd once attempted that very thing, was left admiring Annalee for having remained committed to challenging the ways of the world. When he himself had so failed. And he'd be damned if her family locked her away. Wayland moved his face close to the opening. "Will you help me speak to her? I believe she will not turn me away."

"No gentlemen allowed," she said gruffly, and his hope for this woman being his entry in to Annalee flagged, but was quickly raised once more by her next words. "But if you *were* looking to speak to the lady, you might find your way around the back to the ladies' gardens."

Relief zipped through him as, with that most important of offerings, she shut the door in his face.

Grinning, and flowers in hand, Wayland bounded down the steps and made his way along the side of the residence, following the gated, graveled path that emptied out to a . . . He skidded to a halt, his boots kicking up pebbles, as he stared up at the ivy-covered wall. A veritable fortress suited for a medieval manor surrounded what he presumed were the gardens . . . and the back entry.

Stepping back several feet, Wayland rested his hands on his hips, leaving the bouquet to dangle at his side as he considered his path forward.

You've changed . . .

And yes, she'd been right.

Wayland, however, had been given to scaling trees and even trellises and walls to see her.

With that in mind, he stuffed the flowers he'd brought between his teeth. Several pink petals fell down around his feet. He assessed the thick swath of English ivy climbing along Annalee's wall, eyeing the thickest, densest patch of the plant.

Experimentally testing, he fished around the leaves, searching for the bricks underneath and footholds within.

And with a quiet sigh and a long prayer, Wayland proceeded to climb.

It had been years since he'd done so.

He'd once been rather good at it.

Particularly as, invariably, on the other side of whatever structure he'd been scaling, there'd been Annalee, who would have been awaiting him. This time was no different.

A branch broke under his foot, and he cursed around a mouthful of flowers as his leg slid out from under him.

He was too old for this.

And big.

He'd always been big, but he'd grown even more through the years in height and stone to make entry by climbing—hell, entry by anything other than a respectable door—not only folly but also a dangerous one at that.

At last, he neared the top. He made the mistake of glancing back.

Ten feet were between him and the ground. He'd no doubt survive it, but he certainly didn't want the pain that came with a tumble such as this one.

Catching the edge of the wall, he used all his effort and muscles and energy as, with a grunt, he heaved himself up and shimmied onto his stomach.

Out of breath from his efforts, Wayland paused at that two-foot-wide purchase he found and readjusted the flowers in his teeth. And clasping the edge, he lowered himself.

"Intruder!" someone cried.

Something hit him square in the back.

At that unexpected shout, his grip slackened, and the ground rushed up to meet him.

Oh, Christ.

He closed his eyes, and instead of tensing, he forced himself to relax, and rolled slightly.

Even so, when he landed on his back, all the air was knocked out of him.

"Have we killed him?" That voice, decidedly not Annalee's, sounded entirely too gleeful at the prospect.

"No. No," came another. "See, his chest is moving."

His chest was moving, but his entire body hurt. He'd underestimated how activities which had come so easily, and actions—like a fall—that had once resulted in barely the blinking of an eye, now came harder and hurt like the very devil. Wayland couldn't help it.

He felt a large shadow move over him. "Oh, yes. He is alive." And once more, this youngish voice, belonging to a different lady, contained the greatest disappointment . . . at his being alive.

Wayland opened his eyes. Alas, the hothouse flowers, having landed directly on his face, offered nothing beyond an eyeful of pale pink and fuchsia, silken-soft flowers. Fighting back a groan of misery, he reached up, removed the flowers, and then pushed to his feet.

A group of women formed a line across from him, all ten of them wearing identical expressions of suspicion and fury.

Wayland swallowed hard.

He'd scaled the wrong wall. There was nothing else for it.

Wayland lifted his hand in greeting, and as one, his audience looked to his sorry flowers. Along the way he'd lost another six heads of the peonies, leaving him holding a bouquet of more bare stems. "Uh, hullo?" he greeted dumbly.

And interestingly, a polite hello proved the wrong thing to say.

There came a flurry of cries, more like war whoops of all their cries and shouts rolling together, with only the periodic word peppered through making sense.

And none of them proving good . . .

"Intruder . . ."

"Finish him off . . ."

Cursing, Wayland hurriedly backed away, making for the same wall he'd just tumbled from. And like soldiers in the midst of rushing into battle, they converged upon him.

"Wait!" That cry, piercing through the melee, was a familiar voice, sparing him from being finished off by a bloodthirsty mob of young ladies in mostly white skirts. "That isn't an intruder!" The group parted and his sister stepped through. She cleared her throat. "That is . . . my brother."

Ah, so this was the Mismatch Society. Whenever Wayland had read of Annalee's organization, he'd assumed society's concern and disapproval of it had stemmed from reasons related to the unconventionality of it—daughters of the *ton* assembling to discuss societal norms they wished to break.

In this moment, with bloodlust still brimming from their eyes and the pugnacious stance they'd all assumed, the group, feared by men of all ages, of all ranks amongst the peerage, should be feared for many, many reasons.

"Your . . . brother?" one of the ladies asked hesitantly, breaking the silence.

"I . . . am afraid so," Kitty announced, and moved out from the line of ladies and over to Wayland's side with a reluctance he didn't believe for one moment he'd imagined.

"Another one of those sorts," someone muttered.

"At least he's brought flowers?" a lady piped in.

"I . . . Are we sure they are flowers?" a third lady ventured.

"They are flowers," that familiar voice hissed. Lady Diana.

Bloody splendid. Yes, well, there'd been no way around this.

The group immediately glanced at the offering, and Wayland followed their stares to the forlorn bouquet forgotten until now on the ground.

"They don't look like much of a bouquet," Miss Isla Gately muttered.

The dark-haired girl wasn't wrong in this instant. At this point, one couldn't be certain about the sad stems tied with a blue velvet ribbon.

"Who needs flowers when he is here to remove Kitty from the society?" That hissed query immediately brought a sea of angry stares back his way.

Oh, bloody hell. "I'm not—"

And then intervention came a second time. "What is going on here?"

Oh, thank God.

The line of ladies parted like that infamous sea, and the very clear leader of their ranks swept forward, the queen she was. And for a second time that day, it was like falling all over again and having the air knocked out of him.

Annalee stopped before him. Clad in tight-fitting breeches and a lawn shirt that had been drawn snugly behind her so that the fabric molded to her, she was a veritable Aphrodite.

He felt more than saw every set of eyes swiveling between him and Annalee. Wayland, however, was hopeless to remove his gaze from hers . . . She stopped three paces away, coming up short. "You," she said softly, and with her ocean-blue eyes forming circles, she embodied every aspect of that goddess of legends.

Except he made the mistake of slipping his stare lower and over her. She was all lush curves, accentuated and on display, and they made it impossible for him to form anything beyond one single-syllable utterance. "Me." His mouth went dry and hunger filled him.

God, she was magnificent. But then she could have donned an empty oak sack and been nothing less than the goddess she'd always been, captivating mere mortals.

"What's the problem, Kitty's brother?" another of the Kearsley girls snapped. "Never seen a woman in trousers?" she demanded, thankfully mistaking the reason all the words and thoughts had been knocked square outside his head.

Annalee had donned breeches many times through the years, more often than not pairs which he'd fetched for her. But never, never like this.

Kitty shot an elbow into his side, effectively jolting him back to the moment. "Do not ruin this for me, brother," she whispered under her breath. "Any more than you already have, that is."

He cleared his throat, and assessing the dynamics of this eclectic gathering of women, he opted to speak to the group at large. "Forgive my . . . er . . . entrance?"

He felt Lady Diana's stare burning a hole in him. There was, however, no helping this. He'd speak to her . . . later.

Annalee . . . She came first.

Wayland slid his focus back to Annalee. "I was hoping to speak with Lady Annalee?" He murmured that last part in quiet tones meant for only her.

She frowned. "About what?"

Wayland sent a prayer upward in a bid for patience. She'd not make this easy. He took a step closer. "About . . . a matter of import."

It proved the wrong thing to say. That army of girls moved as one, like a wave rolling forward as they converged around Annalee, forming a menacing line.

"You're here to take Kitty," one of the Kearsley sisters snapped, making devil's horns with her fingers and waving them his way.

"I—" Could not get a word in edgewise.

"Just like all the others . . ."

"Except for the flowers . . ."

Bzzzzz . . .

Their fury and grievances hummed like so many bees.

Wayland blinked slowly.

No, wait a minute . . . that really was a bee . . . He glanced down at a pair of bumblebees circling the last handful of flowers in the bouquet he'd brought. A third bee circled around him, and he swatted it away. "You misunderstand," he said to the group at large.

And Annalee, with the twinkling in her always animated eyes and the dimple made by her devilish smile, was enjoying this.

"They really are misunderstanding the reason for my being here," he called loudly over the din for Annalee's benefit.

She folded her arms. "Are they?"

She was right to her suspicions. He'd been nothing short of blunt to the point of rudeness in sharing his opinions about the Mismatch Society. And as a result, the lady was showing no mercy.

Wayland turned back to her devotees. "I'm not here for Kitty," he shouted over the noise of their chattering, frustration bringing that admission from him. "I'm here to court Lady Annalee." And to accentuate that point, he bent and swiped up the flowers. Too quickly.

A bee stung him for his efforts, pulling a sharp curse from him.

That *was* how this day was shaping up to be.

Silence fell hard and fast, and he'd wager every last pence and property he'd received from the king, and his reputation itself, that this was the first this particular gaggle of ladies had been so effectively quieted.

When still no one spoke and he was left with the awkwardness of more than a dozen eyes all locked on him, he repeated for a second time, "I'm here to court Annalee." He displayed the peonies. What remained of them.

A petal rained sadly down from the bunch, landing atop the tip of his black boot.

These *were*, however, women, he thought, and all women were at least a little bit romantic and were certainly hard-pressed not to sigh somewhat over a suitor who'd scaled a wall, bearing flowers.

Alas, he was reminded all over again that he knew less than nothing where the fairer sex was concerned.

"What kind of suitor arrives with beheaded flowers?" someone whispered from the crowd. "I think it's a threat."

Oh, for the love of God. "It is not a threat," he said, running his free hand down over his face, and through his fingers, he caught Annalee's widening smile. "You're enjoying this," he muttered.

Annalee leaned in, wafting that fragrant rose scent, filling his nostrils and flooding his senses. "Oh, immensely." She winked.

"And furthermore, he cursed at her. Cursed. That is hardly the intentions of a suitor."

Finding no safe harbor in Annalee, he glanced to his sister, Kitty, who at some point had edged away from him and started her return to the bloodthirsty lot. She immediately stopped her retreat. "Will you tell them?"

"They're not wrong, Wayland. If you're here courting, cursing hardly seems the stuff of romance."

Murmurs of assent rolled around the gardens, and he, who'd been praised by society for his respect of propriety and decorum, reached the outer limits and breaking point of his patience. "Because I'm here with honorable intentions."

"Heard that before," a lady in the masses mumbled.

"Do you know what happened to the peonies?" he called, with not a single person present giving an indication that they cared. He gritted his teeth and told them anyway. "The butler beheaded them. Because I tried to make my way through the front door. But alas, I'm a menace. Me, a gentleman with flowers and"—Wayland shot the hand holding the bouquet out toward them—"I got stung by a damned bee and—"

"And he's yelling." A stranger-to-him lady clucked her tongue like a chicken.

"And cursing again," his sister added.

It was official. He was going to lose his damned mind if he stayed here one moment longer.

At last, Annalee took mercy on him and his soul.

She clapped once. "Ladies, if you'll excuse me. There's nothing ornerier than a wounded man."

The group sniggered. His sister included.

The traitor.

"I'm not—" His finger *was* beginning to swell. Except . . . His mind raced. "Er . . . yes, that is . . . that is it, exactly. I am not my usual self because of my grave injury."

Annalee inclined her head. "Ladies, please resume our lessons without me while I save Lord Darlington's life."

With that, she crooked two fingers, indicating he was to follow.

And at last, he was in.

Chapter 22

Annalee and Wayland didn't talk the length of the walk from the gardens to her offices.

In all the years that she'd known Wayland Smith, it was the first silence that had ever existed between them.

And yet, also for the first time, Annalee, who was always ready with a quip and a witty word, found herself . . . speechless.

He'd . . . come here . . . ? For her?

Nay, more specifically . . . to court her?

That didn't make sense. But then, nothing about coming into her gardens and finding the always proper Wayland sprawled on his arse from a fall he'd suffered scaling her wall did.

Had he been Wayland of old, then, yes, nothing about this day would have been unexpected . . . But Wayland, who valued his reputation and his place in Polite Society above all else, was the last man she'd have thought to sneak onto her property.

Except, this *new* Wayland had also bloodied to a pulp Lord Welles, making himself a scandal . . . for Annalee. Because of Annalee.

The same guilt that had dogged her since the Fitzhugh ball reared its head. Mayhap his appearance, and the intentions he had stated, did make sense, after all. Wayland would worry about his reputation and hers—not that there was much left to worry after where hers was concerned—and he'd come to do the right thing.

At last, they arrived at the rooms she'd chosen for her offices, a brightly lit floral chamber that embodied gardens even more than the grounds she and Wayland had just vacated.

The butler, Terrence, stood as a sentry, cracking his knuckles and glaring at Wayland. "Snuck in, did he?"

"Worry not," Annalee said, patting the devoted former fighter's arm. "He was punished, and mightily, by the affront, suffering quite the injury. A fall and a beesting."

Terrence chuckled.

"If you would have a servant bring cold water, some of my tobacco, and a needle?"

The servant nodded, and with a swift bow, he ambled off . . . leaving Annalee and Wayland alone.

Alone.

After . . . everything that had transpired last evening.

Funny that, since Peterloo, she'd lived for sin and scandal and made few apologies for any of it. But being here, with this man who valued his reputation and had worked so hard to rise above the low opinions the world carried about him because of his birthright, she found herself . . . lost . . . to the regret that had riddled her since his rescue. She felt as nervous as she had the moment of her sixteenth birthday when they'd both acknowledged their friendship had been altered by feelings they had, and known from that instant on that everything would be irrevocably changed.

Wayland rocked back and forth on the balls of his feet before coming to a stop. "It was not my intention to force my way inside."

"No, that does not seem to be your preferred mode of arriving at a person's residence." She infused a mock solemnity into her response, grateful to him for speaking first.

An adorable blush climbed his cheeks.

"I see your skill set with scaling walls has not been lost with time," she said softly.

"Alas, my final descent was far below my usual prowess."

They shared a smile, and it felt so very good. After the horror of her latest scandal, and the gossip following it, to find this plane of . . . comfortable ease.

It lasted no more than a moment.

He passed the flowers back and forth between his hands in a distracted and agitated way before stopping himself and extending them for Annalee.

She hesitated, then took them; their fingers brushed, both naked, and the heat sparked electric, tingling at the touch of his skin upon hers. Trembling, Annalee reflexively drew the flowers close and inhaled a scent from . . . what remained of the flowers.

Not just any flowers, either, but the peonies which she'd told him long ago were her favorite. Nay, there was no mere coincidence in that flower selection.

Her heart knocked against her rib cage. He'd been the first man to give her blooms, those he'd picked himself in the fields of Manchester. And he'd also been the last. There'd never been a respectable gentleman to visit. There'd never been a serious suitor.

"They were in far better shape when I set out this morning," he explained. "I purchased them all with heads."

She was certain there were any number of teasing rejoinders she could make. And yet . . . in this moment, every single witty response eluded her.

Annalee was saved when the door opened and a young maid appeared, bearing a tray filled with the items she had requested.

Crossing to the table that held them, Annalee called Wayland over. "Please sit, Lord Darlington."

Wayland joined her, but then paused, eyeing the eclectic mix dubiously. "Should I be nervous?"

"With me, Wayland?" She leaned in, bringing her lips up close to his, so close she heard his slight intake of air, and the sough of his mint-and-chocolate-tinged breath upon her flesh, tempting her with a taste of sweets, and she wanted to taste him more than any of the most delectable confectionaries. "Always," she whispered.

He gulped, and with a little laugh, breathless from the desire she'd inadvertently roused with their nearness, Annalee fell back on her heels. She motioned to the Chippendale camelback sofa. "Now, sit," she ordered, and he promptly fell into the seat.

Joining him, she perched herself on the edge, and setting down her flowers, she reached for a fingerful of tobacco.

He leaned in, examined the items she'd called for . . . and then turned a confused stare back to Annalee. "Are you . . . smoking?"

"I wouldn't dream of so scandalizing you. Furthermore"—with her spare fingers, Annalee plucked a rolled cheroot from within the deep vee of her shirt and held it up—"I come with my tobacco ready for smoking." She tossed down the scrap. "Now, take off your jacket and roll up your sleeves, Wayland."

"What?" he whispered furiously, so endearing in his shock that a smile pulled at her lips.

"You needn't worry too much . . . I didn't tell you to take off all your garments." She pinched the fabric of his sleeve. "Just remove your jacket. I'll also need you to roll up the sleeves of your shirt."

Wayland stole a frantic glance at the closed door.

"Oh, come, Wayland. I am merely tending your beesting, Lord Darlington."

He hesitated.

He really had become . . . laced-up. Odd how shows of such propriety in other gentlemen would have set her eyes to rolling and her annoyance up. Everything with this man, all her feelings for him, had forever been different. Even in these ways in which he'd changed, she found him . . . endearing.

"Wayland, your hand is swollen," she said gently. "And by the redness, it's deuced uncomfortable and painful, and it will remain so until I remove the stinger and release the venom."

With that, he freed the buttons of his jacket, and despite herself, she followed Wayland's every movement. Then he shrugged out of the article, tossing it down over the back of the sofa. He proceeded to shove up his lawn sleeves, revealing arms corded with muscles and sprinkled with a light dusting of dark hair.

Oh, God.

When she'd stated her intentions to care for him, she'd been serious.

She'd not set out to seduce him. Not this time.

She really had intended only to worry after his wound . . . but that had been . . . before. When he'd been fully buttoned up.

Now, with his broad shoulders on display and his biceps rippling, she found herself lost in the sight of him and the memories of how very good it always was between them.

She really was the wanton the world accused her of being. And God forgive her, she had no regrets in that instant. Aside from one . . . that she couldn't climb atop his lap as she used to and ride him until—

"Have you done it before?"

"Oh, yes," she whispered huskily. So many times. But it had always been best with him. She'd lost track of how many times she'd straddled Wayland and freed him from his breeches and pressed herself down until he'd filled her deep. So very deep.

She moaned softly, desire instantly flooding her center.

At his confused look, she fought through the fog of desire. "Yes," she exclaimed quickly. "When I first moved in, Harlow snuck here to visit and suffered such a sting."

When she'd escorted her younger sibling home to their parents, Annalee had fielded just more upset from her mother, about being wholly unable to properly love their family, or look after her sister.

And she hated that sobering reminder of the failure her family—and the world—saw her as. Was there a swifter executioner of desire than thoughts of one's hate-filled mother?

"Now let me see it, Wayland," she said impatiently.

He hesitated another moment, then proffered his hand.

Annalee immediately set to work, dunking a rag in the freezing-cold water; she wrung it out, and then pressed it to the top of his hand. As she tended him, she felt his eyes on her bent head. His gaze had always been compelling, his stare one that moved through her like a physical touch. Trembling slightly, she pressed down too hard on the place he'd been stung.

Wayland flinched. "Are you enjoying this?"

"I've been accused of much, but never bloodthirsty."

"Given the showing from that crowd of ladies, that is doubtful," he said dryly. "Ouch."

Annalee batted her lashes. "Did I prick you too hard, my lord?"

"Minx."

Annalee winked, then resumed drawing back the skin to remove the stinger still stuck there.

"What were you and your membership doing out there?"

She searched for a trace of judgment in his tone but found only curiosity, and for that reason alone, she was compelled to explain what her society had been engaged in, when as a rule, she and the members didn't speak to any man about what they did and why they did it. "Today, we were focusing on self-defense."

"And that is something you are familiar with?" he asked quietly.

"Lila is married to the Duke of Wingate," she said. "As you're no doubt aware, the duke was a former prizefighter. Lila had the idea after . . . after . . ." She bit the inside of her cheek, hating that she'd let that dark day into this moment.

But then, everything ultimately circled back to Peterloo. Everything she'd become, and every action she'd committed prior to that August day, converged.

"Peterloo."

"I kept mentioning the excitement coming to Manchester. I convinced her it would be exciting," she murmured, her gaze fixed on the smooth waters contained within the porcelain bowl. "And afterward, she became a recluse. She found her way out by . . . seeking to learn the skills necessary to disarm someone, should she find herself as she did that day." Taking in a silent breath through her teeth, Annalee forced a casual shrug she did not feel. "And given the precarious way women find themselves so often, it only seemed wise that we provide our membership with the skills necessary to see themselves safe."

She braced for his judgment.

She didn't anticipate the quiet understanding which came next from him. "I think there couldn't be a more valuable lesson to school your members on."

Annalee's head came flying up. "You . . . don't?"

"I'm attempting to live a life free of scandal," he said with a small and pointed smile. "I'm not attempting to see my sister or other women oppressed." Which was what most every other man wished for.

Annalee hurriedly diverted her attention back to the task of caring for his hand. His response showed traces and shades of Wayland of old, who'd climbed parapets and given speeches advocating for a place at the proverbial table. And indicated that mayhap he wasn't altogether different, and she didn't know what to do with that discovery. It was easier to bear the separation that had come when thinking of him as a pompous, priggish lord who cared only about his title, and naught for others.

Annalee dropped the rag, now lukewarm in temperature, back into the bowl. It hit the water with a splash, sending little drops flying over the edge. "Yes, Lila saw the need that I and every other woman should have identified," she said, reaching for the needle. "What she and I . . .

and those other women experienced at Peterloo isn't amongst the threats most ladies face, and yet there is danger all around us, still."

"And . . . have you found yourself . . . in a position of . . . danger before?" There was something ominous and dark. Undercurrents of the same violence that had crackled in the duke's ballroom two evenings earlier, when he'd taken down Lord Welles.

"Most women do," she said, shrugging again. "I didn't have the foresight Lila had after Peterloo . . . to see myself skilled in fighting. I'd been attending—" She grimaced. He'd no doubt see it as her fault. Blame her for the company she'd kept and the attendance that had brought about what had befallen her that night.

Wayland brushed his knuckles in a light caress along her jaw, tipping up her chin and holding her eyes; she made herself say it, his judgment be damned.

Annalee set her jaw. "I was attending an orgy, and a gentleman took my attendance there as consent on my part for anything that would happen."

Wayland's eyes formed thin slits, with rage running from irises nearly perfectly concealed by those long, black lashes. But she saw it. His anger. For her . . . just as it had been directed two evenings earlier. "Did he . . . ?" His words trailed off, strained with fear and pain, and the merging of those sentiments . . . sent a warmth unfurling within her breast.

"He didn't," she said softly. "Lord Willoughby came upon us. He . . . disentangled me, beat the fellow quite handily, and that began our . . . friendship." And a friendship was what it was, and had been . . . with sexual benefits extended to one another.

Annalee felt Wayland's eyes move over her face, and this time, there were no other words or questions forthcoming, and his harshly beautiful, angular features formed a perfect mask she couldn't decipher. Nor did she wish to. Because she didn't want to know in this particular instance what he thought of her and the lovers she'd taken. Or her friendship that was oftentimes more with Willoughby.

"I trust you are wondering why I didn't use those skills to disarm Lord Welles?" she asked guardedly as she resumed plucking the stinger from his hand, and no further words were spoken until she finished. "There," she murmured.

"I didn't," he answered without hesitation. "In those moments . . . there isn't to say when one is under attack what shock . . . or fear does to a person."

No. That was something they'd both learned all too long ago, when they'd put themselves directly in the heart of an impending class-structured explosion.

"Which brings me to why I've come today, Annalee," Wayland murmured.

Annalee's heart fluttered. The courtship he'd mentioned publicly to her friends and society members. "Yes, you . . . mentioned something of it in the gardens."

She was supposed to talk, and she'd always been bright and breezy in dialogue with men. But this time, God help her, it all eluded her.

"Given the nature of the scandal, given what people are saying about you and me . . . it makes sense that we move forward with the courtship you had suggested . . ." His cheeks flushed. "Only until the gossip dies down, and then we can part ways amicably. I will . . . recall other responsibilities that I have, and your name will be spared."

"But . . . the match with Lady Diana. Your reputation."

He grimaced. "We . . . were not a match. Lady Diana is the beautiful, wealthy daughter of a duke who could have anyone. Her interest in me is based on a young girl's fantasy that my rescue makes me her destiny. But I don't love her, Annalee, and she deserves someone who can offer her that."

Yes, he'd said it all so very perfectly: the lady was a duke's daughter, and flawless in every way, and even with her perfection and social connections, Wayland would throw away the possibility of a match with Lady Diana? He'd sacrifice his own reputation and join Annalee in this masquerade. It was the grandest of gestures, one only this man was capable of. And there was no greater gift he might offer, and she should only be grateful and focused on the lifeline he'd extended her, but she'd always been contrary in every way. This moment proved no different.

For what he suggested wasn't real. It was a . . . ruse.

You fool. You thought it was real. You thought he was here for something more. Something that would save his reputation and yours.

Yes, she *should* be grateful.

So what accounted for that momentary madness where she'd believed his visit was real and his request to court her sincere?

Only, after her latest scandal—brought about by his undeserved public defense of her—she could not take what he held forth. Not when, in so doing, he'd also sacrifice the security and stability he sought for his sister. She could not accept this. She knew that now.

"I . . . thank you very much for such a generous offer, Wayland," she said, resting her palms upon her lap. "What the papers are saying today . . . That had nothing to do with you, Wayland."

He tensed, an angry color flooding his cheeks. "Willoughby."

"Nothing happened between us." She grimaced. "Last evening, that is." She didn't know why she told him. It just seemed . . . important that he know that. "Either way, there isn't a need for you to . . . court me. Not any longer. I have decided it is in everybody's best interest that I retire to the countryside until Sylvia has her babe. When she returns, I will have the freedom to return." She made to rise.

"You are rejecting me?" That realization left him with a sharpness that she didn't expect. One that suggested not relief at being freed of a chore he didn't want, but rather frustration at being so denied the role.

Annalee paused. "Wayland, *we* weren't discovered in a compromising position at the duke's. If anyone, Welles—"

"Welles can go straight to hell," he snapped. "Is that what you think I'm here for?" he demanded. "Because I'm worried about my reputation?"

"Yes." His eyes darkened. "In some part?" A vein pulsed at the corner of his temple. She was offending him. And upsetting him, and that wasn't her intention. Particularly after his defense of her honor and his generous overture. "Wayland," she tried again. "I know how dearly you value the life you've built for yourself."

"I didn't build it." He clipped out each syllable between his clenched teeth. "It was given to me."

Leave it to an honorable man such as Wayland to claim as much. Annalee collected his hands. "Either way," she said gently, "it is a life that matters very much to you, and being connected with me?" She shook her head. "That will bring you nothing good." Again, she attempted to stand, but he caught her hand, holding it in a grip that somehow managed to merge strength and tenderness.

"What has changed?" he demanded, his eyes moving quickly over her face. "I'm offering you what you wished for."

She'd offended him. That had never been her intention. Particularly given the sacrifice she knew this proposal to be.

"Between that moment and now, it occurred to me that I'll always be a scandal, Wayland," she said flatly. "I thought I could enlist your help, and that by behaving a certain way and presenting a united showing with you, I would be viewed a certain way." What she'd failed to consider was how his association with her would so adversely impact him. Or Kitty. Or his mother. "But that isn't the case," she said, unable to account for the sadness that realization brought. "It doesn't matter how many proper balls I attend or how modest the gowns I don are or the language I use, society has seen me in one light, and yet, just like the sun, its movement does not change."

"Actually, the sun does move. *Verrrry* slowly, Annalee. Just like the Earth, it rotates on its axis."

Annalee laughed softly, briefly closing her eyes. When she opened them, she found his intent gaze locked on her face. "I'm not going to change," she said with a gentle firmness. "Which is why what I'd proposed and what you're now suggesting? It will not work." Firming her words with a finality meant to end this discussion, she sailed to her feet. "Now, I thank you. I do. But I must decline that offer."

"Do you truly wish to leave the ladies there?" he called out, freezing her as she walked. "I saw you with them, Annalee." His voice drifted closer, indicating he'd moved. "I saw how they admire you, and how you love them, and you don't want to leave them for however long it will be before Lady Sylvia returns."

She felt him the moment he stepped close.

Annalee bit the inside of her cheek so hard she tasted the metallic tinge of blood.

He knew that. How could he know that after a quick encounter between her and the other members?

Because he always knew you.

Because he could always read you.

Even all these years later.

And that scared the hell out of her.

And it also tempted her in ways that were only dangerous. Because like a veritable Eve, she'd always freely surrendered herself to temptation.

It was why, the moment Wayland laid his hands upon her shoulders and guided her back around, she knew what she should do, but also what she would do.

"If there is anything I can do, Wayland"—she spoke fast—"or if you change your mind at any time or—"

He touched a fingertip to her lips, silencing her words, and she wished it was his mouth, ached for his harsh, firm lips on hers.

"I'll not change my mind, Annalee," he said quietly. "I'm not a man who is swayed in his feelings or thoughts . . . A ride in Hyde Park, tomorrow at noon."

"Thank—" And this time, he covered her mouth with his, giving her what she'd craved. All too briefly. Her lashes fluttered, heavy from just a hint of what she desperately ached for more of.

"Until tomorrow, love."

Love.

It had slipped past his lips so very easily and effortlessly, as it once had, doing wild things to her heart's cadence.

She followed his retreat until he'd gone and the door closed behind him.

The moment he was gone, Annalee sagged, wrapping her arms about herself, his deep baritone, alluringly rough and so utterly masculine, echoing in his absence.

I'll not change my mind, Annalee . . . I'm not a man who is swayed in his feelings or thoughts . . .

For with Wayland gone, she didn't know if he'd been speaking in veiled terms about something more . . . or if she had simply heard what she wished.

Either way, she wanted him and this coming time with him, and that . . . could only be perilous.

Chapter 23

Through the years, every moment Wayland had with Annalee had been stolen. Clandestine. A secret they'd been forced to keep from her family. The world.

And Wayland had always despised it. He'd hated a world in which they had to hide their love and keep secret the feelings between them. He'd wanted their relationship to be real and recognized by all. Because he'd loved her. Because to hide it had been to make it tawdry. A sordid secret they could not share.

During those early years, he'd dreamed of the moment they would cease hiding what was between them, and had thought about what life would be like, living freely with the love they had for one another. Where social stations didn't divide them. Where his relationship with her brother didn't complicate what had been special between Wayland and Annalee.

They would have discovered London together, the same way they had explored every corner of Worsley. From the forests to the canals, they'd investigated it all.

Of course, they wouldn't have discovered it together. Not really. For Annalee and Jeremy had been off during much of the social Season, and that fashionable world had been hers. But he would have been part of it with her, and for Wayland, that would have been enough.

So much of what he'd wanted for them had been laid to waste in the fields of Manchester.

But it didn't have to mean that he couldn't steal some of those moments he'd yearned for. That, in this arrangement he'd agreed to, he couldn't help Annalee remember some of what she'd loved in life before his folly had seen it all ripped from her.

Adjusting her parasol, Annalee tipped back her head at the entrance of the grounds.

When she looked at Wayland, surprise lent her mouth a tempting moue.

He offered his elbow.

"I . . . confess to not understanding your selection, Lord Darlington," she said, using his proper form of address for the benefit of the lady's maid she'd brought with her. A servant whose presence made sense—yet at the same time, he'd not thought of having her there with him and Annalee, interrupting this time they had together. "I thought we were to visit Hyde Park, but you've brought us . . . here."

He wavered.

It was a place different from where she was now rumored to frequent. He'd merely made the assumption that she might still like to visit, that it would do her good to see it.

And then she dismissed her maid, who curtsied and took herself off, allowing Wayland and Annalee the privacy he'd craved. When the girl had gone, Annalee placed her fingers upon his sleeve, as he'd long ago yearned for her to be able to do publicly, and followed him inside Vauxhall Gardens.

Walkway after walkway intersected in every direction, lined by piebald-color lamps that lent an added vibrance that was missing at night, when most of the *ton* visited. Her eyes took in the quiet grounds as though it were the first time she'd been here. In fairness, in the light of day, admission was low. It was at night, when the productions were biggest, with fireworks and lit paths and orchestras playing, that the *ton* flocked to Vauxhall.

"You disapprove of my choice," he remarked when Annalee remained silent.

"Not at all," she said, and the instantaneousness of that reply sent a lightness slipping around his chest. "I am . . . surprised," she continued as they headed down the pathway leading to the now empty pavilion where, in the evening, orchestras performed.

"Tell me, Annalee," he called over as she slipped her arm from his and wandered off to the dais. "Where should I have taken you?"

She twirled her parasol as she went, its fabric and pearls and crystals dangling from the fringe, playing with the sun's rays like a kaleidoscope, turning various shadows out upon the stone dance floor.

"Truthfully?"

He nodded, and drawn like the moth he'd always been where she was concerned, he drifted over.

Annalee immediately brought that frilly article to a stop. Snapping the parasol closed, she pressed the tip into the gravel and leaned over it. "I thought you would have taken me on a ride through Rotten Row, Wayland. Or a curricle ride through London. Or the theatre in the evening."

"I intend for us to visit the theatre," he felt compelled to add. Because she'd always loved it. He'd never been with her before, but had instead listened as she'd performed samples of the shows she'd seen, playing all the parts, until they'd both roared with laughter.

"That"—she pointed the end of her parasol at his chest—"that makes sense."

"And what doesn't make sense about this?" he asked, really trying to follow.

"We're not"—Annalee glanced about and then, with her free hand, gestured to the paradise around them—"seen, Wayland."

Of course. Because that was the whole purpose of their arrangement . . . or that was what she expected anyway.

"You like gardens," he said quietly. Didn't she? Or had that changed? She'd used to run barefoot through fields of wildflowers, twirling herself in circles, until she collapsed with dizzying laughter within those blooms.

"And the gardens at Hyde Park . . . where we *would* be seen?" she asked, drifting closer. Annalee of now was a driven woman who knew her mind and what she wanted in life . . . and what she wanted for this arrangement was the benefit it served in establishing respectability.

"Visiting Hyde Park at this hour wouldn't be a place where you could . . . simply enjoy . . . this, Annalee." And twisting the stem of a peony in slow, rhythmic circles back and forth, he freed the bloom and held it out before her.

Her eyes went as soft as they'd been when she was a young girl in the bloom of her innocence, and then she accepted the fragrant flower. Raising it to her nose, she inhaled deep. All the while, she watched him. "You're still a romantic, Wayland Smith."

He wasn't. Not really. Only where this woman was concerned had he been one. Was she?

He knew there had been lovers. She'd all but freely admitted her association with Willoughby, a rake of the first order . . . but also a man who'd saved her, and . . . Wayland breathed deeply, containing the surge of jealousy that had rippled through his being when she shared about her past with the gentleman.

They continued on, deeper into the gardens, which lacked the meticulous tending shown the hedges and blooms in Kew Gardens and Kensington Gardens and Hyde Park. Annalee stopped and, resting a hand on his sleeve, tugged free first one slipper, then the other. She handed the laces over to him as though it were the most natural thing in the world for him to carry her shoes. And there was an intimacy to Annalee's surrendering them to his care.

"Would you have preferred Rotten Row?" he asked, needing to know.

"I prefer this," she stated quietly. "I prefer this." She paused beside a rosebush and, lowering her head, closed her eyes and inhaled.

He watched her as she did, captivated by the sight of her.

In this moment, the walls she'd built about herself since Peterloo, and the time that had separated them, had come down. She was not setting out to shock him. She was simply enjoying this . . . as he'd wanted for her.

Suddenly, she opened her eyes.

Over the top of that bush, their gazes locked, and it was as though the Earth ceased to spin and everything stood frozen in time. And he wanted that for this moment. So that they could block out the past and Peterloo and the present, where her family planned the vilest of futures for her. Where they could remain suspended in the empty gardens of Vauxhall.

But, of course, invariably life continued on . . . and Annalee glanced away.

"I've never been here at this hour," she murmured, more to herself. Wandering off, she headed down a graveled path lined with unlit lights, and Wayland trailed at a slower pace behind her, allowing her that space she sought. "I confess to only coming in the evening."

When the grounds bustled.

Suddenly, she glanced back. "Have you?"

"Evening or day?"

"Either?"

"Never," he confessed, stuffing his hands in his pockets. "This is my first time."

Surprise rounded her eyes. "Come, now."

"Not much one for fireworks," he said gruffly, and then he wanted to call it back. That reminder about . . . that day which neither of them needed reminders of.

Surprise gave way to a dawning understanding. *"Ahh."*

Except, speaking of it also felt . . . right. Important in ways that he'd not considered. He'd resolved to forget everything he could about that August day—an impossible feat. He'd thought to not let it intrude on these moments with Annalee. But . . . mayhap it needed to be spoken aloud. For the both of them. Those pieces they'd begun to explore in the duke's gardens . . . when she'd revealed the small parts she had about her love and need of those fountains that grounded her.

"I hate crowds," he finally brought himself to say. "I hate ballrooms when they're filled with people. I see Peterloo. If it weren't for my mother and the need to ease her way in Polite Society, I'd likely avoid it all."

"Yes, I . . . feel that way, too."

"You?" he asked, sliding closer.

"With the exception about aiming to please my mother, that is." She fastened that teasing part on, adding a wink. However, Annalee toyed with the handle of her parasol, her grip a white-knuckled one, indicating her disquiet. "I've surprised you."

Every day. Then and now. He'd always been endlessly captivated by her for it. "Some," he allowed.

She abruptly stopped fiddling with that article in her hand, lowering it so the tip touched the ground once more, and she stared down upon the graveled stones. "It . . . Peterloo? It is always there for me." For him, too. Likely for every man, woman, and child who'd been dragged into the hell of that day. "But I've found the quiet worse," Annalee murmured. "It's when it is quiet and I'm alone that everything is loudest in my mind."

And then it made sense. "It's why you prefer the . . . the . . ." He stumbled, searching.

A small smile formed on her lips. "The wicked events I do?"

He gave a tight nod, even though she wasn't looking at him. Even though she apparently didn't require any clarification of what he'd really been intending to ask, but was too cowardly to put to words.

"That is precisely why I prefer them. There's shock and scandal and wickedness enough to distract one from . . . *anything.* At the events I attend, with the people I do, one thing a person might be absolutely assured of is that there will be no quiet, but plenty of diversions."

Wayland took in that important piece she'd revealed about herself and how she'd coped with the tragedy. Or rather, how she had failed to cope with what she'd lived through. She still hadn't figured out that she couldn't bury that day completely. She continued to run from it, never confronting what had happened to her. He moved closer, stopping at her shoulder. "But perhaps blocking it out . . . isn't for the best. Not really." A gentle wind rippled through the gardens, stirring the leaves to dancing, and a curl fluttered at her shoulder. Of their own volition, his fingers collected that golden strand, and he smoothed his thumb and forefinger over the silken tress before tucking it behind the delicate shell of her ear. "You can't really confront what happened to you if you're drowning it out with noise, Annalee."

She took a hasty step away from him, putting distance between them . . . and what he said? "Why would I *want* to relive it, Wayland?"

"Because maybe you have to, Annalee. Perhaps we both have to."

Her mouth tightened, and she shook her head. "I gave enough that day," she spat. "To hell with Peterloo and Manchester. And all of it." She pointed her parasol his way, jabbing it with each word she spoke, as though placing exclamation marks upon them. "I'll control what I think of and when I think of it." With that, she whipped around and rushed deeper into the high-hedged gardens.

He sprinted after her, churning stones under the heels of his boots as he went. "But . . . are you really controlling it, Annalee?" he implored, needing her to see that some of the decisions she'd made were ones that had been dangerous to her.

She stopped suddenly. "You're speaking about my drinking?" There was a challenge in her fiery gaze, a warning issued, one that said he'd wandered down a path that she'd no intention of walking with him. "Are you not?"

And he was torn. He wanted to set aside the question which had roused this volatile emotion in her and stolen the soft-eyed joy that had been there the moment they entered the grotto. But he'd run for so very long where Annalee was concerned. And he was done with it. "I'm speaking about your drinking."

"I drink because it's something that I can control."

"You don't control it. It's a vice. It controls you."

She recoiled, and then found her voice. "One who's devoted his life to"—she elevated her nose, pointing it at the air—"propriety and properness would never dare indulge."

"I indulge," he said. "I don't overindulge."

She stomped toward him. "And what of you, Wayland?"

He straightened. "What of me?"

"You speak to me about living a certain way. But are you really living? You've fashioned yourself into a person who cares more about opinions than your own happiness. You don't live. Not like you used to."

"No," he agreed. "I don't. I chose a different course."

"A better course," she jeered.

"I didn't say that, Annalee. I made decisions that day that were reckless. I asked you to meet me there because I wanted you to be there, and what did that get you?" He couldn't stop the trace of bitterness from creeping in. Hatred of himself.

Annalee moved swiftly. Letting her parasol fall, she grabbed Wayland's hands, knocking her slippers free of his grip so that the silken articles tumbled beside her umbrella. "I was there because I wanted to be there."

All his muscles seized up, the pain of it welcome. "To see me," he said, unable to meet her eyes.

"Of course to see you, but also to witness that moment that mattered so much to you, and so much to so many."

God, how unerringly she'd always been able to follow his thoughts.

She tightened her grip upon his fingers, forcing his eyes to hers. "It was *my* decision, Wayland. *Not* yours. And I'd hate you forever if you take responsibility for a choice that belonged solely to me."

Her pronouncement gave him pause. All these years, he'd lived with guilt, having owned her being there. Because it had been his fault. Now, seeing how Annalee had devoted her life to a society of women exacting change over their lives and the lives of other ladies, it made him realize how narrow-minded that view of her and her decision that day had been. She'd been committed to challenging the inequities that existed before, and in ways that he'd not proven steadfast, she had . . . continued those passions through the Mismatch Society. Her devotion to that group and change was so great that she'd even change herself or, as she'd stated yesterday, leave, to preserve it.

Their chests brushed, their eyes locked on one another's mouths.

Then she caught him by the nape and dragged his mouth to hers.

He was lost.

Or found.

Mayhap it was really both.

Wayland surrendered himself to her kiss, a violent meeting that fit with the tension that had exploded in these empty grounds.

He lowered them to the ground, lying down so her form was draped over him. So that her pale-yellow gown was spared stains from the grass.

Her skirts rucked up about them, and he slid his hands up her thighs, gripping and massaging the muscles of her long limbs.

She lowered the bodice of her gown and leaned forward just as he leaned up to worship that swollen pink tip. Wayland flicked his tongue over the crest, teasing her.

Annalee panted, moving against him, rubbing her thatch over the bulge in his trousers. "Please," she begged, gripping his head and anchoring him against her breasts, and he knew what she hungered for, knew she wanted him to suckle deep and long, but he drew out the moment.

Swiping the tip of his tongue back and forth, lavishing attention on each mound, before ultimately giving her what she ached for.

She panted, reaching between them and making quick work of his front falls.

"This isn't why I brought you here," he said, his voice strained as she freed him from his trousers.

She gripped him in her fist, squeezing his length and pulling a low groan from deep in his chest. *"Shh,"* she whispered, concealing his harsh panting with her mouth. "And I know," she breathed between kisses.

Then she sank onto him, sliding herself down in one glorious glide, her channel sodden with her desire, and he filled her.

Sweat slipped down his brow, and Wayland lowered his head to the ground and clenched his eyes tight. This was the homecoming.

And then she began to move, undulating slowly, riding him as she'd always loved.

She moaned, a low, long, throaty rumbling, and a wave of heat and desire all melded into one potent blast that coursed through his veins.

Wayland brought his hands up, gripping her at the waist and stroking over her buttocks, guiding her on to that goal she sought. "That's it, love," he praised, lifting his hips to meet each downward thrust.

She bit her lower lip as she drove herself up and down upon him, and knowing it would drive her to the brink of a happy madness, Wayland stretched up to take the tip of her right breast, swollen from his mouth's worshipping, again.

"Wayland," she rasped, clinging to his shoulders. He felt the bite of her nails through the fabric as she gripped him, leveraging herself forward.

His chest tightened, his breath constricted. "God, you've always been so good at that."

"Have I?" she whispered, squeezing him with clever internal muscles that tightened around his shaft, pulling a gasp from him.

"Annalee," he begged, tightening his hold on her hips and urging her on.

Then she set a frenzied pace, rising and falling over him. Again and again.

Leaning forward, she laid her hands upon his chest, her face scrunched up as she concentrated on the pleasure she found in this moment, and Wayland lifted his head to meet her mouth.

Annalee's body tensed.

She gasped, and he consumed that broken, breathy exhalation.

He felt every tightening of her muscles, and she arched her back, tossing her neck, and climaxed. Her channel pulsed and squeezed as her body shuddered and rippled from the force of her pleasure.

He squeezed his eyes shut tightly, straining and fighting for self-control, as her moment of surrender went on forever and then she collapsed atop his chest.

Gasping, Wayland rolled her off him and then turned sideways, spilling himself into the grass in long arcs, his body jolting and spasming from a release so exquisite it bordered on pain.

And then he sagged.

Annalee came up on her knees and rested her cheek upon his shoulder, and then she placed a series of kisses there, moving that trail higher.

His chest moved hard and quick, his heart pounding in his ears.

"I . . ."

"Don't apologize."

He rolled onto his back and caught her by the waist, bringing her down atop his chest and pulling a breathless laugh from her. "Is it wrong that I wasn't going to?"

She lowered her mouth close to his. "It is *right* that you weren't. I wanted this." Her gaze, still glittering with passion, slipped over his face. "All of this, Wayland," she said with a seriousness replacing her earlier mirth. "This whole day, exactly as it was. I forgot . . . what it is like to be in the gardens." And then she lay down, draped over him, her ear pressed against the place where his heart continued to wildly pound.

Wayland folded his arms around her and proceeded to rub small circles over her back. "How many of us spent so many days trying to forget and, along the way, forgot how to live?"

She stilled. "You're speaking about my drinking," she said guardedly, reality inserting itself into this moment.

"I'm speaking about how all of us coped in a bid to conquer our demons. You weren't wrong earlier, Annalee." Annalee lifted her head, propping her chin on his chest so she could meet his gaze. "I made myself who I am because it was something I could control. I had no control that day. I couldn't stop the mayhem. I couldn't . . ." His voice broke, and he squeezed his eyes shut, letting all the terror of that day wash over him, the panic of fighting his way through a sea of bodies, looking at the trampled and bloodied and battered around him, alternately fearing he'd see her amongst those masses and that he wouldn't. That he'd never find her again.

"Wayland," she said soothingly, sitting up, and he joined her. Hunching his shoulders, he rocked himself back and forth slightly.

"I couldn't get to you," he whispered. He couldn't save her. Ravaged by his failings, all of them in life revolving around this woman, he looked to her and through her. "The one thing I could control after Peterloo was becoming a proper gentleman. There were rules I could follow. There were places I could go and not go. It was a formula. It made sense. But it was also a movement toward one extreme."

"Just as mine," she murmured.

He nodded. "We both went . . . off in these extremes. But alcohol, Annalee? It is . . . will not erase those memories we carry. I want you to give it up. Not for me. But for you. I want you to realize you don't need it. You can and do find fulfillment in other places. Your Mismatch Society. The women who rely upon you. Your sister." *Me.* Why was he only just realizing that this offer he'd put forward hadn't been about easing guilt . . . but that it was about . . . being with her?

Drawing in her knees, Annalee wrapped her arms about her legs. "I don't . . ." *know if I can do it.*

"You just try, Annalee. You just do the best you can. You don't let it control you."

Wayland folded an arm around her, drawing her against his side, and simply held her.

The world existed on the fringe of those high garden hedges. Any passersby might wander in and find them. And yet, he could not care.

He cared only about Annalee and this moment between them, in this walled-in Eden where only they two existed.

Chapter 24

Annalee and Wayland had agreed to a ruse, a pretend courtship. A pretend courtship served its purpose only if the world saw and the world came to believe in that game of make-believe both actors played at.

And yet yesterday afternoon, at the hour when all of Polite Society was riding and strolling down Rotten Row to be seen, he'd met her in the almost intimately private grounds of Vauxhall. He'd recalled her love of nature and gardens. Why, he'd picked her . . . a peony.

And now, today . . . the second part of their most recent act, he'd arranged a meeting at, of all places . . . a museum.

Why would he do that? a voice needled at the back of her mind. Unless . . . what was pretend really . . . wasn't . . . And mayhap, just mayhap, he wished to make that which was fake . . . real.

As she climbed the steps, butterflies danced in her breast.

Those little thrilling flutters she'd come to believe herself too jaded to again feel or know had been resurrected by the same man who'd first given them life within her, all those years ago.

"Suspicious is what it is," Valerie muttered as she stomped beside Annalee up the almost two dozen steps of the Royal Museum. Huffing from the climb and the pace Annalee had set, she shot her friend a sideways glance.

"There's nothing suspicious about the choice," Annalee lied, and tiring of those censorious looks directed her way, she adjusted her bonnet.

"Many, many couples choose to be seen at museums." Obscure ones. On the farthest recesses of the neighborhoods resided in by lords and ladies.

"Do you really know that to be fact?"

"Absolutely." She felt more than a little guilt for how easily that second fib fell from her lips. The undisputable truth was, Annalee knew no such thing of the sort. Wayland had been the only respectable suitor she'd ever had. And back then, he'd been a blacksmith's son, apprenticing and working, and not afforded the opportunity to court her as couples of the *ton* did. They'd entered into a pretend courtship, and yet thus far, the places Wayland had arranged for them to meet . . . were not the ones that would put the most eyes upon them. Rather . . . it felt very much . . . like a real courtship.

"Yes, well, I rather think dashing off where no one is seeing the two of you together defeats the whole purpose of your association with the gentleman. It seems underhanded, as though there is a reason he's keeping you and he a secret," Valerie muttered, effectively popping the bubble on Annalee's foolish dreaming.

They reached the main landing of the Royal Museum.

Collecting the other woman by her shoulders, Annalee drew her in for a hug. "You worry too much."

"And you don't worry enough."

"Yes, well, nothing good comes from worrying."

"That's a ridiculous saying."

Annalee fixed a pout on her lips. "La, I'm offended, given it was a saying I crafted myself."

"I feel his intentions are nefarious, Annalee."

"You feel the intentions of all men are," she reminded her friend. "And that is why we are perfect friends. We balance one another out."

An all-too-familiar worry seeped from Valerie's eyes as she passed her gaze over Annalee, her mouth moving as though she wished to say more, and then she released a sigh.

Annalee patted her arm. "There, that is better."

"Because I'm letting the matter rest," she groused.

"Precisely." And yet . . . Annalee let her smile fade, bringing her features into a mask of solemnity. Her friend had every reason to be cynical and wary of intentions where men were concerned. Given the lies fed her by the man who'd sworn to protect and love her, when all the while he'd been married to Sylvia. "There isn't a better friend than you," Annalee said quietly.

"Because I've let the matter rest about all the reasons I don't trust Lord Darlington and his sudden change of heart in helping you?"

Yes, well, Valerie was nothing if not tenacious. "Because your first worry is always protecting those you love from being hurt." She pressed a kiss to Valerie's cheek. "I know you are worried about me. You needn't."

Valerie winged a brow. "Are you so very sure about that . . . ?"

Was she so very certain? Was she sure Wayland wouldn't hurt her? That his intentions were honorable? A little sliver of unease twisted around her belly.

Valerie moved closer. "You're thinking about what I've said. Why has he suddenly, after all these years, appeared and started whisking you about London to places where no one—"

"Enough," Annalee said curtly, her patience at an end with Valerie's endless warnings that morn. She recalled the hoarse whisperings he'd shared about the changes he'd adopted after Peterloo. "Wayland conducts himself first and foremost with honor."

"No such thing, with men," her friend said in a singsong voice.

There would be no swaying her. Valerie would have to learn and see for herself that Wayland was . . . unlike the men Valerie had dealings with at the fight club she'd been forced into. And he was different from the lovers whom Annalee had taken. "Now, go enjoy yourself. You are at the Royal Museum." And with that dismissal, she collected her hems and rushed on ahead.

"His intentions are probably nefarious, you know."

"Hush, there's my reputation to worry about."

Valerie snorted. "I think that is my point." Annalee increased her stride. "All manner of wicked things happen in museums, you know," her friend called more loudly after her. "Hidden spots for trysting. It's how all rakes and rogues are. Nay, all men! They—"

Not looking back, Annalee lifted a hand, waving off that unending litany of worries about Wayland and his intentions, and let herself inside the museum.

And yet . . . what if it wasn't just a coincidence that, with both outings, he'd chosen the out-of-the-way, private locations he had?

What if—

She stopped abruptly, as she discovered in that very moment there had been something very specific about Wayland's decision for them to meet at the Royal Museum, after all. Annalee shook, the force of emotion rolling through her as she caught sight of the pair twenty paces away.

Wayland . . . and her sister. He and Harlow conversed so effortlessly, Wayland attending whatever it was Annalee's sister spoke about so animatedly. Periodically, he nodded, and said something in return.

Tears clogged her throat and filled her eyes, and through that blurry sheen, she caught the moment Harlow spied her standing there.

"Annalee!"

Sinking to a knee, Annalee threw her arms wide.

Grinning from ear to ear, Harlow came hurtling forward.

Annalee staggered back under the force of her sister's embrace.

"Darlington had the idea that we could go to the museum, Annalee! The museum. Utterly brilliant," she prattled as Annalee kissed her cheeks. "Because he knows I love you and Captain Cook and piracy, but there is no museum of pirates, you know, and there really should be."

Laughing through her tears, Annalee brushed the curls that had fallen loose in her young sister's flight back behind her ears. "There should be. Someday you shall be the one to create such a venture."

Harlow's eyes lit. "Do you know, that is a splendid idea. You do have them often, though. I am ever so excited to see Cook's. I've been asking my governess." She stuck out her tongue. "But you know *that* woman. She's useless. And Jeremy is always occupied with his betrothed, and then . . . well, Wayland." She lifted her right shoulder in an uneven shrug, so casual, when there was nothing minor or trivial about this moment and what Wayland had done.

Annalee looked over the top of her sister's head to Wayland, elegantly clad in his cutaway morning coat and tan trousers. At some point he'd joined them, standing with his fingers clasped behind him, keeping a handful of paces apart from her and her sister, allowing Annalee and Harlow their privacy.

Stroking little circles over Harlow's back, Annalee held his eyes. "Thank you," she mouthed, her lips trembling.

He lifted his head in acknowledgment. "It wasn't just me," he demurred, and she followed his gaze over to Jeremy, hovering off to the side, unseen until now, toying with the brim of his hat.

Annalee stilled, and then hugging her sister once more, she came to her feet. "Jeremy," she greeted cautiously.

It had been the first she'd spoken to her brother since the debacle she'd inadvertently caused at his betrothal ball.

"Annalee." He ceased toying with his hat, returning it to his head. "You look . . . well."

And she'd . . . felt well. She'd not given a thought to spirits or sinning or wagering. How could she ever amend for what she'd done? "I'm so—"

"No. No. That's not why we're here," he said gruffly. "That is done. Darlington thought to unite you and Harlow here and required my assistance to do so. I'd have the day be about that."

"Come on! Come on!" Harlow cried, gesticulating wildly.

When it became apparent Jeremy didn't intend to join them, Annalee frowned. "You'll not stay?"

"I . . . have private matters to attend this morn."

Hearing the heavy thread in his pronouncement, she stepped closer. "What is it?"

"Nothing to worry about, I'm sure. I was summoned by Sophrona's father to discuss the terms of our betrothal. Some . . . final revisions. I knew, however, Harlow would be in good hands with you and Darlington. I'll return when I've concluded my affairs and escort her home."

So that she could have this day that their parents would have never approved of. Another cloud of tears blurred her vision. "I love you."

Jeremy sucked a breath in through his teeth. "And I you, little sister."

"Come on!" Harlow shouted, her child's voice echoing around the empty museum.

Doffing his hat, he nudged Annalee gently in the arm. "Run along before she brings down the ceiling with her shouts."

Annalee laughed, and kissing him on his cheek, she hurried off to join Wayland and her sister. She slid her fingers onto his sleeve. "Thank you."

"It was nothing."

"No, you're right," she said as they walked with their steps in perfect synchrony. "It is everything." Annalee squeezed his arm lightly. "Everything, Wayland."

"I was doing some scouting before you arrived," Harlow said on Annalee's other side. "And we want to go there." She pointed up the center staircase. "For the Captain Cook exhibit." Tugging her arm loose, she rushed on ahead, leading the way as though she were in fact a formal tour operator, and not as though it was her first time in this museum.

Annalee and Wayland followed close behind the happily chattering little girl.

"Some people, you know, think that the most interesting fact about Captain Cook was that he was a mapmaker." Glancing back at Annalee and Wayland as she walked, Harlow pulled a face. *"Borrring."* Her sister redirected her focus forward. "No. The most interesting things about him . . . are invariably the things no one talks about. His run-ins with Britain's enemies at sea. Do you know, an entire *squaddddron* of Spanish vessels detained his ships, but released him? And do you know why?" Harlow asked, her voice more animated than Annalee . . . ever recalled.

"Wh—"

Harlow interrupted Annalee's response. "Because they realized Cook was in command. He was that respected." She stopped suddenly and rubbed her fingers together; a wicked glimmer lit her eyes. "And his death. Do you know he was bludgeoned to death by the very king whom he gifted a sword to? Tossed a blade right into his back"—the little girl skipped on ahead, examining the exhibit as she provided that gruesome lesson about Cook's final fate—"and then clubbed him over and over, and he did . . ." Skipping off to a display of weaponry, Harlow continued prattling on.

Moisture dampened Annalee's palms, and her belly roiled. Her sister's cheer-filled voice, perfectly juxtaposed with that grisly telling, all mixed in her mind with another blood-filled day.

The little boy wailing as a soldier's blade missed the older resister beside him, cutting down the child instead . . . those terror-filled eyes instantly frozen in that moment of his greatest suffering. Unable to tamp down a little moan, Annalee stumbled.

Wayland caught her shoulder and then took her hand, his strong and warm and steadying. He held her eyes. "All right?" he silently mouthed.

She fought to get air into her lungs.

A drink. She needed a drink.

Wayland brought his mouth close to her ear and his breath was warm, soothing against her cheek. A hint of coffee . . .

Think of your conversation at Jeremy's betrothal. How he enjoys coffee . . . anything but—it was futile.

The report of gunshots thundered in her mind, mixing with the jumbled shouts and cries.

Annalee brought her hands up to her head.

"Annalee, you're here."

Wayland.

It was Wayland's voice, calling through the chaos.

"I'm here."

He was here.

"We're in the museum," he said with a quiet firmness that managed to penetrate her rapidly escalating panic. "Where are we?"

She was with Wayland . . . and Harlow. Harlow, who hadn't been present at Peterloo. She'd been a babe. Annalee focused on breathing. "The Royal Museum."

He touched his brow to hers, that physical contact, his touch. His touching her cemented her more in the now. "That's right." His voice, it came soft and filled with a gentle praise.

The horrors receded as she focused on him, Wayland's face and presence proving a lifeline.

And then the present came rushing back to meet her. Annalee sucked in a great big gasp of air.

As with the return to reality, came the rush of shame, coursing through her.

She pressed her eyes closed. This was the part of herself she despised. Gone was the innocent girl he'd fallen in love with, and in her place, this person who didn't even have complete control of her wits. And she wanted to leave. She wanted to run and hide from all her weaknesses.

Nay, that wasn't true. *You want to go back to the moment when you were nothing more than a lady in a museum, meeting your suitor . . .*

But all that had been fake. A carefully orchestrated plan laid out by a man who wasn't a suitor, who wasn't a lover. Who was nothing more than a friend helping her try to present something she would never again be to the world—a normal lady.

Except—

"Annaleee!" her sister cried, gesturing wildly at a glass case. "Look at this! It is a ring . . . made out of a shark's tooth!"

This day was about Harlow, and seeing Harlow. Plastering on a smile for Harlow's benefit, Annalee waved back. "Amazing!" She rushed over, grateful to put some distance between her and Wayland. Wayland, who was studying her with serious eyes and concern, and damn it, she didn't want that from him. Not now. Not ever. Annalee didn't want to be an object of his damned pity. His or anyone else's. But from him, it was worse. With him, she was reminded of all the ways she'd changed, and the fact that he felt guilt for those changes. That remorse he carried, that he'd expressed so vividly in those letters, was almost worse than the pity.

Annalee kept close to her sister's side, listening as Harlow shared all the beloved facts she knew about Cook and his treasures, and sharing in the young girl's excitement for new details she'd not previously learned.

As Harlow pulled away, heading for a feather headdress helmet, Annalee meandered more slowly behind her. Putting space between herself and the military weapons now commanding all of her sister's attentions, Annalee considered the small carvings of turtle figures and the far duller but safer fishing hooks.

Leaning over the case, she glanced at Wayland's image reflected in that glass as he joined her.

"Are you all right?" he asked.

"I'm having a splendid time, Wayland," she said, devoting all her focus to a necklace of beige, brown, white, and black stones. "Again, I cannot thank you—"

"That wasn't what I was referring to, Annalee."

"Oh."

Her skin prickled hot under the somberness of his statement and the stare he'd trained upon her. She didn't need to see it in the crystal panes protecting the artifacts. She felt it on her person like a physical touch.

"You're referring to what happened earlier," she said. She should have trusted he wouldn't let her earlier breakdown go without a discussion. Annalee caught the inside of her cheek between her teeth. He would not. That hadn't been the manner of man Wayland had been. He'd worry. About her. After her. She'd known that years ago. And she'd not wanted his concern then, and she wanted it even less now. "Yes, well, that happens sometimes." She spoke with a breeziness at odds with the pounding of her heart. "As I mentioned when we spoke at Jeremy's betrothal ball." She'd not wanted to discuss it with Wayland then, and she didn't wish to now.

"Is that what happened . . . in the fountain?"

She trilled a laugh. "I never met a fountain I did not love, you know."

Except, he didn't join in her forced humor. He continued to wear that grave mask.

Wayland took her gently by the arm, steering her to the corner. "It's all right, you know."

"I know," she said automatically.

Wayland moved closer, gently taking her chin and angling it higher, bringing her gaze more in line with his, when that was the last place she wished to look. "It is all right that you have those remembrances and respond the way you do."

And something snapped. "It's not all right, Wayland," she said on a furious whisper, taking a quick step that erased all remaining space between them. "It's not. So stop pretending that it is. It's the manner of madness that sees women shut away."

His entire face crumpled, but he was quick to reassemble his features. "You're not mad."

"Yes, I am."

"You're haunted. That's different. You are remembering something no one should have to live through, but you did. And you survived. We survived."

She wrapped herself tight in a hard embrace. Survived. All these years she'd fashioned a fast existence for herself because she'd wanted to celebrate the fact that she'd lived. But what if, all these years, what she could have—should have—taken solace in, found strength in, was the fact that she'd survived? "Does . . . that ever happen to you?"

"Sometimes. Less now than in the first years after. There have been times I've thought I conquered those demons, but they will rear themselves at the most unexpected times. Reminding me that I'll never fully be free of it." Wayland lowered his brow to hers. "It's always there, Annalee. It will always be there. And we can't outrun it."

Or out-drink it. Or out-wager it.

He knew her demons. He'd faced them, too. Nay, he'd battled them far better than she ever had. And something in that, in his presence, and in their different but still shared experiences of that day, allowed her to find her way back from the horrors. She touched her fingertips to the beloved planes of his face, tracing the bold slash of his right cheekbone to his chin. Why had she turned him away as long as she had? Fear had made her fight a friendship that had been the one great, most wonderful thing in her life.

The dark slashes of his brows came together. "What are you thinking?"

"I was just thinking . . . that if I'd returned your letters, how life . . . me . . . us, all of it would be different."

His face twisted, a paroxysm of pain and grief that shredded her heart, a heart that still beat for him. It always would. She'd denied it all these years because it had been easier to tell herself she was over what they'd shared than to meet him again after Peterloo as the changed woman she'd been. Perhaps if . . . she had let him be there when he attempted to, then he would have been her crutch, and not spirits and meaningless assignations and all the other vices she'd freely surrendered herself to.

"Annaleeeee?" Her sister's calls severed the moment, and they glanced in the direction of where Harlow's voice had called from.

And this time when Annalee stepped out from behind the pillar, she stretched her fingers back toward Wayland, and they made the walk to Harlow's side . . . together.

Chapter 25

Wayland's time with Annalee at the museum had been . . . magnificent. Every aspect of every moment spent with Annalee and her sister that morn had been. Witnessing the joy she felt while freely joining the younger girl.

Even the hardest, most painful part . . . Annalee's collapse . . . had seen them joined in a kindred place, born of a shared experience, and had been ideal, for it had been an exchange that was long overdue, one that needed to happen, and also one that had united them.

Yes, everything about the day was perfect.

It was why, immediately following, he'd paid a visit to Lady Diana and made sure, as gently as possible, to explain that his affections were reserved for another. There'd not been the tears he'd feared or anticipated. There'd been a casual . . . indifference from the always stoic lady. And there'd been a . . . freedom when he'd taken his leave.

Whistling, Wayland bounded up the steps, doffed his hat, and skidded to a stop.

The cheerful tune died on his lips.

Or rather, the day had been perfect. All such vestiges of happiness were effectively quashed in this very moment.

His mother stood there in the center of the sundial ornamentation etched within the marble foyer. Just beyond her shoulder, five steps higher and elevated slightly above their mother, Kitty waved frantically. "Run," she mouthed.

And Wayland was more than half-tempted to do just that.

Plucking the hat from Wayland's fingers, his butler ultimately made the decision for him.

"To what do I owe this eager welcome?" Wayland drawled, shrugging out of his cloak and handing over the garment to the servant.

Belding's lips twitched in the hint of a smile.

Descending the remainder of the steps, Kitty shook her head vigorously as she joined Wayland and their mother on the marble floor. "Big mistake, dear brother," she said.

"Splendid. I was hoping I had some nightmare to deal with." His sister giggled. Wayland leaned in with a palm concealing half of his mouth. "What is the magnitude of this catastrophe?"

His sister stretched her arms out on opposite ends. "Huge."

"If you two are quite done with your ill-timed and ill-advised jesting?" their mother snapped. "I quite dislike this lighter side of you, Wayland."

"Well, I rather suspect I know what accounts for the changes in him, and I quite like it," Kitty interjected. "I've missed the more fun version of you."

He grinned. This more fun version of him.

That was . . . certainly what it was. He was lighter. These past days, he'd not given a single thought about how the world viewed him or the image he had to maintain to fit in, in a world that would, as he'd said to Annalee, never truly accept him. And it felt . . . freeing. In being with her, he'd been reminded of how much he'd loved . . . just being with her and laughing and all of it.

"If I may see you in the Rose Parlor, Wayland?"

Ah, the Rose Parlor.

So aptly named for the overabundance of blooms painted upon the pale-white silk wallpaper, and adorning the upholstery of the furnishings, and the regularly installed urns of those blooms. Wayland had found the room nauseatingly overdone . . . until Annalee. Until he'd noted the new fragrance she dashed upon her neck and behind her ears. He smiled. Nay, he'd never again think of a rose without—

"Wayland!" his mother squawked. "Are you daydreaming?"

"Yes," he said. Catching his sister, he swung her in a wide circle around the butler, who didn't make any attempt to hide his grin. "My head, I fear, is firmly in the clouds, and—"

"*Annnd* I advise you to step down to earth once more."

He released his sister, and she twirled off, and a footman caught her before she could bowl him over.

And reluctantly he headed off to join his mother. God, when was the last time he'd been this happy? Years. It had been . . . years. He'd largely existed, and all the while had failed to realize all he was missing.

The moment they reached the parlor, he shut the door behind himself and his mother.

"What is the meaning of this?" she demanded, stopping in the middle of the parlor. "This . . . affair between you and Annalee."

"I don't owe you any explanations, Mother," he said coolly, tugging off his gloves. He stuffed them into the front of his jacket.

"No, but do you know who you owe explanations to?" She stuck out a foot. "The Duke and Duchess of Kipling. The duchess, who came by today and asked the meaning of . . . of all of this."

Oh, bloody hell.

And there it was.

Somewhere along the way, his mother's hopes for a greater connection between Wayland and the most powerful of noble families he'd saved that day had at last materialized into a most real possibility.

He scrubbed a hand over his face.

"I . . . do not have feelings for the lady."

"Bah, what is this?" She scoffed. "You saved her. You were her hero, and from that, feelings will grow," his mother said with a crisp pragmatism born of her ruthless ambition to climb higher than either of them could have dreamed. "You aren't a romantic. Look at what romance got you. Nearly killed. Other people dead." She whisked over. "You, dear son, are now calm and rational and logical, and as such, you know that nothing good can come from a relationship with Annalee, and only everything great can come of a partnership with the duke's daughter. So . . . whatever"—she swirled a palm in the air—"this is between you and Annalee, get it out of your system. Bed her. Make Annalee your lover after you marry, but by God, do your responsibility by this family." Sweeping around him, his mother marched for the door.

A haze of fury fell over his eyes. *Bed her. Make Annalee your lover after you marry . . .*

"This is not over," he said between grated teeth.

"No, but it very nearly was." Whirling back, she glared at him. "The duchess expressed that the duke is quite put out with you. That his daughter has developed affection for you and is quite hurt by your disinterest. And that the only reason he is not giving us the cut direct is because, for reasons I cannot understand, Lady Diana *still* wants to marry you."

"No, that is not what I'm referring to, Mother. I'm referring to this discussion between you and me. I am in love with Annalee."

A horrified gasp exploded from her lips. "What?"

"I have always loved her. And . . . if she'll have me, I intend to marry her."

Horror wreathed her face. "My God. You cannot be serious. That woman is a scandal!"

Yes, she had been.

"She has had lovers," she pressed, four words that in their truth were a lash upon his soul and always would be.

And yet . . .

"I don't care." Not in the way his mother expected he should. He cared that other men had known her in ways that he had, and had hoped to be the only one to know her. "That doesn't matter to me."

"That is different, and you know it. Ladies are to be chaste. Annalee could not be further from that. And an arrangement with her would be selfish," she spat. "Utterly and completely selfish. It is a match that does not take into consideration your sister and her own lack of prospects." Hands on her hips, she stormed over. "Prospects that will be considerably lessened from her already nonexistent ones, Wayland. You'd put your happiness first, and not think of Kitty."

Guilt knotted at his chest, and yet—

"I can't forsake the woman I love. Not for anyone. She is a good woman, Mother," he said, imploring her to see that. "She is a woman of strength who survived something the most hardened soldier shouldn't have to face." And he should have stormed her family's household years earlier when she rejected his letters. To find out why. And to remind her of his love. So much time had passed. But it was not too late.

His mother scoured his face, and then, touching trembling fingers to her mouth, she rocked back. "If you think I will be happy for you, I will not, Wayland."

"No," he said coolly. "I don't think you would or could, because my happiness is secondary to this new life you've dreamed up for yourself and our family. It isn't enough that we have the funds to know safety and security, and that should Kitty wish to never marry, she'll still be financially protected by what we have."

"You don't know that. It's not enough."

"No." He looked down the length of his nose at her. "That is my point exactly. It will never be enough. But I? I will have happiness . . ." That was, if Annalee would have him this time. "I've already paid a visit to Lady Diana."

His mother recoiled. "What did you do?" she whispered.

"I explained as gently as I could that I couldn't offer her the love she wanted."

"No." His mother's voice emerged weak.

Continuing over her interruption, he added a firmer layer of insistence, one that would put to bed once and for all the delusions she'd allowed herself where Wayland's and Lady Diana's futures were concerned. "I reminded the lady that her feelings for me might be misdirected, born of her girlish fantasies and encouraged by two match-making mamas."

His mother cried out. "How could you have said those things to her?" She began to pace frantically back and forth. "The duke and duchess will never forgive this transgression. Never."

He took a placating tone. "You may rest assured, the meeting was amicable." The calm and almost indifference of the lady's response had confirmed the sentiments she'd carried had not been the passionate ones motivated by any real feelings on Lady Diana's part. "I wished the lady much joy and reminded her that she would only have it were she to marry a man who was capable of loving her as she deserved. Which I am . . . decidedly not, as my heart belongs fully and completely to Annalee. She was reserved. Completely emotionally detached."

His efforts at infusing calm proved in vain.

His mother abruptly stopped and stormed over in a whir of skirts. "You selfish, self-centered man. You had your sister to consider, and instead, you've put Annalee first."

"As I will always do from this day forward." As he should have done long, long ago.

If looks could kill, he would have found himself a victim of maternal filicide in that very moment.

And with his mother breaking down into a fit of tears, Wayland stalked off . . . feeling freer than he had since Manchester.

Chapter 26

Entering through the front doors that she'd come through so many times before as a girl, Annalee swept her stare over the expansive marble foyer, expecting to be suffocated, as she inevitably was by her family's residence.

This time . . . her parents had extended her an invitation.

Granted, it had come because her parents believed Wayland was courting her in truth.

And this welcome would go away.

And along with it, so much else would be gone, too.

Her time with Wayland.

Refusing to let herself be bogged down in the misery of what would come when their time together ended, she greeted the butler, murmuring a word of thanks to the servant, who assisted her out of her cloak. "Tanning, old chum."

His eyes twinkled. "It is so very good to see you, Lady Annalee."

She moved her gaze upward to the top of the staircase, where her sister sat, dejected, with her right cheek on her knees and her rapier at her side. Annalee gave a little nod up toward her. "What is going on there?" she murmured in hushed tones to Tanning.

The smile instantly faded from the older man's long face. "I . . . could not say, Lady Annalee," he whispered. "She has . . . been this way for some time now."

Cupping her hands around her mouth, Annalee called up to her younger sibling. "Why so glum, chum?"

Instead of popping up and shimmying down the banister, as was her way, Harlow lifted her shoulders in a jerky little shrug.

Bypassing the parlor, where her family had no doubt assembled, Annalee lifted her hem and headed abovestairs. "You're disappointed because you won't be permitted to play pianoforte when dinner is done?" she asked in a bid to elicit a smile or laugh. The whole Spencer family well knew the younger girl's aversion to instruments.

"I hate playing," Harlow mumbled.

"I know." Annalee leaned in. "That's why it is a jest. If it is any consolation, dearest sister, I feel much the same way about dinner parties with Mother and Father. Look at it this way: at least you are spared suffering through it." That was normally true. Not this night. Not with Wayland present.

Harlow edged away, shifting closer to the wall, refusing to look at Annalee.

A deepening worry took root. "What is it?" she asked softly, taking a seat beside her younger sibling. "Has Mother been harping on your swordplay?"

Harlow hesitated, then muttered under her breath, "She always does. Nothing new there."

No, there wasn't. So then what accounted for this . . . sadness?

"Hey, now. Perhaps it will be good to talk about what is bothering you," she said gently. "I find it always helps to talk to my friends about what has upset—"

"Like you did with Lila?" her sister charged. "When you ran away from Lila during Mother's musical?"

She drew back. Her sister had seen that exchange. And more . . . How much had she heard? Either way, Harlow's words . . . they were fair. Or they *had* been. "I've begun opening up more, too, poppet. That's how I know it is important to not just keep my feelings inside.

Lila and I spoke . . . about my departure." Annalee had eventually gone back to Lila after her breakdown and talked about everything. Every last piece of herself and Peterloo she'd resisted speaking to her friend about: The demons that had haunted her. The vices she'd sought out to cope. The life she wanted for herself.

Her sister looked at her. "You did?"

She nodded. "I did. And it helped." For so long, she'd been pushing away the people who could most understand her experience. She'd depended upon liaisons and other distractions to keep the emotions from overwhelming her. "I've come to appreciate my friendships and learn that talking through"—*my experiences*—"anything"—she substituted—"is a balm." And because of those gifts, her need for other distractions had lessened. "Wayland helped me to see that," she said softly to herself.

Her sister stared at her with stricken eyes, bringing Annalee back to the moment.

She folded an arm about Harlow's small, narrow shoulders. "I thought you should like that I'm coming around more." The time they'd had together since Peterloo had been limited, cut off by their mother and father, who sought to keep their last remaining innocent daughter unsullied.

"I do. But do *youuuu*?"

"I . . . Of course I do."

"You hate it here."

"I love being here because you're here."

"But you were never happy like this before, and . . . what if Wayland wasn't . . . courting you, would you still be happy to visit?"

Annalee sat back on the seat.

"Because it won't last," Harlow whispered.

No, it wouldn't.

"You'll do something to displease Mother and Father, and Wayland . . ." Her voice broke, and something lit her eyes, but then was gone. Her sister looked away.

Annalee frowned. Her sister knew something. Warning bells banged loudly in her mind. "And what of Wayland?" she urged.

Harlow shook her head hard, then made to rise.

Annalee caught her by the shoulder. "What is it?"

"Mother and Father want to send you away," Harlow said, her voice threadbare. "To a hospital. They were going to, but then Jeremy shared their intentions with Darlington."

Annalee's heart pounded in her ears, drowning out the remainder of her sister's words. There it was. That great fear she'd always carried. That eventually her parents would tire of her and send her away. Not just to the country, but to the very place her sister now spoke of.

Her breathing grew labored.

And Wayland had known as much.

It was why he'd had the sudden change of heart. It was why he'd been so insistent. Because he'd known her family would send her away, and he'd have spared her both that fate and that humiliation.

Her eyes slid shut.

He'd been so consumed by guilt; it had been there in his initial letters after Peterloo. Why, it had lived and breathed with a lifelike force, even in their every exchange all these years later.

And because of it, he'd put his reputation and his future marriage to Lady Diana aside . . . for her.

Annalee hugged her arms around her middle and squeezed tight.

She dimly registered Harlow wrapping her slender little limbs around her shoulders. "I am . . . so sorry. I should have told you. Because that is what sisters do. But I was just so worried about keeping you out of that place, but then I saw you today, Annalee, and you were so happy, but I know it is just pretend, and I don't want you to be hurt."

It was too late.

This was a pain she'd not recover from.

Tanning cleared his throat. "His and Her Ladyship asked me to remind you that you are late," the butler called from belowstairs. "That the families have already gathered for the evening meal."

"Go," Harlow whispered. "Before they make it any worse for you."

Could there be . . . a "worse" than this? Than discovering that her parents had intended to shut her away in an institution, and that the only thing that stood between her and that imprisonment was Wayland, who'd jeopardized his reputation and happiness?

Because of me.

Numb, Annalee managed to rise. And with the aid of the railing, she made a slow descent, heading for the dining room.

The sight that greeted her was as happy a tableau as she'd ever seen.

Her and Wayland's mothers, conversing.

Except, if one looked close enough, one saw cracks.

The brittle lines at the edges of his mother's lips.

The worry in his mother's eyes.

His mother, who feared a union between them.

Her mother, who feared a union between them would not be seen to fruition.

And it wouldn't.

Wayland caught her standing there and immediately jumped up, and the rest of the table followed suit.

He'd been the only gentleman to treat her as a lady.

When the whole world had called her a whore and other similar disparagements, he'd offered her kindness and support . . . and . . . and tonight, she'd learned just how much he'd given her.

This was too much.

Annalee clamped down on the inside of her cheek, catching that flesh painfully with her teeth, welcoming the bite of pain, as she made herself walk the remaining way to Wayland's side.

"Hullo, my lady," he murmured as she slid into the seat beside him.

"My lord," she said, her voice thick to her own ears.

She sat there, staring sightlessly at her champagne flute.

It was pretend.

It had always been pretend.

That had always been the game they played at.

She'd just let herself believe.

To be seduced by dreams she'd thought dead.

She stretched her fingers toward that glass, then swiftly yanked them back.

Reaching a hand under the table, Annalee rested her fingers on his thigh. The muscles immediately jumped and bunched under her touch, as did the gentleman himself.

Startling: the fork clattered against the edge of his plate, damningly loud enough to attract brief looks.

But then, with surprising aplomb, the proper Wayland donned an almost bored mask and swapped his fork for a drink.

Annalee crept her palm higher along that marble-hard flesh between his legs.

"Stop," he said from around the rim of his glass.

"Do you really want me to, Wayland?" she whispered, not so much as moving her lips, as with the fork in her other hand, she popped a piece of lamb into her mouth. "Tell me, and I will."

"What are you doing?" he asked quietly. "Why are you behaving this way?"

"What way? *Hmm?* Wicked. It's because it's what I am."

"You're not wicked, Annalee," he said softly.

"You're just telling yourself that because it makes you feel better."

"I'm telling you that because you've placed yourself in that one constraining way, and that isn't you, Annalee. A woman who is wicked doesn't dedicate herself to improving the lives of other women. Or is willing to step aside or make changes so as to save them. The spirits and the smoking and the . . . the . . . ." *Men.* And her heart spasmed; he

323

couldn't get out that admission, and she didn't want him to. She didn't want to think of all the men she'd bedded in the hope of forgetting the one who now sat beside her, compelled by guilt to swap out his future for hers.

"Tell me, did you ever intend to let me know of my family's intentions?" she asked as she sliced a piece of her roast into minuscule pieces.

He stiffened. His leg so near hers that she felt his muscles bunch and tense.

"Or was I never to learn that you were playing the role of hero, attempting to save me?"

At his silence, she slid a glance his way, daring him with her eyes.

His features were frozen, strained, and pale. "Annalee," he tried, his voice emerging as a gravelly whisper.

"Hmm?" Her voice emerged a fraction higher, earning a frown from her parents.

Those traitorous, useless two who'd given her life, and who had spent these past years wishing they hadn't.

Even so, when she spoke again, she lowered her voice, offering him hushed tones. "I didn't ask you to sacrifice yourself for me. I didn't want you saving me then, and I don't want you saving me now." Not in this way. Not with him seeking some kind of atonement which he didn't need. They'd planned to meet on the fields of Manchester that day, and loving him as she did, loving him as she always would, Annalee would do it all over again, even knowing what she knew now about what would happen and how her life would unfold.

She rose.

"What are you doing?" he whispered as everyone looked to Annalee.

She glanced down at him. "I can't do this."

"Annalee?" her mother called.

Wayland gripped her hand, and she covered his white knuckles. "We have to break it off."

"Why are you doing this?" he implored.

"I'll not sacrifice your future with Lady Diana." Before she proved the selfish creature she'd always been, she drew in a shaky breath and looked to the room. "This is not real," she said quietly, the slight clinking of silverware touching porcelain the only sound before the absolute silence. She motioned between herself and Wayland. "This . . . is just pretend." Unable to meet the pain bleeding from his eyes, she glanced to her slack-jawed parents. "He learned what you intended to do, and he attempted to . . . save me, but I'll not be saved that way. By stealing his happiness. I love him too much for th-that." Her voice broke, and she swallowed that sob, burying it in her fist.

"How could you?" her mother cried. "I knew it!"

Annalee shoved her chair; the carved mahogany Chippendale seat bounced back, knocking loudly upon the floor as it fell.

She'd been wrong. Tears blinded her. This was even worse than she could have imagined.

Wayland exploded to his feet. "Stop!" he called, and she needed to keep running, away from this and the pain and now, her future. But something in his voice compelled her back around.

⌘

He didn't deserve her.

She'd been far stronger than he'd ever been.

She'd dealt with scandal and public shaming, and her family's ill treatment, and she'd done it alone.

And with her standing there, tears streaming down the glorious planes of her high cheeks, those ocean-blue pools swimming in sorrow, he loved her all the more.

He took a slow step closer, more than half fearing the wrong word or move would send her fleeing. And this time, when she was gone, there'd be no reuniting. This was the last chance between them.

"I love you, Annalee," he said hoarsely. "I have *always* loved you. You were and are the only reason that my heart beats, and it forgot how after Peterloo, Annalee. It forgot, because you were not in my life."

She trembled, her body shaking like a slender willow being battered by a tempest.

"I was going to tell you," he murmured, drifting closer. "I'd resolved today to tell you all, because I'd not have secrets between us, and because . . ." He stopped before her, and with hands that shook, he captured her face between his palms, cradling her. "Because I didn't want this to be pretend. Not anymore. I wanted it to be real in every way. I want it to be real."

He sank to a knee, earning a shuddery gasp from Annalee . . . and one of horror from his mother.

"What are you doing?" Annalee whispered.

"Wayland, get up this instant," his mother hissed.

"Darlington, you don't have to do this," Jeremy said over her displeasure.

My God, they'd ruin even this moment for Annalee? Her brother? His mother? Her silent and just-as-guilty parents?

And it was in that instant that he snapped, broke completely of the chains he'd let himself be so bound to over the years.

He jumped up. "Do you know what? You people, you're all bloody awful. Each of you is the absolute worst. I'm in love with Annalee, and if she'll have me, I'll spend the rest of my life with her." He looked around the intimate gathering of his family and hers. "And I'll certainly not call family or friends the people who would cut her."

She pressed her fingertips to her mouth. "Wayland—"

Gasps filtered around the room. But by God, he was done caring about familial approval or guilt about Annalee being Jeremy's sister.

"Except you." He pointed to Kitty. "You're fine enough. You've defended Annalee and helped me open my damned eyes to what I was not allowing myself to see."

"Thank you, big brother." His sister offered a pert smile. "And you're welcome," she said with a flounce of her curls.

"But you . . ." He gestured to Jeremy. "My God, what manner of brother have you been? You should have called out any number of bounders over the years, and you didn't. You'd be willing to see her consigned to the worst of fates." Hatred singed his veins. "And you." He turned his wrath upon her parents. "What parents reject their child so?" God, were he to be so blessed as to have a future and babes with Annalee in it, he'd treat those children as the treasures they were. He'd slay goddamned mountains and monsters for them. "A daughter who faced what she faced? You let her to her battles alone."

The earl bristled. "I've never . . ."

"Never what?" Wayland shot back. "Been the father she deserved? No, you haven't. But then"—he glanced about at the guilty parties—"none of us really have been the people Annalee deserved." He paused. "Again, except for Kitty."

"Wayland, sit down right now," his mother ordered.

Ah, and then there was his mother. His self-centered, materialistic, power-driven, dear mama.

"Oh, but you already know what I think of you and your quest for power. I've allowed you to obsess over"—he waved a hand at the elegant dining room—"this lifestyle, and made excuses, telling myself you worried about our family's security, but it was always more about our standing." Wayland didn't bother to hold back the sound of disgust that spilled from his lips. "But you know what? I'm done. With all of it." He found her with his gaze. "I love Annalee." He directed those words for the room at large to Annalee herself, more silent than he'd ever seen her. And absolutely pale. *What is she thinking? Why can't I tell in this moment, when I've been able to tell every other time before this where Annalee was concerned?* "And the people you'd judge her for keeping company with? They've proven more loyal and more loving than the lot of you." He continued to lock his stare with her unblinking one.

"Annalee, at your brother's betrothal ball, you put a question to me. Do you remember what you asked?"

She hesitated, and then gave the faintest of nods.

Even so, he reminded her. Even though he knew she knew and she'd confirmed as much.

He took a step nearer to her so only an arm's length divided them. "You asked . . . what brings me joy, and you rightfully called me out for not knowing happiness." A half laugh, half sob exploded from his lungs. "Nothing did." He cupped her cheek, and she leaned into his touch, and he took faith and found hope in that. "Until you." He let his arm fall. "*You* bring me joy. *You* are my life's pleasure. And my life is dark without you. It has been dark. And empty, and there's only light when you are in it."

She caught a sob in her fist.

Wayland stretched out his fingers toward Annalee. "Let's be done with this place . . . and these people."

"But not Kitty," his sister whispered loudly behind them.

"No," he allowed. "Not Kitty."

Annalee stared at his palm. White-faced, her eyes wide, her lips trembling . . . and she made no move to take his fingers.

Oh, God.

This was agony.

He wavered. His hand faltering, falling, and then she shot out her fingers, catching his palm before it fell.

"Wayland, sit down," his mother cried.

A whistle went up, followed by a lone stomping of feet.

"Enough, Kitty."

Wayland and Annalee shared a smile.

And together, hand in hand, they left.

Epilogue

A fortnight later
Waverton Street

It was a first for the Mismatch Society.

Oh, there'd been marriages within the ranks of members—two, to be specific.

But there'd never been a wedding hosted at Waverton Street.

"Sacrilegious, it is, I say," Isla Gately muttered loudly enough to be overheard from her seat in the second row of the gardens.

"Annalee appears ready to cry. We must stop the affair *nowwww*," Brenna Kearsley cried.

A pair of hands settled over Annalee's shoulders.

Wayland drew her close, so her back rested against his chest, and he folded his arms around her. "What do you think my chances of making you Lady Darlington are this day, given the rumblings of discontent from that lot?" he whispered against her ear.

She giggled, tipping her head and aiding him in his quest to that little spot just below the lobe; she so loved when he teased it with kisses. "I think our outlook is favorable this day."

"Are we certain someone doesn't wish to speak to Annalee . . . ?" Lady Cora suggested.

"You're more confident than I am, my love."

My love.

Closing her eyes, Annalee silently mouthed those two words, letting the syllables he'd spoken roll off her tongue.

How she'd missed hearing him speak that endearment.

It had never been crass or careless, a hurried moniker dropped as it was by the men who would speak it after him. Rather, it had always possessed a husky quality, enlivened with emotion born of that real, purest of love he carried for her.

Turning in his arms, she leaned up and touched her nose to his. "Yes, well, as they are my friends, they know I'll not ever be deterred in following my heart, Wayland Smith." Her eyes slid shut once more as Wayland kissed her. A tender, unhurried meeting that left her heart light and filled her with the most buoyant warmth.

There came the rush of footfalls as more guests arrived, cutting into her stolen moment before the intimate ceremony they'd planned. With a regretful sigh, she opened her eyes. "I thought all of our guests . . . oh."

She stared wide-eyed at the quartet that made up her parents and siblings.

"I did not invite your parents and brother," he said quietly with a slight shake of his head. "I requested Harlow's presence." Wayland took a step closer and slid his fingers into Annalee's, and hers reflexively curled, twining with his, as was their natural place of belonging.

Harlow broke free of their family, and raced headfirst into Annalee's arms. Annalee folded her arms about the younger girl.

Jeremy spoke for the family. "No, Darlington didn't invite us." He paused. "Aside from a letter he sent requesting that I arrange for Harlow to be here, that is."

Tears blurred Annalee's vision as she glanced over her sister's head to Wayland. Once more, he'd thought of uniting her and Harlow, even reaching out to Jeremy, whom he'd not spoken to since that dinner party two weeks earlier, because he'd known Annalee had desperately yearned for her sister's presence that day.

"No one sent for us," her brother repeated into the quiet. "We . . . have no right to be here. Darlington was right," he said, his voice catching. His face spasmed. "About so much. And we are . . . I am"—he took several steps forward and touched a gloved hand hard to his chest—"sorrier than I could ever express. For all the ways that I wasn't there for you."

She bit her lower lip. "It is—"

"It's not fine," he rasped. "You suffered, and you did so alone. You cried out to be seen, and we let you cry alone. Content to let you destroy yourself rather than have to acknowledge what you'd suffered and what you'd lived through."

A little sob escaped her, and Wayland wrapped an arm about her shoulders.

Jeremy stretched an arm toward her. "That isn't why I've come. That isn't why we're here. To bring you more sadness. We wish . . . to share your joy. To witness your union. However, if you'd rather we leave—"

"No!" she cried out. "I . . . I would like that. I would like for you to be here. All of you." Her gaze slipped over to their parents. "If . . . that is something you want as well."

Her mother dashed a lone tear from her cheek. "I'd like that very much, Anna."

Anna.

That name she'd called Annalee when she'd been just a girl. Before Peterloo.

Harlow grinned. "Come along, then; we are holding up the ceremony!" And releasing Annalee, she hurried over to catch her parents and began dragging them forward, out toward the gardens.

As the trio passed by, Jeremy lingered.

The moment their parents and sister had gone, he stretched out a palm toward Wayland.

Wayland, who immediately took that offering, shook the other man's hand.

"You were always a better man and protector and friend to Annalee than I ever was. And I will be forever grateful to you," Jeremy said, and with that, he left.

Wayland remained. He trailed a fingertip along Annalee's cheek. "Are you all right?"

She smiled. "I am." And for the first time in the longest time, she was. There was a joy that was deep. A hope that was real. And a future that was bright.

"Are you ready to live together happily, to have and to hold from this day forward, for better, for worse, for richer, for poorer, in sickness and in health, to love and to cherish, till death do us part?"

Looping her arms about his neck, she drew herself close once more. "There is nothing I want more, Lord Darlington," she breathed against his mouth.

His eyes darkened, and his lashes swept low, forming an inky-black hood. He kissed her deeply, taking her breath away, stealing a sigh that he swallowed, and setting butterflies to dancing throughout her chest and belly.

Sinking back on her heels, she reluctantly ended the kiss. "Off you go, Lord Darlington. So we can begin the future."

He touched a fingertip smartly against his brow.

She followed him with her gaze as he went, taking the walk that soon she'd travel, waving at their guests as he went. Even the hostile members of the Mismatch Society, who still distrusted all men and glowered. And yet, those ladies softened as he continued on. Because he had that effect on everyone. Annalee touched her brow against the edge of the door panel, the glass panes reflecting back her contented smile.

At last he reached the vicar's side, and Annalee straightened.

Down the length of the satin runner that had been laid out as a makeshift aisle, her gaze met his, and across the way, they shared the private smile they'd always known.

They would be together.

For as long as they both should live.

And this time, there would be no separating them.

And with that, Annalee started forward, to meet Wayland and the rest of their future—together.

Acknowledgments

To my endlessly patient, always supportive editor, Alison Dasho. I'm grateful to you for always supporting my vision and trusting me to tell the story that is speaking to me. Having an editor who possesses your level of trust is such a gift.

About the Author

Photo © 2016 Kimberly Rocha

Christi Caldwell is the *USA Today* bestselling author of numerous series, including Wantons of Waverton, Lost Lords of London, Sinful Brides, Wicked Wallflowers, and Heart of a Duke. She blames novelist Judith McNaught for luring her into the world of historical romance. When Christi was at the University of Connecticut, she began writing her own tales of love—ones where even the most perfect heroes and heroines had imperfections. She learned to enjoy torturing her couples before they earned their well-deserved happily ever after.

Christi lives in the Piedmont region of North Carolina, where she spends her time writing and baking with her twin girls and courageous son. Fans who want to keep up with the latest news and information can sign up for her newsletter at www.ChristiCaldwell.com.